The Other Victims

by

Patsy King Hosman

The Other Victims

Cover Art by *Diana Carlile*

The Wild Rose Press, Inc.
PO Box 708
Adams Basin, NY 14410-0708
Visit us at www.thewildrosepress.com

Publishing History
First Edition, 2023
Trade Paperback ISBN 978-1-5092-5112-4
Digital ISBN 978-1-5092-5113-1

Published in the United States of America

Rodney heard the doorbell ring. He hesitated. He knew he wasn't going to answer the door, not after this morning. He stood in the entry and saw the outline of a woman through the curtained window. Glancing out the picture window in the living room, he stared in disbelief as he watched a man with a microphone come out of a van followed by someone with a video camera. With sickened shock, Rodney saw another truck slowly drive toward the house. Then two more.

The doorbell rang again. Rodney tensed. He saw a man and a woman peering into the window. This couldn't be happening. He ran to the garage to get duct tape. From the linen closet Rodney grabbed sheets and blankets. When he returned, Rodney banged on the window and yelled at them. In the background a couple of reporters stood in the yard speaking into microphones, facing cameramen. We've become part of the news, Rodney realized.

Dedication

To the 168 victims of the Oklahoma City Murrah Bombing.

Acknowledgments

When writing a novel for the first time, there are many individuals who should be acknowledged. Thank you, Jean Williams, for your insights into the devastating disease of schizophrenia, for sharing numerous resources, and reading my copy. Thanks to Sergeant Randy Payne for his help with law enforcement scenes. Rosalie and Mark Johnson and their family shared how hunting is more than just a sport, how one can treat God's creations with respect even in death and provide food for the table. Friend, John Shelley, guided me through the process of visiting an inmate in prison. Attorney and close friend, Mack Morgan, explained how to write the legal parts of my story. Bryan Miller, my husband's cousin, taught me about the printing industry and how it is a skill as well as a craft and an art. Thanks also to Norma Jean Lutz who was the first professional who believed in me and guided my initial steps.

I'd also like to thank my pen pal, Kevin Rogers, who was one of the few who knew of my "secret" effort to write a novel. He was a cheerleader, encourager, and constant support. You're next, Kevin!

Thank you to artist, Mike Mitchell, for giving me permission to describe his t-shirt design, "Nothing Rhymes with Orange" in this story. Without it, Flory and Jesse would have never met.

Thank you, Ally Robertson, for being intrigued by my story and being my editor at The Wild Rose Press. I'm still on the journey.

Finally, I want to thank my husband, Tom, for believing in me and supporting me, even though it seemed more like a pipe dream.

Chapter 1

August 6, 2015

On Thursday, Lou Ella Sutton woke up to a cat's paws traipsing over her. She was still in the clothes she had on from the day before. The afternoon sun was at the perfect spot to shine directly into her open window. The screen had a hole in it, and flies buzzed around her and the feral cat, which was now mewing loudly. Lou swung at the cat, and the cat jumped down, just missing the sting of being hit.

Lou rolled over to avoid the sun. The ringing was still there. In her ears. How had they been able to insert a device in her ears? She sat up and hit one side of her head and then the other, like she used to do when she had water in her ears from swimming. But it didn't help. If anything, the ringing became louder. Lou told herself, don't think about anything. Don't think. She reasoned if she wasn't thinking then *they* couldn't steal her thoughts.

Lou's forearms had long scars from her attempts to dislodge the tracking devices that had been implanted. Somehow, they had manipulated the devices, so they dissolved before she got to them. She didn't know how she was going to remove the ones inserted in her ears.

Voices in Lou's head made demands.

Get your headphones and blast the devices. Turn up the volume as loud as it can go!

1

She grabbed her headphones and attached them to her phone. Selecting "Pinball Wizard" by The Who, she turned up the volume as loud as she could stand.

The bass from the song vibrated through Lou's body, and she realized there must be other devices planted in her. She saw insects crawling all over her. A hot shower. That's what she needed. That would get rid of the crawling insects.

Lou stood naked in the tiny bathroom in her trailer, waiting for the water to get hot enough. She was a large woman. She ran her hands over her body, trying to brush off the bugs and to detect any other devices that might have been implanted. She found a small live tick attached under her arm.

Destroy it! It's another tracking device!

Lou removed the body of the tick, leaving the head still attached to her skin.

You must search everywhere! They are tracking you! It's a vast conspiracy.

The voices hissed at Lou. Alarmed, she rummaged through the contents on the shelf in her bathroom. Bottles of expired medication spilled into the sink and onto the linoleum floor. Then she went into her room and emptied the drawers in her dresser, the lone piece of furniture crammed between the twin mattress and the wall. On her hands and knees, still naked, Lou ran her hands through the tumbled pile of under garments—sports bras, underwear, socks, bandanas—in search of anything hard, anything that might be another device. If they could make one to look like a tick, then they could disguise it as anything.

After emptying her closet, Lou proceeded to the kitchen. She let the glasses and plates crash to the floor, hoping to destroy any devices hidden in her trailer. She stepped on a piece of broken glass.

"Shit!" Glass was all over the floor, and she had no shoes on, much less any clothes. Her heart was racing, almost as fast as the thoughts going through her mind.

You've got to get out of here. You've got to stop them!

Lou managed to get back to the bathroom with only minor cuts on her feet. She had forgotten to turn off the water, and steam rose from the shower. She stepped in, and the scalding water burned her back. The pain was unbearable, but she knew any devices implanted in her spine had burned or melted.

Lou pushed her soaked, graying hair from her face as she got dressed. She glanced out the bedroom window to see if there was anyone outside. Listening for any vehicles that might drive up, Lou realized it was just a matter of time before they found her.

The dilapidated trailer where Lou lived was on a dead-end gravel road. No one ever drove past because there was nothing out there, only Lou's trailer. Once a month her landlord came in his pickup to collect rent. But that was it. Lou had little contact with anyone else. She only left the trailer to get more supplies. Stockpiling. That and staying one step ahead of *them* were her goals.

You must find out their plan! And when you do, you must destroy it!

Lou turned on her father's old radio to see if the transmitters would send her a clue. They were her only allies.

"...don't miss tonight's Battle of the Bands featuring the Sonic Wolves at the James B Saloon here in Mineral Wells..."

That's it. They're going to meet in Mineral Wells. If I can catch them off guard, I'll be able to disable these devices and be free.

You must destroy them!

Lou pulled on her work boots and searched for her leather jacket that was buried in the pile of clothing. It was near ninety degrees outside.

You must keep one step ahead of them, you worthless piece of shit! You can't let them know you're on to their plan. Don't screw it up, stupid!

The keys to her dad's pickup lay on the lone table in the front room. Next to them was a birthday card her sister, Alice, had designed. It had three dogs—a beagle, a German shorthair pointer, and a mixed breed—romping in a field of yellow wildflowers. Lou stopped and picked up the card. A flicker of a past memory—of Lucky, Charlie, and Schroeder, her old companions—tried to make its way into her head and her heart. She paused for a moment before the ringing in her ears reminded her of her mission. Alice had put two twenties, a five, and three ones inside the card. Lou grabbed the keys and took the cash, stuffing it in the back pocket of her jeans.

As she opened the door, another feral cat came inside mewing loudly. The first cat emerged from under the vinyl sofa. Lou usually kept extra milk for the cats. But not today. There was no time. She swung her boot at them, but the cats ran past her. The broken glass still on the floor stopped them, and they backtracked.

They've found you!

The cats were spies. She couldn't let them get away. Lou stood at the entrance of her trailer, barring the door. She took a step outside onto the rotting wooden porch.

The cats tried to follow her, but she slammed the door, leaving them stuck inside the trailer.

Get out! They'll send someone or something else. You're so disgusting, they'll want to destroy you. You must annihilate them first!

The voices in Lou's head didn't relent. She knew she had to obey them. Lou climbed into the pickup. The gravel road took her to State Highway 51.

Mineral Wells was about ten miles east down the highway, but Lou turned west and drove toward the interstate, going south. The voices in her head continued to taunt her for the forty-five minutes it took to reach the Waterloo Road exit. Heading east Lou drove past familiar sights—the 7-Eleven, the gas station with the old pumps, and the metal building with a cross on top. An old elm tree with a bend in its trunk seemed familiar, but no memory came.

Lou turned onto a gravel drive and parked in front of an old stone house. A dead rose bush was on either side of the front door. She inserted a key in the lock and opened the door. Inside the air was stale. Everything was quiet. Even the voices. She wandered into the kitchen and opened the refrigerator. An assortment of condiments—ketchup, mustard, a bottle of salad dressing—were on the shelves in the door. Cans of soda, a six-pack of beer, and a block of molded cheddar cheese. Closing the refrigerator, Lou checked out the pantry. A jar of peanut butter, a couple of cans of baked beans, a box of crackers, and a bag of chips. Lou took the chips and a can of Coke with her as she went upstairs.

Her old bedroom was at the back of the house, facing the apple orchard and creek. Alice's bedroom was at the top of the stairs. They had shared a bathroom.

Across the hall were her parents' bedroom and her mother's studio. Lou walked past these and went straight to her room. Nothing had changed. Her room was just as she had left it. Setting the Coke and chips on top of her upright dresser, she opened the drawers. They were empty. She crossed over to the window. A blue jay caught her eye as it flew toward the apple trees. Lou hated blue jays. They pecked at the fruit with their beaks. She stood there motionless, long after the jay had flown away.

Suddenly Lou felt confused. The urgency she had experienced turned into exhaustion, and she couldn't remember why she was here. All she wanted to do was go to sleep. So, she did. The voices had gone silent.

Several hours later Lou woke up. Where was she? From the window she noticed the sky beginning to darken. Lou swung her legs around and sat up. Her work boots left patches of dirt on the plaid bedspread.

Lou went back downstairs. At the bottom of the stairs toward the back of the house was Carl Sutton's study. Lou instinctively inhaled, expecting to smell her father's old pipe, but that smell had long since dissipated. She stared at her father's old desk. When was the last time she had seen him sitting there? Lou ran her hands over the smooth mahogany, disturbing the dust.

What are you doing? You filthy fleabag, you maggot-infested piece of shit! Get the gun!

The voices had returned.

Lou opened the bottom drawer of her father's desk. There it was—his nine-millimeter Glock 19. Where were the bullets? Lou opened the other drawers and dumped out the contents. They weren't there.

The ringing in her ears had returned. Back upstairs

to her parents' room. On the top shelf of the closet was a metal lockbox with a combination lock. Lou took it with her and grabbed a set of keys from a hook by the kitchen door. She ran outside and unlocked the barn. There, she found her father's axe and whacked the box until she had made a cut into it. Rummaging around some more Lou found the wire cutters. She expanded the opening until she was able to get her hand inside. Lou pulled out four magazines and stuffed them in her jacket pockets.

Twenty minutes later Lou was on the interstate. It was almost 8:30. She exited onto State Highway 51 and drove toward Mineral Wells. She passed a Ford dealership on the left. On the right was a giant billboard: *Welcome to Mineral Wells, home of the Oklahoma A&M Combines, Number One Ag School in the Stat*e. As she entered the city limits, Highway 51 became First Avenue. Lou passed the Mineral Wells Medical Center and the County Assessor. There was a drugstore and a local diner called Woody B's BBQ. At Main Street Lou turned left. She rolled down her window and heard the blaring sound of the band. Driving toward the music, she realized the streets had been blocked off, and there was no place to park. Lou backtracked and pulled into an empty parking lot for Mattress King on Fifth and Main. She followed the sounds toward the Battle of the Bands.

Chapter 2

Detective Jeremy Turner glanced at his watch. It was 9:00. Just tonight and tomorrow, then things would be back to normal. He had parked his assigned unit, a black Dodge Charger, on Main Street, just south of Elm. The vibration from the bass pulsated. The crowd had swelled, and the cordoned off area was packed with partiers dancing in the street, Solo cups in hand. It was the one of the few special events Mineral Wells allowed open containers outside, and Jeremy hated it. He knew someday there would be problems. This year had been unusually orderly, and for that he was grateful.

Jeremy's radio buzzed in the holder on his hip. "What's your location?" It was Melvin Pollard, Chief of Police.

"I'm on Elm walking toward the James B," Jeremy said, yelling over the commotion from the partiers and the music. He stepped around a woman sitting on the curb, who was about to pass out.

Jeremy wore jeans and a T-shirt. His dark brown hair curled at the ends. He had decided to grow a beard, only to discover that it came in red. Gina said it made his eyes appear bluer. He wasn't a very large man, but pleasant to look at. He had that aww shucks manner about him, part innocent, part sexy. And he walked with a slight bow-legged gait, as if he had ridden horses all his life, which he hadn't.

Jeremy pulled out his radio. "I'm going to walk the perimeter and do some ID checking." He received the okay from the chief. The street party covered a two-block area, from Sooner Avenue to College Street, the edge of Oklahoma A&M. Jeremy had heard the planners expected over one thousand, up from the previous year.

He walked near the line waiting to get in at the Sooner Avenue entrance. It was mixture of ages, older alums but mainly college students. He scouted the crowd for those under-aged, who were trying to sneak in with their fake IDs. Walking behind the bar, he went past a row of kegs waiting to replace the empty ones. Between the buildings he saw silhouettes of the partygoers moving to the beat of the music. The band played "You're Breakin' My Heart" by Harry Nillson.

Did all bands play that song? It seemed he heard it every year, like the crowds at baseball games who sang "Sweet Caroline" at the end of the seventh inning. Sung, or rather yelled, in unison, the song indicated it was time to party.

Jeremy glanced at his watch as he continued his walk around the perimeter. It was almost 9:30. He had probably four more hours of patrolling. The bar closed, and the band quit playing at midnight, but it took at least an hour to get everyone safely back in their cars. He knew it was going to be a long night.

Jeremy circled past the College Street entrance. Temporary barricades marked the boundaries. He slipped past one and into the frenzy of music and drinking. The Sonic Wolves played on an outdoor stage across from the entrance to the James B Saloon. The sound was deafening. He started to walk toward the entrance of the bar when he heard shots. For the untrained ear, it could have been fireworks or even a staccato from the drummer. But Jeremy knew immediately what it was. He saw two girls collapse. Immediately those nearby panicked and ran. More shots fired. Individuals in the street scattered in all directions, and those inside the bar started pushing their way out. But where was the safest place to be?

Jeremy ran toward the sound of the shots. It was like a fish trying to swim upstream against a current.

He radioed the chief. "Gun shots fired at the James B. I heard multiple shots. I don't know how many are down."

Jeremy heard Melvin yelling for backup. He put the radio back in its holder as he ran into the war zone. That's what it felt like. The chaos and panic and fear were so powerful he could almost taste it. The smell of gun powder mixed with alcohol and sweat and, yes, death was something he knew he'd never forget.

Jeremy entered the bar, or rather pushed his way in. It was a mob scene. Total chaos. People trying to get out of the bar, knocking over chairs and anything in their way, whatever prevented them from exiting. A large man with tattoos covering his arms stood in the middle of the chaos bawling. At his feet was a woman. Broken glass covered the floor. It mingled with the blood that was everywhere. Purses, cell phones, wallets and other personal effects lay abandoned in the effort to escape.

"Gus Walters is going to set up a medical triage behind the bar." It was the chief. "I've contacted the governor. He's sending in state troopers. The OSBI are on their way, too. Tell me, what do you know?"

Jeremy didn't answer immediately. It seemed there were bodies everywhere, and this was just on the first floor. Two sets of stairs led up to a second level—stairs on either side of the entrance and another set at the back of the bar. The second floor was more like an open galley. From up there someone could look down below, or fire a gun, for that matter. A couple of rooms were off to the side and a section of outdoor seating was on the rooftop. He was trying to figure out where the shooting had occurred. It could have happened anywhere.

"Jeremy, are you there?"

"Yeah, I'm inside the bar going upstairs." Jeremy needed to understand what had happened. He didn't know if it was a lone wolf, or if there had been more than one shooter.

He stepped over a large woman face down at the top of the stairs. Blood seeped from underneath her. He checked for a pulse. There was none. "I've found a victim on the stairs. Female," he said into his radio, making a mental note of her location. Jeremy stepped over another victim, a male. Then he heard moaning. He bent down and checked for a pulse. "Injured male," he added.

Upstairs felt like a different place than the chaos he had gone through below. It seemed that only the dead and injured remained. He spotted a young woman on the floor. She sat cross-legged and held the head and shoulders of a man. The blood from his torso soaked her blouse and jeans. Jeremy could tell the woman was in shock. She didn't say anything, just held on to her friend. He examined the young man. His eyes were open, and he turned his head when he heard Jeremy.

"I need some backup upstairs," Jeremy said into his radio. He knelt. Jeremy didn't have the medical background, but he knew enough. This guy was going to make it. Jeremy let out his breath. "You're going to be okay," he said. "Help is on the way." Then he asked the woman, "Can you give the medics a report of what you saw?"

She nodded.

Jeremy continued to make his way through the bar, staying in touch with the other officers on duty. From the rooftop he saw medics treating injured outside below. Three, maybe four bodies were covered with sheets that hadn't been removed. He was trying to piece together a possible scenario in his head. Despite the pandemonium, Jeremy tried to stay in his head. He observed what was going on—the panicked victims, who just minutes ago had been partying, the injured, the dead, the law enforcement trying to create order. He worked to stay focused and not get distracted by the horror of it all. It was tough.

Lance, one of the rookies, caught his eye. He was bent over in the street, vomiting. Poor Lance. Jeremy remembered his first murder scene. He had done the same thing.

Chapter 3

It was around midnight when Jeremy returned to headquarters. About twenty individuals claimed to have information on the shooting. They had all been checked in—any weapons taken, labeled, and kept for evidence—since Oklahoma had a concealed weapons law. He was used to the routine—name, address, where you were, and so on, but not on such a grand scale. He handled domestic issues, petty thefts, and the like. Sure, part of his training was in active shooter scenarios, but he never considered he would put that training into action. Tonight, that was the only thing Jeremy was grateful for—that he had been trained for such an event as this.

The first witness, an older guy, gray hair tucked under a cowboy hat, sat in a folding chair across from Jeremy. He appeared to be a bit shaken from what he had witnessed. Jeremy was used to that.

Jeremy sat behind a cluttered desk. His old chair squeaked every time he moved. Outside in the hall were a handful of the other witnesses sitting in the same folding chairs, waiting their turn. Despite the late hour and the horrific circumstances, Mineral Wells police headquarters maintained a level of orderly chaos. Helicopters continued to hover overhead, disrupting the night sky.

Jeremy made space on his desk for the digital audio recorder. "Thank you for coming, sir." The first rule—

treat everyone with respect. "Your name, please?"

"Stan Warren." So, he was Stan the Man—a visible tattoo on his left forearm.

"Date of birth?"

"January 30, 1952."

"Where are you from, Stan?"

"Amarillo, Texas."

"Address and phone number where we can reach you." Jeremy typed on his keyboard as Stan gave him the information.

"Have you been to the Battle of Bands before, or is this your first time?"

"I was at the original Battle of the Bands forty years ago," Stan said.

Jeremy whistled. "That's impressive. Have you been to every one since?"

"No, I've skipped a few years here and there, but I've got a group of old college buddies, and we try to make it out here. A reunion of sorts since we're from all over now."

"How many of your friends made it this year?"

"Just me and three others," Stan said.

"Can you give me their names, in case we need to talk to them?"

"Joe Roberts, Frank Harper, and Vic Wells."

"Were they with you tonight?"

"Yes."

"Where were you all? Inside the bar, or out in the street?"

"We were in the bar, on the roof. That's the best spot for listening to the band but keeping our distance from all the drunk college kids."

Jeremy nodded. He continued typing, then asked,

"Stan, where are your friends now?"

"I don't know. We kinda got separated when the shooting happened. I can't get ahold of them. The cell phone lines are all jammed right now."

Jeremy rubbed his forehead. He had been trying to call Gina to let her know he was okay, but he couldn't get through either. "Yeah, it's the shits—I mean the pits. Excuse me."

"No, you're right. It's the shits." He shook his head. "I can't get those pictures out of my mind."

"Can you tell me what you saw? Everything you remember?"

"We got to James B early, say, about seven so we could get a place on the roof. We ordered some food, had a couple of pitchers of beer, and settled in for the evening."

"Did you notice anything unusual? Anything out of the ordinary? Did anyone appear to be acting strange?"

"No. But then we weren't really paying any attention either."

Jeremy nodded. "When did you realize something was wrong?"

"The opening band had finished playing, and the Sonic Wolves came on the stage. When they did, the floodlights came on. And the noise level ramped up. Everyone got on their feet and started cheering. It was so loud at first, I didn't know if I heard what I thought I heard."

"And what was that?" Jeremy asked.

"It was a popping sound. You know, like someone had thrown a bunch of black cats. It was hard to tell if it was the drummer or something else…" Stan sniffed and wiped his nose.

Jeremy's own stomach lurched. He knew what was next. "Stan, when you heard the popping sound did you see anything?"

"Yeah," Stan said. "I saw a couple of kids in the street collapse. It was like there was no warning. I heard the shots, and then these two kids just fell." His eyes filled with tears, and he used the back of his hand to wipe his face.

"Then what?"

Stan took a deep breath. "I heard a bunch of people screaming. And I saw people running and falling over—this was down below—"

"Where the band was playing?"

"Yeah, where the band was."

"Go on."

"Then I heard more shots, and this time I knew what it was. That's when I yelled at my friends to get down. I couldn't tell where the shots were coming from. People started screaming and running everywhere."

"Where were you seated on the roof? Were you near the exit?"

"No. We were at the far end, but at the edge, so we could see the band."

"Did you see the killer?"

Stan shook his head. "Once I realized what was going on, I stayed under the table. That's when I lost my buddies. Frank and Vic panicked, I guess, and ran. Joe and me stayed until all the shooting stopped. But we got separated trying to get out of the bar."

"Do you know if there was only one person shooting, or more than one?" Jeremy asked.

"I—I don't know. After I got under the table..." Stan stopped speaking.

"What did you see, Stan?" Jeremy stopped typing, and his tone softened.

Stan buried his face in his hands. He didn't speak for several moments. "I saw a body fall. A young woman." Stan removed his cowboy hat. "She was our waitress, and she was dead."

Oh shit. Not Michelle! He hoped to God it wasn't her. Jeremy opened a desk drawer and pulled out a box of tissues. He handed the box to Stan. "Do you think you can answer a few more questions?"

"Sure. I'm glad to help. I hope you get this guy—whoever he is—who killed all these people. Son of a bitch!"

"Did you hear anything that would lead you to think that this was an act of terrorism? Any shouting in another language?"

Stan shook his head.

"What about any talk of bombs? Did you hear anyone say anything about a bomb that might go off?"

Stan shook his head again. "No."

"Did you see anyone else with a gun?"

Stan closed his eyes, as if trying to visualize the scene. "Maybe. I don't know. As I said, I got down on the floor in a hurry. I thought I saw a couple of guns on the floor."

"What else did you see from that vantage point?"

"Well, Joe and me stayed under the table until all the shooting stopped. The screaming kept going on and on. Then suddenly, it got quiet, just moaning and a cry for help now and then. That's when we decided to try to get out. When we stood up it seemed like there were bodies everywhere. And blood—lots of blood. Everywhere." Stan put his head in his hands. "I hope I never see anything like this again."

Stan took another tissue and blew his nose. He stood up and put on his cowboy hat. Jeremy knew he was finished. He stood up, too, and walked Stan to the door.

"Thank you for your cooperation." Jeremy shook his hand and opened the door. He handed Stan his card. "Here's my card if you think of anything else." Then he turned his attention to the next witness. "Let me get a cup of coffee, and I'll be right with you. Need a cup?" The caffeine was a necessity for Jeremy. He knew it was going to be a long night.

The man sitting in the chair outside his office said, "Sure."

The next couple of witnesses were flakes. They wanted to be part of the action. Jeremy had to go through the questions just the same. Who knew? Maybe one of them had some piece of evidence that would help.

Numbers Four and Six were just plain scared. They had little recollection of what had happened. Number Five wanted revenge. Jeremy was concerned he might become a copycat, so he plugged his name into N.C.I.C, National Crime Information Center. Thankfully, nothing came up.

Jeremy leaned back in his chair and closed his eyes after Witness Number Seven left, shutting the door behind him. He would give anything to be in his own bed right now. Or better yet, at Gina's. How many more witnesses were there to interview? Jeremy and his team of three detectives had been assigned to question the witnesses.

So far no one had identified or seen the shooter. But it seemed there were fatalities in the street, inside the bar, and on the roof. Jeremy concluded the shooter must have entered the bar, gone upstairs, and fired from the rooftop into the street. Then he could have begun shooting inside the bar and on the roof. Hell, they didn't even know if the shooter was dead or alive. According to Melvin, officers had picked up several firearms.

Jeremy sat up and massaged his forehead with the palm of his hand. He felt a headache coming on. "I need more coffee," Jeremy announced to the empty office. He stood and twisted from side to side to release some of the strain in his back.

"I've got a witness who saw the shooter." It was Mike's voice on the radio. He was questioning witnesses in the break room. "Says it was a woman!"

"Detain that witness. I'm on my way." Jeremy ran down the hall toward the break room. He radioed Melvin. "We've got a possible ID on the shooter. It's a goddam woman!"

Chapter 4

The break room held two vending machines. There was a small refrigerator and a counter with a sink, a coffee maker, and a microwave. Two tables seating six each were in the center of the room. Mike Shaw sat at the table farthest from the door. A man in his forties, dark hair, Native American appearance, sat across the table from Mike. Blood was on his face and one arm, like he had been sprayed with a water gun.

Jeremy braked from running and walked in, breathing hard. He pulled up a chair next to Mike and eyed the witness. He set the recorder on the table and turned it on.

Mike said, "Rudy, can you repeat what you just told me?"

Rudy wrung his hands. "Sure. Where do you want me to start?"

"Start with when you got to the bar and where you were."

"Okay. I got to the bar about eight with my buddy, Eddie. Him and me went upstairs in that area where you can walk around and look down. They added a bunch of tables up there for this, you know. We found a couple of seats at a table right by the top of the stairs—the stairs by the front door, not the ones by the bar in the back. We had to share the table with a couple of guys, real nice guys. Lots of people came up those stairs trying to find places to sit. They'd walk all the way around and then go down a different set of stairs. I think we got the last two seats."

"You got there at eight? Did you stay there the whole time?" Jeremy tapped the heel of his boot up and down. He squeezed his hands together like he was washing them. Get to the point, man.

"Huh? Well, yeah, except for when I had to go, you know…" He tilted his head in the direction of the door. "…we were drinking beer."

"Rudy, why don't you tell Jeremy when you saw the woman," Mike said.

"Oh, sure. So, me and Eddie were drinking beer. The other guys at the table were buying pitchers and sharing them with us. We bought a couple of pitchers, too. As I said, crowds of people kept coming up the stairs. A lot of them went out on the roof. From where we sat, we couldn't see the band, but we could hear it. When the Sonic Wolves started playing, it got crazy wild. Everyone stood up and started cheering and yelling. I even saw some young girls get up on the tables and dance."

Rudy stopped telling his story and asked, "Can I have a drink of water?"

Mike went over to the sink. He filled a Styrofoam coffee cup with tap water.

Rudy set the cup down on the table after taking a drink.

Jeremy stood up and walked around the break room. He stood behind the witness and stared at the back of his head. It was all he could do to contain himself.

"Then I saw this woman come up the stairs." Rudy's voice lowered to a whisper. "I noticed her because she

21

had on a leather jacket. It was too hot to be wearing a leather jacket. And she was alone. And she seemed angry. Everyone else was having a good time. She stood out because, well, because she didn't seem to fit in." He turned to Jeremy. "Does that make sense?"

"I think so," Jeremy said. Finally, we're getting somewhere. "Can you describe her a little more? What did she look like?"

"Well, she was a big woman." Rudy flexed his arms to show what he meant. "As I said, she seemed angry or crazed or drugged out, I couldn't tell. She just stood at the top of the stairs for a moment. I thought she must have been looking for someone, like maybe her friend had gone on without her, and she was trying to find where her friend was sitting."

"How old would you say she was?"

"Lemme think." Rudy squinted his eyes and stared at the pock-marked ceiling. "Well, she had gray hair—it was pulled back in a ponytail. I'd say she was fifty or so."

"Any unusual features?"

"Not really, except for her expression. Like I said, she looked real angry. And the way she dressed. She was in jeans and a leather jacket and work boots. Man, who would wear that on a hot night?"

"She stood at the top of the stairs and then what?"

"As I said, I thought she might be trying to find someone. She went out on the roof top, and that's when we heard the popping sound. I didn't know what it was at first. Now I know they were gun shots." Rudy wiped his nose with his forearm. Mike handed him a tissue.

"So, she fired shots from the roof top first. Is that what you saw or heard?" Jeremy's knuckles were white.

He realized he was clenching his fists. Breathe, man, breathe.

Rudy nodded. "My seat faced away from the entry to the roof, so I didn't see anything. But Eddie and the other guys dropped to the floor, and I'm like sitting there, saying, 'What? What happened?'" Rudy took another tissue and blew his nose. "That's when Eddie pulled me down under the table."

"Could you see anything from there?"

Rudy shook his head. Then he nodded. He put his face in his hands, and his entire body shook.

Jeremy waited.

With his face still covered, Rudy continued telling what he saw. "I heard more shots—my ears are still ringing—and then screaming and yelling and crying for help." He stopped and wiped his eyes with the back of his hand. "I saw her boots. She had on big, leather, work boots. They were covered with mud. She stood this close to our table." Rudy held out his hands to show about four feet. "Then she fell. She hit our table and fell to the ground. Right in front of us." Rudy put his head down on the table and sobbed.

Jeremy leaned across the table and turned off the recorder. "Go ahead and find out what else he saw," Jeremy said to Mike. "It sounds like our shooter got shot."

Jeremy stood up and patted Rudy on the back. "Thanks, Rudy. You've been a big help."

Chapter 5

From the initial round of witnesses, Jeremy was able to piece together what happened. Around nine thirty a crazed woman, about age fifty, walked into the James B Saloon and went upstairs. She went on the roof and shot into the crowd of partiers below. Then she came inside and began shooting randomly at the people on the roof, upstairs in the galley area, and down into the crowd on the first level. At about nine thirty-eight she was killed by another patron, not yet identified. It appeared there were several who pulled out their weapons, so an autopsy would most likely reveal who shot her. It would be considered in self-defense.

It was about three in the morning when Jeremy radioed Guy Walters, head of the medical team. "Do you have IDs on all of the dead? We're looking for a large woman, in her fifties, gray hair, ponytail."

"I'll check," Guy said.

"Okay," Jeremy said. "Get back to me with those IDs and the wounded as well. We'll need that information."

"Will do. We just sent several injured to Oklahoma City. Tulsa has also offered assistance with any wounded," Guy said.

"All right," Jeremy said.

Man, why'd she do it? Why did this unidentified woman come into the bar and shoot these innocent people? We may never know, but I'm going to do my damnedest to find out.

Jeremy liked his job. He liked the challenge of solving crimes, piecing together the evidence to form a big picture. He also liked the atmosphere of living in a college town. It would forever be young and progressive and forward thinking. Mineral Wells' low crime record consisted of domestic disputes, petty thefts, and drug and alcohol arrests. There were no local gangs, no organized prostitution, no terrorism. The community had always prided itself in being the safest college town in the nation, one of its major marketing campaigns. Mass shootings happened elsewhere. That is, until last night.

Functioning on caffeine and adrenalin, Jeremy entered the makeshift medical triage located behind the James B Saloon. Guy and his team were still examining the injured and determining who needed additional medical care, and who could be discharged. Those who were conscious were questioned. What did you see? Where did the shots come from? Could you identify the shooter? However, most of the injured were in shock and unable to respond clearly.

Jeremy walked around and observed the system in place. He needed to see the dead victims but didn't want to interrupt their work.

Finally, Guy finished examining one of the patients and saw Jeremy. He nodded and tilted his head toward a cordoned-off area. A large sheet divided the space in two. On one side was where the living were being taken care of. On the other side were the dead.

Guy came over and lifted the sheet, leading Jeremy to the other side. Sounds from the living side became muffled. There were no interviews going on here. No one was checking pulses or monitoring blood pressure. There was no bandaging cuts or wounds, no sending an injured person in an ambulance. Just twelve stretchers with twelve sheets covering twelve bodies. On this side there was going to be no survival, no returning home—except in a casket or an urn—no final caresses or slaps on the back, no more arguments or jokes. It was over for these twelve. There was only the shell of each person who was under a sheet. Whoever he or she had been, they no longer were.

"Death is so final," Jeremy muttered under his breath.

Guy nodded.

The two of them walked among the twelve bodies. There were identifying tags on eleven of the twelve victims. The twelfth one had no tag. That must be her.

Jeremy pulled back the sheet. There she was, just as she had been described—a large-bodied woman with graying hair pulled back in a ponytail, caked with blood. A bullet had entered near her right shoulder. There was a messy hole in the leather jacket she wore. He stared at the lifeless body for several minutes. What caused you to inflict such harm? How did you get to this point? Were you mistreated yourself? Or were you so sick? His chest tightened, and his eyes burned. He squeezed them tight to prevent the tears. Jeremy pulled the sheet farther back and saw more gunshot wounds. It was all so senseless. God, he hated violence. Jeremy pulled the sheet back up so that just her face showed. He took out his phone and took a picture of the presumed murderer's face.

Guy handed him a BPB, brown paper bag. "Here is what we found on her."

Jeremy peered inside the bag. A set of keys and

some cash. No wallet. No phone.

Jeremy turned to Guy. "How many of the injured have been able to ID the shooter?"

"Just a handful. Most of them didn't see anything. It was over before many even realized what was happening."

"And they all said it was a woman who did the shooting?"

"Yep," Guy said. "I've got one guy who sat at a table on the rooftop. His description matched Jane Doe."

"And there wasn't anyone with her?" Jeremy wanted to confirm the shooter was a lone wolf.

"Nope," Guy said.

"What about her injuries? Do we know if they were self-inflicted or not? I'm assuming someone pulled out their own concealed weapon and fired at her." Jeremy paused. "We don't know if anyone was responsible for injuring others, do we?"

Guy shook his head.

More to himself than to Guy, Jeremy said, "We're going to have to find out who else fired shots in the bar and who fatally shot Jane Doe." He rubbed his head. Caffeine and stress were giving him a headache.

Jeremy turned to Guy and shook his hand. "Thanks. Let's send this one to the morgue for holding." He pulled out a pad from his pocket and wrote some notes.

It was sometime between nighttime and dawn when Jeremy left the triage. There was an eerie silence, like the calm before a storm. Only this storm had come without warning. No, it was more like the aftermath of a tornado disaster. Jeremy had had his fill of those. Only law enforcement and medical personnel remained in the area. No helicopters hovered overhead. All the severely injured had already been taken to hospitals. Just a handful of cars and pickups remained parked in streets nearby. One of these vehicles belonged to Jane Doe.

Jeremy walked back around to the entrance of James B. He stared at the remains of the carnage that had occurred earlier that night. But wait—it was now Friday. The street was littered with debris. The stage remained, but stood bare. A single strand of blinking lights from the stage flickered. He turned and entered the bar. Broken glass crunched under his boots. It was mixed with blood and spilt beer, making it slick in places. Jeremy didn't recognize most of those securing the area because so many additional officers had been called in.

He spotted another local, Dylan McCain. He was picking up an abandoned phone from the debris-covered floor. Dylan saw Jeremy and walked over to him. He pointed up toward the galley area upstairs. "We think shots from up there hit the shooter."

"I wonder if there was only one person who killed Jane Doe." In this mess trying to find these people was going to be like trying to find the back of one of Gina's earrings.

"I guess the autopsy report will tell us that," Dylan said.

"Yeah, you're right." Jeremy glanced at the bar at the back. The mirrored glass behind the giant oak bar had been shattered.

Jeremy felt his radio vibrate before he heard the chief's voice. "Jeremy, I've got the media breathing down my neck. What's the latest info you have? I'm not going to share anything with these reporters, but I just need to know if we're making progress."

"I'm pretty sure we've ID'd the suspect. I have a

picture of her on my phone. And I have a set of keys that were on her person."

"So, we need to find the vehicle. What's the make?"

Jeremy peered into the bag without touching anything. "Hold on a minute," he said. He took his phone and used the flashlight to shine into the bag. He jostled the items around until he could see the keys. One belonged to a vehicle, and it said FORD on it. The other must have been a house key. "It appears she was driving a Ford," he told the Chief.

"After we dust it for prints, I'll have Lance work on it. We've set up a staging area for the media on the other side of the barricades at the Sooner Avenue entrance."

"Okay, Chief. I'm on my way." Jeremy left the bar. Satellite trucks lined up, and he saw silhouettes of about twenty individuals milling about. Jeremy hated dealing with the media. He knew they were a necessary part of the system, but he was grateful his interaction with them was limited.

It was early dawn when the Mineral Wells Police had an affirmative identification of the killer from Thursday night's mass shooting. A 2005 Ford pickup was found in the parking lot of Mattress King on Fifth and Main. It belonged to Carl Sutton, who was deceased. The OSBI had found no matches of the dead woman's prints in their data base, but with the truck owner's name, they discovered that there were two living daughters— Lou Ella Sutton and Alice Sutton Bennett. Lou Ella's current listed address matched that of Carl Sutton's residence. Melvin Pollard assigned two officers to go to the presumed residence of Lou Ella Sutton. Jeremy and his partner, Darrell, would go to the other daughter's home later Friday morning, after the two detectives had a couple of hours' sleep.

Jeremy got home at seven Friday morning. He set his alarm for 8:30 and fell asleep.

Chapter 6

Sunday, Monday, Happy Days... Alice Bennett edged toward the side of the bed, turning off her cell phone alarm. It was five o'clock and still dark outside. She sensed Rodney, her husband, stir as she gently lifted his arm from around her. Not wanting to wake him, she slipped out of bed and into the bathroom, shutting the door quietly. Then to the kitchen to make coffee. Alice yawned. Leaning on her elbows, she stared at the coffee as it dripped into the pot.

Wake up, Alice told herself. She rubbed her eyes, smearing the remains of yesterday's mascara and her nighttime eye cream. Alice wore her favorite nightshirt—the one with Snoopy sleeping on top of his doghouse. It hid her figure, which had expanded some with the birth of two babies, who were now in their teens.

What day was it? Friday. The coffee seemed to take longer to brew, just like the alarm seemed to go off earlier, especially in the summer. Finally, it was ready, and she poured herself a cup. Taking a drink, Alice mentally went through her checklist of to-dos for the day. At the top of her list was going to the store. She needed to stock up before she and Rodney picked up the girls from their respective camps on Sunday. But now it was time to go to work. With coffee in hand, she returned to their bedroom. Alice entered her office—what used to be their master closet—and turned on her laptop.

Alice was a graphic artist and designed cards, stationery, and personalized invitations. She and her husband, Rodney, had a small printing company. Originally called Bennett Printing, Rodney had bought the family business when his father retired. When Alice began to design wedding invitations and personal cards, Rodney updated the business, adding digital printing and a webpage. They changed the name to Sutton Cards. Sutton was her maiden name.

Alice spent the next two hours on a project for a museum in Tulsa. They wanted blank notecards with sketches of the gardens and villa that housed the exhibits. Alice glanced at her phone. It was almost seven o'clock. She reached a stopping point on her project and clicked save. Alice got up and peered at her still-sleeping husband as she walked back to the kitchen. Just as she did every other weekday at seven, Alice fixed herself a bowl of Wheat Chex and turned on the television, lowering the volume. A creature of habit, she thrived on routine.

Life was good, Alice thought, crunching on her cereal. Their business was prospering, and both daughters would be at the high school in the fall. Flory a senior, and Phoebe starting her freshman year. On Sunday they would pick the girls up from camp—Flory at basketball camp and Phoebe at band camp. Alice thought of the girls' complaints about no cars or cell phones for a whole week.

The opening music began as the orange rainbow logo for the *TODAY Show* came on the TV screen.

"Good morning." It was Savannah Guthrie's voice. "We have breaking news. A mass shooting occurred overnight around 9:30 at a popular bar in Mineral Wells,

Oklahoma. Twelve known dead, over twenty injured at the annual Battle of the Bands. This is TODAY, Friday, August 7, 2015."

Alice stared at the images on the screen from the night before. Personal videos from camera phones captured scenes from inside the bar and out in the street. Two females in cut-offs ran past holding hands as the popping of what sounded like firecrackers could be heard. Inside the bar a man wearing a cowboy hat leaned against a table that had been knocked over. There was blood on his face, and he had his arm around a young woman who was crying. The ground was littered with bottles and plastic cups and other debris. Outside, helicopters overhead could be heard while law enforcement secured the crime scene. Emergency vehicles departed with flashing lights and sirens.

"Oh my God," Alice said. How could this happen? Mineral Wells was a forty-five-minute drive from where they lived in Junction, Oklahoma. It was too close to home.

"Babe, come here," Alice called to Rodney.

No answer.

"Rodney," Alice shouted. "Turn on the TV in the bedroom. There's been another mass shooting." She turned up the volume to listen to the report.

"…the local affiliate has reported authorities believe the presumed suspect is a woman who opened fire, fatally killing eleven individuals before being killed. The suspect has not been identified, nor has the person who shot her…An estimate of more than twenty being treated for injuries…Authorities do not believe there is any connection to terrorism…the act of a lone wolf. There is no known motive at this time…Law officials are currently interviewing witnesses and gathering data..."

Rodney strolled into the kitchen. What was left of his hair stuck out in all directions. "Alice, I don't want to get sucked into being a lookie loo at someone else's tragedy."

"Shhh!" Alice interrupted him. She put her hand out like a crossing guard signaling stop. On the television a national reporter interviewed the police chief. Alice turned to Rodney. "This shooting happened last night in Mineral Wells." Her face cupped in her hands, she leaned on the kitchen table where her bowl of cereal sat untouched.

"Oh shit! That's bad," Rodney said. He poured himself some coffee and sat down. They watched the report until the commercial break.

Alice pushed her cereal bowl away. "Who do we know whose kids are at A&M?"

Rodney paused. "Let's see..." He rattled off a handful of names. "The Battle of the Bands is going on this week, and it draws a large crowd every year." Rodney stood up with his coffee in hand. "Let me know what you hear. I've got to get ready for work." He kissed the top of Alice's head as he walked past.

"Okay," Alice said, captivated by the news. Without warning, she thought of Flory, their oldest daughter. She could have been there. She could have been one of the victims.

"Rodney," Alice said. "Flory." Her voice cracked. She had a sick feeling in her stomach.

Rodney turned around and put his arm around her. "Hey. We're going to be all right. Nothing's going to happen to Flory or to us." He squeezed her.

"You're probably right," Alice said. But she

couldn't stop thinking about the families of these victims. Who were they? Did they know yet?

After Rodney left, Alice tried to get back to work. She pulled up the project for the museum in Tulsa and stared at the screen. Nothing. She couldn't focus. Sighing, Alice clicked save and wandered back into the kitchen where the television was still on. There was a segment about last minute vacations before school. Across the bottom of the screen, copy scrolled about the shooting in Mineral Wells.

"…injured sent to trauma centers…law enforcement still searching the crime scene."

Alice picked up her cereal bowl and poured the soggy remains down the sink. She didn't feel like eating. Watching the news made her feel sick, yet she was mesmerized. If this had been a normal day, Alice would be in her office working. But seeing scenes from the shooting on TV had disrupted her routine. It was no longer a normal day. She glanced at her phone. How could it be 9:30 already? And she hadn't even showered. Alice turned off the television.

In the bathroom she gazed at her reflection in the mirror. How am I going to lose those fifteen pounds? She peered at her face, smiling then frowning. Were those new wrinkles? She examined her hair for any new gray strands. Sighing, she turned on the water in the shower.

The doorbell rang. Startled, she turned off the water and grabbed a robe.

From the entryway Alice saw two male silhouettes through the curtained window of the front door. The living room, next to the front entry, had a large picture window facing the street. A black Dodge Charger sat in their driveway.

Chapter 7

Why would there be two men at her front door? Alice wrapped the robe around her even tighter, realizing she had nothing on underneath. She wasn't going to open the door to two strangers. Alice backed away carefully, hoping they hadn't seen her. The doorbell rang again, this time accompanied by knocking.

Spooked, Alice moved out of sight, standing inside the doorway to the kitchen.

Once more, the doorbell rang. "Mrs. Bennett," said a voice. "Are you Alice Sutton Bennett? We need to speak to you."

Who are they, and how do they know my name?

"Mrs. Bennett. We're from the Mineral Wells Police Department. Please open the door."

Alice's stomach churned, and she bent over. All she could think of was the last time police had come to their home. At least Rodney had been with her. This time she was alone. She knew whatever the reason was, it wasn't good, and she knew they had seen her.

"Can you wait a minute? I'm not dressed," she yelled. Alice walked past the entry to get to her bedroom. She called out, "Going to get some clothes on."

In the bathroom she found yesterday's clothes, a pair of gym shorts and an old T-shirt. Alice ran a finger through her hair and tried to wipe off the smudged mascara.

Something was terribly wrong. As Alice made her way to the entry, memories of the night her parents had been killed by a drunk driver filled her mind. Two police had shown up to inform them. Carl and Florence Sutton had been on their way home from celebrating their seventieth birthdays when their car was hit head on. Her hands shook as she reached for the door. It wouldn't open. Then she realized the deadbolt was still on.

She opened the door a crack and saw the men. One was tall and muscular, as if he spent his free time in the gym. He was black and wore dark pants and a pale blue shirt with a black sports jacket. He had on a pair of Ray-Ban Aviators. The other man was shorter and slighter built. He had a rust-colored beard and wore pressed jeans and a plaid button-down shirt under his navy sports jacket.

"Mrs. Bennett? May we come in?" It was the shorter of the two, and he showed her his badge.

Alice opened the door, and the officers stepped inside. Alice unconsciously wrapped her robe around her, except she was no longer wearing it.

"You are Alice Sutton Bennett. Is that correct?" The other officer spoke as he removed his sunglasses.

Alice nodded. She backed up a few steps but remained in the front entry.

The shorter one spoke. "Mrs. Bennett, I'm Detective Jeremy Turner, and this is my partner, Darrell Wilson. We're with the Mineral Wells Police. Can we come in? We'd like to ask you a few questions." The detective tilted his head in the direction of the living room.

"Of course," Alice said, "come in." She knew she was shaking. What was going on? Why were the police from Mineral Wells here? What did she have to do with that horrible shooting that happened last night?

"Please sit down." Alice led them into the living room, pointing to the navy and white plaid sofa that faced the large picture window. She sat on one of the coordinating armchairs. There was a rustic coffee table in the center. This was the room where they learned about her parents' deaths, the room they never used.

Jeremy took the seat closest to Alice. "Mrs. Bennett," Jeremy began, "we need to ask you some questions regarding a relative of yours."

"A relative?"

"Yes. Do you have a sister?"

Alice didn't answer. Her heart beat rapidly, and her breathing became shallow.

"Mrs. Bennett?"

"Yes," she said. Alice tried to wrack her brain. What did anything have to do with Lou? Alice didn't even know where she was living. Surely, they had her mixed up with some other Bennett who also had a sister.

"Is Lou Ella Sutton your sister?" Detective Wilson's gaze was kind, but also sad.

Alice turned her head away. She didn't want to know what they had to say. She just wanted to curl up in a ball. She wanted them to go away.

"Please, Mrs. Bennett. Can you answer the question? Is Lou Ella Sutton your sister?" Jeremy repeated the question.

Alice pressed both of her hands over her mouth and nodded. What had happened?

"Can you tell me where your sister was last night?"

She shook her head. She couldn't speak.

Darrell held out a photo of Lou on his phone. "Is this your sister?"

Alice's eyes opened wide in disbelief, but she nodded.

"Tell me, did something happen to my sister? Is she hurt?" Alice feared the worst. *Please, God, not another accident.*

"Mrs. Bennett...Ma'am..." Jeremy's face turned sad.

"Oh, my God! What happened?"

"Are you aware of the shooting that happened last night in Mineral Wells?"

"Lou was shot? Is she okay?" She gripped the chair. Her eyes darted back and forth between the two detectives. This wasn't happening.

"Mrs. Bennett." Jeremy cleared his throat. "We have reason to believe that your sister, Lou Ella Sutton, was responsible for the deaths of eleven individuals last night at the James B Saloon, before she was shot and killed."

Alice moaned. She bent over, burying her face in her hands. This couldn't be. There must be some mistake. She knew Lou would never do something like this. Alice curled into a ball in the armchair and sobbed. All the fears she had tried to push aside about Lou—nothing compared to this.

Alice began to hyperventilate. Panicked, she couldn't breathe.

"Mrs. Bennett. Are you all right?" One of the detectives was talking to her.

Alice heard their voices and saw the alarmed expressions on their faces as the two detectives lay her down on the floor. Soon a paper bag was placed over her mouth.

"Take slow breaths. Breathe into the paper bag." Darrell stayed near her, holding the bag to her face, coaching her to breathe in a calm voice.

Alice tried to breathe slowly, but her heart was still racing.

"Don't talk. Don't try to think. Just breathe…in and out, in and out. That's it. Keep going, Mrs. Bennett. You're doing good."

Alice closed her eyes and listened to his soothing words. She tried to block out what she had heard. Just for now.

Eventually her breathing became normal. Darrell helped her back into her chair. He brought her a glass of water from the kitchen.

Alice nodded as she took a drink. "I need to call my husband."

Chapter 8

In that instant, Alice's life changed. She was no longer Alice Bennett, wife of Rodney, and mother of Flory and Phoebe. She was Alice Sutton Bennett, sister of mass murderer, Lou Ella Sutton.

Eleven individuals—children or parents or siblings, spouses, or soul mates—would never come home. The project at work would never be completed. A baby's first steps, walking down the aisle, the milestones of raising a family would be without a father or a mother or child. A courtship ended. Personal goals never met. Hurts never resolved. So much unfinished business. So many holes and gaps in the lives of those who had died and their loved ones. It was too much.

And Lou. Lou did this? Alice couldn't grasp that as a reality. There was no instruction manual for how to be the next of kin to a suspected murderer.

****

Alice sat in the backseat of her mother's car. It was 1992. Florence Sutton told her to wear her good pantsuit. Alice's father, Carl Sutton, drove. Her parents sat in front, in silence. She wondered why no one was speaking. All she knew was they were going to a meeting at Mr. Armstrong's office. Barney Armstrong, one of Carl's college buddies, was her father's attorney and accountant. At age eighteen and weeks from graduating, going to a meeting on a Saturday morning was the last

41

thing Alice wanted to do. And no one would tell her what it was about. Now that they were on their way, Alice thought her parents were acting very odd.

Carl pulled into a parking space in front of a two-story brick building in downtown Junction. There was the old barbershop on one side and a vacuum repair store on the other side. Alice watched her parents. Carl sat for a moment, as if he didn't want to get out. Just what was the reason for this meeting? Silently all three got out of the car. The door to the building was locked, and there was a hand-written sign on it. *Come to the back door.*

Alice followed her parents down an alley behind the building. Carl, built like a lumberjack, was dressed for work—khaki pants, a white button-down shirt, and a bow tie. His brown hair showed flecks of gray. He towered over Florence, who was petite. She wore one of her church dresses and heels. Her auburn hair curled naturally, and her complexion was like a china doll. Carl rang the buzzer, and soon Barney Armstrong opened the metal door.

"Come in!" Barney's booming voice broke the silence.

Barney Armstrong was a large man. His voice fit his build. The belt on his pants cinched under his belly so that his pants rode low. Alice was afraid one day they would slip down. He always carried a wad of tissues to combat the allergies that caused his nose to be red and bulbous.

"Glad to see everyone. Miss Alice, I'm always happy when I get a chance to visit with you as well." Barney sounded as if he was yelling when he spoke, but in a friendly way. He put Alice at ease.

"Come into my conference room." Barney

chuckled. His conference room consisted of two card tables pushed together with six folding chairs. Set against the wall was a third table with a pot of coffee. "Can I get you some coffee," he paused, glancing at Alice, "or a Coke?"

Alice shook her head. "Thank you, Barney. We're fine," Florence said.

In front of one chair was a manila folder. Other than that, the tables were bare. "Let's get down to business. We don't want to waste precious time on a Saturday as pretty as this one." Barney had positioned himself at the end of the long rectangle. Carl and Florence sat on one side, leaving Alice to the other. She felt as if it was them against her. She said nothing, but kept her hands squeezed between her knees that bounced nervously.

Barney addressed Alice's parents. "As I'm sure you've explained to Alice the reason for this meeting, we can sign these papers, and you all can go."

"Uh...no. We haven't," Carl stammered. "We were hoping you could help us with that."

"So, Alice doesn't know why she's here? She doesn't know about Lou?" Alice jerked her head toward Barney. "I guess not," he said. His voice became softer.

Again, Barney addressed her parents. "I think it should come from you, but I'll be glad to help with the legal aspects of it."

Carl and Florence turned toward each other. "Alice," Carl said, "you may have noticed some things different about Lou."

"You know how you used to ask me questions about Lou Ella, why she didn't have friends, and why she went to the hospital," Florence added.

Why was her mother calling her Lou Ella? Where

was Lou, and why wasn't she at this meeting?

"That's right," Carl continued. "Lou has a disorder that affects her brain, and so it affects that way she behaves. We've been getting help for her condition once we realized something was wrong."

Alice felt like someone had socked her in the stomach. Something was wrong with Lou's brain? What did that mean? She didn't say anything. She didn't know what to say.

There was a long pause. If her parents expected her to say something, it wasn't going to happen. Alice felt betrayed, as if her parents had caused this to happen to Lou. And now they were trying to explain it away.

Barney finally spoke. "Alice, Lou is schizophrenic." He opened the folder and pulled out some papers. "Here is a copy of the medical reports your parents gave me for legal purposes." Barney pushed the papers toward Alice. She stared at them but didn't pick them up. It was as if they were contaminated.

More awkward silence followed. Alice stared at the table, not the papers in front of her. She didn't want to see what was written in the report. Maybe if she didn't read it, it wouldn't exist. Maybe Lou was just strange. Maybe the doctors made this up. Maybe her parents did something to Lou—accidentally, of course. Alice didn't know what to think. She felt numb.

Barney cleared his throat. "Because of Lou's condition, your parents have had to make some legal decisions should something ever happen to them." Carl and Florence nodded but said nothing. "Someday your parents will not be here. They'll be...dead. And, uh, they decided they need to make legal provisions for you and Lou when that time comes." Barney turned toward Carl and Florence, but they remained silent. "Your parents have set up two trust accounts—one for you and one for Lou. They have also designated you—and me—as executors of their estate if they are no longer here or capable of managing their affairs." Barney paused. "Do you understand?"

Alice shook her head. "I don't know what this means." Those were the first words Alice had spoken.

"This is hard for all of us," Carl said. "None of us like what we're doing. We don't want to be here making these difficult decisions. But we want to do what is best and make sure you and Lou are cared for."

"We wish we didn't have to have this meeting," Florence said. It seemed as if when Alice spoke, the dam of silence broke. "But we don't know what Lou's future will hold. And we felt this was the best thing to do. I hope you understand."

Alice nodded. But she didn't understand. Not at all.

"Alice, you and I will be co-executors of the estate of Carl and Florence Sutton, should anything happen to them. What that means is the two of us will jointly make the decisions regarding all the physical possessions—the farm as well as their bank accounts. Any and everything." Barney paused and looked directly at Alice. "We will be a team."

Again, Alice nodded, but said nothing. Papers were signed, and the three of them left. Nothing was ever spoken of the meeting again.

****

Alice had been eighteen when she learned about Lou's schizophrenia. At the time Lou was twenty-four and living at home. Alice had pushed the memory of that meeting out of her mind for almost twenty-five years. It was something she had tried to bury. This would not define her life. She would not let it interfere with her own happiness. No one ever needed to know about Lou's problem.

Chapter 9

Ten minutes later Rodney arrived. Alice heard the door from the garage to the kitchen slam. She hadn't told him why the police were here, and for a moment, a feeling of relief washed over her.

"Alice, what's going on?" Rodney came into the living room. He appeared out of breath, as if he had run home. The two detectives stood up.

"Mr. Bennett, I'm Jeremy Turner, and this is my partner, Detective Darrell Wilson."

Rodney shook their hands and repeated, "What's going on? Why are you here?"

"Please, have a seat, Mr. Bennett," Jeremy said.

Rodney sat on the sofa facing the large window, where Jeremy had been sitting. "Would someone please tell me what's going on?"

"Rodney," Alice tried to tell him. But she couldn't say it. She started crying again. She saw his frustration, but she couldn't explain what had happened.

"Mr. Bennett, can you identify this woman?" Darrell showed him the photo of Lou.

"Yes. That's my sister-in-law, Lou. What happened?"

Alice got out of her chair and scooted next to him on the sofa. She clung to his arm.

"You're aware of the shooting that happened in Mineral Wells last night?" Darrell's voice softened.

"Yes."

He continued, "We have reason to believe your sister-in-law was responsible for the deaths of eleven individuals before being shot and killed herself."

"Oh, my God!" Rodney slumped in his seat, and Alice clung even tighter to his arm. "Oh, my God!" Rodney shook his head. For a moment there was silence. The reality was incomprehensible. Alice watched Rodney struggle. Then he sat up. "I need to call Barney," he said.

The Bennett family lived on a quiet cul de sac in a modest neighborhood. Junction, a middle-sized community, had a single high school and perhaps every fast-food chain available. There was a small state college—Central Oklahoma College, COC, where Alice's father had taught economics before the accident. The college had the tallest structure in town, a bell tower, which rang on the hour.

Interstate thirty-five, the north-south route that began at Duluth, Minnesota and ended at Laredo, Texas was the eastern boundary for Junction. Railroad tracks divided the east side from the west side of town, and outlying acreages of the neighboring community of Persimmon butted the city limits on the west side. The town had that spread out feeling as if you had the entire sofa to yourself, arms stretched out on either side. To the north were open fields and more acreages. Beyond that was the town of Guthrie, the first state capital of Oklahoma. To the south was Oklahoma City, the current capital. Strategically or accidentally placed between the former and current capital, their town acquired the name of Junction.

Alice stared out the window in their living room.

Mrs. Callahan's son was visiting. His car was parked in their elderly neighbor's driveway. Soon Barney's old tan Chevy Impala pulled in behind the black Dodge Charger.

The doorbell rang, and Alice watched Rodney let Barney in. She remained seated, unable to get up.

"Hey, Rodney. I came over as soon as I could. Where's Alice?"

Barney Armstrong's voice, always loud and always a voice of assurance, was a momentary source of comfort for Alice. Barney had been her father's attorney and accountant, and now he was theirs. If anything could be fixed, Barney could do it. But was this fixable?

Alice could not grasp in her mind what Lou had done. It was unfathomable. There was a part of her trying to hang on to her old reality, thinking this had to be a case of mistaken identity. Once they were able to clear things up, surely Alice would be able to resume her life. Her brain was unable to accept others had died at Lou's hand.

Barney strode toward Alice, bent over, and bear-hugged her. "I'm so sorry," he whispered in her ear. She went limp, and tears filled her eyes.

Jeremy cleared his throat. He had moved to the armchair that faced the entry. "I'm sorry for having to bring such terrible news to you, Mr. and Mrs. Bennett. But I need to ask you a few questions about Lou Ella." He looked at Alice and Rodney and added, "I know this is hard."

Alice stared at this man. This couldn't be happening.

"Can you tell me Ms. Sutton's other relatives? Are there any other immediate family members?"

Alice struggled to concentrate. The questioning seemed surreal. She shook her head, and her eyes pleaded with Rodney.

Rodney glanced at Alice, then answered. "Just our family. Alice and I have two daughters, Flory, who's seventeen, and Phoebe, who's fourteen."

Jeremy wrote the information on a small pad. He paused. "I understand your parents are no longer living. Is that correct?"

Rodney took a deep breath. "Yes. They were killed in an automobile accident two years ago."

Jeremy stopped writing. "I'm so sorry," he said. "What happened?"

Alice watched Rodney struggle. This was hard for him, too.

Barney gave Jeremy the information. "They were killed by a drunk driver on their way home from a concert in Oklahoma City. A drunk kid crossed the median and hit them head on."

"Oh shit!" Jeremy looked at Alice and said, "Pardon my French."

Rodney nodded. "That's how we feel, too."

"Can you tell me about your sister's friends, who she hung out with?"

Rodney continued to answer for Alice. "Lou really didn't have friends. She was more of a loner."

"Can you think of a motive she might have had for going into the bar last night and…"

Alice grabbed Rodney's arm. She dug her nails into his skin.

"Please, don't say it," Rodney said. "We're still struggling with what happened. But, no, we have no idea. That wasn't who Lou was."

Alice watched Jeremy scribble something on his pad. "You call her Lou. Is that right?"

Rodney said, "Yes. Lou. That's what we call her, I mean, called her."

"I need some background information on her—date of birth, education, medical history, any police record she had…"

Alice bit her lip to keep from exploding. Lou had been reduced to a list of statistics. Just the facts, ma'am. But then she didn't even know who Lou was any more. Suddenly Alice realized, Lou *wasn't* any more. She was gone. Dead. Not only that, but others died because of her. She wanted to bolt.

"Alice?" Rodney jostled her. "Are you okay?"

She shook her head.

Barney had a file in front of him that he opened. "Lou Ella Sutton was born on July 31, 1968. She was diagnosed with paranoid schizophrenia in…" Barney flipped through the pages until he found what he was looking for. "In 1988."

"Can you tell me more about your sister's mental health issues?"

Alice covered her mouth and shook her head.

"Was your sister ever hospitalized?" Jeremy asked. "Did she ever have any run-ins with the law?"

Alice's eyes glazed over. What do I say about Lou to this stranger? Does he want to know how we used to make Sutton cookies together, or how she taught me how to ride a bike, or how she loved animals, or how many times Mom and Dad had to hospitalize her, or how I completely ignored her once she moved away? Or how I could have reached out to her more and maybe prevented this thing from happening? Does he need to know about those times Lou's behavior scared me? And scared Mom and Dad? How much do I say?

Alice shook her head and began to cry. She covered her face with her hands.

Jeremy put away his pad. "Okay. I think I have enough for now." He glanced at his phone, clicked on it, answering a text he had received. He stood up, then stopped. "Lou Ella—Lou—was living on Old Farm Road. Is that correct?"

Alice's stomach lurched. She grabbed Rodney's arm. That was her parents' address. How did they know that? For that matter, how had they found them?

"That was Carl and Florence's home. Lou lived with them most of the time, until the accident," Rodney explained. "Then she disappeared."

Barney stood up. He gave Jeremy his business card. "Why don't you call me if you have any more questions. I've known the family longer than Alice has been around." Barney and Jeremy exchanged information.

Jeremy and Darrell shook hands with Rodney and Barney, nodding to Alice. "Thank you for answering our questions. We are so sorry for your loss. Our condolences to you," Darrell said.

As Rodney walked the three men to the door, Alice remained stuck on the sofa. She wanted to crawl into a hole.

Chapter 10

Rodney watched Barney and the two detectives leave. He pulled at his golf shirt that clung to his body. He was soaked. Nerves.

Now what? His life, as he knew it, no longer existed. Rodney scratched his head, sending his reddish-blond comb-over in all directions. What was he supposed to do? In the living room he saw Alice in a ball on the sofa. No use in getting her up.

Rodney changed his shirt and put on a pair of shorts. He knew he wouldn't be going back to work. Average build, Rodney had lost much of the muscle mass he had when he played baseball. Too much sitting all day. He had considered growing a mustache, but Alice had complained it was prickly. Like his father, Rodney had fair skin and reddish hair. And freckles. He hated them. But it was his eyes, clear blue, that first attracted Alice to him.

He wandered into the kitchen, turning on the television and lowering the volume. At the bottom of the screen ran an announcement: *Mineral Wells Press conference, 11:00, for updates on mass shooting.* He didn't know whether to watch it or not. Friday's newspaper was on the kitchen counter. Unfolding the paper, in large bold type, the headline read, "Mass Shooting at Mineral Wells Bar." He tried to read the article, but his mind couldn't compute.

Rodney's phone vibrated in his back pocket. It was Barney.

"Hey, Barney," he said.

"Rodney, can you talk?"

"Sure," Rodney said. What else was he doing?

"I want you and Alice to know I'm here for you. If you all need anything, just holler."

"Thanks, Barney."

"I'm sorry I didn't stick around, but I thought you two might need time to yourselves," Barney said.

"Alice is pretty shaken up, and I don't think it's sunk in with me yet. I'm not sure what to do." He paused. "What's this going to mean for us?" Seeing mass shooters on the news was one thing. Being related to one was a completely different matter. Rodney couldn't begin to comprehend what the victims' families were going through.

"Uh…Rodney, I think it may become more serious than you realize. The other reason I called is to let you know that there's a press conference at eleven, and…"

"Yeah, I saw that on the news."

"They're probably going to announce the identity of the killer. That means Lou's picture is going to be on national TV. Once they do that, your lives, well…they'll never be the same."

Rodney didn't say anything.

"Just remember I'm a phone call away. Call me."

"Sure," Rodney said.

"Anytime. I mean it!"

The two men hung up, and Rodney set his phone on the kitchen counter.

One crucial thought surfaced. "Oh, my God. Flory and Phoebe!"

Entering the living room Rodney saw Alice still curled in a ball. He sat on the edge of the sofa.

"Alice, we need to talk."

Alice stirred, moaning. "Go away. I don't want to talk." She turned, so that her back faced him.

"What about our girls?"

Alice sat up. Her red eyes filled with tears. "Do you think they know?"

Rodney shook his head. "I don't know. I don't think so." He swallowed the lump in his throat. "I hope not—not yet."

Rodney held her, saying nothing. There was nothing to say.

Alice turned toward Rodney. She looked terrible—red eyes, splotchy face, smashed hair. "I'm going to bed." She got up and left the room.

Rodney watched her leave. Hopelessness washed over him. He felt abandoned. He had no idea what the rest of the day would bring or how they were supposed to move forward. However, he knew crawling into bed when their two daughters were coming home from camp in two days wasn't going to help.

"I should probably call the guys at work," Rodney said to himself. He had left his phone in the kitchen. There were eight voice messages and fifteen texts. He glanced at them to see who had called. One was from Becky, his bookkeeper. She had left a message.

"Hi Mr. Bennett. This is Becky from work. I'm sorry about your wife's sister. We just heard about it on the radio." There was a pause on the line. "Uh, I have to go, and so is everyone else, except for Mr. and Mrs. Nguyen. They're still here, and… I just wanted to let you know."

Rodney stared at his phone. That was strange. What was going on? Surely it didn't have to do with Lou, or did it? Rodney slammed his fist into the wall.

At least he didn't have to call the shop. Rodney listened to the other voicemails. Four had no identification. One call was from the local paper. He certainly wasn't going to call them back. One was from the OSBI, Oklahoma State Bureau of Investigation, and there was Barney's number.

"Hi Rodney. One more thing. I wanted to give you a little legal advice. If the police or the media try to call you, don't answer any questions. You understand? Let me talk to them for you, especially the media. They're going to want a statement, so we'll need to work on that. Anyway, I'm a phone call away."

What would we do without that guy? Rodney knew Barney was going to be their lifeline. He was basically retired, except for a handful of clients with whom he'd worked for years. Rodney knew he would do anything for Carl's family, and Alice was all that was left of it.

Rodney heard the doorbell ring. He hesitated. He knew he wasn't going to answer the door, not after this morning. He stood in the entry and saw the outline of a woman through the curtained window. Glancing out the picture window in the living room, he stared in disbelief as he watched a man with a microphone come out of a van followed by someone with a video camera. With sickened shock, Rodney saw another truck slowly drive toward the house. Then two more.

The doorbell rang again. Rodney tensed. He saw a man and a woman peering into the window. This couldn't be happening. He ran to the garage to get duct tape. From the linen closet Rodney grabbed sheets and blankets. When he returned, Rodney banged on the window and yelled at them. In the background a couple of reporters stood in the yard speaking into microphones, facing cameramen. We've become part of the news, Rodney realized.

Dragging one of the kitchen chairs into the living room, Rodney taped a blanket over the window. He watched the street fill with more reporters and camera crews. Vehicles parked on both sides of the street. It was a circus, and they were the freak show on display. With the media outside, he became a prisoner in their home.

Rodney returned the chair to the kitchen and saw Lou's face on the TV screen. Rodney's head pounded. How had her disease taken her so far, that she felt she had to kill innocent victims? He couldn't understand what must have gone through her mind.

"Authorities have positively identified the suspect of last night's mass shooting in Mineral Wells. Lou Ella Sutton…Her only living relatives reside in Junction."

That's us. They're talking about us. Rodney walked away from the television. He didn't want to hear any more. He collapsed into his recliner in the den. His mind couldn't reconcile the events of the past fifteen hours. And he had no idea what was going to happen to his family, or what to do next.

He leaned back in the recliner and closed his eyes. The television in the kitchen was still on, but Rodney couldn't make out what was being said. The clicking sound from the refrigerator reminded him it needed repairing. Down the hall he heard Alice sobbing. Could you run out of tears? he wondered. Rodney hadn't shed a tear. He was too numb. That eleven innocent victims were dead because of Lou was beyond comprehension.

There it was again, the doorbell. The sound startled him, and he tensed. He felt trapped inside his own home like a caged animal. The house phone rang. No one called on the house phone.

"We can't come to the phone right now, so would you please leave a message after the tone? Thank you." It was Phoebe's ten-year-old voice. They had never changed the message.

"Go to hell, you murderers!" No caller ID. Rodney got up and unplugged the phone.

His cell phone rang. It was Larry, his older brother, who lived in Los Angeles. He never called. Rodney realized he must have heard what had happened.

"Hello," Rodney said.

"My God! What did that woman do?"

Rodney didn't answer.

"Rod, are you there?"

"Yes."

"What happened? Couldn't you stop her from doing that? I mean, how did she kill all those people?"

"Listen, Larry—"

"Lawrence! Call me Lawrence."

"Okay, Lawrence. We don't know what happened. We just found out ourselves, and—"

"This is bad. Really bad, man." Rodney heard a woman's voice in the background. "Hold on a minute," his brother said.

Rodney waited. Some things never changed. Which girlfriend was this? In that moment he resented his brother. Larry, or Lawrence, as he now preferred to be called, could go on with his life. This was just a nuisance for him. But for Rodney, he knew his life would never be the same.

Lawrence came back on the phone. "Say, Rodney, this news isn't going to sit well with the people I work with. So, I'm not going to say anything about it here. And I need you to make sure Mom and Dad don't go bonkers about it, 'cause then they'll start calling me. You got that?"

"No! I don't get that. You just go on with your life, *Lawrence.* We'll sit in this pile of shit without any help from you." Rodney clicked off his phone. It wasn't the same as slamming down a receiver.

His phone rang again. It was his brother. Rodney didn't answer.

"Sorry about that, Rodney. Didn't mean to sound quite so crass. But I'd appreciate it if you'd talk to Mom and Dad for me. Try to leave me out of it for now. Thanks, pal."

"Thanks for nothing," Rodney muttered. He realized he did, in fact, need to call his parents, who lived in Arizona now. But not yet. I need to—what did he need to do? Rodney was at a total loss.

He needed to call his parents. His employees had left. For good? How were they going to tell Flory and Phoebe? When would the media leave? He couldn't stomach the news, so he had no idea what was being reported. Were they considered suspects? Did the whole town know about Lou now? Of course, they did.

Maybe we should leave. But where would we go? What about the girls' school? It would be starting soon. What was it going to be like for them? Rodney's head hurt.

The hours seemed to drag. Wandering into the living room, Rodney pulled the blanket over the window aside. He saw reporters milling about, smoking, chatting on their cell phones, talking into microphones, and pointing toward their home. Then he saw his neighbors, Ron Martinez and Doug Harris. They must be coming home from work. Reporters ran toward them as they pulled into their driveways.

"Don't talk to them. Please don't," Rodney whispered, as he saw his neighbors about to be sabotaged. He felt so helpless. He watched, with relief, as they drove into their garages and shut the doors.

Rodney collapsed into the armchair in the living room. Was it after five o'clock already? What had he done all day? He had talked to Barney, and he had called his parents, but other than that, he was clueless. Alice hadn't left the bedroom.

Rodney thought of his call to his parents. It hadn't gone well. His mother was hysterical, but not about how they were. Like his brother, she didn't want any of her friends to know she was related to Lou in any form.

"Well, actually we aren't related," she had told Rodney. "You are. But we aren't." Thanks, Mom.

His father said little. That was how he was. "I'm so sorry, Rodney." He said nothing more. But Rodney knew he was sad for them.

"Hey." It was Alice.

"Hey, back to you," Rodney said. She came into the living room. It was strange being there. They never came in here.

Alice pulled her legs under her as she sat on the sofa. She grabbed the needlepoint pillow her mother had made and hugged it. "Gross," she said as she smacked her lips. "I need to brush my teeth."

Rodney's stomach rumbled. He hadn't eaten since breakfast. And they hadn't talked about Lou or their girls. He hadn't told her about his conversation with Barney. But when it came to initiating anything, he couldn't. Any attempts for conversation evaporated.

Neither of them had listened to the news, so they didn't know what was being reported about the shooting. Had any of the injured died? What information were they saying about Lou? About us? What had they found out? How had Lou done it? Where did she get the gun? Rodney realized they knew less about the shooting than anyone.

Together Rodney and Alice sat in the living room. Neither spoke. The television in the kitchen was still on, like background noise. The refrigerator continued clicking. Gradually the room darkened. From the outside Rodney imagined their house appeared empty. The front porch light hadn't come on. There was no glow of indirect light from other rooms because no lights had been turned on, and the windows were covered. No cars in the driveway, indicating teenage friends visiting.

Flory and Phoebe. What were they going to do about them?

"Alice, we have to talk about Flory and Phoebe," Rodney said. "We're going to have to tell them what happened. Hopefully, they don't know."

Both camps were located on COC's campus in town. Flory and her basketball team were having a skills training camp. Phoebe was at band camp. As an incoming freshman, she was almost guaranteed a spot in the marching band because she had been first chair in her section in middle school. Attending the camp cinched the deal. Both had been looking forward to this week, being with their friends and doing what they loved. The camps ended on Sunday.

Alice shook her head as tears formed.

"I think if they knew what had happened, we would have heard from them by now," Rodney said.

Silence.

Rodney got up and sat next to Alice. "How do you think this news is going to affect them at school?" He could take whatever was dished out, but he didn't want his daughters hurt by this.

Alice shook her head again. She didn't answer.

"We're going to get through this. I don't know how, but we will." He squeezed her hand, and she squeezed his back. The two of them sat shoulder to shoulder on the sofa. Neither Rodney nor Alice could even begin to grasp what the victims' families were going through. It was all they could do to manage their own pain and hell.

Eventually they were sitting in darkness. "Come on." Rodney stood up and took Alice's hand. "Let's go in the kitchen." He turned off the TV. He pulled out two bowls from the cabinet and a box of Wheat Chex from the pantry. They sat at the table—the round oak table that had been in the Sutton family kitchen when Alice was growing up, where she had eaten her meals with Carl, Florence, and Lou—and ate cereal for dinner.

Chapter 11

"Let's come back every year, no matter where we live," Kathryn Randolph said to her boyfriend, Paul, as she climbed into his Range Rover. The Battle of the Bands had been their first date the summer before their sophomore year.

Now a senior, Kathryn had returned from a summer internship in New York City. She was going to apply for jobs in Dallas upon graduation, and Paul planned to go to law school. They would still be able to see each other on weekends. Her life was all planned out.

They hadn't talked specifically of getting married, but Paul had said everything but the word marriage. That evening was going to be a great way to celebrate the beginning of the end of their college years.

****

Robert and Elizabeth Randolph had been at a fund raiser for the new Art Center in downtown Oklahoma City the evening of the shooting. They knew Kathryn was in Mineral Wells with Paul at some party. Their younger son, Robbie, was with a group of friends for the evening. Life was good.

It was almost eleven o'clock when they returned home. Robbie was in the family room watching a movie. Elizabeth leaned over and kissed the top of his head. "Good night, Robbie. We're bushed and going to bed."

"Turn out the lights when you come up," Robert

called as they went upstairs.

Robert Randolph was a man of habit. He did not like messes, especially messy situations—all that emotion and chaos. The next morning, he watched the news in the bathroom while shaving. The opening music began, as the orange rainbow logo for the *TODAY Show* came on the television screen. "Good morning." It was Savannah Guthrie. "We have breaking news. A mass shooting occurred overnight around 9:30 at a popular bar in Mineral Wells, Oklahoma. Twelve known dead, over twenty injured at the annual Battle of the Bands at the James B Saloon…This is TODAY, Friday, August 7, 2015."

"Elizabeth!" Robert yelled from the bathroom. He had a towel wrapped around his waist, and half of his face was still covered with shaving cream. He found Elizabeth in the kitchen in her robe, drinking coffee. The newspaper, still in its plastic bag, sat on the table.

"What's the matter?"

"Did you ever hear from Kathryn last night?" Robert turned on the small flat screen television on the kitchen wall. While waiting for it to come on, he opened the paper. There, on the front page was the headline, "Mass Shooting at Mineral Wells Bar."

Elizabeth stared at the headlines and shook her head. "I didn't expect to hear from her. I thought…" She pushed the paper away. "Where's my phone?"

On the television a reporter spoke. "Behind us you can see the temporary triage unit that was set up last night after the shooting began. Authorities have not yet identified a suspect…"

Elizabeth pulled her phone out of her robe pocket and stared at it. Robert stood behind, looking over her shoulder, hoping to see a missed call from Kathryn. He saw her hands shaking as she dialed Kathryn's number. It went straight to voice mail.

Robert's face contorted. In his effort to maintain control over this uncontrollable situation, he clenched his fists until his knuckles turned white and his nails dug into his palms. "Try Paul."

Elizabeth dialed Kathryn's boyfriend's number, but then handed the phone to Robert. "I can't do it. I can't talk."

A voice answered, but it wasn't Paul. It was his father.

"Robert, have you heard from Kathryn? We're with Paul in the hospital. They brought him to Oklahoma City in a helicopter. But he doesn't know what happened to Kathryn."

Something in his chest dropped. When he opened his mouth to speak, no sound came out. He cleared his throat, as he tried to control his emotions. "Uh, no. I just saw it on TV. We can't get ahold of her."

"Well, it's a madhouse there." There was a pause on the other end of the phone. "I don't know what to tell you."

Robert hung up the phone.

"What did he say?" Elizabeth pulled on his arm.

Robert shook his head. "Paul's in the hospital. He doesn't know what happened to Kathryn."

"Oh, my God." Elizabeth buried her face in her hands.

It wasn't until nine thirty that they learned Kathryn was among the dead. A deputy arrived at their home. By then, Robert had gotten dressed, but he knew he wouldn't be going in to work that day.

****

Mickey Martinez was nervous. He changed his shirt three times before he finally decided on the Phish T-shirt. Jamie Coverdale was the only other person he knew who was a fan of the band. Maybe that was why he liked her. They had been lab partners in biology spring semester, and he had developed a crush on her, even though she had a boyfriend. Toward the end of the semester her boyfriend had broken up with her. Their friendship developed, and now he was finally going out with her. The Battle of the Bands would be a fun first date.

"Let's stay in the street near the stage," Mickey said. He took a selfie of Jamie and himself. On a whim he sent it to his dad.

****

Jose Martinez wiped the sweat from his brow. The heat from the kitchen was unbearable. "Order up," he shouted as he placed sizzling chicken fajitas on the pick-up bar. Jose helped his brother, Marco, who owned a Tex-Mex restaurant in Oklahoma City. He had raised Mickey solo after his wife died. He heard his phone ding in his back pocket. The restaurant was swamped. He'd check it later.

The next morning Jose learned of the shooting when he turned on the news. Mickey had mentioned a party, but was this it? Jose tried to call Mickey, and his phone went straight to voice mail. Then he noticed the text. It was a photo of Mickey and a nice-looking girl. Jose didn't even know who she was. Why didn't Mickey answer his phone? Did something happen? Surely, he wasn't at that bar. Oh, how he wished Camilla were still alive! She would know what to do. She would go to Mass and pray. Never had Jose felt so alone.

****

Jamie Coverdale checked her make-up one last time. Her phone dinged. Mickey was on his way. She decided to wait for him outside her apartment because they were just friends. But he had been awfully nice when she came to class after her break-up. And he was kind of cute. She was ready to go out and have a good time.

Mickey suggested they stay in the street near the stage. It wasn't long before the street was packed with partiers. He pulled out his phone and took a selfie of the two of them. Jamie was having a good time, and she didn't want the feeling to end.

****

Jamie's parents were in bed when Rick Coverdale's phone woke them up. "Hello," he said.

"Turn on the TV." It was their neighbor. "There's been a shooting at a bar in Mineral Wells." The neighbor knew Jamie was living there for the summer.

Rick and Diana sat up in bed. On the television a local reporter described the events.

"We are working to confirm reports of exactly what happened tonight here at this bar…The OSBI has been called in to help with the investigation. As of right now, we can tell you shots were fired at the James B Saloon around nine thirty. We cannot tell you how many victims there are, or if the shooter is still at large. There are unconfirmed reports that the shooter is one of the victims. We will get back to you as soon as we know more."

Rick and Diana spoke simultaneously. "Call Jamie." But she never answered her phone. She was already dead.

****

"Aren't we getting a little old for this?" Ken joked as he and several of his fraternity brothers found a table on the rooftop of the bar. "We used to try to get as close to the band as we could, but now it's just too loud." Ken remembered the first Battle of the Bands forty years earlier.

Michelle Fisher, one of the wait staff, brought two pitchers of beer to the table and a stack of Solo cups. "If you're planning to eat," she said, "it's burger, cheeseburger, hot dog, or chili dog—all served with fries."

As they drank their beers and waited for their food, one of them commented, "You know, we could get a lot better food and be able to hear and crash at Ken's house instead of fighting this crowd of pubescent teens in twenty-one-year-old bodies."

"Well, if you want to," Ken said, "we can have our reunion someplace else. We've got plenty of bedrooms."

It was decided. This would be the last year for the group to attend the Battle of the Bands. Next year, they would find a different destination. But in the meantime, they were determined to make the most of the evening, drinking as much beer as they could and telling old stories until they were ready to crash at the Holiday Inn. Ken never made it back.

****

Ann Goodson finished reading the book for her book club and set it on the table. Now what? She went out to the back yard and surveyed her flowerbeds. Ann took the hose and watered her marigolds that were parched from the heat. She noticed some weeds and crouched down to pull them. Then she saw the bird feeder was empty and filled it with birdseed. She discovered a couple of ripe cherry tomatoes, and she picked some sweet pea blossoms climbing on the fence.

No need to fix dinner, since Ken wasn't going to be home. Just a tuna fish sandwich would be fine. Ann sat at the kitchen table with her tuna sandwich, a glass of iced tea, and another book to start reading. It seemed so quiet in the house without Ken. There was no TV blaring from the other room, no sound of the lawn mower or edger outside, no interruptions of conversations about cars, or how to repair something, or politics.

Ann was already asleep when her son called.

"Mom, have you heard from Dad?"

Trying to wake up, Ann answered, "No. Why?"

"There was a shooting at the Battle of the Bands. Several people were killed."

By then Ann was awake. "I'm going to call Ken now. I'll call you right back."

"I've already tried several times. His phone goes to voice mail."

The tone of her son's voice alarmed Ann. Surely something hadn't happened to Ken.

****

Michelle Fisher loved the annual Battle of the Bands at the bar. Most of the staff dreaded the event because of all the people, but not Michelle. She knew how to work the crowds. She could keep multiple orders in her head. And besides, they only served beer and soda on that night, and everything was disposable. The menu consisted of either hamburgers or hot dogs. Keeping it simple had been the key, especially when they were expecting over a thousand attendees during the week.

Michelle was grateful her parents lived a few blocks from her apartment. They were able to watch her son,

Seth, when she worked. She was finally going back to school. Juggling work, school, and parenting kept her busy—and sober. She had been sober for thirteen years, ever since she found out she was pregnant with Seth. Her sponsor couldn't understand how she could work at a bar, but alcohol was no longer a temptation. Her focus was staying sober and giving her son a good life.

It was going to be a long night. She wouldn't get home until after three in the morning because she was going to help close.

Michelle had one concern, and that was the argument with Seth before she left for work. It had to do with him not finishing his chores. He'd talked back to her in a way he never had before. And what was worse was it reminded Michelle of herself. She didn't want her son going down the same path she had taken. Seth had slammed the door without saying good-bye. It was still bothering her.

"Michelle! Over here."

Michelle heard her name. Some of the regulars called out to her, and it wasn't long before other groups began calling her, too. It was going to be a busy night, and that meant making some good money. She depended on this event.

Michelle decided to call Seth while waiting for the food orders, but his phone went straight to voice mail. "Hey, Sethy. Listen, I'm sorry I got so upset with you for not finishing your chores. I didn't let you explain why. I had my mind on other things, but that's no excuse. I won't get home until late, so I'll pick you up when I wake up in the morning. Love you, Seth." And she hung up the phone.

Michelle never came home.

****

When Seth woke up the next morning, he thought of his mom. He wanted to apologize. He didn't know what had gotten into him. His mom was cool, and he had acted like a jerk. Then he intentionally ignored her phone call and didn't feel like listening to her message. He checked his phone and clicked on his voicemail. After listening to her message, Seth called his mom back, even though Gran had said not to—she needed to sleep—but the call went straight to her voicemail.

Seth lay back down. He was in his mom's old room. He liked staying there. He heard the doorbell ring. Who would be coming to Grandpa and Gran's at this hour? he wondered. He heard voices and something about a shooting.

****

Taylor Almon picked up two-month-old Lizzie and kissed her cheeks. He was in love with his daughter. He had no idea fatherhood would be like this.

"Maybe I shouldn't go," he said to his wife, Angie. "What if you and Lizzie need help?"

"Go. We'll be fine. Besides, if we need anything, I'll call Mom and Dad."

Taylor kissed Lizzie one more time before putting her in the crib.

Angie walked him to the door. "You'll have a great time with the guys. You always do."

"You're right," he said. It was a ninety-minute drive to Mineral Wells from Tulsa. Going to the Battle of the Bands had become an annual tradition for Taylor and some of his fraternity brothers. He had been out of school ten years now, but it was still something he looked forward to.

So why did he have this nagging feeling?

****

Angie heard Lizzie cry in the middle of the night. She sleepily reached over and patted the mattress where Taylor was supposed to be. "Taylor, it's your turn to get the baby," she said. But, of course, he didn't answer. He wasn't there. The clock by her bed said it was one o'clock.

She had an eerie feeling as she went into Lizzie's bedroom. The house felt empty. Something wasn't right. She picked up Lizzie and padded down the hall to the den and sat in the chair that was perfect for nursing. As Lizzie nursed, Angie turned on the television and muted the volume. Switching channels, she caught a scene from one of the cable news stations. She read the trailer along the bottom of the screen. "Shooting at James B Saloon in Mineral Wells, Oklahoma…unconfirmed reports of multiple deaths and injuries…unknown if shooter is still at large…"

Angie gasped and accidentally squeezed Lizzie. The baby began to cry, and Angie did, too. Something inside her knew Taylor wasn't coming home.

****

"Let's make a bet to see who is the first to pick up a guy at the Battle of the Bands." Kayla Merrell and her best friend, Danielle, shared an apartment, and they both had jobs at the university. Kayla's dark hair and dark skin contrasted with Danielle's fair complexion and blonde hair. Together, they attracted attention, and they knew it.

Kayla and Danielle had met freshman year, living on the same hall in the dorm. They were opposites in many ways—Kayla was black, and Danielle was white.

Kayla was from Dallas, and Danielle was from Wewoka, with a population of only three thousand. Kayla's father was an attorney, and Danielle's father collected disability unemployment. But the two of them became best friends when they discovered they had both played soccer in high school.

Kayla and Danielle lingered by the kegs of beer, hoping someone would buy one of them a beer. "You'll win the bet," Kayla told Danielle. "Blondes always have more fun." She laughed.

One of the football players approached the kegs. His dreadlocks danced around his face. "Can I buy you ladies a drink?"

The girls laughed. "Of course, you can," Kayla said. The bet was over.

****

David and Bianca Merrell were celebrating their anniversary with a trip to Las Vegas. David loved to play blackjack, and Bianca went along for the shopping and the shows. On Thursday night they had gotten tickets to the latest Cirque de Soleil show. It had been sensational.

As they walked back to their hotel, Bianca leaned against David, feeling his firm body against hers. She stood on her toes and kissed him. "Happy anniversary, David. Let's keep going."

David embraced his wife of twenty-five years. "We will," he said. "We have great kids, my law practice is going well, your interior design clients love you. What could go wrong?"

They bypassed the bar in the lobby of the Bellagio and went straight to their room. They were both tired. Bianca fell asleep immediately, while David stayed up to watch the news. There was a report about a mass shooting that had happened in Mineral Wells.

"Bianca," David nudged his wife. "Wasn't Kayla going to something this weekend at a bar?"

Bianca, half asleep, answered, "No, I think it's next weekend."

Ten minutes later David, too, was asleep as the television continued to show videos from the crime scene at James B Saloon.

It wasn't until the next morning that Kayla's parents began to feel uneasy. Although they didn't expect to hear from her, the continuing news of this mass shooting alarmed them.

"I've tried Kayla three times, and her phone keeps going to voice mail," Bianca said.

"Try her roommate," David suggested. He picked up the paper delivered to their room. The front page showed the exterior of the bar where the shooting had occurred.

Bianca set her phone down. "I don't have her number," she said. Panic rose in her like bile in her throat. "David," Bianca's voice trembled. "What if something happened to Kayla?"

****

"You're going to win the bet if you wear that," Danielle Eckles said when she saw what Kayla was wearing. She laughed. She loved sharing an apartment with her best friend. They were going to the Battle of the Bands and were ready to meet some hot guys.

Danielle constantly worried about money. She had a loan to pay for her schooling, but she also worked twenty hours a week during school. Now that it was summer, she had a fulltime job. Kayla knew there were money problems, but Danielle hadn't told her she might not come back in the fall. Things at home had gotten worse, and her mother needed her help. Besides, no one else in her family had ever gone to college. But Danielle had been ready to get out of Wewoka, and college had been her ticket.

****

Danielle's father, Roger Eckles, was still hung over when his wife aroused him. He swung his arm, barely missing her face, like he was trying to swat a fly. "Leave me alone, woman," he bellowed. His mouth was parched, and his head throbbed. He was sprawled on the threadbare sofa in the front room. He hadn't made it to the bedroom before passing out the night before.

"Roger, there was a shooting at a bar in Mineral Wells last night. I've tried to call Danielle and can't get an answer." Danielle's mother, Frances, sounded panicked. The drawn curtains over the windows of their rent house hid the sun that was already up. Frances was supposed to be on her way to work.

Roger, who was on disability, sat up. "What's she doing hanging out at a bar when she's supposed to be saving her money for school?" He almost said it served her right but stopped himself. Suddenly he seemed to sober up. "Gimme your phone. I'll call her." The phone rang until he heard his daughter's voice. "Hi. This is Danielle. I can't come to the phone right now. Please leave a message at the tone and have a great day."

Roger had never listened to her voicemail message. "Hey, Danielle. This is your dad. Your mom's kind of worried, so give us a call." He paused and almost added, "I love you." Roger clicked the phone off and handed it back to Frances. "Go to work." Unsteady on his feet, he walked his wife to the door, practically pushing her out. He thought about kissing her on the cheek but changed his mind. He needed a drink.

****

Amber Cottingham drove south on I-35. Leaving Kansas, she crossed the Oklahoma state line. Amber had been on the road about four hours. She hadn't eaten since breakfast, and it was close to six o'clock. She took the next exit and drove east on State Highway 51.

Her phone buzzed periodically, but she ignored it. All she wanted to do was get as far as possible from her parents and their *talk*. A divorce? After all these years? Her dad already had an apartment, and her mother was putting their house on the market—the only home she'd ever known. Her little brother, Sammy, cried the whole time. Amber couldn't take it. She had to get out of there.

The billboards on the highway read like the old Burma Shave signs, advertising the Battle of the Bands at the James B Saloon. That sounded like a place where Amber could go, disappear, and drown her sorrows for a while. Maybe meet a nice guy. No, that wasn't going to happen. Maybe after she cooled down, she would drive back and try to make sense of what was happening to her family. The thought of it made her sick.

****

Leslie Cottingham stood at the door behind the screen and watched Sammy get into a car with his father. She closed the door and turned to survey the house. It was empty. Amber had left in anger a couple of hours ago, and now Tony, her soon-to-be ex, had taken Sammy to spend the night.

Leslie sighed. Amber's angry, but she'll cool off, she reasoned. She wandered around the house, picking up a stray sock, an empty cup, a discarded envelope that missed the trash. She hadn't eaten, but she wasn't hungry. Feeling like there was nothing else to do, Leslie turned on the television and found an old movie to watch. Periodically, she tried to call Amber, but to no avail.

Three days later Leslie still hadn't heard from Amber and filed a missing person's report. Sammy was still with his dad. She was in the laundry room, folding towels—anything to keep her hands busy—when the doorbell rang. Two police officers stood on the other side of the screen door.

****

Blake Youngblood wasn't supposed to be in a bar. He was only eighteen. There were seven eighteen-year-olds, who had gotten fake IDs to get into the James B Saloon. Blake had told his parents he was going to Mineral Wells—which was true—to meet up with some guys who were going to be freshmen in the fall—true also—to get a pizza—not true. He had also told his parents he was spending the night in Mineral Wells at an upperclassman's apartment, so he wouldn't have to drive back late at night. That was also supposed to be true.

Blake was nervous and excited at the same time. He had never been to a party at a bar. He had never used a fake ID. Sure, he and his friends drank beer in high school, but this was different.

There was a line to get beers by the time Blake and his group arrived.

"Just keep your ID in your wallet. Don't show it unless they ask you for it," one of the upperclassmen told the seven.

Blake's phone vibrated in his pocket. He pulled it out and glanced at it. It was his mother. He put the phone back in his pocket.

Blake never got his beer. He was dead before it

77

arrived.

****

"Why won't Blake answer his phone?" Cheryl Youngblood asked her husband, Kevin.

Kevin rolled his eyes. "Do you remember when you were going off to college? Did you want to talk to your parents?"

"Okay. You're right. I won't try to call him again," Cheryl said.

They were at a neighborhood cookout. Cheryl watched her two younger sons, now in their teens, throwing a frisbee. Kevin sat at a table with other men discussing the upcoming football season. She missed Blake, her oldest. She sighed, and her chest tightened. Everyone said the first one was the hardest. She quickly wiped a tear away. This is silly. He's going to be forty-five minutes away.

Cheryl glanced at her watch. It was half past nine. As she collected their belongings, she wondered what Blake was doing. I'll try and call him one more time, she decided, even though she had promised not to. Again, he didn't answer.

As they were leaving one of the men called out, "I just got a text that there's been a shooting in Mineral Wells at some bar."

Cheryl suddenly felt sick to her stomach. She looked at Kevin. His face was blank. If he was thinking anything, he didn't betray it. But surely that wouldn't affect Blake, because he was having pizza and then hanging out with some upperclassmen.

Once they were in the car Kevin pulled out his phone. "I'm calling Blake to make sure he's okay." It went straight to voicemail.

****

Olen Cummins decided to make the drive from Joplin, Missouri to Mineral Wells one last time. For his dad. They had attended the Battle of the Bands annually since Olen had followed his father to Oklahoma A&M. Burl Cummins had died that winter of a heart attack.

"Come on, Hannah, it'll be fun," Olen said, trying to convince his twin sister to join him. "Dad would love it."

"I wish I could, but I can't get anyone to switch hours with me at the hospital," Hannah said. "Bring me a mug or a T-shirt, will you?"

Leaving early Thursday morning, he drove the three-hour trip to Mineral Wells. First stop was getting a T-shirt for Hannah. Then he planned to have lunch with an old college buddy, Jeff, who lived in town. He would crash on Jeff's sofa and head back to Missouri the next day.

Olen never made it home.

****

Sylvia Cummins sat at the kitchen table in her bathrobe. Her hair appeared as if she hadn't combed it in days. She had a cup of coffee, a pack of cigarettes, an ashtray nearly full, and the newspaper. God, how she missed Burl! He should be in Mineral Wells with Olen. Sylvia lit a cigarette and opened the paper. The headlines on the front page read, "Mass Shooting at Mineral Wells, OK Bar." The cigarette fell out of her mouth as she cried out, and the ashes started to burn a hole in the paper. Sylvia poured coffee on it, and the tiny flame hissed as it went out, leaving a burned spot on the table.

"I've got to call Olen," Sylvia said. Her phone was in her purse, which was perched on the kitchen counter next to yesterday's mail. He didn't answer. She tried Hannah next. She didn't answer her phone either.

Sylvia lit another cigarette and tried Olen several more times. "Answer, damn you!" Salty tears slid down her face and into the sides of her mouth. She poured herself another cup of coffee, and her hands shook.

"Please, God, not Olen, too! I can't bear this." It had barely been six months since Sylvia had buried her husband, and now she couldn't reach her son. She feared the worst.

As if on cue, her phone rang. It must be Olen. But it wasn't. She didn't recognize the number, and so she let it go to voicemail. Sylvia stared at the phone. Eventually she set the phone on the table and put it on speaker.

"Hi, Mrs. Cummins. My name is Jeff Wilson. I'm a friend of Olen's. Can you give me a call?"

Sylvia waited until her daughter, Hannah, stopped by after work to call him back. By then, she already knew Olen was dead.

Chapter 12

Detective Jeremy Turner stood outside the old, two-story stone farmhouse. It was well-built but appeared abandoned. Was this where Lou Ella Sutton lived? The tactical team had given clearance, and two other officers had already gone through the house, but Jeremy wanted to check it out for himself.

Two dead, thorny bushes stood on either side of the entrance. Wooden steps led up to the door, and Jeremy's boot almost fell through a loose board.

He opened the front door slowly and stepped inside. Cobwebs hugged the corners, and dead bugs lay on the window ledges and the floor. Slipping on shoe covers, he surveyed his surroundings. From the large entryway, he saw footprints on the hardwood floors. Heavy boots, most likely caked with mud. Jeremy followed them to the left, through a swinging door to the kitchen. Putting on rubber gloves, he opened the refrigerator. Cans of soda and beer were on the shelf, condiments on the door, and a block of molded cheddar cheese in the refrigerator drawer. In the pantry he saw a box of crackers, a jar of peanut butter, and a couple of cans of baked beans. There were windows along the eastern wall of the kitchen. A fine layer of dust covered everything, including the gingham curtains. They reminded him of curtains his mother had made.

Jeremy stepped out of the kitchen, and he followed

the tracks to the living room on the other side of the entry. Sheets draped over heavy upholstered chairs surrounding an old walnut table. The room seemed to be frozen in time. The walls were painted a Wedgewood blue, and landscape paintings hung on the walls. There was a fireplace against the northern wall.

Jeremy noticed a door to another room, the study. It had dark-paneled walls, bookcases, and an oversized desk in the middle of an old Persian rug. Blinds on the windows facing west were closed, making the room unusually dark. The stale air was hot. This was not what he had expected to find in this farmhouse outside of Junction.

When Jeremy walked behind the desk, he discovered the contents of the drawers spilled onto the floor. He combed through the papers and miscellaneous stuff. This must have been where the gun was.

Jeremy retraced his steps back to the entryway and followed the fading prints up the stairs. At the top of the stairs was a single hallway with two rooms on the right and one large room and a smaller room on the left. The footprints appeared to go in all directions.

To the right, the first room from the stairs appeared to belong to a young girl. The bedspread and curtains were made of matching pink gingham. The dresser was empty, and the drawers in the desk contained old mementos. On the wall were posters of bands from the eighties and nineties and a bare bulletin board. Faded outlines showed where cards and photos had been displayed. Dust covered everything.

A bathroom connected the adjoining room. Jeremy inspected the bathroom to see if anything appeared out of place. Then he entered the next room.

The first thing Jeremy noticed was the space on top of the upright dresser where the dust had been disturbed. He sent a message to one of the guys on the force who had been through the house earlier that day. An open can of soda and a bag of chips had been there. There was nothing on the walls and no evidence of personal items. A red and blue plaid bedspread covered the bed. Again, the curtains matched the bed cover. Jeremy saw dirt on the bedspread at the end, as if someone had been lying on top of it.

"This ain't no Goldilocks," Jeremy said out loud.

A couple of drawers had been opened, but they were empty. Nothing else seemed like it had been disturbed.

Jeremy walked across the hall to the two rooms on the other side. The back room was smaller. Jeremy figured it could have been a nursery at one time, but now it appeared to be a studio. There was an easel with an unfinished landscape on it. It resembled the artwork in the living room. A stack of canvases leaned against the wall underneath the window. With gloved hands, Jeremy flipped through them. These are nice, he thought. Mostly scenes of the plains—wildflowers and larges skies with billowing clouds, oil derricks, wheat fields.

In the stack one painting differed from the rest. It was of two girls, holding hands. They were walking away from the painter in a field of wildflowers. One was taller and older than the other. The older one wore blue jeans and a T-shirt. Her brown hair was pulled back in a ponytail. The younger one had pigtails and wore overalls. Their heads tilted toward each other as if sharing a secret. A mutt of some kind was up ahead of them. It turned and faced the girls, waiting for them to follow.

Jeremy's eyes stung as he stared at this painting. He pulled out his phone and took a picture of it before putting it back in the stack of canvases. He had a feeling he knew who those girls were.

The last room upstairs was the master bedroom. Again, like the pink bedroom, it appeared mainly untouched. However, the drawers of the dresser were not empty. Jeremy saw men's and women's clothing—all neatly folded—as if they had every intention of returning. He wondered if the room had been untouched for two years.

The closet had sliding doors. One side was open. Everything was in place, except for an empty space on the top shelf. This was where the lockbox had been.

He combed through the rooms again before going downstairs. Walking through the dining room behind the kitchen, Jeremy entered a screened porch. Two worn wicker chairs faced each other. From there, he had a view of the land. A vegetable garden, neglected, was immediately outside the porch. Beyond that was a grove of trees.

To the left was the barn. The corrugated roof had rusted red, and Jeremy found the double doors ajar. This was where they had found the lockbox that was back at headquarters. He peered inside the dark interior. He saw evidence of where Lou must have pried open the lockbox. It was all falling into place, but it wasn't pretty.

Chapter 13

Junction was a tight-knit community. Everyone knew one another, and they watched out for each other. There were two Baptist churches, one Methodist, one Episcopal, and one Catholic. The people of Junction knew the difference between good and evil, right and wrong. There was no question about it.

From this environment the community struggled with the savage actions of one of their own—Lou Ella Sutton. How could such evil come from their town? She must have been a bad seed. And if she was, then so was her family.

Judgement was immediately thrust upon Alice and her family, and they were totally unprepared. Like the rest of Junction, Lou's actions horrified and caught them off guard. But they became guilty of the murders by association.

****

Alice woke up Saturday still in the clothes she had worn the day before. For the briefest moment she thought Friday had been a nightmare. Then reality came back like a blast of heat from an open furnace. As she stared at the wall, her back toward Rodney, she sensed him stirring.

"Alice? Are you awake?"

She shut her eyes and didn't answer. Alice wished she could climb out of her body and become someone else. What had occurred thirty-six hours ago didn't seem real. She was incapable of grasping the truth, and completely unable to comprehend anything about the victims. That her sister had committed such a heinous crime was too painful to understand.

Alice heard the bedsprings squeak as Rodney sat on his side of the bed. She continued to feign sleep as Rodney went into the bathroom. He shut the door, and she heard the water from the shower. She envied his ability to function. A few minutes later Rodney reappeared, letting steam escape from the bathroom. He was wrapped in a towel, his hair combed over, covering the ever-growing bald spot. He smelled fresh, not dirty and contaminated like she felt.

"Alice, I'm going to make some coffee. Want some?" Rodney had put on shorts and a T-shirt. She didn't answer.

Alice heard the television come on in the kitchen. Then she heard Rodney's voice. Who was he talking to? She tried to get out of bed, but her body felt like concrete. When she finally got up, it was like she had entered a tunnel with no end. Why did she feel so drained?

Rodney was still on the phone when she reached the kitchen. He poured her some coffee, cradling the cell phone between his ear and his shoulder.

"Yeah, she just walked in," Rodney said as he indicated with a tilt of his head to have a seat at the table.

Alice stared at her coffee. The smell made her gag. Here was Rodney perfectly capable, and she was bordering on incompetence.

"Okay. I'll tell her. See you around ten o'clock." Rodney set his phone on the table and refilled his mug. "That was Barney. We're going to his office this morning at ten. He's made a list of things we need to take care of."

"What time is it?" Alice had no idea.

"Almost nine o'clock," Rodney said. He got up and rinsed the cereal bowls from the night before. "Hungry?"

Alice didn't answer. Normal conversation felt wrong. She didn't deserve… She didn't know what the answer was, but she sensed she should be paying some form of penance for what had happened. Yet, Alice couldn't go there. She couldn't think of Lou, of what she had done, of all the people who had been affected.

"Hon, you might want to take a shower before we go," Rodney said. He had his back to her as he put the bowls in the dishwasher. "I think you'll feel better."

Alice tried to break the fog in her head. "What?"

"A shower. Go take a shower. You'll feel better." Rodney pulled out her chair and helped her up, practically pushing her toward their bedroom.

She did feel better, almost normal. Alice dried her hair and put on a clean top and a pair of Bermuda shorts. She added a little mascara and lipstick before she got her purse.

"I'm ready," Alice said as she entered the kitchen. Again, for just a moment she forgot about the past thirty-six hours.

Going out to the garage through the kitchen, the two of them settled into Rodney's extended cab Ford pickup. He pushed the garage door opener and backed out. Almost immediately reporters and photographers surrounded the truck. Someone banged on the back of the truck, and Rodney braked. Another person ran up to the window on Alice's side. He was shouting at her, but she put her arms over her head.

"Stop it. Get away," she screamed. Reality had

returned.

Rodney backed out slowly, honking his horn continuously. "Get the hell out of the way." A woman with a microphone chased the car as he backed out. A cameraman followed her, videotaping the entire scene. As soon as Rodney came to the intersection, he stopped then sped away, leaving the media behind.

By the time Alice and Rodney arrived at Barney's office, they were shaken and unnerved by the experience with the press. Barney's office was located off Broadway in downtown Junction near the local college. Situated between the barber shop and Vintage Treasures, they were all part of a single two-story building. A young architect had recently moved in on the second floor.

They parked behind the building to avoid being seen, and Alice felt like a criminal. Rodney pushed the buzzer at the back door, and Barney let them in. Not much had changed. The card table where she had sat with her parents for the meeting when she was eighteen was still in the back room.

"Come into my conference room," Barney said, referencing the card table and folding chairs.

Rodney took Alice's elbow and led her to a place at the table. Alice never dreamt she would be back at Barney's office because of Lou. It had been almost twenty-five years since that first meeting. Her head pounded.

Barney had a folder and a couple of legal pads on the table. "Coffee anyone?"

Alice shook her head, but Rodney said yes.

Barney brought two Styrofoam cups of weak coffee and sat down. He pulled out a large handkerchief and blew his nose. "Allergies," he said. Then he cleared his throat. "I hate that we're having this meeting, you know. I don't think any of us ever thought something like this would happen."

Barney opened the folder. "I'm not an expert on schizophrenia, but your parents wanted me to keep a file of Lou's treatments, hospitalizations, medications, and the like, in the event they were no longer able to care for her. They made that decision after the meeting when they told you about Lou." He added, "I didn't read her file until yesterday."

Barney closed the folder and pushed it across the card table toward Alice. "I made a copy of everything for you. I think you should contact her psychiatrist to get a better idea of what was going on with Lou," Barney said. "This is something you'll want to do when you're ready. But in the meantime, there are some immediate issues that need to be addressed."

Barney glanced at the list he had written on the legal pad in front of him. "I'm sorry." His eyes said everything.

Alice knew he was sorry for what Lou had done, for how it was going to affect her family. She knew he was sorry her parents were dead, that maybe if they were still alive this could have been prevented.

"I'm sorry for you all. But I'm sorrier for the victims' families. It's a tragedy."

He peered at the two of them over his reading glasses. "This isn't going to go away anytime soon, you know."

Barney handed a legal pad and pen to Alice and Rodney, and Rodney pushed the pad toward her. Did he not realize she was paralyzed, her brain was barely functioning?

"I can't do it," she said.

"Yes, you can," Rodney said.

"Don't worry about it. You don't have to write anything down," Barney said. He retrieved the pad from them. He pulled out his handkerchief and blew his nose. "Okay, the first thing we need to do is put together a statement to give to the press."

"But we didn't do anything," Alice said.

"This would be a statement of condolence. Here's something I wrote down. See what you think." Adjusting his glasses, he read, "The family of Lou Ella Sutton expresses their deepest condolences to all the families affected by the shooting. We give our sincerest apologies for her actions. Please know our prayers are with you. We will be cooperating fully with the investigation."

As Barney read the statement, Alice turned toward Rodney. They both nodded. It worked.

"Barney, that sounds good. Thanks," Rodney said.

"Okay. I'll get that sent out," Barney said. "I've already told you not to say anything to the press or to the police. Let me be your spokesman. There could be lawsuits and threats to your family." Barney wiped his forehead. "You know, I'm more of an accountant than an attorney, so I don't want to lead you astray. But I want you to know I'm here for you."

None of this made sense to Alice. Threats? What kind of threats?

As if reading her mind, Rodney asked, "What kind of threats are you talking about?"

"I'd probably say all kinds—vandalism, anonymous phone calls and letters, threats to harm your family members. Do you still have a dog?"

"No, Maggie died last year," Rodney said.

"Good. I don't mean good that she died. I just mean sometimes people poison pets to threaten individuals."

Someone would do that? Alice covered her mouth. She felt like she was going to throw up.

"You might consider calling the high school to see if they think the girls are going to need security."

"You've got to be kidding!" Alice could tell Rodney was upset.

"I'm just trying to prepare you for the worst. Most likely you'll just get a few harmless anonymous calls, but you need to keep track of the numbers, and when they call. Have you received any yet?"

"I've had a few," Rodney said.

Barney asked, "What about you, Alice?"

"I—I haven't looked at my phone. It's still in my office on the charger."

"I'll check it for you."

Barney checked his notes. "I have one last item we need to discuss. Jeremy, the detective who came by the house, gave me the number for the coroner's office. I haven't heard back from them yet. But you'll need to decide what you want to do with Lou's body."

Alice let out a moan. She was going to have to bury the last member of her family. How do you have a funeral for someone who murdered eleven people?

Alice was exhausted when they finally left Barney's office. She couldn't process anything they had discussed at the meeting. All she wanted to do was crawl into bed. She pulled her feet up onto the seat, wrapping her arms around her legs. Neither of them spoke on the way home.

When they turned on their street, Alice saw the satellite trucks and cars still parked. "I can't do this," she said.

"We have no choice." Rodney's hands gripped the steering wheel. "What I don't need right now is you getting hysterical. I don't want to hit one of these yo-yos. So, just sit there and don't say anything."

Alice put her hand over her mouth to stifle a sob and watched as it seemed like people swarmed like ants from the cars and vans.

Rodney drove slowly up the driveway. He had to brake to avoid a person who ran in front of his truck.

"They won't go into the garage, will they?" Alice couldn't believe what was happening.

Rodney didn't answer. He blasted the horn, keeping his hand on it. As the members of the press backed away, he pushed the garage door opener, drove the truck in, and shut the door behind them. The two of them sat in the truck and didn't speak. Alice noticed Rodney was breathing like he was out of breath. Adrenalin had kicked in.

Finally, Rodney spoke. "Come on. Let's go inside."

Chapter 14

Jeremy knocked on the open door of Melvin Pollard's office. Chief Pollard glanced at Jeremy over his bifocals and nodded, then resumed writing. Jeremy took a seat. He liked Melvin. He was a good man to work for. A little gruff, especially with the rookies, but fair. He had the respect of his force. Jeremy worried he would retire because of health issues. But that thought was for another day.

He looked around the familiar room. The two flags, the American and the Oklahoman, in the corner; his diplomas hung, always crooked; and an A&M sign next to the Mineral Wells Police insignia. There was an unidentified dying plant on the credenza along with his police hat and a framed photo of his family. Jeremy hoped to have a family himself someday.

On the wall next to the diplomas was a large map of the city of Mineral Wells. Jeremy walked over to examine it. He saw where the James B Saloon was, the location of the outdoor band on Sooner Avenue, and a pin that marked where they had found the pickup registered to Carl Sutton, father of the suspect. Then with his finger he followed Highway 51 out of Mineral Wells west toward the interstate. But the map stopped short of showing where the trailer was. He had received a call from Lou Sutton's landlord, who recognized her photo on the news.

Jeremy had just returned from there with the tactical team. He washed his hands in the men's room, but he still felt grimy from investigating the trailer.

It was rundown, the kind of place where someone would live only if they didn't want to be found. The wooden deck abutting the entrance was rotting. There was a front room with a vinyl couch and a table with one chair. The kitchen was small—a sink, a two-burner stove, and a refrigerator that must have been at least twenty years old. Broken plates and glass were on the floor. A narrow hall led to a single bedroom barely big enough to hold the mattress on the floor. At the end of the trailer was the bathroom. The place appeared to have been ransacked by someone. It didn't make sense. And the two half-dead cats nearly clawed the guys on the team when they first opened the door. Flies were everywhere. Besides the broken dishes in the kitchen, the bedroom and bathroom both seemed to have been torn apart, as if someone was looking for something.

There were fingerprints everywhere, but they all belonged to the suspect. Jeremy sighed and sat back down. Was Lou Sutton was searching for the gun? Why did she decide to go to Mineral Wells? What was her motive? Or did her disease cause her to inflict this violence?

Jeremy stretched his legs and leaned back. He needed to talk to—what was his name? He dug into his pocket, but he didn't have the card. Jeremy also needed to get organized. He hadn't even had a chance to get back to his own office.

"So, what do you have?" Melvin had finished his task. He had on the white short-sleeved version of their uniform, the buttons pulling across his chest. It was still too hot for black or long sleeves. His desk looked like chaos, with papers covering it, but Jeremy knew better. Melvin knew where every single piece of paper was and what was on it.

"I just returned from the trailer Lou Sutton rented."

"Did you find anything?" Melvin asked.

Jeremy explained the condition of the trailer. "At first, I thought someone had gone through the trailer, but we only found the suspect's prints."

Melvin pushed his glasses on his forehead. "So, why do you think she did this?"

"That's what I'm trying to figure out. When I went to interview her sister and husband, they said she was schizophrenic, but wouldn't go into it. I've got their attorney's card. I'm going to give him a call."

"Okay. Let me know what you find out. We've got our next press conference today at one thirty. I'm going to be there, but Ron is conducting it." Melvin leaned back and put his hands behind his head. "I plan just to give updates on the condition of the injured and tell the media about the release of the victims to their families."

Jeremy said, "I bet the press was all over the sister's house after yesterday's announcement."

"I wouldn't be surprised," Melvin said. "You know, there's no protocol on how to handle these mass murders. I mean, how much information to share, and what is best to withhold. Once the suspect's name is out, it's hell. It makes it harder to do our job, and I don't think it helps the victims' families either—although for them it feels like it does."

"What about the person who shot the suspect? They're going to want to know who he is," Jeremy said.

Melvin put his glasses back on and read the paper in

front of him. "We've identified the person who shot and killed the suspect, Lou Ella Sutton. It was an act of self-defense. That's all they need to know."

Jeremy nodded then stood up. "I'm going to call the family's attorney and see if I can get a better idea of a motive." He readjusted his side arm. "But I have a feeling they don't know any more than we do. I think it was probably her mental illness."

"And you know what that will do, don't you?" Melvin pointed his finger at Jeremy. "That will set off a storm about the mentally ill being violent, and our media will pick it up, and the whole culture will come to some crazy—pardon my pun—conclusion and want to lock up every single person who has some form of mental instability." He paused for a moment. "Damn laws. Families try to get help for their loved ones, but we can't do anything until they hurt someone or themselves. And then it's too late." Jeremy could tell Melvin was on a roll. "Let me tell you something else. The mentally ill get a bad rap. People don't realize treatment and medications can manage their symptoms. But when they refuse their medication, that's when there are problems. And that's when the law won't help these families."

Melvin waved his hand, as if to shoo Jeremy out the door. "Go on and let me know what you find out."

Jeremy walked down the hall toward his office. He stopped to get some coffee in the break room. Who made this coffee? he wondered, as he poured it down the sink.

He stood at the entrance and stared at his desk. Like Melvin's, it was covered with paper. Unlike Melvin, he had no idea where that business card was. He'd emptied his pockets last night, but was he at home or at Gina's? Jeremy pulled out his cell phone.

"Hey," he said, "did I leave my stuff at your house last night?"

"Yep. I knew you'd be calling." Jeremy heard a chuckle on the other end of the line. "What do you need?"

"It's a business card. Take a picture of it and send it to me."

"Hold on a minute and let me find it," Gina said.

Jeremy heard the screen door open then shut. She must have been outside. Gina loved being outside.

"Okay. Is it Barney Anderson?"

"Yeah, that's him. Send me a pic," Jeremy said. He heard the click, and a couple of moments later his phone dinged. "Thanks, Gina. When this mess is all over, we'll do something special."

"Okay. I'll start saving." He heard that chuckle again. "Love you."

"Love you, too." Jeremy held his phone in his hand for a minute. Gina got it. She understood his work, and she seldom got mad when he had to cancel at the last minute. She also knew the salary for a police detective, which was less than hers as a nurse. That's why he loved her. Early on in their dating, he had explained why he loved being a detective so much, and she had accepted it. What she didn't know was he had planned to propose to her on Thursday after he got off work. That never happened. The ring had been in his pocket during the shooting, the interviews, the entire night. He knew where the ring was now, and he wasn't going to lose it.

Jeremy sat down at his desk. He opened the file on his computer. Then he called Barney Anderson.

Barney's phone went to voicemail.

"Hello, Mr. Anderson. This is Detective Jeremy

Turner from Mineral Wells. We met yesterday at the Bennetts' residence regarding Lou Ella Sutton. I would like to speak with you about the suspect. Please call me at this number." Jeremy left his cell phone number. He leaned back in his chair, staring at the screen on his computer. His phone rang.

"Hello," Jeremy said.

"Jeremy?" It was Barney Anderson.

"Mr. Anderson, thank you for returning my call so promptly."

"Call me Barney," he said. "Sorry I didn't answer the phone when you called. I've gotten so many calls from the press since I released the family's statement, that I'm letting the calls go to voicemail."

"I understand," Jeremy said. "I wish I could do the same." He thought of all the calls he received about leads on crimes. So many were usually a waste of time. "Listen, we need to get some background information on Ms. Sutton to help with the investigation. We want to make sure she wasn't part of a bigger plan, a terrorist plot or some other dangerous cause."

"Yes, that makes sense," Barney said.

Jeremy waited for him to continue, but he didn't. "Mr. Anderson, I mean Barney, you and your clients indicated that Ms. Sutton suffered from schizophrenia, but no one elaborated. I found a couple of run-ins with the law, but none recently. It would be helpful to understand her condition better, hospitalizations, medication, treatment."

"Lou's parents gave me a file on her which they continued to update until their death. They wanted her records in a safe, known location. Of course, they didn't know they were both going to die when they did, but they realized Lou would most likely outlive them. I'd like to get Alice and Rodney's consent before I release them to you."

"Unfortunately, your clients don't have any choice. We can get a court order to get the records if you refuse to release them," Jeremy said.

"Is there any way this information can be withheld from the press? When Lou was diagnosed, her parents were very private about the matter."

"I can't make any promises," Jeremy said. "The victims' families will feel they have a right to know everything."

There was silence on the other end of the line.

"Did I lose you?"

"No," Barney said. "I'm still here." Jeremy heard him sigh. "I'm just trying to protect my clients. I have a feeling they will become victims, too. That they'll be tried and found guilty of a crime they didn't commit and was beyond their control."

"I understand," Jeremy said, and he did. Again, he heard Barney sigh.

"I'll get a copy of her records to you," Barney said.

"Thanks," Jeremy said and hung up the phone. He rubbed his temples. This case touched him on a personal level. Bipolar disorder and depression could also be deadly. He called Gina.

"Now what did you forget?" He heard the playful taunting in her voice.

"Nothing," Jeremy said. "I just called to see how your brother was doing."

Chapter 15

Rodney couldn't sleep. He was aware of Alice tossing and turning during the night and knew she wasn't sleeping either. Finally, about five, when Alice's alarm would have gone off, he fell asleep. The vibration of his phone on the bed table woke him sometime after nine o'clock. Rodney slipped out of bed, taking his phone with him to the kitchen.

Who had called him? Thom Ellis, his sister's husband. Do I really want to know why he called? Rodney checked his phone. He had seven other missed calls and twenty-three texts since last night.

Coffee first. Rodney dumped the last of the coffee into the filter, assuming there was more in the pantry. While waiting for his coffee to brew, he scrolled through his texts. It was about fifty-fifty, half of them were from friends expressing their shock and regret, the other half were angry, hateful messages from phone numbers with no ID. He forwarded the negative texts to Barney, then deleted them.

Rodney poured himself coffee and went into the living room to see if the vehicles were still parked outside their home. He pulled the blanket aside. Cars and vans lined the street as they had the two previous days.

The house was so dark it seemed like a dungeon. It had been about forty-eight hours since they had found out Lou was responsible for the mass shooting in Mineral

Wells, yet their life before that seemed ages ago. From now on, Rodney realized that they would define their lives by before and after the shooting.

He still couldn't understand what had prompted Lou to murder all those people. Barney had called him yesterday about giving consent to release Lou's medical records to the police. Rodney knew it was the right thing to do, but Alice didn't want to. It had been hard trying to convince her. When he asked Barney if the information could be kept confidential, he said he couldn't promise that. Rodney didn't tell Alice.

If this had been a normal Sunday, they would have been on their way to church. But it wasn't a normal Sunday. He didn't know if they would ever have a normal one again.

His phone vibrated. It was an incoming text from Thom Ellis. *Did you get my message?* Sighing, Rodney listened to his brother-in-law's message. "Hello Rodney. This is Thom Ellis. Listen, we were real sorry to hear about Alice's sister. Man, that's a scary thing. She could have come after you guys, you know? Anyway, Kristin is pretty upset about it. She's worried her clients will find out there's a slight connection. Also, Isabel heard about it at her school. She called, crying, but we didn't tell her we knew who the killer was. So, if you could, don't contact us until this blows over. Thanks, pal."

Rodney was tempted to call his brother-in-law because there were so many things he would like to say. Keep your home in Connecticut and your fancy jobs in Manhattan and your boarding school for your daughter. We'll pretend we're not related to you, if that will make you feel better. Don't worry about us. Just make sure your image doesn't get tarnished.

So much for support from his family. It hurt. But he had heard from his fishing buddies. Each of them had called or texted. Ben even tried to come by. The media had swarmed his car, so he turned around and left.

Rodney sighed and wandered back into the kitchen. What he really wanted to do was fix himself a couple of fried eggs and read the morning paper. But he didn't dare go outside and retrieve the paper. Rodney opened the refrigerator and pulled out the carton of eggs. There was a single egg in it. When he opened the pantry, it appeared almost bare. Alice always kept the refrigerator and pantry stocked. It didn't make sense.

Rodney heard a knock on the door and froze. He went into the living room and pulled the blanket aside. He saw his neighbor, Doug, leaving the porch. Reporters came out of their cars, but he waved them away and kept walking.

Rodney opened the front door, knowing full well he was taking a chance of being bombarded by the media. At his feet were his mail, newspapers, and a casserole dish covered with foil. He felt like crying. Rodney gathered the mail and papers and put them on top of the dish. He shut the door and locked it before anyone reached him. Gratitude filled his heart for the first time in at least two days.

Rodney fixed a single egg, poured another cup of coffee, and seated himself at the table with the newspapers. That was a mistake. The front page of both Saturday's and Sunday's editions were dominated by the shooting. Lou's face stared at him from the paper. He couldn't read it. Not now. He knew at some point he would need to, but this wasn't the time. Rodney gathered the newspapers and put them in his briefcase, a safe, out-of-the-way spot, for the time being. Then he went through the mail, searching for anything appearing suspicious—just bills and junk mail.

Now what? Rodney felt like he was in limbo. There was so much he needed to do, yet there was nothing he could do. The girls' camps both ended at one that afternoon. Until then, he was stuck inside their house. He couldn't leave because the media would follow him, and if he went anywhere, he was afraid he might be recognized. Surely their photos weren't in the paper. Maybe he should call one of his pals to find out what had been reported. At least he'd know what the family was up against.

Rodney got up and put his dishes in the sink. The house was too quiet. He missed the constant chatter of his daughters, the back-and-forth banter. He missed hearing about Alice's day, her latest projects, and her asking him about his day. What was the future going to be like for their family? He had no idea. And at this point Rodney, like Alice, was incapable of even letting his mind go to what the victims of Lou's rampage were going through. He was in survival mode, just taking one step at a time.

And his next step was picking the girls up from camp.

At 12:30, Rodney backed his pickup out of the driveway. Immediately reporters and photographers came out of their vehicles. It was like a horde of wasps coming in for the kill. Once again, he put his hand on the horn and held it until he was at the end of the street. A couple of cars pursued him. This was the last thing he needed—to be followed as he picked up Flory and Phoebe. Rodney went the opposite direction of the college campus. He accelerated, hoping there was a cop nearby. Please pull me over, he begged. The two cars continued the chase, and Rodney realized this was dangerous. He pulled into an empty parking lot and got out of his truck as the two cars pulled in on either side of him.

A woman, probably in her thirties, came out of one car. In the other car were a reporter and a photographer taking still shots.

"Please leave our family alone!" Rodney felt hysterical.

The woman had a microphone, and she shouted questions at him. "Why did Lou Ella Sutton murder those eleven innocent victims? Why didn't your family take any precautions toward preventing her access to guns? Can you tell us your sister-in-law's mental condition at the time of the shooting?"

Rodney was close to tears as he got back in the truck, and his breath came in gasps. He needed to get ahold of himself before he saw his daughters. Rodney pulled into a McDonald's drive-thru and ordered some coffee. He didn't see either car as he left. With relief, Rodney drove toward the college. He picked up Phoebe first, then drove across campus to get Flory.

Once the bedrolls and bags were thrown in the back seat alongside Phoebe, she asked, "Where's Mom?"

Rodney hesitated and took a deep breath. "Uh, she couldn't come. There's something I need to tell you…"

"What's wrong? Did something happen to Mom?" Rodney could hear the alarm in Flory's voice.

"No. Not really." Rodney pulled over and cut the engine. Turning to face them both, he said, "Girls, there was a shooting in Mineral Wells at a bar, and…"

"We heard the coaches talking about that. It sounded awful," Flory said.

"Well, yes. It is. I mean, it was. But they identified the shooter, and…" Rodney struggled to get the words out. How should he tell his daughters their aunt had murdered eleven people? Rodney squeezed his eyes to prevent the tears. No father should ever have to say what he was about to tell his daughters.

"Aunt Lou."

"What about Aunt Lou?" Phoebe asked.

Flory figured it out. She clapped her hands over her mouth and screamed.

"Aunt Lou shot them?" Phoebe bent over and cried. When she sat up her face was streaked with tears. "How could she have done that?"

"I don't know. We don't understand what happened. We don't know why she did it. We don't know anything. I'm so sorry." Rodney tried to hug his daughters at the same time. Phoebe climbed over the backseat and reached for him.

Eventually Rodney released his embrace. With his fingers, he brushed the tears first from Phoebe, then Flory. "Your mother is having a hard time with this. She couldn't come." He paused. How did he tell his daughters what he anticipated their future to be? "Our lives are going to be affected by what happened, and I'm so sorry for you girls. But we'll get through this. We'll be there for each other. Okay?"

Flory and Phoebe both nodded.

Rodney felt guilty giving a pep talk he didn't believe in himself. What else could he do?

As Rodney turned onto Redbud Lane, he realized the media trucks were still there.

"What are all those vans and cars doing on our street?" Phoebe asked.

Flory read the sides of the satellite trucks. "CNN, ABC, CBS. Oh my God!"

As if on cue, individuals came out of the vehicles—video cameras propped on shoulders, microphones in hand.

That evening there were several prayer vigils. Each community that had lost a member held one. The churches in Junction were open for prayer services, but Rodney knew his family wouldn't be welcome.

Chapter 16

Ever since coming home from basketball camp, Flory had not spoken to her best friend, Marta. They had been roommates at camp and had promised to shop for school clothes together. When Flory tried to call, Marta's phone went to voicemail. Every time.

The night before school started Flory borrowed Alice's car and drove to her friend's house. Marta's dad answered the door when Flory rang the doorbell. He didn't even open the screen door. He stood behind it, as if the barrier between them would protect him from whatever disease or defilement Flory carried.

"I'm sorry. Marta can't come to the door. She's busy. And please, don't come back." Then he shut the door. He didn't greet Flory or say her name. It was as if she was contaminated, and he couldn't close the door fast enough.

The next day Flory drove Alice's car to school, and her stomach began to flip flop as if she had just gotten off a roller coaster. Junction Memorial, the school she loved became a place she dreaded entering. As Phoebe opened the passenger door, Flory grabbed her arm and said, "Let's not go in yet. Let's wait until the bell rings."

"Why? I want to make sure I know where my classes are."

Flory watched her enter the school. No one knew Phoebe. She was just another new freshman. She hoped

Phoebe's day would go well. She wasn't so sure hers would.

When the first bell rang, Flory got out of the car. She stood and stared at the old building. This was where her parents had gone to high school. They had met in English class on the first day of their senior year. Her grandmother, Florence Sutton, for whom Flory was named, had taught art at Junction Memorial until the car accident. There were a lot of reasons this place meant something to Flory. But today, she only saw the shell of an old building and a trashcan already overflowing.

Flory walked upstairs to her first period class. Lockers slammed and startled her. They sounded like gunshots. The door to room 2ll was already shut, and Flory entered her class as the final bell rang, finding a seat toward the back of the room. Her teacher glanced up when he heard the door shut. The dry-erase board had his name, Mr. Hutchison. He was new. Flory glanced at the backs of heads in front of her. She saw a few acquaintances and recognized almost everyone. Mr. Hutchison called role, finding each student as he or she answered.

"Florence Bennett?"

"It's Flory. Here." It was too late. The rest of the class noticed, and they all turned around to stare at her. She glanced out the window at the black tar roof of the lower level, pretending to be bored and unconcerned with the stares she received.

It was the same the rest of the morning. Each time during roll call, Flory felt the stares of her classmates when her name was called. She tried to act nonchalant, but inside she was anxious and seething.

At lunchtime Flory turned on her phone. She hadn't

seen Marta all morning.

—*I'm in the foyer. Where r u?*—

Why hadn't she texted back? Flory placed herself so she had a view of almost everyone who walked through, but out of the line of traffic on the far side of the trophy case, hoping to be inconspicuous. She had never felt the need to hide before.

Flory had a feeling someone was staring at her. Across the foyer she saw Katy Lewis, the Senior Class President, walking toward her. She was dressed like she was going to a business meeting instead of the first day of high school. But why did she appear to be so angry?

Katy marched toward Flory as if on a mission. She was. She pointed her finger at Flory. "You! You shouldn't be here," she said. "You should leave. You don't belong. That's the way we all feel." Katy choked down a sob. "Your family makes me sick." The tension in the foyer stung like a giant rubber band had stretched until it broke, separating Flory from the rest of the students. All conversation and commotion seemed to stop. Katy turned and walked back toward a cluster of her friends, who tried to console her.

Then someone from the group lobbed a bombshell at Flory. "Her brother's best friend is still in the hospital because of your aunt."

Flory's only option was to leave. She ran out the front door, almost knocking over another student.

"Just shoot me!" Flory said as she ran toward the car. "I wish I was dead." Flory got in and shut the door. "I hate you, Aunt Lou," she screamed.

Flory didn't return to school until it was time to let out. She found a parking spot in the senior lot and texted Phoebe her location. Her stomach growled. She hadn't eaten. Instead, she had driven around, finally driving to Buffalo Springs State Park, a thirty-minute drive away. It was a favorite spot of her family's.

Flory's phone dinged.

—*I'm on my way.*— It was Phoebe.

Flory glanced at her face in the rearview mirror. Yes, her eyes were still red, and so was her nose. Like her parents, Flory had not been able to grasp the enormity of the destruction her aunt had committed. It was too much for her brain and her heart to hold. She had grown up under the guise that they were good people. It was those *other* people who did bad things. It wasn't until she returned from basketball camp, that she learned about Aunt Lou's mental condition. Schizophrenia. It was a disorder that happened to other families, not hers. Flory wondered how she would feel if one of her friend's relatives was schizophrenic.

"Oh, my God!" Flory realized she would probably want to avoid that friend. She clapped her hand over her mouth.

Phoebe opened the passenger door. "What's wrong?"

Flory shook her head. "Nothing and everything. I don't want to talk about it. How was your day?"

"Better than yours, I'm guessing." Phoebe dropped her full backpack at her feet and pulled her phone out. "Sadie and I have two classes together, and we have the same lunch hour. She told me she was going to be my shield and armor in case anyone tried to be mean to me. I had a couple of teachers who asked if you were my sister, but other than that, no one said anything to me."

"I'm glad," Flory said.

"Well, that is, until I got to band. They posted the

names of those who would be in the marching band, and my name wasn't on the list."

"I thought you were almost guaranteed a place in the marching band by going to band camp. You said you scored Superior on all your performances. What's the deal?"

"I don't know," Phoebe said. "I didn't ask Mr. Fixley. Sadie said I should have, but I was too nervous. What do you think?"

"I think they aren't letting you march in the band because of Aunt Lou," Flory said. "That's what I think."

"Really? Could they do that?"

"I don't know, but nothing else makes sense." Her own day took a backseat to Phoebe's problems. No one was going to hurt her little sister.

"Well, let's ask Mom and Dad what they think when we get home," Phoebe said.

"You mean Dad. Mom is pretty worthless." Flory's voice had a mixture of resentment and sadness. She knew her mother was upset, but she wasn't there for them. It was like she was so wrapped up in feeling sad that she couldn't see it was hurting them, too.

When Rodney came home that evening, he had two white paper sacks in his hands, take-out from Johnny's, one of their favorite hamburger joints. "To celebrate the first day of school," he announced, as he pulled out four foil-wrapped hamburgers, two orders of fries, and an order of onion rings.

Phoebe set out four placemats, four plates and grabbed the ketchup from the refrigerator. Flory got out four glasses and put ice in them.

"Will one of you girls tell your mother dinner is on the table?"

"You tell her," Flory said to Phoebe. She slammed the glasses on the table. Getting napkins out of the drawer, she slammed that shut, too.

"Hey! Settle down," Rodney said. He came up behind Flory and wrapped his arms around her. "I know it's hard," he whispered in her ear, "but let's try to have a nice dinner."

Flory didn't answer.

"We can talk about everything after dinner, I promise."

Phoebe returned to the kitchen. "Mom said she isn't hungry."

Flory turned to Rodney as if asking, now what.

"Girls, sit down. Phoebe, you say the blessing. Then start eating while it's hot. I'll talk to your mom."

Phoebe closed her eyes and bowed her head. "Dear God, bless this food to the nourishment of our bodies. Thank you for this day. And God, please help Mom. And please be with the other families who lost someone in the shooting. Amen."

Flory ate her food in silence. Phoebe did the same. Rodney had left the kitchen to speak to Alice. So much for the first day of school. What a great way to start my senior year.

Rodney returned and sat down.

"Where's Mom?" asked Phoebe.

"She isn't coming." The rest of the dinner was void of any conversation. The normal chatter about school, especially the first day, didn't happen. The silence hung like a dark thundercloud hovering above them.

Chapter 17

When Rodney left the bedroom, Alice rolled over and pulled the covers over her head. She lay there, expecting to hear the murmuring of dinner conversation, but there was silence. Presently she heard the chink of dishes and running water. More silence. One door shut, then another. Never had the house seemed so quiet. It was too quiet, and now she was awake.

It had been over two weeks since they had learned what Lou had done. It still seemed like a nightmare. Alice hadn't left the house but once, which made her life surreal. Everything that had happened since August 6 was more of a blur. What had she been doing? Did she pick up the girls at their camps? Alice had no recollection of what had been going on the past couple of weeks. And it was too difficult to try to think about it or even care.

Her phone sat plugged in, but untouched, on the desk in her office. She had not ventured in there since that dreaded morning. She wasn't aware she had been asked to resign from the Women's Charity Auction Committee, or that the Boys and Girls Club had called to say they no longer needed her to teach art classes. She didn't know the latest project she had been working on had been cancelled.

To her family, it appeared Alice was wallowing in self-pity, whereas she was physically and mentally paralyzed. She was incapable of instigating the energy necessary to go forward. It was as if her limbs had been severed, and she couldn't physically move, much less mentally or emotionally function. It was too painful to grasp what had happened, and so Alice merely shut down.

Now awake, Alice shuffled into the bathroom. A glimpse in the mirror caught her by surprise. Dark circles hung under her eyes. Her hair, part of it stuck to her head, and part of it stood straight up. When was the last time she had taken a shower? Alice splashed some water on her face and brushed her teeth. She tried running a comb through her hair. Maybe I should take a shower, she thought. But she rejected the idea. It was too much trouble. I'll take one tomorrow.

A pile of her clothes lay on the floor in front of the dresser. She picked through them, searching for something to put on. Changing one set of dirty clothes for another seemed logical to her.

Alice wondered what day it was. They all seemed to run together. Phoebe had come in to tell her dinner was ready. Then Rodney. She shrugged her shoulders. It was as if she was balancing on the fallen tree limb she and Lou used to walk on to cross the creek. Any thoughts of what had happened might send her slipping over into the muddy water. She tried so hard not to think about anything. Sleep was her sole companion—until the nightmares came.

Alice's stomach growled. When had she last eaten? Barefooted, she entered the kitchen, walking past the girls' bedrooms. Both doors were closed. In the kitchen was a plate on the table with a hamburger, still wrapped in foil, a small pile of fries, and three onion rings. An overflowing pile of mail sat on the kitchen counter. Alice glanced at it, then turned her head.

The kitchen, usually the hub of activity, was dead. Alice unwrapped the foil from the hamburger and, without sitting down, took a bite. It was cold. She tried a French fry, cold as well. Suddenly she had lost her appetite.

Alice wandered into the den where she found Rodney sitting in front of the muted television, studying his laptop. A newspaper spilled over the edge of his chair, and Alice could see a headline. It read, "Mineral Wells' Victims, continued…"

"What does it say?" she asked.

Rodney looked up. "What?"

"The article in the paper. What does it say?"

Rodney gathered the paper and rolled it into a roll. "Nothing. I mean, I didn't read it."

Alice knew he was lying. Rodney didn't lie.

"I left a Johnny's hamburger for you in the kitchen," Rodney said.

"Thanks. I saw it." Their conversation felt stilted. It was as if they were trying too hard to be polite. What needed to be said wasn't being said.

Rodney let out a sigh. "You missed the girls' first day of school."

"What?" Alice couldn't believe what she heard him say.

"I said, you missed the girls' first day of school. Phoebe's first day of high school, and Flory's senior year."

"Oh, my God!" She collapsed onto the sofa. "I can't believe that." She put her head down and shook it.

Rodney crossed his arms and stared at Alice. "I think you need to get some help."

Rodney's words stung. How could she ask for help when no one wanted to have anything to do with her? "I can't. Besides, who would see me? I've been branded." Alice shook her head. "No, I can't do that."

"Well, what are you going to do then? Spend the rest of your life in bed?"

Alice had never seen him look at her that way. She didn't know what to say.

He closed his laptop and turned off the television. Standing up, he gathered the newspaper and took it in the kitchen to recycle.

Alice waited, to see if he was going to return. He did. He picked up his laptop.

"I'm going to the shop. Don't wait up for me." She heard a door slam, and she flinched.

Stunned, Alice sat in the den and stared at the blank screen of the television. Then the door from the kitchen to the garage opened. She heard Rodney's shoes squeak on the kitchen floor.

"Alice." Rodney spoke abruptly. He stood at the doorway but didn't come in the den.

"What?" Maybe he was going to apologize.

"You need to go talk to Flory and Phoebe. They miss you." Rodney's voice softened.

"But what do I say?" Alice felt at a loss.

"You're their mother. You'll know what to say."

"Will you come with me?" Part of Alice wanted nothing more than to crawl into bed. On the other hand, part of her was trying to do the right thing, what the former Alice would have done. But she didn't know if the former Alice existed anymore.

"Okay," Rodney said, relenting. "But then I have to go back to the shop."

Phoebe's door was covered with sayings, pictures torn out from fashion magazines, and cards from friends. There were even a couple of Alice's designs taped to the door. From inside the room came the sound of a clarinet.

Band, thought Alice. Marching band. I wonder how it's going. Alice tentatively knocked on the door. The music stopped. "Come in." Phoebe's voice sounded different—grown-up, yet still her little girl.

When Alice opened the door, she saw Phoebe standing with the music stand in front of her. Followed by Rodney, Alice entered the room.

"Hi, Phoebe. You sound great. Gearing up for marching band?" Alice said.

"I don't think I get to march."

"What do you mean? What happened?" It was Rodney, not Alice.

"I don't know, Dad. My name wasn't on the list."

"Did you ask your teacher? I thought you were practically guaranteed a spot."

"Dad, I'm only a freshman," Phoebe said. "And besides, I was too scared to ask Mr. Fixley. Maybe there were too many clarinets. Maybe I wasn't good enough. Maybe…" Phoebe glanced at Alice. She didn't finish what she was going to say.

Alice was silent. She didn't have anything to contribute, and she was oblivious of Phoebe's insinuation.

"I'll call the school tomorrow and get to the bottom of this," Rodney said.

"Dad, please don't. I'll ask Mr. Fixley about it."

Alice didn't have the energy to try to participate, but she had to say something. "Well, I think you sound just wonderful." She gave Phoebe a kiss on top of her head.

"Good night."

Phoebe gave Alice a strange look. "Mom, it's only seven thirty. I'm not going to bed."

"No, of course you aren't. I just meant…well, you know…" Alice felt like an outsider, like she was a guest in her own house. She didn't know what was going on. She hadn't even known what day it was. As her voice trailed off, she quietly shut the door.

In the hall Alice's eyes pleaded with Rodney, as if to say, do I have to do this again? She tentatively knocked on Flory's door. There was no answer. She shrugged her shoulders and glanced at Rodney. Was that good enough? Rodney knocked harder, and then opened the door.

Flory sat cross-legged on her bed, headphones on, scrolling through her phone. "Oh hi," she said, and then went back to looking at her phone.

Alice went over and sat next to her on the bed. "Hi Flory. How was school?"

Flory took off her headphones. "What do you care?"

"Flory!" Rodney said.

"Oh, it's okay." Alice tried to sound upbeat.

Flory put her headphones back on, ignoring her parents.

"Flory, your mother asked you a question."

"Do you really want to know, or are you just trying to make conversation because you don't know what to say? Because you have no idea what's been going on with us while you spend all day in bed!" Flory ran out of the room.

Alice began to cry. "I don't know what to do. Flory's right. I don't know what's going on with my own family. What's worse, I don't know if I want to know, because I can't take anymore," Alice said. She watched Rodney get up and leave her sitting on Flory's bed. She heard the door to the garage open, then slam shut.

Chapter 18

Today wasn't what Phoebe had thought high school was going to be like. But then that was before the shootings. Phoebe couldn't get the victims' families out of her mind. What would it be like to lose Mom or Dad or Flory? she wondered. What if they had been at the bar? What if someone else's relative had shot those people? Did any of the victims have a fourteen-year-old daughter or sister? What were they doing right now?

Phoebe rolled over to her back and stared at the black ceiling. They're not sleeping either. She had googled the names of the victims and read about them. She wished she could do something to help them. She wished she could at least tell them how sorry her family was. How would she feel? Empty. Horrible. Beyond sad. And mad. Yes, she'd be mad.

Phoebe had never understood Aunt Lou, and she thought she was kind of creepy. But Phoebe remembered she loved animals and would nurse injured or abandoned animals back to health. How could someone who loved animals have killed those people? It didn't make sense.

It seemed like Phoebe had just fallen asleep when she heard her name being called. At first, she thought she was dreaming. It sounded like her dad was calling her though a long tube. It echoed.

"Flory! Phoebe! Wake up!" It was her dad. "School starts in thirty minutes."

Phoebe sat up immediately. Surely, she had set her alarm. She heard a thud from Flory's room followed by cussing. Phoebe pulled back the sheet. She had to hurry to get into the bathroom. Otherwise, Flory would lock the door. The door was already shut and locked.

"Unlock the door, Flory. I have to get ready, too," Phoebe yelled as she banged on the bathroom door. She continued banging until Flory finally let her in.

Flory ran out. "I'm leaving in ten minutes," she said, followed by a slam of her bedroom door.

Eight minutes later Phoebe ran through the kitchen. Her backpack straddled one shoulder as she tried to pull her tangled curls into a ponytail. She swirled toothpaste in her mouth and spit it in the kitchen sink. Opening the refrigerator, Phoebe grabbed an apple and some string cheese.

"Bye, Dad," Phoebe said as she ran out the door to the garage. A couple of minutes later she returned. "Forgot my clarinet." She kissed him as she ran past a second time.

"Bye, Phoebe, have a good day," Rodney said.

"Yeah, sure." She sounded sarcastic.

From the garage Flory yelled, "Come on. We're going to be late!"

The drive from their house to school took fifteen minutes, that is, if they were speeding and hit the lights just right and didn't have to slow down for school zones. It wasn't going to happen. Phoebe knew they were going to be tardy. And on the second day of school.

"I can't believe I forgot to set my alarm last night," she said. Phoebe turned and asked Flory. "Did you forget, too?"

"Yeah. Kinda weird, isn't it?"

Phoebe watched Flory navigate the morning traffic. The light at Cherokee turned yellow. Flory sped through it.

"You didn't tell Dad good-bye," Phoebe said.

"What?" Flory knitted her brows and shook her head.

"I said, you didn't tell Dad good-bye."

"I heard what you said." Flory's tone was annoyed. "So? I didn't say bye. I didn't go and tell Mom good-bye either. Did you?"

"No, but…"

"Don't pick on me about this minutia shit. I'm just trying to get through the day. I don't need you to add to my aggravation."

Phoebe didn't say anything for about a minute. Then she asked, "Flory?"

"Now what?"

"Did you know Aunt Lou was schizophrenic?"

Flory hesitated. "No. Not until on Sunday when we came home, and Dad tried to explain why she did what she did."

"Do you understand what it is? I mean, I googled it, but…"

"Yeah. Me, too," Flory said.

Phoebe noticed her sister glance at the clock on the dashboard. They might make it before the tardy bell—that is, if Flory could find an open parking spot.

"I read it's genetic." Phoebe was afraid to ask the question.

"I know," Flory said. "I know what you're thinking, Phoebe, but I don't know the answer. Yeah, it scares me, too. It scares the shit out of me."

Phoebe started to cry. She couldn't help it. "What if

we become like Aunt Lou?"

They had arrived at school, and Flory drove up to the front entrance to the school. "Come on, Phoebe. We can't talk about this now. Don't even think about it, okay? I'll see you after school."

Phoebe got out of the car. She turned to ask Flory why she had dropped her off, but she saw Flory drive away. She ran toward the building just as the final bell rang and realized she had no time to go to her locker. Her shoes squeaked as she ran down the empty hall to her first period class. She slid into a vacant seat in the back of the class. Phoebe felt the stares from the other students who turned to see who was late.

Mrs. Mitchell, her history teacher, glanced at Phoebe then resumed roll call. "Class, open your textbook to Chapter One."

Horrified, Phoebe realized her book was in her locker. She stared at her bare desk. Phoebe could feel her face flush. What was she going to do? Mrs. Mitchell was calling on students to read. Please don't call on me.

"Phoebe, can you continue with the next section?"

She stammered. "Uh, uh."

"Yes?"

"I don't have my book," Phoebe said. She watched Mrs. Mitchell open a folder and put a mark on the paper inside the folder.

The rest of the class was a blur for Phoebe. When the bell rang, she didn't see Sadie in the hall, so she hurried to her locker before her next class.

At lunch Phoebe walked toward the table where she and Sadie had sat the day before. Sadie wasn't there, and she didn't recognize anyone who was seated at the table. Looking around she saw her at a table on the other side of the cafeteria. There were four or five girls seated with her and a couple of boys standing behind. Phoebe hesitated before walking over. Why wasn't Sadie at the table they had deemed as theirs?

"Hi Sadie. I didn't see you at first," Phoebe said. "Is there an extra chair where I can sit?"

Phoebe saw her best friend's face turn red. "Uh, no. I think all the chairs are taken. Sorry Phoebe." Sadie turned away and began talking to the girl next to her. Phoebe stood there.

Finally, she said, "I don't get it. Why didn't you save me a seat?"

Phoebe watched Sadie get up slowly. "I'll be back," she said to the other girls. "Save my place."

Sadie walked away from the table. She turned toward Phoebe but wouldn't look her in the eye. "My parents told me I can't see you anymore. They said your aunt was schizophrenic, and it can run in families. Sorry." Sadie turned away from Phoebe and returned to the table.

Phoebe couldn't move. Her lunch sack fell out of her hands onto the floor, and the apple rolled out of the bag. She stared at the table full of freshman girls where her best friend was sitting. She felt like someone had stuck a knife into her chest. Phoebe picked up the apple, now bruised and sticky, dropped it in the trash, and left the cafeteria.

Squeezing her eyes to prevent herself from crying, she accidentally bumped into an upperclassman. "Sorry," she said.

The tall boy backed away. "Whoa. Stay back. You're Flory's little sister, aren't you?"

Phoebe nodded. She didn't like the way he talked to

her.

"Don't touch me again. I don't want to get *Sutton-ized.*" He laughed as he walked away. Phoebe's ears burned. "*Sutton-ized!*" She could still hear him saying it.

When the final bell rang, Phoebe hurried back to the band room dodging students as she ran down the halls. She wanted to talk to Mr. Fixley before he left. He was locking the door when Phoebe rounded the corner.

"Mr. Fixley, can I talk to you?" she called out as she ran toward him.

"I was on my way out. Can it wait until tomorrow?"

Phoebe hesitated. Normally, she would have said yes. But, no, this couldn't wait. "No. I need to know why I'm not in the marching band. I was first chair last year. I went to band camp, and I scored Superior on all my performances."

Mr. Fixley unlocked the door to the band room. "Come in, Phoebe. I'll see if I can explain this to you." He was a tall, thin man, like an extension of the baton he used to conduct the band. His face was narrow, and it often appeared as if gravity pulled down his eyes and the sides of his mouth.

He seated himself behind his desk and pointed to a chair for Phoebe. He cleared his throat. "Phoebe, you're an excellent musician, and I look forward to working with you the next four years." He paused and adjusted himself in his chair. Phoebe sat motionless. "However, the School Board informed Mr. Webb, our principal… Some of the parents are concerned about your relationship to…well, you know." Mr. Fixley's eyes seemed to droop even more. "They feel the marching band represents our school, and they gave me no choice. I'm sorry."

Phoebe sat fixated. Behind her were the rows of chairs arranged for band. She faced the dry-erase board on the wall with the diagram for marching. Again, Phoebe felt tears form. She stood up and ran out of the room.

Chapter 19

The first week of school had been disastrous for Flory and Phoebe. Each of them tried to manage in their own way the fallout from what seemed like a war-torn week. After the conversation in the car with Phoebe about Aunt Lou, Flory kept her problems to herself. No one in her family knew her secret, and she hoped to keep it that way. At some point she knew it would catch up with her, but she wasn't going to think about that for now.

After the first day of school, Flory took Phoebe to school and picked her up, but she never entered Junction Memorial High School. What was the point? she asked herself every day.

Each morning when they arrived at school, Phoebe asked, "Aren't you going in?"

Each morning Flory found a new excuse for lingering. On Monday Flory had driven around, eventually ending up at Buffalo Springs State Park, a small oasis of natural springs feeding into creeks, hiking trails, and a buffalo pasture. Located at the base of America's oldest mountain range, the Arbuckle Mountains, Flory and her family often went for the day, just to get away.

Tuesday afternoon when Flory's stomach rumbled, she went in search of a place to eat. She turned west, away from the high school toward the other side of town and found herself in front of Okie Bowl. There was a lone van in the parking lot, and the neon sign flashed open.

Why not. Bowling alleys served food. She entered, and country western music blasted from the speakers. The alleys were lit, and the pins lined up ready for the next round, but no one appeared to be there.

"Can I help you?"

Flory heard a voice but didn't see anyone at first. Then she saw a guy standing behind the shoe rental counter. Appearing to be in his twenties, he had longish hair pulled back in a ponytail and a beard. He wore a button-down shirt that had *Okie Bowl* on the pocket.

"Oh! Uh," Flory stammered.

"Did you want to bowl," the Okie Bowl guy asked. He smiled.

"No, not really," Flory said. She had the feeling he was laughing at her, and she felt flustered. To the left she saw arcade machines, and beyond that was a counter for food and drinks. "Do you have any food?"

"Well," Okie Bowl guy stroked his beard, "unless all of that stuff over there is fake food, I'd say we do." He tilted his head to the left.

And so, it began. The Okie Bowl guy had a name. It was Mitch. He had been working at the bowling alley since he graduated from high school four years ago. He was now the day manager. The job was a breeze because no one hardly came in until two or three, unless there was a kiddie birthday party.

Flory dropped off Phoebe at school every morning, then drove away. She returned in the afternoon in time to pick her up. At first, she sat at the counter eating a hot dog. Then Mitch offered her a beer. Then one beer became a pitcher of beer. Then the pitcher of beer led to his van in the parking lot.

There was something exciting about her rendezvous with Mitch each day. He didn't care about what had happened, telling Flory the kids at school were treating her like crap. He seemed to tell her what she wanted to hear.

On Friday Flory selected her outfit with care. She wore a halter top underneath an open work shirt, tied at her waist, and a pair of cut-off jean shorts. Phoebe noticed and commented, but Flory ignored her.

Okie Bowl didn't open until eleven, but Mitch arrived at 10:30. Flory was already waiting. He parked next to her.

Mitch grinned. "Happy Friday. Are you ready to celebrate?"

Following him inside, Flory sat at the bar and watched Mitch open the bowling alley. Presently he came over and poured two beers. Mitch leaned across the counter and kissed her. Her head felt light. It felt good having someone pay attention to her.

Mitch grabbed a pitcher and filled it after he downed his glass. "Follow me," he said as he went outside to his van.

After the second pitcher of beer Flory said, "I have to pee." She tried to sit up and tie her halter-top. "I feel dizzy," she said, laughing. Flory stumbled out of the van and into the bowling alley to relieve herself. When she weaved back to the van, it was empty. Where is Mitch? Maybe I'll just close my eyes.

Flory woke up wet and sticky. Her hair was matted, and the front of her halter-top was covered in vomit. She reeked. Flory tried to sit up, but her head felt like someone had hit it with a mallet. Then she felt sick again. This time Flory opened the van door in time. She staggered out and almost slipped on the wet asphalt. Standing made her head spin. She needed to lie down.

The back seat was covered with her vomit, so she wasn't going back into Mitch's van. Next to it was her mother's car, but it was locked.

Flory realized she had left her keys inside the bowling alley. Groping her mother's car, she considered crawling because she didn't know if she could make it. Once inside, the neon lights and loud music made her feel worse. Flory used the wall for support as she lumbered to the bathroom. She felt disgusting and humiliated as she tried to clean herself.

Mitch was at the food counter, and there were two guys bowling. He saw Flory and said, "Sorry. I had a call, and you were asleep, so…"

Passed out was more like it. "I need to go. I just came in to get my keys."

Mitch walked past her, patting her on the butt. He returned with her purse. "I put it in the office for safe keeping, but are you sure you're okay to drive?"

Flory took her purse but stepped back. She didn't want him to get a whiff of her. "I'll be fine," she said, "and thanks."

"See ya," Mitch called out.

Not likely. Please don't get sick again. She tried to walk without weaving. As soon as she got to her mother's car, she climbed in, rolled down the windows for some fresh air, and fell asleep.

Chapter 20

"Alice!" She opened her eyes. Rodney stood over her. "Has Flory been home?"

Behind Rodney, Alice saw Phoebe. Her eyes were red, like she had been crying. Where was Flory? She sat up. Alice wiped the drool on the side of her mouth. Her right hand was numb from lying on it, and she had no idea how long she had been asleep on the den sofa.

"No. Wasn't she at school? Where is she?" None of this made sense.

"We don't know where she is," Rodney said. "When school let out, Phoebe couldn't find her or the car."

"I must have dozed off. She could have come in and not wanted to wake me."

"No, Mom." Alice heard the annoyance in Phoebe's voice. "We've been trying to call Flory, and she hasn't answered. And she's not in her room."

Alice closed her eyes to clear her mind. "When did you realize Flory was gone?" she asked.

"When she didn't pick me up after school," Phoebe said. "She always texts to say where she is parked. But I never heard from her, and when I went out to the parking lot, I didn't see your car anywhere. I waited until almost every car was gone. Then I called Dad."

The sick feeling in her stomach returned. What happened to Flory? Oh my God!

"We were hoping she was home," Rodney said. "I

checked her room. Nothing."

"Do you think we should call the police?" Phoebe was near tears.

Rodney shook his head. "Not yet," he said. "I'm going to drive around and see if I can find her." He gave Phoebe a squeeze. "Don't you worry."

"I'm going with you," Phoebe said.

"I'll get my shoes on," Alice hurried back to her bedroom. She didn't notice the unmade bed, or the pile of clothes that continued to grow. She wasn't aware that she was wearing the same clothes she had put on the day before, the ones she fell asleep in, or that she hadn't brushed her teeth or combed her hair. Alice, who normally woke up before everyone, had breakfast ready, already on her second cup of coffee when her daughters appeared in the kitchen, hadn't made it out of bed all week. She didn't know how they got to school, or that everyone overslept on Tuesday.

Alice slipped on a pair of flip-flops, and the three of them climbed into Rodney's pickup. It was a relief to leave the house without a hoard of cameras and microphones chasing them. The media had departed after the first week.

Rodney's words hung in the air. *We'll find her. Don't you worry.* But Alice was worried. What if they didn't find her? What if something horrible had happened to her? What if? Alice didn't even want to think about it.

Rodney drove to the school hoping the Honda Civic would be there. He went by all the hangouts—the strip shopping mall on Bryant, Starbucks, Dairy Queen. He even drove past Maddie's home and through the neighborhoods where other friends lived. All the while

Phoebe kept phoning Flory.

"Flory, it's me. Where are you? Call me." Phoebe's voice cracked.

Sandwiched between Alice and Rodney, Alice observed Phoebe, sitting up straight, searching through the windshield for any sign of Flory.

They had been searching for Flory for almost an hour when Phoebe said, "What about Buffalo Springs? Maybe she drove out there."

"Good idea," Rodney said. He turned the truck toward the interstate, and thirty minutes later they arrived at the park. It didn't take long to drive through. They stopped at the Nature Center, the stone bridge, the buffalo pasture, and Bromide Hill, but there was no sign of Alice's car.

"I think I'll drive around Sandy Point," Rodney said. It was the small town adjacent to the park. Still no car.

Alice had been silent for most of the drive. Her parents were dead. Lou was dead, along with eleven others. And now Flory was missing. She couldn't take it.

Please, God, we must find Flory. I can't take another loss, she prayed.

When all efforts to find Flory seemed exhausted, Rodney turned back toward Junction. "I'll call the police and make a missing person's report when we get home," he said.

Alice heard the despair in Rodney's voice, and she choked back a sob. Her family. It was all she had. Rodney stared stoically at the road, brushing away a tear from time to time. Phoebe had curled into a ball, her knees pulled up and her head down. No one spoke.

Rodney pulled into the drive and pushed the remote to open the garage. There was the car. The three of them erupted in cheers. Alice was flooded with relief.

Phoebe pushed her way past Alice and was the first one inside. Alice and Rodney followed quickly behind. She heard Phoebe ask, "But why didn't you call?"

Alice and Rodney found the girls in Flory's bedroom, sitting on her bed. The room reeked with an odor she recognized immediately.

Rodney stopped abruptly. He must have gotten a whiff, too, Alice surmised.

"Flory, where were you? Why didn't you answer your phone?"

"I'm sorry, Dad. My phone went dead."

Alice said, "We were worried sick!" She instinctively went over to hug her daughter.

Flory stood up and walked away. She crossed her arms and didn't answer.

"Flory, what's the matter?" Alice tried to resume her role as mother.

"What do you mean, *what's the matter*? My aunt murdered eleven people. My mother can't even get out of bed. My friends have all disowned me—all of them! What's the point of going to school?"

Alice took a step toward Flory. She reached out to touch her arm.

"Don't touch me! It's all your fault. You could have done something to help Aunt Lou. And then when it happened, you just felt sorry for yourself. You forgot the rest of us are dealing with it, too. Maybe we're struggling, too. Did you think of that? Have you asked Dad how work is?"

"Flory, stop," Rodney said.

Alice stared. She couldn't move.

"And what about Phoebe and me? Did you know

they didn't let Phoebe in marching band because of Aunt Lou? You haven't gotten out of bed for over two weeks. Two whole weeks! We've done our own laundry, fixed dinner, gone to the store. But you wouldn't know. The few times you did come to the table for dinner, you didn't even pay attention to what you were eating. Phoebe and I were fixing dinner. You've done nothing," Flory screamed. "Nothing!"

Chapter 21

Rodney pulled into the parking lot behind Sutton Cards on Monday morning. It was a nondescript, concrete block building located on the other side of the railroad tracks in the industrial part of town. A row of storage units had recently been built in the vacant lot next door. On the corner was a 7-Eleven. When the wind blew from the east, Rodney could smell the dog food manufacturer nearby.

There was one other car in the parking lot. It belonged to the Nguyens. It seemed strange not to see any other vehicles. How was he going to run the business with only two employees? How much business would he have? he wondered. Rodney watched the elderly couple slowly get out of their old Pontiac. They bowed when they saw him. "Good morning, Mr. Rodney," Liem Nguyen said.

"Good morning, Liem. Good morning, Ha. How are you this morning?"

"Very good," Liem said, which meant *honest one* in Vietnamese. "And you? Are you good, or are you not so good?"

Rodney shook his head. "Not so good today." He unlocked the metal door at the back entrance and followed them inside.

Ha, which meant *sunshine and warmth* in Vietnamese, patted his arm. "We stay with you. We help you."

"Thank you," Rodney said. He watched the Vietnamese couple walk toward the break room. They put their lunch in the small refrigerator.

Rodney had initially felt relief leaving the house, but now being at work, he felt overwhelmed.

It had been strange not attending church on Sunday, but Rodney wasn't ready to face the public. And he wasn't sure they were ready to encounter his family. It was so awkward. What did someone say to an acquaintance whose relative had murdered eleven people? Those were the ones who sympathized with his family. What about those who considered them guilty?

Yesterday he had felt so aimless. It was like the four of them were locked together in their house, but each in their own private prison. At least Rodney had accomplished something over the weekend. He had gathered all the cell phones, read every text and email, and listened to all voicemails since the shooting. It had been daunting, and it made him sick to his stomach. On Alice's emails he had found messages from the school about Flory's absences. But since she had literally shut down, she hadn't checked her phone. Her inability to cope added to the pile of garbage—no, the pile of shit—he had to go through.

Number one on Rodney's list that morning was to call the school and figure out what to do. Rodney had dropped Flory and Phoebe off before he came to work, insisting Flory go to school this morning, but he wasn't sure it was the right thing to do. Rodney checked the attendance policy online, and it made his head swim. This was, and always had been, Alice's area. He felt completely out of his league, but there was nothing else to do but take care of it.

Rodney closed his eyes and pressed his palms against his forehead, applying as much pressure as possible to prevent the ever-persistent headache from returning. He sat up and took a breath. "Okay. Let's do this," he said out loud. He called the attendance office. Then he made an appointment with the school counselor.

The appointment with Ms. Grady was at eleven. He hoped she could help them find a solution for Flory. Memories of Friday afternoon when he was convinced they had lost her made him tear up just thinking about it. She'd always been a good student, active at school, playing basketball, and finding time for her boyfriend, Blake. But after last week, he didn't know what to think. Was this something temporary because of Lou, or was this the path Flory wanted to take? Either way, they had to put a stop to it.

Rodney's cell phone vibrated, interrupting his thoughts. It was Alice. "Hello?"

"Have you had a chance to talk to the counselor?"

"No. I scheduled an appointment for eleven this morning," Rodney said.

"Oh, good. I was afraid you had already talked to her," Alice said. "I'm coming with you."

"O-kay?" Rodney said, surprised at what he heard. "That's good?" He asked, as if he wanted to add, "and you're coming because? Are you sure you're up to this? I don't need a melt down at the school."

"I'll pick you up at ten thirty. Bye." Alice hung up.

Rodney stared at his cell phone. That almost sounded like the old Alice.

Rodney's exposure to the high school had been limited to Flory's basketball games, parent-teacher conferences, and Meet the Teacher Nights. Alice's awareness of the ins and outs of the school was a relief to him. She knew where the administration offices were, and she had met Ms. Grady at a meeting about college prep.

Ms. Grady was a thirty-something, hip woman. It was obvious she could relate well with the students. She seemed young enough to understand their challenges, yet old enough to have the needed authority. She greeted Rodney and Alice and invited them into her office. It was 11:01.

Ms. Grady's office had a sense of organized chaos— Alice could relate to that, Rodney thought. One wall was covered with sayings, such as, "You are responsible for YOU!" Pennants from colleges and universities covered another space. There was a bookcase behind her desk, and a small seating area to the side. That was where she directed Rodney and Alice.

Ms. Grady picked up two copies of Flory's records from the printer. She handed one to them. "Mr. Bennett," she said, "I'm glad you called this morning. It was on my list to contact you today." It was as if this was merely a meeting about Flory's class schedule.

"The attendance office notified me on Friday of Flory's absences," she said. "They also told me they had contacted the parents," she paused, studying them, "and never heard back." She waited. It was their turn to talk and explain why.

Rodney cleared his throat. "As you know, I'm sure, our family has had a very—what should I say— unsettling past couple of weeks. None of us are functioning as we normally do. I must confess I didn't know Flory wasn't going to her classes until late Friday afternoon."

Alice interrupted Rodney. "The school contacts me—my cell phone and email address—when there is an issue. I dropped the ball."

Rodney noticed Alice wringing her hands. "You see," he said, "we started getting threats." He had no idea if he was getting across to this woman the desperate state they were in. "Flory stopped coming to school because one of her classmates knew someone who had been hurt."

"It took us awhile to get it out of her. Flory, I mean," Alice said, "but the student told Flory she didn't belong, that she should leave. I'm sorry, it's my fault. It was my sister. We're all trying to come to terms with it. You have no idea…" Alice's voice trailed off.

Rodney eyes watered.

"This is a very difficult situation, for all of us," Ms. Grady said. "Yes, there are several students who knew individuals who had been there or were injured that night. But that doesn't give them the right to bully another student. However, I understand Flory's state of mind, that she might feel uncomfortable here." Ms. Grady studied Flory's record. "Flory's an excellent student, as you know. I would hate for her to lose everything she's worked so hard for." She laid the paper down on the small table in the middle of the seating area. "Does she have a good friend she can rely on right now?"

"No. Not really. Her best friend dropped her, and her boyfriend broke up with her," Rodney said.

"This is tough," Ms. Grady said. "We want all of our students to succeed. And we want them to complete their education here at Junction Memorial. But sometimes that's not the best answer to a situation." Ms. Grady paused. "What do you think? What would be best for Flory?"

"That's the problem," Alice said, "we don't know. We really have no idea."

"Flory's behavior last week was totally out of character for her, as far as we're concerned," Rodney said. "I have a feeling she felt like all the doors had been shut."

Ms. Grady nodded. "Let me give this some thought," she said. "I want to discuss this with Mr. Webb, our principal, and Mr. Doty, our VP. Obviously, we've never had a situation like this before at our school, and we want to do what's best for all the students. In the meantime, I'm going to personally talk to each of Flory's teachers. I think they will give her extra time to complete any missed assignments. These were certainly circumstances that don't fall into any of our prescribed boxes." She studied Flory's record and added, "Have you thought about home-schooling her?"

Rodney raised his eyebrows. Alice almost chuckled. "I don't know how successful that would be, but I guess that's certainly an option." That was the first time he had heard Alice laugh in over two weeks.

"What about concurrent enrollment?" Ms. Grady asked.

Rodney and Alice turned toward each other. "What is that?" Rodney asked.

"It's also called dual enrollment. The student is enrolled simultaneously in two schools. Flory could take some of her classes at the community college, but she would have to take the required courses for graduation here." Ms. Grady studied Flory's file. "She needs to take Senior English and a Civics class here. U.S. Government is what she's enrolled in."

Rodney asked, "Isn't it too late to enroll in classes at another school?"

Ms. Grady went over to her computer and scrolled through information. "I see there is a deadline for late enrollment of September 3rd, that is, assuming the classes aren't filled."

Alice asked, "But what if the classes are filled? What is Flory supposed to do then?"

"There's also the option of taking classes online." Ms. Grady added, "As I said, I'll discuss this with Mr. Webb and Mr. Doty, and then I'll let you know what they recommend."

Ms. Grady stood up. "Is there anything else you needed to discuss with me?"

Rodney asked, "What about Phoebe, our other daughter? She's a freshman."

Ms. Grady stopped, her hand on the doorknob. "I wasn't aware of…is she having problems, too?"

"Phoebe didn't get into marching band," Rodney said.

"Oh, that's normal for incoming freshmen. They have to attend band camp to qualify."

"She did. She went to band camp and got Superior on all her performances. She was first chair in her section in middle school. Phoebe was under the impression those guaranteed her a spot. When her name wasn't on the list, she asked the band instructor. He said the School Board didn't want her to march with the band." Rodney's heart pounded in his chest. He knew he was getting angry, and he needed to calm down. Deep breaths.

Ms. Grady walked over to her desk. She took out a post-it and wrote on it. "I'll ask about that, too, when I meet with Mr. Webb. I wasn't aware of what you just told me, and I really don't know if there's anything we can do. But I'll find out." Ms. Grady studied Rodney and Alice. "Mr. and Mrs. Bennett, are you aware we have a crisis counselor? Mrs. Mullins is wonderful with the students, and I think Flory and Phoebe could benefit from seeing her."

Again, Rodney and Alice looked at each other and shook their heads. This time Alice spoke. "We've just been trying to get through each day. And I personally haven't been doing a very good job as their mother. I didn't even think about that." She glanced at Rodney, and he nodded. "I think that would certainly be helpful. I'll tell them about it, and suggest they talk with her."

Ms. Grady glanced at her watch. "Thank you for coming by. I hope we can get Flory's classes adjusted. And please be sure to talk to them about making an appointment with Mrs. Mullins."

Rodney extended his hand, and Ms. Grady shook it. "Thank you for your time," he said. Alice followed his actions.

"Thank you, Mr. and Mrs. Bennett. I'll be in touch," Ms. Grady said, and she ushered them out of her office.

As they stepped into the hall, they were almost run down by the mass of students pouring out of the classrooms. Rodney and Alice pressed themselves against the wall to let the teens pass. Thankfully, no one paid attention to them. They were too busy visiting with each other. Lockers slammed, and the chatter accelerated. Rodney's eyes widened. He didn't remember the halls being this crowded when they were in high school. His cell phone vibrated in his pocket, interrupting his thoughts. It was Barney.

"Hey Rodney, do you have a minute?"

Rodney held the phone close to his ear as he and Alice inched their way down the hallway. "Can I call you back? We're about to be run down by a bunch of teenagers." He had to shout to be heard over the noise. "I'll call you back in about five minutes."

Rodney felt Alice tug on his arm. She tilted her head in a direction, indicating the way out of the crowd. Once outside, Rodney pulled at his shirt. It was soaked.

"Damn," he said. "I didn't know there were so many kids at that school!" As they walked toward the visitor parking lot, he noticed students coming out of the building. He heard car doors slam and engines rev. They must be the seniors leaving campus for lunch. He wondered where Flory was. He knew she didn't have a car, and hoped she went to lunch with someone.

Once they were back in Alice's car, Rodney returned Barney's call. "Hi Barney. What do you need?"

There was a pause on the other end of the line. "Well…" Barney hesitated. "I'm in a quandary. I'm a small-town lawyer and accountant. I do wills and estate planning. And I file people's taxes. I've never had to work on a lawsuit, but as of now, seven of the eleven families of the victims have filed suits against Lou's estate."

Now it was Rodney's turn to hesitate. Oh my God. He hadn't even thought of that. "Does that mean they can come after us?"

"As I see it, it's pretty cut and dry. Lou killed the individuals. There's no doubt. She's dead, so she can't be defended. As executor of Lou's estate, I will allow default judgements to be taken. Her assets will be divided among the plaintiffs, or they will compete

144

against each other. So, basically, it's out of our hands."

"What about us?" Rodney asked.

"They can't come after you and Alice, as long as your assets are separate from Lou's."

"Okay." Rodney's head pounded.

"You hang in there. We'll get this handled."

"Thanks, Barney." Rodney placed the phone back in his pocket and stared out the window as Alice drove out of the parking lot.

"What was that about?" Alice asked.

"I'll tell you later." Rodney didn't want to talk about it. He thought of the one asset Alice and Lou had that wasn't separate—the farm.

Chapter 22

The bell rang for first lunch. Bile rose in Flory's throat. How was she going to get through the day? She was stuck here. No car, no way to escape. Prison. That's what it felt like. Kind of like being at home, except there were all these people around. They didn't want her here any more than she did. This was not how her senior year was supposed to be. Instead of being the best year, her life was cascading downward.

After the fiasco with Mitch at the bowling alley, her parents were never going to trust her again. Flory felt like she was grounded for life. What was there to look forward to? She had no friends. Most likely no basketball—certainly not varsity—now that she had been branded. Boyfriend? Blake broke up with her by text. What a jerk! No one would get near her now. Classes? Well, what was the point? Life sucked!

Flory waited at her desk until most of her classmates were gone. Then, keeping her head down, she left the classroom from the back door. Flory felt like there was no one on her side, and she hadn't done anything. She hated Aunt Lou.

Flory stood in the hallway, undecided. Her stomach growled, which was better than feeling like she was going to vomit. She couldn't go out to lunch because she didn't have a car, and no one was going to ask her. And there was no way she was going into the cafeteria. She decided to take the apple she brought and go to the library. It was better than hiding in the restroom.

When the bell rang for the end of school, feelings of relief and dread covered Flory. Now what? she wondered. In the past, she stayed after school for club meetings or student council. Basketball practice began in October, but Flory didn't know if she would be on the team, or if she wanted to. Now, there was nothing to do but go home. Leaving one prison for another.

Her phone dinged. It was Alice.

—*Hi girls, I'll meet you on Perkins Street.* —

At her locker Flory gathered her books for her missed assignments. Thankfully, her teachers had been discreet, and one or two seemed sympathetic. That helped.

Her phone dinged again. It was Phoebe.

—*Where's Perkins Street?*

Flory texted back. —*Meet me at the back entrance, and I'll show you.*—

Five minutes later the two of them walked together to meet Alice. Neither spoke much. Flory was relieved. She didn't feel like talking. There was nothing to say. But she knew once she got in the car, her mother would ask how their day was. At least Mom was out of bed. Flory wondered if she was back to her old self, or if this was a temporary thing. There was nothing predictable in her life now, not even her mother—especially her mother.

"Hi girls, how was your day?"

Well, that was predictable, Flory thought. But she didn't answer.

"It was okay," Phoebe said. She slid into the back seat.

That meant Flory had to get in the front with Alice. She'd give anything to crawl in the back, but that would be strange. She sighed as she opened the passenger door, never making eye contact with her mother.

Alice turned toward Flory. "How was school?"

Flory shrugged her shoulders but didn't answer. As her mother pulled away, Flory glanced at her. She was dressed and wearing make-up. That was surprising.

After driving past the strip mall and the Mexican restaurant, Alice finally broke the silence. "Your father and I met with Ms. Grady, the school counselor, today."

Flory was curious but didn't say anything.

"We are trying to figure out what is best for you, Flory, going forward."

What did that mean? Flory wondered.

"Ms. Grady came up with some different options that might work," Alice continued.

Options for what? Flory had no idea what Alice was talking about. But she remained silent.

"At first she mentioned homeschooling, but I doubt you'd want to do that."

Oh my God! That would be torture.

Alice continued, as if she was having a conversation instead of a monologue. "Then we discussed other ideas, like concurrent enrollment or online classes."

What does that mean?

"Concurrent enrollment is when you're enrolled simultaneously in two schools." The stoplight at the intersection turned red, and Alice turned to Flory. "You could take the majority of your classes at COC, except for U.S. Government and Senior English."

Why was that?

As if she was reading her mind, Alice answered,

"Those classes are the only two on the required list for graduation at Memorial that you haven't taken. You have to take them at the high school."

The light turned green. Flory didn't answer her mother, but she thought about what she was telling her. Maybe if she was able to go someplace where no one knew her, she could have a life. She let out a breath, the only sign she gave to indicate she had heard what Alice was telling her.

"Oh, and one last thing. Ms. Grady mentioned something else both of you could benefit from."

Now what? Flory stared out the window.

Alice continued, "She told us about Mrs. Mullins, the crisis counselor. Both of you could make an appointment to talk with her. I think it's a good idea. What do you think?"

Flory was silent.

"I don't know, Mom. I figured that would be for the other kids," Phoebe said.

"Well, think about it," Alice said.

The remainder of the ride home was in silence. Alice pulled into the garage. Once the ignition was turned off, Flory got out of the car, went to her room, and shut the door. She dropped her backpack on the floor and flopped onto her unmade bed. She gazed up at the ceiling, staring at a single crack that extended from corner to corner. Did that mean her ceiling might fall in? That would fit with everything else in her life. She rolled over and glared at the pile of books that spilled from her backpack, as if it was their fault for her misery.

Sighing, Flory sat up and gathered the load, arranging them on her bed in order of importance. Calculus first. She had to do her calculus, or she'd never catch up. A pestering voice in her head asked her what was the point. Flory's dream had been to go to nursing school, but now she didn't know what she wanted to do. What if no one would hire her because her aunt was a murderer? Of what if she got a job, but the patients were afraid of her because of Aunt Lou?

Flory felt herself in a downward spiral. All she wanted to do was climb into bed. That would be so easy. Flory sat cross-legged on her bed and stared at the unopened calculus textbook. It was as if she was staring at a massive boulder, too heavy to pick up. There was a tension between the appeal to crawl into bed and the reality of all the homework she had. She felt paralyzed.

Oh my God! This is what Mom has been doing. But Flory resented her mother's behavior. So, how could she justify it in herself? She felt pulled into a paradox— resentment yet understanding. Flory hated how weak Alice had been the last two weeks. Yet, here she was, ready to crawl into bed herself. But she couldn't go there. If she did, then she was accepting her mother's behavior.

Her only choice was to forge ahead and throw herself into her studies until something better came along. She resolved to do whatever it took to ward off despondency if she could. Flory picked up her calculus book.

****

There was a knock on her door. "Flory." It was Alice. "Dinner time."

Had she been studying that long? She had made quite a dent. She put a strip of paper in her U.S. Government textbook to mark the page.

"Coming," she said. Then she remembered she was angry, at her family—especially Aunt Lou—at the school, and everyone in her hometown. But wait. Mom fixed dinner? That must have been the first time since the...Flory didn't let herself go there.

She entered the kitchen. Phoebe was pouring water into the glasses. The table had been set. Her mother pulled meatloaf out of the oven. It smelled delicious, even though Flory didn't especially care for it.

She resumed her scowl and sat in her usual place. Rodney came up behind her and squeezed her shoulders, then kissed her on her cheek.

"How was your day?" Rodney whispered in her ear.

Flory couldn't help herself. She gave him a half smile. He cared. But she didn't say anything, just shrugged her shoulders.

Alice put the plates on the table and sat down. "Whose turn is it to say the blessing? Flory?"

Flory shook her head. How could she thank God for anything? Where had He been? Why hadn't He stopped Aunt Lou?

"I'll say it," Rodney said. He closed his eyes and bowed his head. "Dear God, bless this food to the nourishment of our bodies." There was a long pause before he continued. "And God, we don't understand why all those lives were lost. We really don't. Be with those families who are grieving." Flory heard Rodney sniff. "God, we're hurting, too. It's awful, and we don't know what to do. Please help us, God. Please?" The silence lingered. "In your Son's holy name, Amen."

Flory opened her eyes. She realized she wasn't the only one who was hurting.

Rodney squeezed Flory and Phoebe's hands on either side of him. Then he reached across the table and held onto Alice's hand. "We'll get through this," he said.

"I know we will. It won't be easy, and we can't do it on our own, but we'll find a way, God willing."

Flory and the rest of her family had no idea what their future held. It was going to be one day at a time for a long time. But for this one meal, there was a feeling of hope.

****

After dinner that night Phoebe remained in the kitchen and helped put away the food. Rodney grabbed a beer from the refrigerator and announced he was going to watch football. It seemed like old times. Just plain normal. What a relief. Phoebe hoped that meant her family would be okay and everything would be back to the way it used to be. There was a calm silence as the three females worked side by side to put the kitchen back in order.

But the calm silence shifted to a communal sense of panic. No one said anything, but Phoebe could sense the change. The mindless distraction of putting the dinner dishes and food away ended, and Phoebe, along with Flory and Alice, were back to their new normal. It frightened her.

Without a word, Flory walked out of the kitchen to her bedroom. Phoebe heard the door shut. She watched her mother turn and drift down the hall. It was like watching a ghost float away. In the den she could hear Monday night football on the television. Occasionally, Rodney let out a yell. Suddenly she felt all alone.

Chapter 23

The private memorial service for Lou was scheduled for eleven on Saturday. Bud Weirich, an old friend of Carl's, had offered his services to Alice. Alice's grandfather had helped Bud's father get his start in the funeral business years ago. When her parents were killed in the auto accident, Bud had been there for her and her family. Now again, he provided the needed help. Alice was grateful for her parents' invisible hand in this ordeal.

Since Carl and Florence had been cremated, it made sense to have Lou cremated, too. It also solved the dilemma of what to do with her body. There was no risk of vandalism. Alice and Rodney decided not to ask their pastor to officiate the service for his own benefit. They didn't want to tarnish his reputation with Lou's actions.

Weirich's Funeral Home was located on Broadway, the main north-south street in town. It stood out from the big box stores and strip malls along Broadway with its Mediterranean styled building and terra cotta roof. A circular sidewalk surrounded a fountain in front of the entrance. The sound of water was supposed to soothe the grieving who came.

Alice and the family arrived at 10:45. She glanced at her daughters, dressed in their Sunday clothes. They seemed so grown-up. Flory pulled her straight dark brown hair into a ponytail that was elegant rather than casual. She appeared so poised and mature. Alice wondered what Flory was thinking. It had been a horrible four weeks.

Phoebe's mass of auburn curls tumbled about her face. She had on the slightest amount of make-up—a little blush and mascara. Alice could see Rodney in Phoebe's clear blue eyes and thick eyelashes. Was she really going to be fifteen soon?

Bud walked toward them with his arms extended. "Come back this way," he said, as he led them to the chapel. He spoke in a soft voice, as if he didn't want to disturb the dead. Alice wondered if Bud had made funeral arrangements for any of the victims. She cleared her throat in order not to cry.

The four of them followed Bud silently. Upon entering the chapel, piped in organ music played. The haunting notes to familiar hymns disturbed Alice. She wasn't expecting it, and it didn't leave her with the peaceful feeling it was intended to give.

The chapel was an interior room, so there were no windows for natural light. It seemed dreary to Alice. There were contemporary-styled benches that could be added or removed, depending on the number of attendees. Bud ushered the Bennetts to the first of only three benches in the chapel.

On the wall at the front of the chapel hung a simple cross. On either side of the cross were pedestals, reserved for floral arrangements. There was an elegant all-white arrangement on one pedestal, and a small colorful bouquet on the other.

Rodney reached over to take Alice's hand, and he squeezed it. That was her signal to squeeze back, but she didn't. Again, she felt paralyzed and numb, as if she was having an out-of-body experience, peering down on the four of them from above. What she saw was a family who didn't want to be there.

Presently she heard the door to the chapel open. Someone else was here. Then the door clicked shut, and it felt like they were locked in. Alice experienced a rush of panic. Her breath became shallow as she tried to calm herself down.

"Are you okay?" Rodney leaned over and whispered to her.

Alice nodded.

She heard the shuffling of bodies as the bench behind them became occupied. There were handshakes and shoulder squeezes and heads nodding as Barney and Rodney's three best friends seated themselves.

The door opened and shut again. Soon Alice felt someone's arms around her and the fragrance of gardenias. It was Sandra Snyder, an old friend from grade school. Alice's rigid stance melted. How grateful she felt to have her there. What a blessing and a surprise.

The final taped hymn ended, and Bud walked toward the podium in front.

"Welcome," he said. "We are gathered here to honor the life of Lou Ella Sutton. Lou Ella was born on July 31, 1968. She died on August 6, 2015. Lou Ella was preceded in death by her parents, Carl and Florence Sutton, and two stillborn siblings. She is survived by her sister, Alice Sutton Bennett, husband, Rodney, and two daughters, Flory and Phoebe." Bud nodded to Flory and Phoebe. "And now we will have the Scripture reading."

Alice watched her daughters walk together toward the podium.

Flory stood behind the podium. "Here is the reading from the Old Testament," she said. "Psalm 139, verses thirteen through sixteen. Hear the word of the Lord. 'For you created my inmost being; you knit me together in my mother's womb. I praise you because I am fearfully and wonderfully made; your works are wonderful, I know that full well. My frame was not hidden from you when I was made in the secret place. When I was woven together in the depths of the earth, your eyes saw my unformed body. All the days ordained for me were written in your book before one of them came to be.' " Flory looked at her parents. "This is the word of the Lord."

"Thanks be to God," they replied.

Phoebe then took her place behind the podium. "Here is the reading from the New Testament," she said. "John, chapter fourteen, verses one through three. Hear the word of the Lord. 'Do not let your hearts be troubled. Trust in God; trust also in me. In my Father's house are many rooms; if it were not so, I would have told you. I am going there to prepare a place for you. And if I go and prepare a place for you, I will come back and take you to be with me that you also may be where I am.'" Phoebe kept her head down. "This is the word of the Lord," she said, wiping her face.

"Thanks be to God."

Bud returned to the podium. "Is there anyone who would like to say a few words about Lou Ella?" He waited.

Alice froze. What could someone say about her sister? She felt the back of the bench pulled as someone behind her used it to stand up. Barney walked toward the podium.

He regarded the small gathering. "Well, I hadn't planned on saying anything, but all of a sudden I stood up, and here I am." Barney took out his handkerchief and wiped his brow. Then he focused on Alice, as if he was speaking only to her.

"I've known Lou longer than anyone here. I remember the day she was born," Barney said. "She was a big baby. She had big hands and big feet, kind of like a puppy that was going to become a Great Dane or a Lab. Carl and Florence loved Lou." Barney blew his nose, then stuffed the handkerchief back in his pocket. "Then when Alice was born, Lou was so excited." Barney looked at Alice. "She loved you so much, you know."

Alice nodded, wiping a tear.

Barney continued, "Lou became her mother's helper with Alice. I can remember going out to the farm, and there would be Lou sitting on the back porch in the rocking chair, holding her baby sister. Lou loved her family, and she also had an affinity for animals, especially stray or injured ones." Barney paused. "It was a sad day when they discovered what was wrong with her. It answered many questions but didn't provide the answers Carl and Florence would have liked. It was a struggle, more so than anyone expected or anticipated." Barney wiped his eyes and sighed. "But I can tell you this: Lou Ella Sutton would have been devastated if she knew what she had done. That was not who she was. She was a kind and gentle soul, tormented by a horrible disease that caused her to commit a horrible crime." Barney choked on his last words and sat down.

A stunned silence followed. Alice's vision was blurred. She felt Flory hand her a tissue. On the other side Rodney sniffed and wiped his nose.

"Please bow your heads for our closing prayer," Bud said.

Alice closed her eyes, but she didn't hear the prayer. Barney's words came back to her, "…that was not who she was. She was a kind and gentle soul who was tormented by a horrible disease."

Chapter 24

"Mom is acting like such a loser," Flory said. "She thinks she's the only one who's having problems."

"I kind of feel sorry for her," Phoebe said. The metal spatula scraped the cookie sheet.

"Of course, you would."

"Well, don't you?"

"No," Flory said. "It was *her* sister. She should have known this was going to happen. She should have done something to stop her."

Rodney entered the kitchen, and the conversation stopped. Phoebe put the last of the Sutton cookies on the rack to cool. Flory held a mustard-covered knife in midair. On the counter were eight pieces of wheat bread, half of them with ham and a slice of Swiss cheese.

"Just make three sandwiches, Flory. Your mom's not coming," Rodney said.

"Again?" Flory rolled her eyes. "I feel like Mom's becoming the drama queen."

Phoebe put the spatula down and slumped. "I tried so hard."

Rodney asked, "You tried so hard for what?"

"I wanted to find something to get Mom out of bed and happy again. I thought a picnic at Buffalo Springs would do it."

Rodney hugged his youngest. "Phoebe, that's what I love about you."

After sandwiches and Sutton cookies, bottles of water and orange cuties were packed, the three of them climbed into Rodney's pickup. He didn't tell Alice they were leaving.

As they approached the interstate, Flory suggested they go by the farm. Rodney turned left instead of right toward the farm. Phoebe sat in the middle of the bench seat and turned on the radio. Turning up the volume, she and Rodney sang along with Merle Haggard as he sang "Okie from Muskogee." Flory covered her ears but grinned.

Rodney turned down the gravel driveway. Up ahead was the old farmhouse, where Alice and Lou had grown up, where Carl had lived as a boy, and where Alice's parents had lived until their tragic death two years ago. The family hadn't been there since Lou murdered the eleven victims.

Rodney turned off the engine, and they stepped out of the truck. "The house needs some cleaning up, doesn't it?" he said. There was a tear in the screen covering one of the windows. The steps leading to the front porch had decayed from neglect. A loose shutter banged in the breeze. The place seemed abandoned.

Flory and Phoebe slowly walked toward the house. "Dad, do you have a key? Can we get in?" Phoebe asked.

Rodney shook his head. "No. The key is back at the house." He shrugged his shoulders. "Sorry, girls. I didn't know we were coming. But we can walk around outside. Come on. Let's go down to the creek." Rodney led the way, walking past the barn. He noticed it was open but didn't think anything of it.

The three of them explored the land around the old farmhouse. It was full of memories and stories their mother had told them of when she was growing up. At the creek, Phoebe took off her shoes and waded into the cool water. Flory walked along the edge of the creek with a long stick, poking the water in search of frogs. Rodney stayed back a few yards and observed his daughters. The shadow of a lone hawk flew overhead.

A small garter snake slithered past Flory. She screamed, and it disappeared into the fallen leaves. Flory ran from the creek bed, and Phoebe followed, grabbing her shoes.

"That was just a harmless garter snake," Rodney said. "I'm sure it was more afraid of you." He paused, thinking of Lou. "She loved this place," he said, more to himself.

"Who?" Phoebe asked.

"Your Aunt Lou." Rodney watched a squirrel run up a scrub oak. It scolded them from its perch on a branch. They were invading its territory. "She loved traipsing through the wooded area. If there were any injured animals, she would find them. It was as if she had a sixth sense for them."

"Remember the baby rabbit she found?" Flory picked up an acorn and tried to toss it up to the squirrel. "The mother was dead, and she took care of it."

"Or what about the owl with a broken wing," Phoebe said. "Aunt Lou loved animals, didn't she?"

"I think she probably got along better with them than with people," Rodney said.

The three of them were silent as they walked back to the truck. Rodney thought of Lou, how sullen and anti-social she could be. Yet, put her near animals, and she lit up. Yes, she would have been a great vet, he thought sadly. What a tragedy. Rodney wondered what it must have been like for Lou. What a waste of a decent life.

They drove in silence to Buffalo Springs, each in their own thoughts. Rodney kept his eyes on the road. Traffic was heavy on the interstate for a Sunday afternoon. Flory stared out the window. The trees hadn't started to turn yet. Oil wells dotted the landscape. Phoebe sat in the middle and scrolled through her phone.

"Dad," Phoebe said, breaking the silence. "I googled schizophrenia, and it scared me. I don't understand it."

"I don't think many people do," Rodney said.

"Well, I've read it can be hereditary. That's what Sophie's parents told her. That's why she stopped seeing me. Is that true?"

"It can be, but not always. That's my understanding." Rodney changed lanes.

"Did anyone else in Mom's family have schizophrenia?" Flory asked.

"No. I don't think so… Mimi and Granddad didn't talk about it much, but I think I would have known if there was."

"It was a lot easier when Aunt Lou wasn't around. She scared me sometimes," Phoebe said.

"Where was she when she wasn't home?" Flory asked.

"She lived in a group home for a while. And sometimes she was in the hospital."

The three of them fell silent again. It seemed to Rodney perhaps his daughters didn't want to know too much about Lou. At least, not yet. That was fine with him. It was a hard subject to discuss.

They spent the afternoon exploring their favorite spots at Buffalo Springs—hiking to the natural springs, climbing Bromide Hill, and looking for buffalo. They picnicked near the stone bridge by Rock Creek, and for one afternoon Rodney put his worries aside. He felt relaxed for the first time since the murders. He had needed this.

"Thank you, Phoebe," he said as they drove back.

"For what?"

"For coming up with the idea. I didn't realize how much I needed it." Rodney leaned over and kissed his youngest on her cheek.

****

"Alice, I have an appointment this morning," Rodney said. It was seven-thirty on Monday. "I can't take the girls to school, so you'll have to."

There was no response.

Rodney left their bedroom and knocked on Flory's door.

"Don't come in!" A voice on the other side yelled.

"I won't."

Eventually the door opened. "What do you want?" Flory had a towel wrapped around her. Bra straps and flip-flops were visible.

"I'm leaving soon for a meeting. If your mom doesn't get up, you can take Phoebe and yourself to school."

"Okay. Fine," Flory said.

"But you have to go straight from school to the library. No messing around." Rodney had to restrain himself from wagging his finger at her.

"I won't," Flory said. "I promise."

Rodney fixed himself some coffee. Glancing at his watch, he realized he needed to go. Driving to downtown Oklahoma City in eight o'clock traffic was going to take some time.

Rodney picked up his briefcase. "Good-bye," he shouted to his family as he left. He had an appointment at nine o'clock with Michael Schell of Morgan & Schell Attorneys at Law. Their offices were downtown in the Mercantile Building on Hudson.

It had been a long time since Rodney had been to downtown Oklahoma City, especially during rush hour. It seemed there was construction on every other block. There were detours and roadblocks, towering cranes, and leveled spaces where old buildings used to exist. He hardly recognized parts of it.

Rodney knew of a parking garage on Walker Avenue. He turned in and found a space on the top floor. Around the corner and two blocks east, Rodney found the building. It was one of the newer ones, a thirty-story, all-glass building. After the tornado that destroyed half of downtown, they replaced glass with glass. That didn't make sense to him, but then a lot of decisions didn't make sense to him anymore.

Like the reason he was going to see this attorney. His brother, Larry, had been a fraternity brother to Michael Schell and had called him. "Hell, I've never been sued before," Rodney had told Barney. "I tried to google what was involved in getting sued, but I stopped reading after I saw it was 'a complicated process, full of unpleasant surprises.' "

Rodney and Alice weren't getting sued, but because Alice was Lou's next of kin, they had to make decisions for her estate, which consisted of the trust fund Carl had set up and half the farm.

The lobby of the Mercantile Building had polished travertine floors and walls. The elevators were in the center, and the lobby circled around them. The office building was on a corner, and there was a courtyard behind it, making it accessible on all four sides—two entrances from the street, and two from the courtyard.

Rodney examined the directory and found Morgan & Schell on the twenty-third and twenty-fourth floors. Which floor should he choose? A woman in tennis shoes and a business suit carrying a pair of heels waited at the elevator. Two men discussing football came up behind him. A couple of women holding disposable cups of coffee, and more men preoccupied with their phones, joined Rodney. The red arrow pointing upward lit up, and the elevator dinged as it opened. The group surged into the elevator. Four, six, eleven, nineteen, twenty-seven. Everyone else on the elevator knew where they were going. Rodney stared at the numbers. Which floor? Finally, he chose the twenty-third floor. As the elevator went up Rodney stared down at his shoes, the ones he wore to church. They appeared shabby and unpolished. The collar of his shirt felt tight. He would give anything to unbutton the top button and loosen his tie.

The button for the twenty-third floor lit up, and the doors opened. Two mahogany-stained French doors greeted him. The Law Offices of Morgan & Schell. Rodney felt like his heart was in his throat. His palms were sweaty. He took a deep breath and opened the French doors.

Rodney had the impression he was entering a posh hotel lobby instead of a law office. A large circular marble table with an elaborate arrangement of fresh flowers in the center dominated the room. There were a couple of small seating areas off to one side with large paintings on the walls. A set of stairs leading up to the next floor was on the other side. Doors on either side of the large marble table indicated there were offices and conference rooms behind them. At the other end of the entrance Rodney saw a petite woman sitting at a desk peek her head around the vase, which obstructed her view of him and his view of her.

She waited until Rodney approached her desk before addressing him. "May I help you?" she asked. The nameplate on the desk said Felicia Reneau.

"I have an appointment with Michael Schell," Rodney said.

She checked her computer. "Rodney Bennett?" She peered at him over her glasses.

"Yes."

Ms. Reneau picked up the phone. Rodney heard her tell the person on the line, "Mr. Schell's nine o'clock appointment is here." She put the phone down and turned to Rodney. "Mr. Schell's assistant will be down in just a minute. Have a seat." She indicated the sitting area off to the left of her desk.

Rodney sat on a leather loveseat. Men and women walked past, punching numbers into keypads that opened doors on either side of the lobby. He noticed a stray thread hanging from his shirt. He didn't pull it for fear something would unravel.

Five minutes turned into fifteen, then thirty. Rodney glanced at his phone. It was 9:58.

He stood up and walked to Ms. Reneau's desk. She either didn't notice or ignored him. Rodney cleared his throat.

"Yes?"

"I'm here to see Michael Schell. My appointment was for nine o'clock, and you said someone would be down in a minute. I was wondering if there was a problem…" Rodney's voice faded under the stare of Ms. Reneau.

She let out a sigh and picked up the phone again. This time she spoke with less formality and more annoyance. "Betty, Michael's nine o'clock is waiting."

There was no apology or explanation. He had been waiting an hour. Did she think that was okay? Rodney forced a smile and said, "Thank you," returning to his seat.

Five minutes later a pair of heels, the highest he had ever seen, walked down the staircase. A young woman in a tight-fitting dress greeted him. "Rodney Bennett? Please follow me."

Rodney followed the woman upstairs. They walked to the far end of the hall, and she opened the door to a corner office. "Mr. Bennett to see you," she said, closing the door behind him.

There was a large desk angled in front of the over-sized corner windows. An L-shaped credenza sat below the windows. Framed photos of family clustered in one area. Trophies—for golf, tennis, and fishing—were arranged in another area. Directly behind the desk were stacks of paper. On top of the desk were more papers.

The man seated at the desk, Michael Schell, stood up when Rodney entered. He had silver hair, neatly trimmed. His suit was immaculate, and his face was tanned, as if he spent more time outside than behind a desk. Rodney felt drab and frumpy as he walked toward the extended hand. It was a strong handshake, probably the firmest grip he had ever felt. Rodney winced.

"Come in, Rodney," Michael said. "Have a seat."

There were two leather armchairs. Rodney picked the one on the left.

"Larry told me about your situation. It was all over the news for while, wasn't it? Tough deal, real tough." Michael took a sip from a mug with the letters M&S on it and shook his head. "Sorry to hear you're in such a mess. Coffee?"

"No thanks," Rodney said. "I wanted to—"

"Rod, I might as well get straight to the point. These lawsuits against your sister…"

"My wife's sister," Rodney corrected.

"Oh yes, your wife's sister. These lawsuits against your wife's sister—there's not a damn thing you can do about them."

"What?"

"These people are going to get big judgments, and that's that. You're wasting your time and money if you try to defend your sister."

"My wife's sister," Rodney repeated.

Michael nodded his head. "Your wife's sister." Rodney half expected this man to pull out a cigar and light it up. "You can't win. And you can't afford to pay us what it would cost you."

Rodney sat cemented to the chair. This wasn't what he expected to hear. He didn't know what he thought Michael Schell was going to tell him, but this wasn't it. "So, what do I do?" he asked.

"Nothing. Let the victims' families take the default judgment. They can fight over her estate. Get the estate in order, all her assets. They'll take those, but they shouldn't be able to touch you."

"Lou's assets." Rodney spoke to himself out loud. That would be her trust fund and half the farm. He was about to ask how they would handle the farm but stopped himself.

"Lou Sutton," Michael said. It was as if it registered about whom they were talking. "What a shock. That was an awful thing that happened. Bad for our state." He studied Rodney. "No offense intended. But, man, did you know she was capable of this? I mean, she shot eleven people in cold blood. If she was my relative, I don't know what I'd do."

Rodney had heard enough. He stood up and extended his hand. "Thank you for your time, Mr. Schell."

"Michael. Call me Michael. Glad to help. Sorry I couldn't do more." He shook Rodney's hand. "Tell that crazy brother of yours to get his ass back here for a visit. Betty will show you out and get billing information." His phone rang, and he turned his attention to the call.

Rodney rubbed his sore hand. He couldn't get out of the building fast enough. He pounded his fist on the steering wheel as he entered I-35 back to Junction.

Chapter 25

Flory sat at the table eating cereal when she saw Alice enter the kitchen. "Mom, what are you doing up?"

"I'm taking you and Phoebe to school instead of Dad."

"But why?" Flory asked between mouthfuls.

Alice poured herself coffee. "I need to run some errands. Does anyone need anything while I'm out?"

"If you want to come by the office, I'll give you some checks to deposit." Rodney put his empty bowl in the sink. The key to his truck was on the counter. Kissing his daughters, he said, "Bye, girls. I'll see you after work." He kissed Alice and left.

Alice was miffed. No thank you. No appreciation. Everyone acted as if it was normal for her to drive the girls, which it was. But the last couple of months had been anything but normal. They had no idea how hard it was for Alice to get out of the bedroom, get dressed, and leave the house.

When Alice returned to the kitchen with her purse and clothes for the drycleaners, Flory and Phoebe weren't there. Then she heard the horn honk. "Come on, Mom," a voice yelled.

Phoebe sat in the front seat, scrolling through her phone. Flory was in the back, earbuds on to avoid conversation.

Alice glanced at Phoebe. "I thought you weren't on

social media anymore."

"I'm not," Phoebe said. "I'm reading articles."

Alice was tempted to ask her what they were about, but she kept her mouth shut.

About a block from the school, Phoebe said, "Pull over at the corner. That's where Dad lets us off."

Alice stopped at the corner.

"Thanks, Mom." Phoebe got out of the car. Flory had already left without saying a word—no goodbye, no thanks, nothing.

When the girls left, the distraction departed, too. The empty car brought back her anxiety. Her errands seemed pointless to her now, and she wanted to crawl into bed. Being out of the house felt like freefalling without any support. This is ridiculous. She had errands to run. Still parked at the corner, Alice pulled out her list. She scribbled *Rodney-bank* at the bottom.

Downtown Junction consisted of a four-block section of 1940's buildings connected to one another. The newspaper, post office, and City Hall were on Main Street. Broadway intersected Main Street, and there were retail shops, restaurants, bars, and a local pharmacy. Barney's office was nearby. The local college, where Carl had taught, was about a half a mile away, making downtown a destination where students frequented. Old-style streetlights were installed, and small wrought iron tables and chairs had been positioned in front of restaurants.

Alice found a parking spot near the pharmacy. Second Avenue Cleaners was around the corner. This was where Florence used to take Carl's shirts to be laundered. Alice thought of her father in his pressed shirt and bowtie, his trademark, as she entered the cleaners.

She was dropping off the clothes they wore to Lou's funeral. It didn't seem right.

Alice pushed the door open with her arms full.

"Good morning, may I help you?"

"I need these dry cleaned, and the shirt laundered," she said.

"Name?"

Alice froze. She didn't want to say her name. "Bennett."

"First name?"

"Rodney." That was as far from being Lou's sister as she could get.

The woman gathered the laundry. "They will be ready on Friday after four."

"Thank you."

Once outside Alice noticed a poster taped to the window. It was a black and white photo of Lou, with the words: *DON'T LET CRAZY PEOPLE OWN GUNS!* She stood, petrified, unable to move.

Should she retrieve her clothes? Fight or flight? Alice chose flight.

When she got to her car, she saw the same poster taped in the pharmacy window. Desperate to get away, Alice rummaged through her purse for her keys. They weren't there. She dumped the contents on the sidewalk. Still no keys. Alice peered inside her locked car, hoping they were there. She saw nothing. She knew they had to be somewhere because she had driven and parked her car. If the keys weren't in her purse, and they weren't inside the car, then they must be at the cleaners. That was the last place she wanted to go.

Alice had no choice. She stuffed everything back into her purse and returned to the cleaners. From the window she saw her keys on the counter. Alice slipped in. One of the workers looked up. "I forgot my keys," she said as she picked them up from the counter. The worker nodded, and Alice left. She felt relieved. But what to do about the posters? Were there more around town? Alice didn't want to find out.

Suddenly, Alice felt incredibly sad for Lou. She had been deprived the opportunity to live a normal life. Instead, this horrible disease had betrayed her and convinced her she needed to destroy other lives. Alice thought about the victims' families. Their lives would never be the same. Yet, Lou was a victim, too. Wasn't she?

Alice's head pounded. Seeing Lou's face plastered on the posters and thinking of the victim's families was too much. She wanted to drive home and crawl into bed. But a voice in her head reminded her Flory and Phoebe went to school every day, and Rodney had to go to work.

"I'll go to the store then deposit the checks." she said, trying to convince herself.

It was the first time Alice had been to Sutton Cards since the shooting. She was surprised to see only two cars in the parking lot. She entered the back door, and the smell of ink and freshly printed paper greeted her. It seemed quiet, only the hum of a single machine. It used to be so loud that you had to yell to be heard.

She saw a silver-haired head peep from behind the stitch machine. It was Ha Nguyen. She bowed. "Mrs. Alice, so good to see you."

Alice smiled when she saw the older woman. "Thank you and thank you for working." What would we do without Ha and Liem? They were the only two employees who had stayed. But Alice didn't realize how much business they had lost. "I'm looking for Rodney. Is he in his office?"

"Yes. Mr. Rodney is in there," Ha said as she resumed her task.

Rodney sat at his metal desk—crowded with ink samples, a mound of rubber bands, stacks of invoices, an open box of Cheez-Its, and two bobble heads—staring at his computer. A second desktop was on the credenza underneath the window. On the windowsill set a dead Boston fern and an overgrown airplane plant. Their wedding picture and outdated school photos of Flory and Phoebe hung on the wall behind his desk.

Alice studied Rodney. His brows wrinkled in concentration. He didn't even know she was there. She tapped on the door, and his head lifted with a jerk.

"I'm here for the checks you wanted me to deposit," Alice said.

Rodney plucked a small stack of checks clipped together and handed them to her. "Thanks," he said, then returned his attention to what was on the computer screen.

"Do you need anything else?" Alice wanted to tell him about the posters of Lou, but he seemed preoccupied.

"No. That's all," Rodney said, his eyes back on his task.

Alice picked up the checks and left.

The bank and the grocery store were near each other. Alice wondered if there would be posters displayed at either of these locations. They were meant to be a public service announcement about the dangers of guns. Instead, she felt it was a vicious attack on Lou, and a way of shunning them. Was it intentional? She didn't know.

For that matter, Alice didn't know much about the murders and the investigation. It was too painful.

I don't even know the victims' names. She knew nothing, but she wasn't ready to face this information. She was barely surviving.

Alice turned the corner onto Cherokee Avenue and pulled into the parking lot of Corsin's Grocery Store. She hadn't even been to the store. Rodney or the girls had done the shopping. Alice scanned the windows for the poster. She didn't see it. Relieved, she went inside.

"Why if it isn't Miss Alice!"

A familiar voice boomed, and Alice turned to see Leo Porter, manager of the grocery store. Leo, who had started as a bag boy, then promoted to the stock room, then to cashier, then butcher, then manager, had known Alice and her family since she was a teenager. His wife, Edith, who worked at the hospital, had brought a casserole over during the early weeks after the shooting. Leo and Edith knew. They understood.

Leo gave Alice a giant bear hug. "It's good to see you," he said. A tall, wiry black man, Leo put his arm around Alice and held her tight. He stepped back and examined her. "How are you doing?"

"I'm fine. I'm okay," Alice said. She noticed his hair was starting to gray. He had on the white apron he always wore, and his glasses sat slightly crooked on his nose.

"Alice, I'm real sorry about what happened. Me and Edith, we know Miss Lou wouldn't have hurt a flea if she'd been in her right mind."

No one had said words like that to Alice—except for Rodney and Barney. Few had given Lou any credit for being a human being.

He led her away from the customers in the store.

"You know, some people came to the store and wanted me to put this poster up. It had a picture of your sister on it. But I wouldn't do it." He gave her a squeeze. "I just wanted you to know."

Alice felt tears forming. "Thank you," she whispered.

"And I want you to know you are safe to come in here. If anybody tries to give you any trouble, you just holler. Leo Porter won't stand for it."

Alice nodded. Her vision blurred from the tears.

Leo pulled out a grocery cart and rolled it toward her. "You go ahead and do your shopping." He winked at her and left.

Carl had helped Leo and Edith after they were first married. He had given them a loan for Edith to go to nursing school. When they tried to pay him back, he wouldn't take their money. He said their role in the community would be the only payback he needed. And they never forgot that.

Alice walked up and down the aisles, getting the items on her list. She found herself glancing around for anyone who might recognize her. After checking out, she waved good-bye to Leo and put her groceries in the trunk of the car. The bank was across the street on the corner. Alice went through the drive-through and deposited the checks. She drove home, put the groceries away, and climbed into bed.

Chapter 26

1988

The Great Reading Room was a long narrow space with a high ceiling and elongated windows located on the second floor of the college library. Shelves of books lined the walls, and in the center of the room were rows of tables where students studied. It was spring semester, and Lou was studying for her biology exam. She was a sophomore at the college where Carl taught economics.

They're watching you.

Lou looked up from her biology notes and turned around.

Don't turn around! Idiot!

She moved her eyes from side to side without turning her head. Who was talking to her? And who was watching her? She sat motionless for a couple of minutes, unable to resume studying and uncertain what to do. Very slowly she put her hands on the edge of the chair.

Don't stand up!

A male voice practically screamed at her. Lou glanced at the man at the other end of her table. He wasn't screaming at her, and he obviously hadn't heard anything. Neither had anyone else.

Lou cupped her hand over her mouth and whispered, "What am I supposed to do?"

There was no answer.

Lou sat toward the back of the room, and she had a view of the others who were studying. She heard a muffled cough. Across the way, two students whispered, their heads together. A book slammed shut, and a pencil fell. But no more voices.

Eventually students began to leave. The long tables in front of her were empty, and it was quiet. Lou glanced at her watch. It was almost seven, and the sky was turning golden. No one else was in the room.

Lou closed her books and left. Silence followed her.

****

Lou was anxious about her biology exam. She knew the material and understood the concepts, yet she kept second guessing herself. What if her mind went blank? What if the professor asked something she hadn't studied? She had an A in the class, yet she had this irrational fear she was going to fail. And what about the person who had screamed at her when she was studying? That had been unsettling. Who was that person? She never even got a glimpse of him.

Her exam wasn't the only thing Lou was worried about. She was afraid she was going to lose her job. She didn't know why she felt that way, but Lou sensed some of the employees at Anne's Doggie Day Care wanted to get her fired. She wasn't sure exactly who was in charge of this plan, but she could sense it. And someone kept moving her truck in the parking lot so she couldn't find it.

Then there was her family. Why were they trying to confuse her? Florence would send her to the store for something. Then when Lou came home, she was in trouble because she brought home the wrong items. But she hadn't. Florence had changed the list without telling her. Carl kept asking her questions that were none of his business. And Alice was just plain annoying. They had never been close anyway.

Lou had a suspicion something *bigger* was behind everything, but she didn't know what. Someone or some organization was trying to prevent her from doing what she was supposed to do.

Lou parked the pickup in the student parking lot. She didn't ride with Carl anymore, since she had bought his old truck. She liked the independence. Lou got out of the truck, but she couldn't remember what building her class was in. What if she missed the test?

Finally, she found the building. The class was on the third floor. When she reached the room, the door was already shut. She went inside and found a seat at the back of the room. The professor handed her the exam. Why was he frowning at her?

Lou read the questions on the exam. Something was wrong. It seemed like every other question was in a different language. Why would he do that? Lou did the best she could, but on the ones written in a foreign langue, she wrote, "This doesn't make sense. Put all questions in English, not in another language!"

Lou turned in her exam and left the classroom. She was hungry, but she didn't want to go to the Student Union. She didn't trust the students who ate there. She couldn't quite put her finger on it, but she knew something sinister was going on there. Lou decided to see if her dad was in his office. Carl's office was across campus on the second floor of the Business School. Lou heard voices behind the closed door. They must be talking about her. Lou turned to leave as the door opened. A student walked away.

"Lou, come on in." Carl smiled at her. "I'm glad to see you. I had an appointment, but now I'm about to get some lunch. Would you like to join me?"

"Well, it depends on where you're going," Lou said.

"How about grabbing a bite at the Student Union?"

"No. I can't go there." Lou shook her head.

She noticed Carl regarded her as if he didn't understand why she couldn't go there. But he should.

"Okay. What about getting a hamburger across the street?"

"I can do that." Lou knew the hamburger place was safe.

Carl locked his office, and they walked across campus to Joe's Burgers.

"How was your biology exam?" Carl asked after they ordered their food.

"I don't understand why he did what he did, but he made the test very confusing."

"What do you mean?"

Lou leaned across the table and whispered so no one else would hear her. "He wrote half the questions in another language."

"Who did?"

"My professor. He stared at me when I walked in. So, I don't know if everyone got a test like mine, or if I was the only one."

"Lou, that doesn't make sense."

"I know, Dad. I feel the same way. But that's what happened. So, I'm probably screwed."

"What makes you say the questions were in another language? Could you pick out words you recognized that were, say, French or Spanish?"

"No. It was more like they were written in Russian.

I couldn't even tell what the letters were. But not every question. Just about half of them."

Carl didn't say anything else about her exam. But she sensed he didn't believe her. Maybe he was part of this bigger plan, too.

"What time is your next class?" Carl had finished his lunch and was gathering his trash.

"I have a lab at two," Lou said. She, too, gathered her trash. "Thanks for lunch, Dad," she said, as they left the restaurant. Lou hoisted her backpack on her shoulders.

Chapter 27

1988

Carl was confused. Lou's comment about her biology exam made no sense. Why would she think half her exam was written in another language?

As they parted ways, Carl watched Lou walk away. Her gait was heavy, more like a man's. He felt a twinge of sadness. Florence was right. She didn't have any friends. She kept to herself. The closest she came to friends were some of the co-workers at Anne's Doggie Day Care. Was she happy? He didn't know.

Carl thought of when she was younger, when the four of them did things together. Every Friday Lou and Alice helped Florence make Sutton cookies. Then it stopped. He wasn't sure why.

Lou was like the son he never had. They both loved being out-of-doors. Setting traps for wild boars, repairing fences, cutting down the invasive red cedars. Carl and Lou spent many hours roaming the farm. He also shared his love of hunting with Lou. He taught her how to respect the animals and how hunting was not a sport but part of God's way of providing food for man. Hunting created a natural bond between them.

****

On Lou's twelfth birthday, Carl got her a 20-gauge shotgun, her own hat and vest in safety orange, a hunting license, and an upland game permit for hunting quail.

She took the Hunter Safety Course, and Carl set up a target between two scrub oaks beyond the barn. They took their shotguns and went behind the barn for target practice just about every day. Charlie, their German shorthair pointer, often joined them. He sat in the shade near the barn and didn't cower or flee when a shot rang out. Carl realized Lou was a natural. She had a good eye, didn't flinch, and stayed calm.

Hunting season for quail didn't begin until November. Carl and Lou checked the weather and picked a date for her first outing. The night before, they packed their supplies—thermoses of water, sack lunches, a first aid kit, an extra gallon jug of water for Charlie, and his bowl. The shells stayed separate from the shotguns. Carl stressed safety.

At five the next morning Carl gently nudged Lou from her sleep. "It's time to get up."

Lou dressed quickly, putting the orange vest over a sweatshirt. When she came into the kitchen, Carl handed her a mug of hot cocoa.

He motioned to her to be quiet as they tiptoed out to his pickup. It was a two-hour drive and then some to the WMA, Wildlife Management Area. Neither spoke much in the truck. Once they entered the WMA, Carl parked the truck and turned off the ignition. He turned toward Lou. "You okay?" he asked.

She nodded her head. In the back seat Charlie whined. He was ready to get out.

"Not yet, Charlie." Carl spoke softly. "We need to wait until it's light enough to see."

When sun rose, a majestic show of pink and orange-tinged clouds hung in the sky. Yes, this was what made the early morning rise worth it. Carl wondered who else was admiring this view of God's glory.

The Oklahoma prairie stretched before them—tall grasses and sage brush with plum thickets, juniper, and low-lying mesquite trees—the perfect habitat for bobwhite quails. Charlie jumped around like an over-sized rabbit in his excitement.

"Settle down, Charlie," Carl said.

The three of them walked through the grassland. Every so often Charlie ran ahead in search for the quail, then would stop. Off again he went, nose to the ground. It had rained the day before, making the scent easier for him to follow.

They spent the day traversing the land as Charlie sought out coveys of quail. Every so often they heard the call of the quails, "Bob white! Bob white!" Carl loved that, along with the sound of their wings fluttering as they took flight and the rustling of the dry grasses as the quails scurried away. Sharing this with Lou was something he would always treasure.

By the end of the day after many attempts, Lou got a quail, and in total they bagged five. Carl considered it a success.

****

But something was different about Lou, and he couldn't put his finger on what it was. Lou had always been quiet, not social, like Alice, but she seemed content. Her first love had always been the dogs—Lucky, Charlie, Schroeder. Getting a job at Anne's Doggie Day Care had been the perfect outlet for Lou. Then she decided to study to become a veterinarian. Carl hoped that goal would keep her focused. But lately, she seemed distracted. By what, he had no idea. The motivation Lou had when she started college had dissipated.

Florence commented about Lou's personal hygiene, and Carl was beginning to agree with her. She wore the same clothes almost every day and unfortunately often emitted a strong odor. Was she showering regularly? Carl hated the feelings these changes in Lou conjured in his head. It was almost as if he was embarrassed by her. He would never feel that way, yet a part of him did. And sadly, the good memories seemed to be overtaken by the current bizarre behavior.

Chapter 28

"Lou, I can't find my latest copy of *SEVENTEEN* magazine. Have you seen it?"

Fourteen-year-old Alice popped into Lou's bedroom. Lou stared at her, but she could only see a mouth chomping on gum, one eye then the other, a nose, then a chin that moved up and down. Lou knew it was Alice, but she only saw parts of her. It was terrifying, and it was all she could do to keep from running out of her bedroom.

"Lou! Did you hear what I said?"

Alice stomped her foot, like a child, but it sounded more like a load of bricks had been dropped. Lou put her hands over her ears because the sound was deafening. She tried to focus on Alice. She could see her lips moving as she spoke, but the words weren't making sense. Lou squinted her eyes, hoping that would make Alice become herself instead of separate parts. But nothing changed.

"Never mind," Alice said. She turned and left.

Lou was relieved. That was exhausting.

****

Lou was in her pickup on her way to work when she heard the voices again. Anne's Doggie Day Care was about six miles south of their farm on the interstate access road.

Get off the road now!

The voice startled Lou, and she braked, glancing in the rearview mirror.

I said now!

Lou swerved and crossed a lane to get over. Horns honked and brakes squealed. A car passed by and shot her the finger. Parked on the side of the road, Lou was breathing hard. Now what?

Lou waited, but she didn't hear the voice. She turned on her radio.

"This is KROV, 97.7 in Oklahoma City. There's still time to call in. I'll repeat the question. For ninety-seven dollars and seven cents, what was Elvis Presley's first big hit?"

Don't answer. It's a trick.

It was the voice again. She turned off the radio. Maybe it was okay to go now. Lou signaled left and waited for an open space, then pulled back onto the highway.

You stupid! Don't go! They'll find you.

"I'm just going to work," Lou told the voice.

You can't go. Didn't you hear me?

"But why?" Lou didn't understand.

Because, dummy, I told you. They'll find you.

"Who?"

Loser! Just do what I say, or you'll regret it!

Lou took the next exit and turned around. She drove back to the farm.

When she arrived, Florence came outside. She had a speck of bright green paint in her hair. "Lou, Anne called. She said you didn't show up for work. What are you doing home?"

"I couldn't go. They'd find me," Lou said.

"Who? What are you talking about?"

Lou shrugged her shoulders and walked past Florence, upstairs to her room and shut the door.

The next time she heard voices, Lou knew. The government had hired spies to follow her. They planned to remove her thoughts and perform experiments on them. It was up to her to evade the spies, but they were everywhere. She didn't leave her room for days. She couldn't go back to school, and she didn't take her finals.

****

Your shoes are on the wrong feet.

"No, they aren't."

Yes, they are.

Lou entered the kitchen. Florence was frying salmon croquettes in the electric skillet.

"Lou, can you set the table for me?" Florence put the croquettes on the paper bag to absorb the grease.

Your shirt is on inside out.

"No, it's not."

Yes, it is.

"Lou, what are you talking about? I asked you to set the table."

Don't open the drawer. There are snakes in there.

"No, there aren't."

Yes, there are.

"Lou, stop your mumbling and set the table."

Don't do it.

"Why not?"

Because.

"Because why?"

Because I said so.

Lou chuckled. "I'll show you." She opened the drawer with the silverware. "See, no snakes."

Florence stopped what she was doing and put her hands on her hips. "Never mind, I'll do it myself."

Chapter 29

1988

"You go talk to her," Florence said. It was half a whisper and half an angry hiss. "She won't listen to me, but she listens to you."

Carl had been sitting on the back porch, enjoying a quiet moment after spending the day driving around the property seeking out the water-sucking red cedars. The pile of cut down trees in his truck gave off a fragrance deceptive to the harm they caused. He shook his head as he stood up. Lou hadn't agreed to come along with him as she normally would, so he wasn't confident he could talk her into anything. Carl climbed the stairs with effort. It wasn't that he was tired from the day's chores. Instead, the exhaustion came from the dread and uncertainty of having to confront Lou.

Why was she acting so strange? Carl's heart palpitated. Surely nothing was wrong with her. But he couldn't explain her behavior. It had been outright odd all spring.

He knocked on the closed door to Lou's bedroom. He heard her talking, but she stopped when he knocked.

"Lou," he said. "Can I come in?"

Carl heard the heavy footsteps. She had her work boots on. Florence wasn't going to be happy about that.

Lou opened the door. Her hair was pulled back in the usual ponytail. It was greasy, as if she hadn't showered in days. He noticed she had on the same clothes she had worn the day before, and the day before that. But he didn't say anything. Lou didn't come out of her room except for meals. Her face was expressionless.

It was all Carl could do not to recoil from the smell of her. Lou, who had been a loving, gentle daughter and big sister, seemed to have withdrawn. But it was more than that. Lou wasn't herself.

Carl let himself in as Lou stepped back. He patted her arm as he walked past her, and she flinched from his touch. She stood by the door, as if she was ready to bolt if he did anything she feared.

"How are you doing, Lou?"

"I'm fine," she said.

"Are you?" Carl's brow furrowed. "Are you really fine? Or is there something you'd like to talk about?"

"No."

No, she wasn't fine, or no, she didn't want to talk? Carl wasn't sure. He decided to try another tactic.

"Lou, what are your plans for this summer? I think it's too late to sign up for summer school. What about work? Aren't you going to help Anne at the day care?"

Lou sighed. At first, she didn't say anything. Then she spoke. "Nine...eighteen...twenty-seven...thirty-six...forty-five...fifty-four...sixty-three...seventy-two...eighty-one..."

Carl sucked in air and almost choked. What was going on? Trying not to act alarmed, Carl slowly walked back toward the door. Lou did not move from her position.

****

Carl was sitting on the front steps when fourteen-year-old Alice came out and sat next to him.

191

"What's wrong with Lou?" she asked. Alice, who had just finished eighth grade, had started experimenting with make-up and all sorts of strange hairdos. Currently, she had attempted a side ponytail with tall bangs. The smell of hairspray was overpowering. She linked her arm through Carl's.

"She's been working too hard. I think she needs a break." Carl wished that was the case, but a part of him knew something was wrong with Lou. And he had no idea what it was.

"Well, she's been acting weird. I hear her talking to herself. Sometimes I hear growling from her room, and it scares me." Alice turned toward him. "Do you ever hear her?"

Carl shook his head. He had, but he didn't want to admit it. He feigned sleep when he heard Lou talking, so he didn't have to admit it, even to Florence.

"Dad." Alice smacked her chewing gum. "Mom said to ask you to take me to Mary Lyn's house. She's busy."

Carl realized Alice had already moved on. Lou's bizarre behavior was low on her priorities. "Sure. Let me take these trees out of the back of the truck, and then I can take you."

When Carl returned from taking Alice to her friend's house, he smelled fried chicken. He came up behind Florence and put his arms around her. "Smells delicious." He picked up a chicken leg and ate it. Florence made fried chicken and homemade biscuits as good as his mother's.

"Where's Lou?" he asked.

"Upstairs, I guess." Florence placed the flour-covered pieces of chicken into the electric skillet. "Did you talk to her?"

"I tried, but I didn't have much luck." Carl wiped his mouth with the back of his hand. He reached for another leg, but Florence swatted his hand.

"What did she say?" Florence looked up from frying the chicken. She had a splotch of flour on her nose and forehead.

"She didn't really answer me. I asked what her plans were for the summer, and she didn't say anything." Carl took his finger and wiped the flour from Florence's face. "Have you talked to Anne? Do you think she got fired?"

These were discussions Carl never imagined having a year ago. Lou was conscientious almost to a fault. Yet, who was this stranger who had inhabited her body?

Chapter 30

1988

By the end of the summer Carl and Florence began to worry about the fall semester. Lou wasn't enrolled in classes. They both had to go back to work teaching. What was Lou going to do? Every time Carl or Florence brought up school, Lou began counting by nines. What did that mean? And sometime in August Lou started wearing an old bicycle helmet and leather gloves whenever she left her room.

Classes at the university started the next week, and Carl began spending his days on campus, preparing for his fall courses. His office phone rang not long after lunch. Now what? Either Florence or Alice called continuously, always about Lou.

"Hello?"

"Carl, I'm going to the high school, and I'm taking Alice with me. She's afraid to be alone with Lou. Do you think it's safe to leave Lou by herself?"

Carl gripped the phone. Perspiration ran down his back. What had their life come to? They had to babysit their twenty-year-old daughter? He wanted to reassure Florence Lou was fine. But was she? Her muttering about the government spies made no sense. And what was the deal with the helmet and gloves?

"You have to go to school, and Alice wants to come with you. I'm sure Lou will be fine. Tell her you're going. She can call me if she needs anything. I'll try to get home early today." After Carl hung up the phone, he couldn't concentrate. All he could think of was what if something happened?

It was a twenty-minute drive from the college back to the farm. Carl decided to go home and check on Lou. When he turned onto Waterloo Road, he drove past the old elm where Lou had taught Alice how to climb a tree. It had low hanging branches, and one branch was L-shaped. He recalled the time he saw them sitting side by side in the tree on his way home from work. They whooped and waved their arms when he backed up. Carl smiled to himself briefly. But the tree was empty. No one had climbed it in years.

From Old Farm Road he took a left onto the long gravel driveway. Carl noticed the front door was wide open as soon as he pulled up to the house. And Lou's truck was gone.

Carl felt like a boulder was in the pit of his stomach. Lou hadn't left the house all summer. And now she was gone. Where would she go?

It had been such a strange summer. Carl and Florence had taken turns being at home, except for Sundays when they went to early church. Neither of them wanted to leave her alone. They were afraid of what she might do. It was the unknown they were afraid of. The strange sounds coming from her room at night, how she took to wearing a helmet and leather gloves whenever she left her room, the mutterings about government spies who were stealing her thoughts, her refusal to eat certain foods because they were poison, her unwillingness to bathe regularly. What did it all mean?

Was Lou on drugs? That didn't make sense. But

what could it be?

"I've got to find her," Carl said out loud. But where? Carl drove back into town. He stopped at Anne's Doggie Day Care, the park, Johnny's Burger Joint. He drove past the shopping mall. He went back to the college, thinking maybe she decided to sign up for late registration. But there was no sign of the pickup. Finally, Carl drove to the high school.

He found Florence and Alice in the art classroom.

"I can't find Lou."

Florence was checking her supplies. "What do you mean you can't find Lou?"

"I went home after you called. I couldn't concentrate. When I got there, the front door was open, and her truck was gone. I've driven all over town. I can't find her."

Carl saw the same panic he felt in Florence's face. Her eyes widened, but she didn't say anything. Instead, standing behind Alice, she indicated their daughter was listening with a nod of her head.

As if on cue, Alice said, "She's probably at Buffalo Springs." Then resumed drawing her picture.

Carl kept his eyes focused on Florence, waiting to see her response. He felt a small amount of relief with Alice's matter of fact statement. Once Florence nodded, Carl spoke. "You're right, Al-Pal. I'll bet that's where she is—at Buffalo Springs, checking out the freshwater springs, looking for buffalo, taking a hike. She'll come home when she's ready." He smacked his lips loudly and made an exaggerated motion with his hands. "Catch it," Carl said, indicating the kiss he blew to Alice.

She reached up and grabbed the imaginary kiss and pressed it to her cheek. "Thanks, Dad."

"Bye, ladies."

Florence followed Carl out the door into the hallway.

"You stay here with Alice and finish getting your room ready. I'm going to drive to Buffalo Springs and see if I can find Lou."

"Okay." Florence said. She kissed Carl on the cheek. "I hope you find her, and she's okay."

"Me, too."

Once on the interstate, Carl took the Sandy Point exit and drove ten miles east to the park, which abutted the town. Upon entering Buffalo Springs, Carl drove past cars and trucks parked alongside the narrow road. Families waded in the creeks and floated along the current toward the waterfalls. A couple of tents were pitched in the camping area, and picnickers had set up coolers in preparation for dinner.

The park itself wasn't very big, and it didn't take long for Carl to drive through the main area. He pulled into the parking lot at the base of Bromide Hill and remembered there was a service road going to the top.

Sure enough, the road wound around the backside of the park and ended several hundred yards from the trail leading to the top of Bromide Hill. There was his old 1972 Ford pickup. The hood was up, the front bumper smashed into an oak tree, and the driver's door was open. Carl got out quickly in search of Lou, but there was no sign of her. He walked toward the trail and saw a family sitting on the limestone ledge.

"Excuse me," he said, "have you seen a woman, about age twenty?"

"Describe her," the father said, eyeing Carl warily.

"Well, she may have been wearing a helmet..."

"That one. Yeah, we saw her." The man stood up and approached Carl. He didn't like the way the man looked at him. "She was screaming and running around up here. I sent my son down to find a ranger because I was afraid she was going to jump." The man shook his head. "Man, she's looney."

Carl's knees buckled, and he tumbled to the limestone.

"Hey. Are you okay?" The man changed his expression and bent down to help Carl.

"No. Not really. That's my daughter, and we don't know what's wrong with her. Do you know where she is now?"

"I saw them put her in the sheriff's car and drive away. I tried to keep my kids from seeing what was going on."

Carl and the man discussed the situation some more. They checked the damage done to the truck. Then Carl shook the man's hand and climbed into his pickup. He found the ranger's office not far from the base of Bromide Hill. Yes, Lou had been taken away. She was in the emergency room of the Sandy Point hospital.

****

It didn't take long for Carl to find the hospital. The single-story brick building sat on a piece of property absent of the trees that were prolific in the park. The exterior gave the impression it was not well-maintained—dead grass, shrubs untrimmed, trash blown into the corner of the entry. There was a single empty chair in the ER waiting room. He went to the reception desk to find out if Lou had been admitted.

"I'm sorry, but we can't give out information on our patients." The woman at the desk said.

"I was told by the ranger's office they had brought my daughter here." Carl couldn't understand what was going on.

The woman repeated herself.

"But I'm her father, for God's sake!" Carl felt like he was about to lose it. He started pacing in front of the reception desk. The woman picked up the phone, keeping an eye on Carl as she dialed an extension. Presently a uniformed security guard entered the area.

"Sir," he said, "can you come with me?" The security guard indicated a small office to the side. "Maybe we can discuss your problem over here." The man was a good six inches taller than Carl, and he appeared as if he could burst out of his buttoned shirt if he flexed his muscles.

Carl felt like he was going to be arrested for disturbing the peace. This didn't seem like the solution he was hoping for. Somehow, he was considered the problem. All he wanted to do was find Lou.

Carl followed the man—his nametag read Ray—into the room. Ray shut the door and pointed to the chair. Carl sat down.

He didn't wait for the man to speak. "I'm trying to find my daughter. Her name is Lou Sutton. I found her truck at the top of Bromide Hill, and she wasn't in it. A family told me there was a woman who matched Lou's description screaming up there. I'm worried about her. I don't know what's wrong, and I don't know where she is."

Ray sat behind a desk with his hands folded. "Have you contacted the police?"

"Yes. Well, no. I don't know. I talked to the Ranger in the park. He told me she had been brought here. And now no one will help me." Carl paused. He studied Ray, figuring he was old enough to have children. "What would you do if you couldn't find your daughter?" Carl noticed his own hands were shaking.

For a moment Carl thought he was going to tell him the same story as the woman at the reception desk. Instead, he picked up the phone and dialed a number. "Say, did the sheriff bring in a woman from Buffalo Springs earlier this afternoon? Do you have an ID on her?" He pushed a pen and paper toward Carl. "You say you have a woman, but no ID. Can you describe her?"

Carl wrote *LOU SUTTON* on the paper. Then he added, *HELMET AND GLOVES???*

"I think we may have an ID on her. I have her father with me…Okay. I'll tell him." Roy hung up the phone. "The sheriff brought in a woman matching your daughter's description, wearing a helmet and leather gloves. She had no ID but was disturbing the peace."

"What do you mean by disturbing the peace? Just exactly what was she doing?"

"I'm afraid you'll have to talk to the officer who brought her in," Ray said. "I'll take you back, but they told me she's been sedated. So, she probably won't be awake."

Carl followed Ray through the closed doors to the Emergency Room. A nurse took Carl to the partitioned space where Lou was. She pulled back the curtain, and Carl saw Lou lying in the bed. She had a bandage on her forehead and was hooked up to an IV. A heart monitor beeped.

Carl took her hand. He gently brushed her hair back. He could see a bruise was starting to form on her cheek below the bandage. He asked the nurse, "How is she?"

"You'll have to talk to the doctor. He's busy now."

No one seemed to want to give Carl any information. The nurse left and pulled the curtain closed. He dragged the lone chair up next to the bed and sat down, still holding Lou's hand. Carl glanced at his watch. It was almost five o'clock. He needed to call Florence, but he didn't have any information about what had happened. Carl gazed at his daughter, trying to grasp what was going on in her mind, what had caused her to do whatever it was she had done. "What's going on, Lou?" he whispered. Standing up, he bent over and kissed the cheek that wasn't injured.

Carl stepped out of the partition and asked for a pay phone.

Florence answered after the first ring. "Did you find her?"

Carl could hear the urgency in her voice. "Yes. She's in the hospital in Sandy Point," he said.

"But why? What happened?"

Carl took a deep breath. It was going to be difficult to explain what he didn't know. "I found the truck at the top of Bromide Hill. It had hit a tree. But Lou wasn't there. A man told me the sheriff had taken her to the hospital. She's in the ER now, and..."

"Is she hurt? How bad is she? Did she tell you what happened?"

"She has a bandage across her forehead, and her left cheek is scraped. They have her sedated, so I couldn't talk to her."

"What did the doctor say?" Florence kept firing back questions, and Carl had no answers.

"I haven't seen him yet. I'm waiting to talk to him, and then I'm going to the police station to find out what happened. I also need to get the truck taken care of." Carl felt his head pounding. "I'll call you back when I find something out."

"How can I reach you?" Florence asked.

"I'm calling from a pay phone. I'll let you know as soon as I have any information."

Carl walked back to the doors leading to the ER.

"Wait a minute. You can't go in there." It was the same woman.

"My daughter is in there. You saw me leave. You're the one who told me where the pay phone is." Carl felt like pulling his hair. This was exasperating.

"This is the emergency room. You can't go back and forth at will. Let me call and see if you can go in."

Carl waited. He watched the woman until she nodded her head and pointed to the closed doors. He was seething. It was difficult to stay calm.

"Is the doctor available?" Carl asked the nurse.

"He's with another patient right now. He'll come see you when he's finished."

Carl went back to Lou's partitioned area. Nothing had changed. Lou was still out, and the heart monitor continued beeping. He sat down and waited.

Carl studied Lou. Her hair was plastered to her head. When was the last time she had showered? He had no idea. She smelled. He lifted the sheet covering her. She was dressed in a hospital gown. Carl saw her arms had scrapes, and she was strapped in bed. He stepped back and stumbled into the chair. Why was she strapped down?

Carl pulled back the partition. "I need to see the doctor," he said.

A nurse came by. "He'll be with you shortly."

"No. I need to see the doctor now! My daughter is strapped in her bed, and I need to know why. What's going on? No one will answer my questions!"

A middle-aged man with a mustache that seemed to cover half his face stepped out from the partition next to Lou. He had on the white jacket doctors wore, and part of a stethoscope peeked out of his pocket.

"I'm Dr. Rogers. How can I help you?" He held open Lou's partition for Carl and followed him in, closing the curtain behind him.

"I need someone to tell me what's going on with my daughter. I found her truck run into a tree. Then I heard the sheriff brought her to the hospital, but no one would tell me if she was here or not. When they finally agreed to let me see her, I couldn't find out what was wrong with her or why she was strapped to her bed. All I know is she's been heavily sedated, so I can't talk to her." Carl took a couple of breaths. "Can you tell me what's going on?" He collapsed into the chair next to Lou and accidentally jostled the bed, causing Lou's body to pitch to one side and setting off the heart monitor.

A nurse rushed in and reset the monitor, and the beeping resumed.

"I'm sorry for all the confusion. Your daughter had no form of ID on her when she was brought in, and she was very agitated. We used an antipsychotic medication to calm her, but had to add restraints until the meds kicked in. We've kept her arms strapped as a precaution. She's only been here a couple of hours. As you can see, it's gotten busy."

"But that still doesn't answer my question. What's wrong with my daughter?"

Carl felt close to tears. His eyes burned, and he

blinked several times to keep tears from forming.

"That's what we need to find out. Does she use drugs of any kind?"

"No," Carl said. "Not that I know of. She lives at home and hasn't really been out of the house all summer. Besides, that's not who she is."

"Is screaming about government spies after running into a tree—is that who she is?"

Carl slumped into the chair. "No. That's what I don't understand. What's wrong with her?"

"We'd like to run some tests on her and get a proper diagnosis. It should take two or three days. Then we'll know more of what's going on." Dr. Rogers replied as if this was a simple solution, and life would be back to normal in no time. Carl didn't feel the same confidence.

The doctor patted him on the back as he left. Carl felt like a child who had been sent to the office.

Now what? Should he stay with Lou, or go to the police station? Maybe someone there could tell him what had happened. Carl stood up. He watched Lou's chest rise and fall. Carl took one of her hands. He uncurled the fingers and turned her hand over so that his palm touched hers. He leaned across the bed and hugged her. "I love you, Lou," he whispered in her ear. Then he left.

****

By the time Carl got home that evening, he had gotten the truck towed to the Ford dealership in Sandy Point and filled out the accident form at the police station. The sheriff, who had assisted with transferring Lou to the hospital, had already left for the day. Carl was exhausted.

The next morning, he called the hospital to see how Lou was doing. He poured himself some coffee and sat down, letting the cord from the wall phone extend to the table. Florence sat beside him.

"What did they tell you?" she asked.

"Nothing much, really," Carl said. "She had a good night, and she knows where she is."

"What does that mean?"

Carl took a sip of coffee. "I'm not really sure," he said. "They suggested we visit her this afternoon, so I'm going up to school this morning. Then I'll go by and see her." Carl eyed Florence. "Do you want to come?"

She shook her head. "No. You go. Tell her we love her and let me know how she is. I'll go tomorrow. That way one of us is with Alice."

"Good idea," he said.

Carl was in his truck when he saw Florence running toward him, still in her robe and curlers. "What do we tell Alice?"

He sat for a moment, turning the volume of the radio down so the morning talk show was just a whisper. "Tell her Lou was in an accident with her truck. She's in the hospital."

"You're right. That's true." Florence leaned into the open window and kissed Carl. "You're my strength," she said. "I love you."

****

Lou was released from the hospital after two days. She had a prescription for medication and a recommendation to make an appointment with a psychiatrist in Junction.

When Carl made the drive back to Sandy Point to pick up Lou, he brought clean clothes—one of her favorite T-shirts, a pair of gym shorts, tennis shoes, and socks. He relaxed once he saw Lou. She was showered and dressed and appeared to be fine. The bandage on her forehead had been reduced to a large Band-Aid.

As they drove away from the hospital, Carl turned to Lou and asked, "How are you feeling?"

"Oh, much better," Lou said. "The people were very nice there, and the food was good. I'm glad I had a chance to visit." Lou looked out the window as they drove past the old buildings of downtown Sandy Point. "Are we going to stop at Buffalo Springs? I'd like to see if the buffalo are out today."

Carl was confused by what Lou said, but he didn't say anything. He was just relieved they were having a conversation, instead of the silence they had experienced all summer.

"I think we'll just head home. Your mother and Alice are eager to see you."

"Okay. That sounds fine."

Carl kept his eye on Lou as they drove down the interstate back home. She seemed pleased to be out, taking note of scenery. It must have been because she hadn't left the house for almost three months, he reasoned.

"Look at the cows over there," she said. She started counting the cattle, but they went past them too quickly. "Oh well."

Carl cleared his throat. "The hospital sent some medication home with you, and they want you to make an appointment with a psychiatrist in two weeks.

Lou laughed. "I know. Isn't that funny? I'm fine."

This wasn't making sense to him. "I don't understand. Why would they send home medication?"

"I think it was left over from what I was taking while I was visiting there. They probably didn't want to waste it."

Lou's logic must have made sense to her, but it certainly didn't to Carl.

"Lou, do you have your discharge papers? I'd like to see them when we get home." Carl wanted to see what they said.

"Really, Dad? Don't you trust me? I'm fine now. I was having a little stress. Maybe it was the classes that I was taking. But I'm much better now. Can't you tell?"

Carl decided to try a different tactic. "You know, school starts next week. Do you think you're ready?" Carl thought of how she had flunked biology in the spring, and how she didn't sign up to take it during summer school. None of this made sense.

Lou's face darkened, like a cloud had cast a shadow on her. She scowled. "The professor didn't like me, and he gave me trick questions on my test."

"But if you want to get into veterinary school, you have to pass biology," Carl said. He was still trying to have a logical conversation with an illogical daughter.

"No, I don't," Lou said. "And besides, I may not do that anyway." She put her head back against the headrest. "Whew, I'm tired." And with that, Lou closed her eyes.

What did all this mean? Nothing Lou said made any sense to Carl. A kind of terror grabbed him. What was wrong with her? He could think of no explanation. He turned and glanced at Lou. She was snoring, her mouth open, drool forming in the crease of her mouth.

The two of them rode the rest of the way home in silence.

Chapter 31

1988

Early one fall morning Carl slipped out of bed. The wood floors felt cool on his bare feet. He went downstairs and made a pot of coffee. In his office he pulled out a leather-bound journal and a book of devotions from his desk drawer.

Back in the kitchen, Carl poured himself some coffee and put on his heavy jacket hanging on the hook and his work boots by the back door. Books in one hand and coffee in the other, he sat on the screened porch. The sun wasn't up, and he sat in the still, cold morning looking out at the land. He saw only silhouettes. The remains of the tomato plants looked like scraggly skeletons. The apples on the trees were invisible. Only the early morning sky had any color—violet and blue.

Schizophrenia. How could a God who created such beauty allow such a disease? He couldn't understand it, and it devastated him. He had never experienced such a period of darkness as he felt now.

"What am I supposed to do?" Carl whispered those words. He didn't know if he was asking God, or if it was a rhetorical question. The books lay idle in his lap. In the darkness, Carl saw a wisp of steam rise from his cup. He took a sip. It tasted good and felt warm going down.

God, what am I supposed to do? Again, Carl posed the question, but this time he directed it to the Creator of the universe. The sun began to lighten the sky. He heard the first chirps and peeps as the birds began to wake up. Then a thought came to him out of nowhere.

Just love her.

Chapter 32

Printing was a craft. It required a passion for perfection and a keen eye for color. A printer also had to be a chemist and a mechanic, and Rodney had the skill set it took to be a good, no excellent, printer. As a teen, when he wasn't playing baseball, he was at his dad's print shop. Before he was old enough to legally drive, he was doing odd jobs at Bennett Printing, loading the press, cleaning up, even running deliveries. His fingers were permanently ink-stained, and he loved it. Almost more than baseball. Under the guidance and training of his dad, Larry Bennett, he learned everything there was to know about the printing business. When Larry retired, he sold the business to Rodney.

In the beginning Bennett Printing was a small, moderately successful, commercial printing company. Rodney adequately provided for his family with the clients he had. As the business grew, he added a small sales staff to recruit business, and, of course, Alice's graphic art talent created a new line of products—personalized invitations, stationery, cards, and more. By then, he had changed the name to Sutton Cards. Creating a website increased their sales, as orders came in online.

However, having the same name as a murderer created unintended consequences for Sutton Cards. Many of their customers decided to have their printing done elsewhere. Plus, all the employees left, except for the Nguyens.

By fall, business at Sutton Cards had leveled out, but it was barely able to cover expenses. Rodney still received orders for printing invoices and purchase orders for small businesses, envelopes and business cards, fliers and labels, and the like. But there were no orders for the invitations and cards Alice had designed, and there was no new business.

Rodney faced the prospect of not making ends meet. Would he have to sell? If he sold, what would he do? Who would hire a forty-two-year-old man whose sister-in-law had murdered eleven people?

Rodney wondered if he would treat someone the way they were being treated. Would he judge someone because of what an extended family member had done? That didn't mean that we were murderers. We're common, decent folk. And so were Carl and Florence. And for that matter, Lou was, too. It was the disease, schizophrenia, that had caused her to act out.

But that wasn't completely true. Rodney realized the mentally ill were getting a bad rap because of Lou's actions. He understood when Lou stopped taking her medications, when her disease went untreated, the consequences were often disastrous. He had observed the struggle his in-laws had had, the vicious cycle of Lou's psychotic episodes, hospitalization, prescribed medication and treatment, Lou deciding she didn't need the medication, and it started all over again.

Rodney realized when Carl and Florence died, the safety net for Lou disappeared. He and Alice didn't pick up the slack. They were so caught up in their own grief and their own lives Lou didn't even enter the picture. She took Carl's pickup the day after the funeral and left, which didn't help. They had no idea where Lou lived until after the shootings. Alice tried calling her from time to time, and they knew she returned to the farm every so often, but there was no contact. Lou still received her disability payments, but the money her parents set aside in a trust remained untouched. Rodney and Alice never saw Lou after Carl and Florence's funeral. Not until her own funeral.

Rodney never knew the *real* Lou, Alice told him. But he heard stories. She must have been great. And then she got sick. Schizophrenia was to the brain what terminal cancer was to the body. It had no cure, and it lasted a lifetime. How could a loving God allow such a horrific disease? It was a question he couldn't answer.

Rodney stared at the bobble heads on his desk. There were too many things on his mind.

Which one had priority? Business? Lawsuits? His family? Rodney felt responsible for everything. He had to hold it together. He couldn't lose it, like Alice had. Their family couldn't handle both parents unable to function. One was enough. One was too many.

Since August 6, the day everything changed, Sutton Cards had lost almost half its business. Hell, I've got two girls I need to provide for. Flory will be graduating, and then there's college. How am I going to pay for that?

Rodney pushed back his office chair and let it swivel around until he faced the metal file cabinet on the opposite wall. Where was that folder Carl had given him?

****

Carl came by Sutton Cards late one afternoon and asked Rodney if he wanted to get a beer. The two men met at Father Tom's Pub. Carl picked a table away from the noise, and they each ordered a beer.

Carl, not one for small talk, got down to business. "I want you to know I've set aside a college fund for the girls."

Rodney set his beer down. "Are you saying…?"

"I'm saying you don't have to worry about Flory and Phoebe."

"But why?"

Carl took a sip of beer, then placed it on the coaster, lining it up so the bottle was exactly in the middle, and the coaster was square to the table. "When we realized we would be taking care of Lou the rest of her life, and she would probably outlive us, I made a decision not to leave your girls out of the equation."

Carl took another sip. The coaster stuck to the bottom of the bottle. "As you know, I set up trust funds for Lou and Alice. I started investing when Lou was born, and I've done well in the market. But I wanted to do something for my granddaughters."

Carl pulled out a folder from his briefcase and slid it across the table. "Here is everything you need to know. Just file it for now. I'll remind you about it when the girls get older." He winked.

****

The two of them finished their beers and never spoke of it again. After Carl and Florence were killed by the drunk driver, there was so much sorrow and so many things to take care of, and Rodney forgot about the folder.

Chapter 33

It had been nearly three months since the mass shooting in Mineral Wells. Pumpkins, propped on front porches, waited to be carved for Halloween. Children shuffled and crunched dried leaves on their way to and from school. Life had gone on, but not for the Bennetts, and not for the families of those killed.

Alice was still skittish after seeing the posters with Lou's face on them. She hadn't had a chance to tell Rodney. She knew he had a lot on his mind, but they hadn't discussed anything. That wasn't like them. Alice and Rodney talked about everything.

The school had rearranged Flory's schedule so her required classes were in the morning. In the afternoon, she went to the library for her online classes. Alice did the driving to and from. Having this routine helped, but Alice still struggled. Some days it was exhausting just getting dressed. She had no energy and no initiative. The routine kept her out of bed, and that was important.

Flory had been pestering them about driving Phoebe to school. It was a logical solution, but Alice knew how easy it would be for her to climb back into her hole. However, was it fair to make Flory a prisoner to her depression?

One day, before Halloween, Alice went to the hardware store. Amid the pumpkins, bales of hay, and stacked rakes, Alice noticed a poster for the Women's

Charity Auction in the window. She was supposed to have been chairman this year, until she received the email saying her volunteer services were no longer needed. Having designed the posters and invitations in the past, Alice examined the one in the window. It was a knock-off of one of hers, but not as good.

Alice needed birdseed and lightbulbs. Picking up a twenty-pound bag of birdseed, she pushed the cart toward the aisle with the light bulbs.

"I told you I needed lights that twinkle. White lights, not colored. And I need them in one hundred-foot lengths."

Was that Mary Lyn? What was she doing here? Alice heard a man's voice trying to explain something, but she didn't wait to hear. She wanted to get her items and leave so she didn't risk running into Mary Lyn. They had been close friends in high school, but Alice was sure Mary Lyn had been behind the decision to take her off the committee for the Charity Auction.

****

"Hey Al-Pal," Carl called out. "Miss Mary Lyn Rah Rah Sis Boom Bah is on the phone."

"Dad!" Fifteen-year-old Alice took the phone from her father and covered the mouthpiece. She whispered, "She'll hear you."

Suppressing a chuckle, Alice cleared her throat. "Hello? Oh hi, Mary Lyn. Tonight? Well, I have a math test tomorrow and…Sure, I understand. I'll get my mom or dad to drive me over. See you in a few."

Alice hung up the phone slowly. She felt her father's eyes watching her. As she turned around, she shrugged her shoulders as if that explained it all.

Carl folded his arms and did not take his eyes off

Alice. "What does she want this time?"

"Oh, just a few signs for the boys on the basketball team. It shouldn't take very long. Can you take me over to her house? She likes to do them there."

"You mean she likes to watch you do them and claim she made them herself. Am I right?"

"Please, Dad, just take me to Mary Lyn's." Alice felt like crying, but she didn't know why.

"If it means that much to you, I will." He gave his daughter a quick hug.

"Oh, and can we stop by Hyde Drug so I can pick up some extra poster board and paint?"

****

Alice flushed. How could she have been so blind? Alice got in line to check out. There was an older gentleman in front of her with a cart full of plumbing materials and a toilet seat. The cashier was in a chatty mood. Please hurry, Alice thought. She wanted to be out of the store before Mary Lyn saw her. She wished she were invisible, even at age forty-two.

"I wanted to support our local businesses, but I guess I'll have to go to some big box store in the city to get what I need." Mary Lyn walked past her. She stopped and turned her head to stare at Alice. Without a word, she left.

Alice thought of Sherry Mashburn on the school bus. All the sixth graders knew she had cooties, and they called her Sherry Mashed Potatoes. No one would sit next to her, so she always sat by herself in the back of the bus. How could we have been so cruel?

Alice drove home and didn't bother to get the items from the car. Seeing Mary Lyn had undone everything Alice had been trying to do. Once inside, she climbed into bed. She hated that she did that.

I should be able to resume a normal life, she thought. But what was normal about living with the aftermath of eleven dead who had been murdered by her sister? How would she feel if someone had killed Rodney, or the girls, or her parents? She sat up in bed. She knew what they were experiencing because she felt the same way about the man who drove his car across the median and hit her parents head on, killing them instantly.

Suddenly, Alice wanted to know who the victims were. She realized she didn't know if they were male or female, or how old they were. She didn't even know their names. Alice searched for her phone. It wasn't on the bed table. Alice got out of bed and went to the kitchen. There it was.

She noticed four missed phone calls and a voice message.

"Mom! Where are you? Come get me!" Flory had called.

Alice slipped her shoes back on and ran to the car. She called Flory as she drove to the high school.

Flory was waiting outside in the cold October wind when Alice drove up. Fuming, she got into the car.

"Flory, I'm so sorry," Alice said. She didn't want to admit she had climbed back into bed. "Are you hungry? Let's pick up something before I take you to the library."

Flory didn't say anything. Alice glanced at her.

"Mom," she said finally, turning toward Alice, "it would be so much easier if you would let me use the car. I could take Phoebe to school. Then I could drive myself to the library and go back to pick her up when school was out."

Alice saw Flory watching her, waiting for her

response.

"You don't have to worry," Flory added, "I'm not going to do anything stupid. I promise."

Alice turned into parking lot of the local deli. "I want to believe you, Flory. Because what you did was so out of character. Can we trust you?"

Flory started crying. Alice didn't know if it was frustration or sadness. "Yes. You can trust me. I promise. I'm so sick of my life right now. But I don't want to screw up. I just want things to be right again."

Alice pulled a twenty-dollar bill from her wallet and handed it to Flory. "Get two California clubs and two drinks." Alice gave her another five. "And get one of those giant cookies we can share."

Flory wiped her face and opened the car door. She stopped. "Don't you want to come inside, and we'll eat here?"

"No," Alice said. "Let's eat in the car." She didn't want to tell Flory she'd had enough of the public for one day.

When Flory dropped Alice off at home, she went to her office and turned on her desktop. Alice had not ventured inside her office since the day after the shooting. For a moment, Alice hesitated. But no, she was on a mission now.

Alice's office had been the master closet. It was a long and narrow space with the door at one end and a small window at the other. Her desk, covered with a fine layer of dust, was pushed against one wall, and above it were samples of her work displayed on corkboard. There was a small drafting table close to the window with a swing arm lamp attached to it and a metal stool underneath it. Charcoal and pastels, ink, acrylics, brushes, and pens were organized in a small cabinet.

Alice googled Mineral Wells Mass Shooting. Immediately, numerous links to articles and images popped up. Alice's heart raced. Her hands shook. She opened one article, then another. She glanced at the headlines. No, these weren't what she wanted. The articles were going to take her back into the cave she was trying to crawl out of.

She changed her search to Mineral Wells Mass Shooting Victims. Up popped the names of the eleven victims, plus Lou. Alice took a deep breath. Just focus on the victims. Don't think about what Lou did. She read their obituaries and several articles. She clicked on images and saw their faces. Alice did some copying and pasting and soon she had their obituaries and other material next to each photo.

What to do with this? she wondered. Alice leaned back in her chair. She examined the faces on the screen. Who were these people? What had their dreams been? How were their families handling their grief?

Alice closed her eyes. Were they able to get out of bed each day? How did they function? How did they handle their new normal? What was the main force that kept them going? Was it anger or revenge or grief? Did they have others to care for, a reason to live? What would they want from Alice, the sister of the murderer? I wish I could tell them how sorry I am. I wish there was a way to let them know.

What could she do for them? What would *she* want? Alice wanted more than anything for her parents to be alive. But no one could bring them back.

"I have something in common with these families, yet I can't do anything to help them."

Chapter 34

Thanksgiving, the one time of the year Americans set aside for gratitude, was fast approaching. Christmas decorations had been up since Halloween and overshadowed the images of families around the table, heads bowed, giving thanks. Most families were preparing for that solitary day of feasting in the name of gratitude. It was but a brief interlude before the shopping season arrived. But for the eleven families and the Bennetts, there was little to feel thankful for.

Alice announced she wanted to spend Thanksgiving at the farm. It sounded like a good idea. They needed to get away. Rodney thought of the last time they had had Thanksgiving there. As was their tradition, Alice and Florence spent all day in the kitchen preparing the Thanksgiving meal. Flory and Phoebe, fifteen and twelve at the time, played board games. They went into the kitchen from time to time to help peel potatoes, stir the gravy, or sample the cornbread dressing. And it was their job to set the table. Rodney and Carl stayed out of the way and in front of the television, watching as much football as they could. Lou was upstairs in her room. She remained there until Florence or Carl called her down for the meal.

Several months later they were killed. If we had known they were going to die, I doubt we would have taken certain things for granted. It was our last

Thanksgiving with Lou as well, Rodney realized. After her parents died, Lou disappeared. We had no idea what was to come. We were totally blindsided. Could they have prevented Lou from stopping her meds and becoming psychotic? He didn't know. What could we have done? Plagued with guilt, Rodney asked himself that question nearly every day.

Yes, getting away was a good idea. Even the girls seemed excited. A different setting would be good for all of them. Maybe they might spend the entire weekend at the farm. No one had been inside the house since the shooting.

Rodney sat at his desk at Sutton Cards. He stared at the computer, but his attention was elsewhere. When he was at work, he thought of problems at home. When he was at home, he thought of the issues at work. And always the victims' families were not far from his mind. How do you tell them you're sorry when it was your own relative who murdered their loved ones?

Lou had not been an evil person. There was no way she would have committed such a heinous act if she hadn't been in the grasps of this disease. Schizophrenia had to be the worst illness because it took a healthy mind and body and destroyed it. Medication had improved, and that was good, but for those who stopped taking their meds or refused to altogether, the outcome was unpredictable and frightening.

Rodney remembered one of the few times Carl had discussed Lou's condition. They were tinkering with the old pickup Lou used to drive. It was the one she wrecked during her first psychotic episode.

****

The hood was up, and the two of them peered under

it. The battery appeared to be good. So did the spark plugs. There was plenty of oil.

Rodney took his rag and wiped a grease smudge from the hood. He glanced at the place where the bumper belonged. The front end of the old pickup was smashed in, but it still worked. "Say, Carl, why don't you get this front end repaired?"

Carl pulled his head out from the hood. "I don't see the point. It may get smashed again. So, I figure, what's the use?"

Rodney wasn't sure he understood, but he didn't say anything. He had moved on to the tires. He took a clean rag and began to wipe the hubcaps.

Carl straightened up and leaned to stretch his back. "The body damage—it's kind of my reminder. You see, this pickup still works fine, but it's changed. It's become damaged. Same way with Lou." He wiped his brow. "I'll never forget what the doctor said to me—the one who gave us Lou's diagnosis." Carl cleared his throat and paused, as if to gain control of his emotions. "He told me, 'This daughter of yours, she's never going to be the same. The daughter you knew...she's gone.' " Carl wiped his eyes on the back of his sleeve.

Rodney was silent. Carl had never spoken about Lou in this way.

"But you know what?" Carl continued, openly letting the tears fall. "I couldn't accept that. I couldn't give up on Lou." He blew his nose. "So, this old truck is my reminder. She's in there. I know she is. Somewhere underneath all the fog and bizarre behavior is my precious daughter. Sometimes, I catch a glimpse of the old Lou..." He sniffed. "And I hang on to that." Carl repeated, in a whisper, "I hang on to that."

****

They never spoke of Lou again, but Rodney never forgot that.

Since the shootings almost four months earlier, Rodney had had no peace. There were times he wanted to shake his fist at God. How could He take away the two people who were sustaining their sick daughter, then two years later allow *this* to happen? There was no way to make sense of the tragedy, and it consumed him.

He knew his entire family was affected. Alice was incapable of functioning. Flory was angry at the world. And sweet Phoebe was trying to fix everyone and everything, so they could be happy again. What was he doing? Rodney was just trying to hold everything together—the business, his family—and now the legal issues. Which brought him back to the families of the victims. How were they managing?

Rodney's phone vibrated and interrupted his thoughts. It was Barney. "Hey, Barney. What's new?" There was silence on the other end. That wasn't a good sign.

"Well, uh, I think I have a realtor who would be interested in listing the farm."

Listing the farm? Rodney didn't remember them discussing this. "So soon? I had no idea. I haven't mentioned it to Alice yet." That wasn't going to be fun.

"Well, I started asking around, and the name, Archie Robinson, kept coming up. So, I gave him a call. He wants to see the place tomorrow.

"Tomorrow! Does that mean he's going to put a sign up tomorrow?" Rodney panicked.

"It's a process. He wants to check out the property and see what you have. Then he'll know what market to gear it toward. He's a pro. He's sold a ton of acreages around here, places families want to get off their hands."

"But that's not what we have." Rodney felt like he needed to defend Alice's property.

Barney didn't say anything for a moment. "Rodney," he finally spoke. "You know the farm has to be sold. Otherwise, you could lose the entire thing to these settlements. There are other options, but I think selling the farm is the best one. Alice will get half from the sale, and the other half will go into Lou's estate. Lou's half and her trust fund will make up her estate. That's all the victims' families will get. Whatever that amount is will be divided among the litigants."

Rodney knew Barney was right. He wasn't expecting it so soon. Plus, they were spending Thanksgiving at the farm. "Okay. Let me get this straight. This Archie guy wants to meet tomorrow. Then what? When will he put it on the market?"

"I don't know exactly," Barney said. "With the holidays coming, he'll either want to go ahead and put it up for sale or wait until after the first of the year. It depends on what the real estate market is doing."

"Can we request it not be put up for sale until after the new year?"

The two men went round and round, trying to figure out the best options. In the end Rodney agreed to meet with Archie Robinson on Tuesday at ten-thirty.

"Oh, and Rodney," Barney hesitated. "Have you been out to the farm since…?"

"Not really. I mean, I took the girls, and we walked around. But I didn't have a key. We didn't go inside the house. Why?"

"Well, I'm sure you realize the police searched the

place after the shooting. I don't know what condition it might be in."

Rodney tensed. "What are you trying to say?"

"I'm not sure. But you might want to get there early and make sure there's not a big mess inside the house." Barney added, "I'll be glad to meet you there ahead of time."

Shit! That had never entered his mind.

"Yeah. You're probably right. I'll go over and make sure the house is okay." He sighed. "I hadn't thought much about the logistics of what happened that night…" Rodney's voice faded. "But she had to have a gun, and she would know where Carl kept his." He rubbed his head. These were things he never wanted to think about.

The next day Rodney sat in his truck in front of the old Sutton home. He felt like a traitor. It was ten. Rodney heard tires on the gravel and saw Barney's old tan Chevy Impala. Barney parked next to him.

"Hey pal," Barney said, as he joined him, "nice day for some shitty business." The two men zipped up their jackets to block the wind.

Rodney nodded his head. He pulled out the keys from his pants pocket and walked toward the house. "I guess I might as well open up the house." He worried what he might find inside. The two men walked slowly toward the house, neither wanting to be there, doing what had to be done.

As Rodney approached the front of the house, he noticed the paint peeling from the front door. There was a tear in the screen covering the window on the left side, and the window on the right had a large crack. He didn't remember it being quite so run down.

The house itself, which had been built of Oklahoma

sandstone, stood firm and solid. Yet everything around it seemed dead or overgrown. The two rosebushes, which Florence had nurtured, were merely thorns and dead branches. Virginia creeper, now out of control, had wrapped itself around a volunteer redbud tree. How had it become so neglected in two years? It made him think of Lou. How had neglecting her led to violence in the same two years?

"I guess you have to take care of the things you love." Rodney spoke more to himself, but Barney heard.

"It takes a lot of work to maintain a place like this," Barney said.

Rodney nodded, but he wasn't thinking of the farm.

One of the steps leading to the front door had rotted through. Rodney avoided it. The key struggled inside the lock, but finally opened the door. Stale odors greeted the two men. Rodney could smell a hint of rancid grease, probably left over from frying fish there last summer. That was the last time they had been at the farm. Then a month later, disaster had happened.

Rodney rubbed his hands together, trying to stay warm as he searched for any evidence of foul play. "I sure hope this thing works," he said as he turned the heater on. There was a rumble, a musty odor, then the familiar sound of the furnace kicking in.

From the main entry, the house appeared untouched. Then he noticed the tracks of dried mud on the wood floor. They seemed to go in all directions.

"Tracks," he said. He knew they belonged to Lou, and he shuddered as he thought of what had happened. When had she come to the farm? Was it the same day she went to Mineral Wells, or were these tracks of no consequence? He went into the kitchen to grab the broom and dustpan.

"Here, let me do that," Barney said. "Go ahead and check out the rest of the house."

"Thanks," he said and gave Barney the broom.

Rodney followed a set of prints into the living room where he lifted the sheets he and Alice had draped over the furniture. The dining room table made of pecan wood from their property and other family heirlooms stood frozen in time, as if a sense of history was slipping away. He still hadn't told Alice.

Rodney entered Carl's study and saw the contents of the desk drawers on the floor. His stomach churned. This must have been where Carl's gun was. He got on his knees and crammed items into the drawers and fit them back into the desk. Shaken, Rodney returned to the main entry where he found Barney sweeping the tracked mud from the stairway.

"I'm going upstairs to check things out." He dreaded what he might find in the bedrooms. He wished he could cancel the appointment. "Will you let Archie in if he arrives before I come back down?"

"Sure. Take your time," Barney said.

The stairs creaked in all the familiar places as Rodney slowly trod upstairs. He thought of the time he had sneaked into Alice's bedroom when they were dating. She had shown him which steps to avoid so her parents wouldn't hear him. How long ago that seemed! They had been just kids, barely older than Flory. Surely not, he thought.

There were four bedrooms upstairs, two on each side of the hall, and two bathrooms. Alice and Lou's bedrooms were on one side of the hallway. Lou's room faced the back of the property, overlooking the orchard, and Alice's room faced the front. Rodney remembered seeing Alice from her window as he drove up to the house. Those had been happy times. Carl and Florence's bedroom was across the hall from the girls, and they converted the second bedroom into a studio for Florence. Before that, it had been the nursery.

Rodney wanted to avoid Lou's room. He had an eerie feeling. Everyone who had lived in this house was dead, except for Alice. He didn't know if he was treading on hallowed or haunted ground. He stood at the door and glanced inside. At first glance everything appeared to be normal. Then he noticed that the bedspread was wrinkled, as if someone had slept on top of it. That could have happened at any time, though. The queasiness returned. He closed the door to her room.

Rodney examined Alice's bedroom. It appeared untouched. So did Florence's studio. There was an unfinished painting on the easel. How come he never noticed this before? His eyes stung, and he squeezed them tight.

When he entered Carl and Florence's bedroom, he sensed he was going to find something amiss, yet everything seemed in place. Rodney stepped into the bath and closet area, and there he found an open closet door with an empty space on the top shelf. Before he had a chance to speculate, Rodney heard voices downstairs. His search was interrupted.

Archie Robinson had arrived and stood at the foot of the stairs with Barney.

"Hi Rodney. Archie Robinson here," he said as Rodney walked down.

"Hi Archie. Nice to meet you." The two men shook hands. Silence followed. Rodney couldn't speak. He was afraid he was going to start crying. It certainly wouldn't cut it to get all emotional in front of this guy.

Barney cleared his throat.

"Nice place," Archie said.

"Yes, it was a good home. Hate to let it go."

"On the phone Barney told me it was thirty-six acres, with a barn, a small apple orchard, a pond and wooded area, and land for grazing or planting a small crop." Archie walked toward the kitchen, running his hand over the dusty counter.

"Yes. They used to have chickens and a couple head of cattle. And Carl kept the pond stocked with fish. The house was built in 1918. It's almost a hundred years old, but the wiring and plumbing were updated in the nineties. So, it's fairly current."

"The kitchen looks outdated," Archie said. He peered into the cabinets. A box of crackers, cereal, and some cans of baked beans, probably forgotten from the summer, sat on a shelf.

Rodney felt himself get defensive. "It works fine. My in-laws were impeccable and kept everything in top condition. He watched Archie open the refrigerator, the oven, and the dishwasher. The yellow Formica countertops seemed dingy, even to Rodney.

Archie walked through the living room and eyed the furniture. "Does the furniture go with the house?"

Rodney was caught off guard. He started to say no when Barney interrupted him. "It's negotiable."

Archie nodded his head. He went upstairs. Rodney froze. He didn't want to watch this man open and close the closets and drawers. He stood in place, as if nailed to the floor, and tried to scan the area for any other evidence of misdoing he might have missed. Archie returned and walked around the rest of the downstairs.

There was a screened-in porch off the back of the house with two wicker chairs. Archie let himself out onto the porch. The barn was to the left of the house, and directly behind the house was where Florence had planted her vegetable garden. Behind the yard was an apple orchard. Most of the property was hidden from view.

Archie unlocked the screened door. It creaked then slammed shut behind him. Rodney stood on the porch with Barney and watched Archie pulled out a cigarette and light it. He inhaled then glanced at his watch. "I'd like to come back, walk the property, and take some photos. Then I can give you an idea of what it's worth. Are we talking farmland or development? How about Friday?"

"I don't think that will work," Rodney said. He wanted to put off the inevitable as long as he could. "I know my wife will want to come out and spruce the place up before you take any photos."

"Okay. Then next week sometime." Archie had his phone out checking his calendar.

"Uh, no. Next week is Thanksgiving." Rodney was stalling, and he knew it was obvious.

"It's just one day. There are six other days in a week." Archie held out his hands in disbelief. "I don't really care about how the house looks. That's not what's going to sell the land. Do you want to sell the place or not?"

Did he really want to know the truth? Rodney was tempted to ask. Instead, Rodney said. "I don't think you understand. We haven't been out here since..." He stopped. He didn't know if he could go on. "...well, since August. And my wife doesn't know we're selling the home where she grew up. I just need some time."

Barney stepped outside and joined Archie. "I doubt you're going to get much interest in selling property like this between now and Christmas. Are you?"

"You never know. The right person comes along, and…"

Barney turned back and glanced at Rodney, who still stood on the porch. "How about the week after Thanksgiving? That should give Rodney some time."

Archie dropped his cigarette butt on the ground and smashed it with his boot. He checked his phone again. "Monday, the thirtieth at one o'clock?"

Rodney agreed to the date and time. He watched Archie drive away, and he realized he had been clenching his fists. "Asshole," he muttered under his breath.

Barney came back inside the porch, and the two men closed the house, covering the furniture, turning off the furnace and locking the doors.

"I want to check out the barn before we leave. I noticed it was open. It's usually locked." Rodney walked toward the barn. Again, that eerie feeling came. The doors were ajar, and there was no sign of the padlock. He peered inside hoping not to find any signs of foul play. Thankfully, he found nothing out of the ordinary. It didn't dawn on him the evidence had been removed.

"I don't look forward to telling Alice about this," Rodney told Barney. He was also thinking of the work that needed to be done to make the farm more presentable—replacing the rotted boards, repairing ripped screens and the broken window he had discovered, painting the front door, and general cleaning.

And he needed to get a new lock for the barn.

Barney gave him a pat on the back. "I'm sorry. I know this will be hard."

The two men parted. Rodney watched the dust swirl behind Barney's car as he drove away. Then he turned and stared at the old stone house.

Chapter 35

"What do you mean we have to sell the farm?" Alice sputtered, her mouth full of a ham sandwich.

It was the Friday before Thanksgiving, and Rodney had come home for lunch in case Alice needed his truck.

"I should have told you. Barney called me on Monday. We met with Archie the next day, and—"

"Archie! What kind of name is Archie? It sounds like a comic book character." Alice crossed her arms, glaring at Rodney across the table. "Tell me again why we have to sell the farm, and why we have to do it now." She had lost her appetite.

"We have to sell the farm so Lou's half will go into her estate. That and her trust fund will go to the litigants in the lawsuits."

"Lawsuits? What are you talking about?" It felt as if her heart was in her throat. What was he going to tell her next?

"According to Barney, there are seven lawsuits against Lou's estate."

Alice stood up, knocking her chair over. Her breath became shallow. "What's this going to cost us? We don't have the kind of money for a lawsuit! What are we supposed to do?"

"Hon, they aren't suing us." Rodney righted the chair and helped Alice sit. "But they are suing Lou's estate. Since Lou owns half of the farm, that means we must sell the farm so her half can go into her estate. Otherwise, a judge could take over the entire farm, and who knows what we'd get, if anything.

Alice stared straight ahead. She didn't speak.

Rodney went to the refrigerator. "I think I need a beer," he said.

In the middle of the day?

"Yes," Rodney said, as if reading her mind. "In the middle of the day." He opened the can and took a long swallow. "Business is bad. Each month I don't know how much longer I can keep Sutton Cards running. I have no payroll except for the Nguyens, and I still struggle to come out even at the end of the month. Our sales are down. I have been trying to figure out if it would be better to sell the business or declare bankruptcy and start over again. But our choices are not good."

"You never told me this."

Rodney said to her, "We're outcasts. No one wants us to do their printing. A few of our clients who've been with us forever didn't leave. But any new business we had is gone. I'm keeping the Nguyens on because they need the money, and they're loyal."

Alice didn't know what to say. She had no idea.

Rodney continued. "And then there's Flory. What's she going to do next year when she graduates? I found the letter from Carl about money for the girls' college, so that will help." Rodney took another drink from his beer and set it on the table. "Selling the farm is shitty, but it could give us some needed cash to help us stay afloat until things settle down. I guess we could blame Lou for this, but what good would that do," he said. He shrugged his shoulders when she looked at him.

"I can't believe you said that." Alice got up and left

the table. She walked toward her bedroom. She just wanted to crawl into bed.

"Alice! Don't get in bed." She could hear Rodney shouting at her, but she didn't care. How dare he say that about Lou? It was like he had put a dagger in her chest and turned the blade. She heard his footsteps coming up behind her. He grabbed her elbow.

"Let go of me!" Alice tried to pull away from his firm grasp.

"Listen to me, Alice. Things aren't going well. We need to talk."

"I can't. Not now." Alice felt his grip lighten, and she retreated to the bedroom, closing the door.

Mentioning Lou had put Alice in a tailspin. Did he not realize she felt responsible for the deaths of the eleven victims? Alice played the same tape over again in her head. If only I had been more aware of Lou's situation. If only I had reached out to her. If only I had been a better sister when she started having problems. If only I had known what to do. She began to cry.

Despite the door being shut and a blanket over her head, Alice heard sounds in the kitchen. Cabinet doors slammed, dishes clattered in the sink, a chair banged against the table. Then angry footsteps came toward their bedroom. The door opened, and Alice lay still, her head under the blanket. She knew Rodney was in the room, but he didn't sit on the edge of the bed, like he often did.

"Alice." Rodney's voice was sharp.

"Leave me alone. Go away." Alice kept the blanket over her head.

"Alice, sit up." It was a command, not a request.

Alice pulled the blanket down. She saw Rodney with his arms crossed. His eyes were sad, but his mouth was pulled down in anger. She dragged herself to a sitting position.

"Don't you see what you're doing? You're punishing yourself. *You* didn't pull the trigger. *You* aren't the one who killed eleven people."

"Don't say that!" Alice put her hands over her ears.

"Don't say what?"

"That word." Alice had her eyes squeezed shut and her hands still over her ears. She curled herself in a ball.

"What word?"

"That word," Alice repeated. She heard Rodney let out a sigh.

"Are we going to play this guessing game? Because I have no idea what horrible word I said."

"Just don't say it anymore," she said.

"Okay. This is going nowhere. I said some word you don't want me to say, but you won't tell me what it is." Rodney stopped. "Open your eyes and look at me." She opened her eyes. "Now, take your hands off your ears and sit up." Alice sat up.

Rodney continued to stand. "I can't do this much longer. I know you're struggling with everything, but the girls are suffering, too. I'm having problems. You have no idea what's going on with the rest of us. You've dug a hole so deep, I don't know if you can claw yourself out."

Alice stared at her hands. She had bitten her nails to the quick.

Rodney continued. "I don't know if I can sit around and wait for you to figure out you have a life worth living. Think about it." He turned and slammed the door behind him. The framed photo of the seven of them toppled over.

Chapter 36

"Flory, wake up." Phoebe shook her. "You promised you'd take me."

Flory opened one eye, then rolled over. Phoebe was already dressed. "If I could drive, I would go by myself," she said, "but you said you'd come with me. You promised."

"All right. I'm up. Now leave me alone so I can get dressed."

Twenty minutes later they backed Alice's car out of the garage. Phoebe left a note on the kitchen counter.

"Tell me again why you talked me into taking you to some church in the city." Flory glanced at her sister as she entered the interstate. Phoebe wore her nice jeans and a sweater under her coat. Her thick, curly hair was clipped back, and she wore the slightest amount of makeup.

"I heard they served a Thanksgiving meal and needed volunteers. I wanted to find out more about it. Besides," Phoebe added, "I wanted to get in the thankful spirit."

"I can't think of anything to be thankful for myself," Flory said.

Phoebe didn't say anything.

They exited the interstate and turned down a tree-lined street in a neighborhood closer to downtown. There was a park on one side of the street and older homes on the other side.

"It's the church with the tall steeple. You know, the one we can see from Broadway as we drive to the city," Phoebe said.

"I know which one it is," Flory said. "Don't you remember? Mimi and Granddad took us to a concert there in the sanctuary. They had a mini orchestra and even bagpipes."

Phoebe remembered. That was why she decided to play in the band.

There was an early service at eight-thirty. Phoebe chose it because they could leave before their parents woke up. Ionic columns graced the exterior entrance to the sanctuary.

As the girls entered, an usher greeted them, handing them a bulletin for the service. Quiet organ music played as they walked down the carpeted center aisle. The sanctuary's tall windows let the sunlight stream in. It felt bright inside on the cold November morning. Flory nudged Phoebe toward an empty pew in the back of the sanctuary.

The pastor stood in the chancel wearing the traditional long black robe with a green stole. A large wooden cross hung around his neck. He stated the Call to Worship and welcomed all who were there. "May the peace of Christ be with you and all of your loved ones."

The congregation responded, "And also with you."

Phoebe and Flory watched as the worshippers greeted one another. There was laughter and handshaking, reaching in front of and behind the pews and across the aisle. An older gentlemen walked toward them.

"The peace of Christ be with you," he said, as he

extended his hand.

Phoebe shook his hand. "And also, with you." Flory followed.

"Please stand and join us as we sing our opening hymn, 'For the Beauty of the Earth.' " The organist began playing, and the congregation stood. Phoebe's heart swelled. She loved that old song.

Phoebe followed along in the bulletin—the Prayer of Confession, Assurance of Forgiveness, Apostle's Creed—so much of it was familiar and comforting. They stood when they were supposed to and bowed their heads during the prayers.

"Our New Testament scripture comes from the book of Matthew. 'Come to me, all you who are weary and burdened, and I will give you rest. Take my yoke upon you and learn from me, for I am gentle and humble in heart, and you will find rest for your souls. For my yoke is easy and my burden is light.' This is the word of the Lord."

"Thanks be to God," the people said.

The sermon was on being thankful, even when it seemed there was nothing to be thankful for. Phoebe felt as if the pastor was speaking directly to her.

Before the Pastoral Prayer, a woman read the list of members who needed prayers—a new baby, cancer treatment, lost job, ailing parent, recovery from an injury in rehab. "Please pray for Anthony Wilson," she said. "He is in rehab now. Pray he can walk again. He's still recovering from the gunshot wound he received at the Mineral Wells shooting."

Phoebe glanced at Flory as she slid down in her seat. She wanted to bolt. Flory grabbed her arm and stared straight ahead.

"Please bow your heads," the pastor said. "Dear Lord. There is so much to be thankful for on this bright, crisp morning—our neighbors and families, our community, our church which embraces both the helper and the helpless. Remind us, Lord, of the many gifts you bestow on us. We also pray for those who are hurting, like Anthony. We pray for supernatural healing for him. We also pray for those who are hurting on the inside. We pray for forgiveness to those who need it. Lord, you know in the hardest of times is when we need you the most, and that's when we need to say thank you. Please help us to be grateful for you and for your Son, Jesus, who died on the cross for us. In your Son's holy name, Amen."

"Now join us for our closing hymn." The organ began to play, and the congregation stood. Phoebe and Flory stood up and walked out. They couldn't get out of there soon enough.

"Well, that was a mistake," Flory said, as they got in their car.

Phoebe, still holding the church bulletin, was pensive. She thought of the closing prayer. *Lord, in the hardest of times is when we need you the most, and when we need to say thank you.* She pulled out the insert about the Thanksgiving dinner.

"You're not still interested in helping with that, are you?"

"I don't know," Phoebe said. "There's a list of things still needed. It says here, 'Desserts of any kind.' " She paused. "We could make Sutton cookies."

"I don't want to make our cookies and go back to that church," Flory said. "Aunt Lou shot one of their members. If they found out who we were, they'd kick us out."

"You're probably right," Phoebe said. But she didn't let go of the idea. "What do you think we'll do for Thanksgiving? Mom talked about having it at the farm, but I haven't heard anything else about it. Have you?"

"No. As far as I know, she hasn't done anything."

Phoebe heard the disgust in Flory's voice. "I wish I had a credit card. Then I'd go to the store and get the food for Thanksgiving. A credit card and a car. That's all I need." Phoebe leaned back in the seat and sighed. Being fourteen was no fun. She couldn't do anything on her own, and there was no one to ask for help. In the past, she might have called Sadie, but that wasn't going to happen now. "Say, let's stop by the farm."

Flory passed the exit to their house and kept going north. At the Waterloo exit, she turned and drove past the odd-shaped tree where Alice and Lou used to climb. She turned left onto Old Farm Road. About a mile down, the farm was on the left-hand side. There wasn't another house in sight.

"I love this place," Phoebe said. "I don't ever want to sell it."

Flory nodded her head. She turned onto the gravel drive and parked in front of the house. The two girls got out. They buttoned their coats and turned up the collars to block the wind.

"I wish we had the key, so we could go inside," Phoebe said. She walked toward the house and jiggled the doorknob, hoping it was open, but nothing happened. The two girls walked around the house, peering into the windows.

"Come on. Let's go. I'm cold," Flory said.

Soon they were back home.

"We forgot to plant daffodils," Phoebe said.

"What?"

"Daffodils. We forgot to plant them for Aunt Lou," she said.

"I don't get it," Flory said.

"Don't you remember? After Mimi and Granddad died, we planted daffodils for them—some here, and some at the farm."

"What made you think of that?" Flory pushed the remote for the garage door.

"It was around Thanksgiving when we planted them. Mom said you had to plant them after the ground was cold, and they'd come up in the spring. They did, and they still do. I think of them when I see the daffodils."

"Yeah, but who's going to want to remember Aunt Lou?" Flory turned off the ignition and got out of the car. She opened the door to the kitchen.

"She's family, isn't she?" Phoebe followed her.

"Who's family?" Rodney sat at the kitchen table, drinking coffee and reading the paper. Alice was nowhere in sight.

"Aunt Lou," Phoebe said. "She's family, and we didn't plant daffodils for her."

"Daffodils? What are you talking about?" Rodney asked.

Flory rolled her eyes. "She wants to plant daffodils for Aunt Lou like we did for Mimi and Granddad after they died."

Rodney set his cup down. "You're right, Phoebe. We didn't. Do you think we should?"

"Yes. But is it too late?"

Flory was scrolling through her phone. "It says

daffodils can be planted through mid-November." She shrugged her shoulders.

Phoebe slumped. "All my plans fail. Everything I try to do doesn't work." She opened the refrigerator, hoping to find something to eat. Nothing appeared appetizing. "Has Mom made any pumpkin bread?"

Flory rolled her eyes. "What do you think?"

Phoebe ignored her. She opened Alice's recipe box. After finding what she was looking for, she wrote down ingredients on a separate piece of paper. At the bottom of her list, she added daffodil bulbs.

"Dad, can you take me to the store?"

Rodney had resumed reading the Sunday paper. "What do you need?"

"I want to get the ingredients for pumpkin bread and Sutton cookies, and I want to see if I can find daffodil bulbs," she said. "If I could drive and had my own money, I wouldn't have to ask someone all the time. But I can't and I don't, so I do." She chuckled at what she said.

Rodney pushed back the chair and stretched. He was in an old T-shirt and boxers. "Let me get dressed." He tousled Phoebe's hair as he walked past her.

Rodney and Phoebe drove to Corsin's. Phoebe pushed the cart, and Rodney walked beside her. As she found the ingredients for pumpkin bread and her grandmother's cookies, she noticed the advertised specials for Thanksgiving. "Dad, what are we doing for Thanksgiving? Has Mom gone shopping yet?"

Rodney sighed. "I'm not sure." He hesitated. "No. I don't think she has."

Phoebe stopped short, and another customer bumped into her. The store was crowded, even on a

Sunday. "We have to get food for our dinner while we're here." Phoebe's mind began to race. At fourteen, she hadn't paid attention to what Alice bought for the meal, but she knew they needed a turkey.

"Come on, Dad, let's get a turkey. And potatoes. We always have mashed potatoes. Or should we get sweet potatoes? What about dressing? I don't know what goes into Mom's dressing. And cranberries and pie? Pumpkin or apple? I don't know how to make a pie."

Phoebe continued to think out loud as she walked up and down the aisles. Rodney followed her.

"Okay. Let's get a turkey," Rodney said. They walked over to the freezer section and discovered the selection was slim, at best. Their choices were twenty-pound turkeys or boneless turkey breasts.

"What does Mom usually get?" Phoebe asked. The twenty-pound turkeys seemed too big.

As the two of them tried to decide what size turkey they should get, Phoebe sensed someone staring at them. She saw Sadie and her mother. Immediately, Sadie turned and walked the other direction. Phoebe's face burned. She could tell by the way they were dressed they had come from church. Phoebe was still in her nice jeans, but Rodney was in a pair of sweats and unshaven. Another reminder of their status because of Aunt Lou.

"Wasn't that your friend?" Rodney noticed Sadie and her mother walk away.

"Ex-friend, Dad." Phoebe didn't feel like shopping anymore. "Let's forget the turkey. I just want to leave."

Rodney paid for the ingredients in the cart, and they left. "Do you want to see if we can find daffodil bulbs?" Rodney asked. There was a local nursery nearby.

"I guess," Phoebe said. She had lost her enthusiasm.

At the nursery Rodney asked one of the employees if they had daffodil bulbs.

"I'm sorry, but we're all sold out. They're usually gone by the first of November."

Back in the car Phoebe felt deflated. "Nothing I try to do ever works."

They returned home with the ingredients for Sutton cookies and pumpkin bread, but no daffodils bulbs.

Chapter 37

By Monday Alice hadn't done any shopping for Thanksgiving. Rodney decided to take things into his own hands and order a dinner for four. The local cafeteria was the only place Thanksgiving meals were still available.

Everything changed when Carl and Florence were killed, including Thanksgiving. After Lou disappeared, Alice tried to call and invite her to join them, but the phone always went to voicemail. This year brought even more changes. No one was in the mood. There was no feeling of gratitude—for anything. Their front porch, which usually overflowed with seasonal decorations, remained bare. No aromas came from the kitchen as Flory and Phoebe came home from school. No bags of groceries covered the countertops, waiting to be put away. No one felt like having the traditional Thanksgiving meal, except for Phoebe. And Rodney decided to do something about it.

On Wednesday Phoebe made six-dozen Sutton cookies and convinced Flory to take her back to the church to deliver the cookies for the next day. That night Phoebe and Flory made pumpkin bread, and the next day the four of them went to the farm with their catered meal. Alice and Phoebe rode in the Honda, and they brought the food. Rodney and Flory took the truck. He brought his tools and some cleaning supplies. He still hadn't mentioned they were going to have to sell the farm.

"Dad, what's all the stuff for in the back of the truck?" Flory asked.

"There's some repairing to do, and I figured the house might need a good cleaning."

Flory shrugged her shoulders. "Whatever."

The plan was to stay at least through Friday, if not longer. The girls would sleep in Alice's bedroom. Rodney and Alice would take her parents' room. Lou's room would not be used. It never was.

Rodney and Alice had not discussed the sale of the farm since their argument. No decision had been made about how to tell the girls, but Rodney knew he had to do it while they were there. His appointment with Archie was on Monday.

This was not a trip he was looking forward to. If he could sense the tension, then he knew everyone else could. Why couldn't they just call off Thanksgiving? Flory, who was normally silent, didn't disappoint him.

Finally, she turned to Rodney and said, "What's going on? Something's not right."

"If you mean none of us are in a real thankful mood, then I would say that's what's going on."

"No. It's something else. I can feel it." Flory persisted.

Just then Rodney turned onto the gravel drive. He parked the truck near the barn. Turning toward Flory, he said, "We'll talk later." He squeezed her shoulder and gave her a sad smile.

"Watch out for the rotted board on the steps. I'm going to fix it while we're here," Rodney said. He led the way and unlocked the front door. It was the first time any of them, except Rodney, had been inside since Lou's killing spree.

Rodney watched Alice and the girls tentatively enter the house. How ironic and sad, he thought. This was the place they had felt the safest. Yet, here they were, nervous and anxious. And for good reason. None of them had been inside the house since the summer. And their lives had been turned upside down since then.

Rodney had been in the house briefly the previous week. Only Alice was aware of that. His meeting with Archie had been the tipping point, because selling the farm would take away the false sense of safety they had placed in that spot.

Rodney wanted to shake his fist at Lou, but what good was that? She was dead. Suddenly, he felt very alone.

"Dad!" It was Phoebe. Rodney had this image of her when she was about four or five, trying to get his attention by pulling on the leg of his pants. She had been so little then.

He shook his head to bring himself back to present. "Sorry. What do you want?"

"Can you turn on the heat? It's cold in here."

"Sure," Rodney said. At least he knew the heater worked.

Food and clothing were brought inside the house. The sheets were taken off the furniture, and everyone started to settle in. Flory and Phoebe took their bags upstairs and reappeared moments later.

"It felt creepy up there," Phoebe said. Flory rolled her eyes but didn't disagree.

Rodney checked the television to see if he could get any of the football games. Then he remembered they had turned off the internet after Carl and Florence died. So much for watching the games unless he wanted to drive home and retrieve his laptop.

Alice was in the kitchen putting things away. Rodney glanced in at her. It seemed so normal, like old times. He wondered what was going on in her mind. They had hardly spoken all week. Cordial. That was how they had been toward each other. But not honest. And not intimate. Rodney ached.

"Hey," he said, peering into the small kitchen. "What'cha doin'?"

"I'm putting the food away. You know, busy, trying to be useful." Alice looked at Rodney. There was a rawness to her expression.

He came in and folded his arms around her. She sobbed on his shoulder. Neither spoke. They didn't have to.

Alice pulled back and said, "We have to tell the girls."

"I know," he said.

"We need to do it at dinner. Together."

Rodney agreed. "Yes." This was the Alice he knew and loved. He hoped she was back. Or at least that she didn't crawl back in bed.

It was early afternoon when they sat down to Thanksgiving dinner. Flory and Phoebe set the table, like they used to. Pinecones and sprigs of cedar were the centerpiece for the table. Alice pulled out her mother's good serving dishes and put the prepared meal in them.

The four of them sat at the massive, pecan wood table that Alice's grandfather had built. With seating for twelve, they positioned themselves opposite each other in the middle of the table.

"Let's pray," Rodney said. He bowed his head.

"Dear Lord, on this day of thanks, we feel empty. But we have much to be thankful for. They're here around this table. We have each other, and for that I'm deeply grateful. We ask that you walk beside us during these hard times. Be our supporter and comforter. Bless this food to the nourishment of our bodies. Amen."

Opening his eyes, Rodney looked around at his family. His heart swelled. He loved each one of them.

"Pass your plates, and I'll serve this delicious meal." Rodney stood up and went to the end of the table where Alice had placed the platters of food. There was turkey, dressing, mashed potatoes, sweet potatoes, green bean casserole, gravy, rolls, tabs of butter, and cranberry jelly.

There was silence as they ate. Flory was the first to speak. "This isn't very good," she said and put her fork down.

Rodney, chewing on a piece of dry turkey, said, "The sweet potatoes are good."

Phoebe pushed her food around her plate. "It tastes nothing like what we usually have. Mom, your food is so much better."

Alice nodded. "This is probably the worst dinner I've had in a long time."

Rodney swallowed the dry turkey and washed it down with water. He stared at the pile of food remaining, knowing none of it would be eaten. What he realized was in the past, before Lou's shooting, they would have said those exact same words and then laughed about it. That wasn't going to happen today.

Should I get the rest of the bad news over with? Rodney glanced at Alice, and she shook her head no. He signaled back by shrugging his shoulders.

"What are you all doing?" Flory asked. "It looks like

some kind of sign language."

"You mother and I have something to tell you." Rodney ignored Alice as she vigorously shook her head.

"Not now, please," Alice said finally.

"What do you have to tell us that you don't want to say?" Flory persisted. "What's going on?"

Rodney sighed heavily. "Well," he started, "we have something to tell you."

"You already said that," Flory said.

"We—I mean, I—met with a realtor last week, and…"

"We're selling our house?" Phoebe interrupted. "What's wrong with our house?"

"Not our house," Rodney said slowly. "We have to sell the farm." There. He said it.

Flory and Phoebe broke down crying. They left the table and ran upstairs. Alice glared at Rodney and followed them.

Rodney sat at the empty table, surrounded by unwanted, horrible tasting food.

"Talk about bad timing," Rodney muttered. He had certainly made a bad situation worse. He stared at his plate of food. The gravy had started to congeal on the dried turkey and instant potatoes, and the smell was starting to make him gag.

"Let's get rid of this stuff," he announced to himself. Rodney gathered the plates and serving dishes and took them into the kitchen. He dumped all the food into the trash. Soon the dishes were washed, and the kitchen cleaned. There was no evidence of the Thanksgiving meal, except for the emptiness in his stomach.

Flory was the first to come downstairs. "I'm hungry," she said.

Rodney was in Carl's study, examining the shelves of books along the wall behind the desk. He held a book by C.S. Lewis. When he saw Flory, his heart melted. He wondered if that was how Carl felt whenever he had looked at Lou. And when had their lives changed? His heart ached. How could he protect his daughters from what life threw at them going forward? Rodney closed his eyes briefly. "*Help me*," he whispered.

Rodney set the book down and walked over to Flory who stood at the doorway. He put his arm around her. "Me, too," he said. "Let's see what we can find to eat."

As they walked toward the kitchen, he told her, "I threw away all the food."

Flory opened the refrigerator and surveyed what she saw. Rodney watched her. She was devising a plan, he could tell.

"What do you think? Can we salvage a meal out of any of this?" Rodney liked the idea of relying on Flory to solve the problem.

"I think so. We have bread, milk, and eggs. All we need is some syrup, and we can have French toast. Do you think that 7-Eleven down the road is open?"

Rodney smiled. "Let's check it out."

Thirty minutes later Alice and Phoebe entered the kitchen. "Something smells good," Phoebe said.

Flory stood at the stove, flipping pieces of bread soaked in egg and milk. "French toast," she said.

Soon the four of them were seated back around the large dining room table. Laughter replaced the previous silence. It almost felt normal. Rodney wondered if he should bring up the sale of the farm. It would ruin the mood, so he decided not to.

It was Flory who broached the subject. "So, that's

what was going on. I mean, that's why you were acting all weird when we were driving here. You knew we had to sell the farm. Am I right?"

Rodney nodded. He looked at his daughters, then at Alice, who signaled him with a sad smile. An honest conversation, explaining the reason for the sale, was followed by more tears. But Rodney felt better. There were no more secrets.

Chapter 38

On Monday the farm was in good condition. Rodney had been able to get the repairs done, and Alice had cleared out a lot of personal items. Flory and Phoebe had cleaned, dusted, and polished the old farmhouse from top to bottom. Rodney felt it was ready to show.

He glanced at his watch to check the time. It was almost noon, and he was meeting Archie at one thirty. He decided to call Alice to see if she wanted to come with him.

"Hey, Alice. I'm meeting Archie at the farm at one thirty. Do you want to come?"

"Let me think about it," Alice said.

"What's there to think about?" Rodney didn't get it. "I think you should come. You can meet Archie and tell him about the history of the house."

"Well." Alice hesitated. "I guess I can."

"Great. I'll come home for lunch, then we can go."

Rodney and Alice arrived at the farm with enough time to unlock the house and air it out. He watched as Alice ran her hand along the banister as they walked up stairs. It was as if she was trying to capture memories from her touch. This was another good-bye she would have to face.

Rodney followed her from room to room, letting her make any finishing touches. Back in the kitchen, Alice lit a citrus candle. Rodney went outside and opened the barn. He had raked the dirt floor to get rid of any incriminating footprints and had gotten a new padlock.

"Hello. Anybody home?" Archie entered the house with a black case on his shoulder. Rodney and Alice emerged from Carl's study.

"Hi, Archie. This is my wife, Alice."

The three of them exchanged greetings. Archie then opened the case and pulled out a camera, attaching a wide-angle lens. "I'll take some pictures now, if you don't mind," he said.

Rodney let Alice take Archie around the house. She explained the history of the house, how her grandfather had built it almost one hundred years ago. The floors were oak planks from trees he had cut down. The light fixture in the entry had come from Pennsylvania, where her great-grandparents were from.

"What do you think our prospects are for selling?" Rodney asked, after he had led Archie outside to the barn, through the grove of apple trees, down to the creek and beyond.

"It depends," Archie said. "The way I see it is you're going to have two kinds of buyers: the ones who want to tear everything down and subdivide the property, and the ones who want to preserve what you have here." Archie paused and pulled out a pack of cigarettes. "Do you mind if I smoke?" he asked.

Rodney saw Alice bristle, but he answered, "Just outside. Be sure to pick up your cigarette butts."

Archie nodded. He lit up and inhaled. He continued. "The best chance you have for selling this place is to find a buyer who wants to turn this into a new subdivision or a commercial development."

"That means they'll tear everything down." Rodney

heard Alice's distress.

"Yes, that's true," Archie said. "But if you want to find someone who wants to live out here, you're going to wait a long time." Archie took a puff and blew out smoke. "And you won't get as much money for it. But it's up to you. If you want to sell this quickly, or if you want to sit on it. It's up to you."

"We haven't discussed the price yet," Rodney said.

"You'll need to get an appraisal," Archie pulled out his phone, with his cigarette hanging from his mouth. "I've got a good appraiser who can check out the property. He costs, but he's worth every penny."

Rodney only saw more expenses as Archie talked. He tried to follow Archie's conversation, and at the same time was keenly aware of Alice's rising anxiety.

"I'll do a comparison of properties that have sold recently, and I'll check to see what the land is zoned for. If it can be developed commercially, then you'll get a better price. Let's cross our fingers."

Archie wrote the appraiser's name and number on the back of one of his business cards and handed it to Rodney. "Here you go, Rod. Give him a call."

Rodney hated being called Rod. His name was Rodney.

"I'll get back to you on comps. If you don't hear from me by the end of the week, call me. Just not in the evenings. I work when everyone else is off." He winked and dropped his cigarette butt in the dirt, smashing it with the toe of his boot. He started to walk toward his car.

"Pick up your butt," Alice said.

Archie stopped. He turned around and eyed Alice. He picked up the butt and left.

"I don't like that man," Alice said. She and Rodney walked toward the house to close it up.

"I know. I'm not too sure about him, myself. But he came well-recommended," Rodney replied.

"By whom? Who told you to use him?" The conversation continued as they went upstairs and turned out lights.

"Barney got his name from someone," Rodney told her.

"But does Barney know him personally?"

"I don't know the answer to that," Rodney said.

"I'd like to know. Because I'm not sure I want him to represent us. I mean, I don't want him to be our face to prospective buyers. I would prefer someone who appreciates the history of my home."

"Alice," Rodney said, "you have to realize what the *history* this house may be for people who live around here."

"What do you mean? Oh." Alice stopped. Her shoulders sagged momentarily, then she straightened herself. "Okay," she said, "so what do we do?"

Rodney switched off the light in the entryway and turned off the heater. He locked the front door. "Well, according to what Barney heard, Archie can sell just about anything. He doesn't care if a murder happened in the house, or…" He looked at Alice. "Or if a murderer lived here."

She didn't say anything. The two of them walked to the truck, the familiar sound of the gravel crunching underfoot.

"Bottom line, for Archie," Rodney continued, "it's about making the sale, closing the deal." The two of them climbed into the truck. "And that's what we need—like it or not." Rodney started the ignition.

It wasn't until they were on the highway that Alice spoke. "You're right," she said. "I don't like it. But I guess that's what we must do. We need the money, and we have to get Lou's part of the estate…" Alice's voice trailed off.

"That's right." Rodney reached over and squeezed her shoulder. "We have to sell the farm for Lou's estate. It will be dispersed somehow to most of or all the victims' families. And we want to get as much as we can for her estate, for the families, and for us."

Neither spoke until Rodney exited the interstate.

"Rodney," Alice said.

"Yeah?"

"Do you ever wish you could go back in time? I mean, do you ever wish you could have done some things differently?"

Rodney shrugged his shoulders. "No, I've never really thought about that. Why?"

Alice sighed. "Well, sometimes I wish I had been more attentive to Lou when she lived here. I wish I had been more involved with Mom and Dad in her care. You know, learned about her meds, gone to some of her appointments." Alice paused. She tried to suppress a sob. "I never visited her when she was hospitalized."

"But your parents told you not to."

"I think they were trying to protect me," Alice said.

Rodney pulled into the driveway and put the truck in park to let Alice out. He watched her go inside before driving away.

Shit. This thing never goes away. It's going to follow us the rest of our lives.

The more he tried to get away from the murders Lou

committed, the more they engulfed his family. Rodney gripped the steering wheel. His jaw clenched. Damn you, Lou.

Chapter 39

1996

Alice and Rodney were getting married at the farm in a week. It had been exhausting for Lou—hearing about the plans, constant chatter about the guest list, flowers, the photographer, the ceremony, the reception. Hors d'oeuvres with the cake or not? Champagne or punch? Formal or informal? Ad nauseum. Florence had wanted Lou to be a bridesmaid. The idea itself made Lou anxious. Having to wear some uncomfortable dress and shoes and parade in front of a bunch of people she had no desire to expose herself to would have been pure torture. But thankfully, it wasn't going to happen.

Lou stayed in her room or outside roaming the land to avoid Florence. Even Carl seemed preoccupied with the upcoming wedding.

It had been eight years since Lou was diagnosed with schizophrenia. But she knew she wasn't sick. Sure, she had had problems, but they were worked out at the hospital. Occasionally, she needed to take some medication to get better. But once she was better, she didn't have to take the pills anymore. Her parents didn't understand that. Especially Florence. Every morning she insisted Lou come down for breakfast. The pill would be sitting on Lou's plate. At first Florence watched Lou to make sure she was taking it. But recently with the wedding plans, she had become distracted.

Lou slipped the pill in her napkin and threw it in the trash. Sometimes she washed it down the sink. Either way, she wasn't going to take it because she knew it was poison.

Lou had a plan. She was going to open her own wild animal care center. First, she needed to round up some animals who were injured and heal them. Then they would let other wild animals know about her. It was going to be great. But she had to make sure the government spies didn't find out. Lou kept her helmet in her bedroom closet in case *they* were searching for her. And she had a box of aluminum foil for her windows if she needed to protect herself.

It was early on the morning of Alice's wedding. Outside the birds were waking up. Lou was still in bed, and the house was quiet. Something tickled her nose, and she brushed it away. It happened again. Lou swiped at her nose. Then she felt something crawl across her arm, on her neck, and up her scalp. Soon bugs of every kind were crawling all over her body, and they began multiplying. She sat up. Her bed was covered with crawling creatures. They were climbing on top of each other and tumbling onto the floor. They began to climb up the walls. Once they reached the ceiling, they dropped down, covering Lou.

They got tangled in her hair. She could feel them inside her nightshirt, under her armpits, between her toes, and in her ears. They were in the sheets and on top of the blankets. Her room darkened as the bugs covered everything. Soon, Lou realized, she, too, would be completely covered. They would get inside her body, slithering down her throat and consume her from the inside out.

There was nothing she could do to stop them.

Chapter 40

On Christmas Day Robert and Elizabeth Randolph and their son, Robbie, sat in a hotel room at a resort in the Cayman Islands. None of them felt like celebrating, but it was better than being at home surrounded by memories of Kathryn. Her life had been taken on August sixth by a mass shooter, Lou Ella Sutton.

****

Jose Martinez spent Christmas by himself. His brother, Marco, had invited him to come over, but he declined. First, he lost his wife two years ago, and then, Mickey. He would have been the first one of their family to graduate from college.

****

Rick and Diana Coverdale woke up on Christmas morning. While Rick filled two thermoses with coffee, Diana gathered a fresh evergreen wreath. They put on heavy coats and gloves and drove to the cemetery to spend the day with Jamie.

****

Ann Goodson was in her nightgown when her son called. "Mom, aren't you coming over? Kenny and Bailey want to show you what Santa brought them."

"I'm sorry, Craig, I don't think I'm going to make it," Ann said. Ken had been gone nearly five months. She just wanted this day to be over.

****

Twelve-year-old Seth Fisher woke up to the smell of bacon and homemade sweet rolls. He knew his grandmother had made them for him. They had been his mom's favorite. He felt that now-familiar ache and tightness in his chest. He squeezed his eyes to stop the tears.

****

Six-month old Lizzie was crying. Angie Almon rolled over and patted the side of the bed where Taylor was supposed to be. When would she stop that habit? It made waking up so much harder, realizing Taylor was gone. It was Christmas morning. Angie hadn't put up a tree, and Santa didn't come.

****

David and Bianca Merrell stared at the tree in their living room. It had been professionally decorated. As one of the partners of a prominent law firm in Dallas, there had been the obligatory holiday gathering. David had thought planning the annual event would help ease the pain they felt after Kayla's death. Never again.

****

Frances Eckles woke up Christmas morning. She knew Roger was passed out on the sofa in the living room. Her two sons were probably hung over, too. Oh, how she missed Danielle!

****

Leslie Cottingham's fourteen-year-old son, Sammy, knocked on her bedroom door. "Come on in," she said.

"Merry Christmas, Mom."

Sammy gave her a package, and she started to cry. She knew her divorce was the reason Amber drove away that day.

****

Cheryl and Kevin Youngblood watched their two teenage sons open their Christmas presents. They were all failing at their attempts to act like this was just another Christmas, because it wasn't. Blake had been taken from them, and he never got to start college.

****

Hannah's phone rang. She knew it was her mother. "You should have spent the night here," Sylvia Cummins said.

"Merry Christmas, Mom," Hannah said. There wasn't anything merry about the day, and she didn't look forward to spending it with her mother. Hannah missed her twin brother, Olen, more than anything, but she wanted to spend the day alone with her own memories.

****

Jeremy Turner had the ring in his back pocket. He had talked to Gina's parents the week before. When he picked her up on Christmas Day, they drove to the park near the university. It was cold and windy. Jeremy held Gina's hand, and they walked toward the statue of Will Rogers. He pulled out the ring and got down on one knee. "Gina, will you marry me?"

****

Jordan Hall sat on his cot in his cell. The guards handed out candy canes to the inmates for Christmas. One stupid mistake had spiraled his life downward. He wanted to die. After his conviction of vehicular manslaughter, his parents had disowned him. Only his sister, Rachel, kept in contact with him. He hadn't meant to get so drunk. He'd been accepted to medical school, and his celebration ended everything, including the lives of that older couple.

****

Alice sat in the front seat of the pickup next to Rodney. The girls were in the back. On her lap was the wooden box containing Lou's ashes. The four of them drove in silence to Buffalo Springs where they planned to scatter her ashes.

Chapter 41

The New Year, 2016, arrived. Initially Alice felt some relief that the old year was gone. Perhaps she could make a new start. However, the first weeks of January were overcast. Days passed without seeing the sun, and the darkness reflected her mood and pulled her back into the cave she had created for herself.

Lately Alice had been having a reoccurring dream. Someone was falling, and she was trying to rescue the person. Each time she tried to reach for the person, she woke up. On this frigid Friday morning, Alice woke up startled and in a sweat. This time the person had a face. It was Lou. She opened her eyes and stared at the dark ceiling, waiting for the panic attack to pass. She had seen Lou's face, and she had watched her fall. Alice couldn't get that picture out of her head.

She glanced at the mound under the blanket next to her. She wanted to wake up Rodney, but what was the point. He'd only tell her it was a dream and to go back to sleep. But she couldn't. Sleep, which was sometimes her only means of escape, now eluded her. She was awake and now waited for the morning dread that greeted her daily.

Alice glanced at her phone. It was four o'clock. Did she really used to wake up at five every morning? That seemed like a different life, ages ago. It was. She shivered as she pulled back the blanket and climbed out of bed. She searched for her slippers with her bare feet. Then she made her way to her office. She turned on the light once she shut the door. It felt so foreign and out of place to be there. When was the last time she had been in her office?

Lou's face haunted her. What could she have done? she asked herself, as if the dream had happened. But the reality was Alice struggled with what she could have done to prevent Lou from spiraling down to the place where she ended. The paranoia must have been so powerful Lou's only recourse was to resort to violence. It was her only means of protecting herself in her distorted reality.

"Schizophrenia." Alice spoke the word that had never been said in her home. She typed it in on her laptop. So many links popped up it was overwhelming. She started at the top and clicked on each link, reading about this disease that had imprisoned Lou for almost thirty years. Delusions, hallucinations, paranoia, psychosis—words that had never been part of Alice's vocabulary or life, defined what Lou had endured. Lou and Alice had existed in two different worlds. Alice's parents, especially Carl, had cared for Lou and tried to penetrate Lou's world. But Alice had remained oblivious, content to live her life free of any obligation to Lou. Because of this, her guilt for Lou's actions consumed her.

Alice was still at her laptop when she heard Rodney's alarm go off. Hearing the shower come on, Alice clicked save and went down the hall to make coffee. Just like she used to.

Alice heard a hairdryer coming from the girls' bathroom as she returned to the bedroom with two mugs of coffee. Rodney was out of the shower and wrapped in his towel when she handed him his coffee. It seemed like such a normal morning.

"Thanks, Alice," Rodney said. "Have you been in the kitchen all this time?"

"No, I was looking up something on the computer." Not sure why, but Alice didn't feel like telling him about the dream or what she was doing. Besides, she could tell Rodney had things on his mind.

"I need to make some deliveries this afternoon. If you need the truck, I can drop it off after the deliveries," Rodney said.

"No. I don't need to go out," she said. Flory was still using Alice's car for school.

"Okay, that's great." Rodney patted the shaving cream on his face and began to shave.

Alice stood and watched him for a moment.

****

Carl stared at his face in the mirror. It was covered with shaving cream. Behind him, he saw ten-year-old Lou and four-year-old Alice sneaking up on him. Suddenly he turned around and roared. Lou laughed out loud, while Alice squealed. He grabbed both girls, as they pretended to try to get away. It was part of the game. Before they ran off, Lou and Alice both had dabs of shaving cream on their noses.

****

Alice found herself brushing the tip of her nose.

"We're out of milk," Phoebe shouted from the kitchen.

Alice touched her nose again, as if to lock that memory in her mind. "Coming," she called.

"Oh, I didn't know you were up," Phoebe said, as

Alice entered the kitchen.

"Well, I am," Alice said. The mood was lost. She opened the top drawer and found a pen. A magnetic pad Alice had designed was stuck to the refrigerator. It had a floral design on the bottom. "Milk," she said as she wrote it down. "What else do we need?"

"I don't know what we need. I thought that was your job." Flory was in one of her moods. Alice ignored it because she didn't have the energy to do otherwise.

"Come on, Phoebe, we've got to go." Flory grabbed a granola bar and an apple and stuffed it in her backpack. "Granola bars," she said as she slammed the kitchen door to the garage.

"Bye, Mom." Phoebe gave her mother a peck on the cheek. "Coming," she yelled. The door slammed a second time.

Rodney came in the kitchen. "Sorry I missed the girls." Alice could hear the disappointment in his voice. He opened the pantry and got a box of cereal.

"We're out of milk," Alice told him.

Rodney sighed and put it back in the pantry. "Never mind," he said. He stuck two slices of bread in the toaster. "Looks like we might need more bread, too."

Alice added bread to the list. What was it Flory said we needed? She'd already forgotten. Milk, bread, and something else.

Soon Rodney was gone, and Alice was left to her thoughts, which was not the best place for her. She wandered back to her office and stared at the words on the laptop. It made her head spin. She closed the door to her office and climbed back into bed.

When Alice woke up, she had no idea what time it was. Picking up her phone, she saw it was almost three o'clock. Quickly she got dressed, putting on a pullover sweater and jeans instead of the sweats she so desperately wanted to wear. She brushed her hair and applied a little make-up. Then she went into the kitchen.

Dinner. What can we have for dinner? Alice opened the refrigerator. She didn't see anything. In the freezer she found a package of frozen chicken and pulled it out.

Then she went back to her bedroom to make the bed.

When Flory and Phoebe came home, there was a package of frozen chicken sitting on the counter.

"Gross," Flory said. She pulled out a bowl and put the chicken in it, running cool water over it. Then she sprayed the counter with anti-bacterial spray.

When Alice came in the kitchen Phoebe had her head in the refrigerator searching for something to eat. Flory sat at the table with a bag of pretzels.

"Hi girls. How was school?"

"Same." Flory and Phoebe spoke in unison.

"Any homework?"

"A little," Phoebe said.

"What about you, Flory?" Alice asked. There was no answer. "It's Friday night. What are you all doing? Any plans?" Both girls shook their heads.

"You keep forgetting. We have no friends," Phoebe said.

"Surely you have someone."

"Not really," Phoebe said.

"Well, I got some chicken out. We can fix chicken fingers tonight."

"The chicken is still frozen." Flory stared at her with her arms crossed. "So, I guess we can't."

Alice went to the pantry to see what was there. "We can have macaroni," she said as she pulled out a box.

"If I have to have boxed macaroni again, I'm going to vomit," Flory said.

"Me, too," Phoebe said.

"Then what?" The three of them stared at each other. Flory kept her arms crossed. Phoebe opened the pantry, then the refrigerator, then back to the pantry. Alice watched the process, unable to come up with any ideas of her own.

Flory grabbed her backpack and went to her room. "If I had any cash, I'd go get myself some food," she yelled as she left. "Just go to the store and get something!" The door to her bedroom slammed.

Alice watched Flory leave. She felt like crying, but not in front of Phoebe. What a failure.

"Mom, don't leave. I'll be back." Phoebe ran to her room. Alice wondered what this was about.

Phoebe returned with a brochure.

"What's this?" Alice asked.

"Do you remember when Flory and I went to that church in the city? I found this insert inside the bulletin." Phoebe handed it to her mother. "Read this."

"Stephen Ministers," Alice read aloud. *"Are you grieving? Have you lost your job? Do you have an ill family member? Are you going through a divorce? We can help with these situations and more. Contact our Stephen Ministry team, and we can set you up with a one-on-one caregiver to walk with you during your period of struggle."* Alice set the paper down.

"I think you should call them," Phoebe said. "Remember when you told Flory and me about the crisis counselor? You know I see her every Monday, and it helps."

"I don't know," Alice said. She stared at the words

on the paper. Would someone really be willing to help her? "It doesn't say how much it costs." That was a major issue. Rodney had told her they needed to cut back their expenses.

"Just call them and find out." Phoebe took the bulletin from her. "Here's the number," she said. "What have you got to lose?" She shrugged her shoulders.

Chapter 42

Alice dialed the number. She sat at the kitchen table with the start of last Friday's grocery list—milk, bread.

"First Presbyterian Church. How may I help you?"

"Uh, hello. I was interested in the Stephen Ministry program." Alice spoke tentatively.

"Certainly," the voice on the other end said. "Are you wanting to know about volunteer opportunities, or did you need information about having a caregiver?"

"I think I want to know about having a—what's it called?" Alice stammered.

"A caregiver," the woman said. There was a pause. "I think one of our Stephen Leaders is here around the church right now. Can you hold a minute, while I try to find him?"

"Sure," Alice said. The line clicked. She leaned her elbows on the table as she held the phone to her ear. What am I doing? This is never going to work. I should hang up.

"Hello, this is Jim. May I help you?"

"Yes, I think…I hope so. I'm interested in the Stephen Ministry program," Alice said.

"Okay. Fine. Did you want to volunteer, or are you in need of a caregiver?"

This time Alice had a better idea of what to say. "I'd like to know more about having a caregiver."

Jim proceeded to explain the program, how it was a

volunteer, one-on-one caring ministry. He told her one volunteer was assigned to a care receiver, and the relationship between the two was strictly confidential.

"What is the cost?" Alice asked, starting to feel a little better about the program.

"There is no cost," Jim said. "We are all trained lay volunteers."

"Oh!" Alice couldn't believe what she was hearing.

"What is your name?"

Alice froze. Did she have to tell this man her name? Finally, she said, "Alice."

"Are you a member of our church, Alice?"

She knew there was a catch. "No. I—we belong to a different church." There was a pause on the other end of the line. She knew it was too good to be true.

"I don't have my information here in front of me. But if we have a female caregiver available, I don't see why we can't help you. What is the issue you're struggling with?"

Alice paused. "My parents were killed in a car accident almost three years ago, and my sister died last year at the end of the summer." That sounded safe. If he knew who she was, Alice feared he might hang up. But maybe not. She couldn't tell. She hoped not.

"I'm so sorry! Can you give me your phone number? I'll have one of the female leaders contact you."

Alice hung up. What if there was someone out there who would be willing to help her? She almost felt energized. She walked back toward the bedrooms and glanced into the girls' rooms. When was the last time those sheets were washed? Alice stripped the beds and then did the same with their bed.

Alice was putting clean sheets on the beds when her

phone rang. She didn't recognize the number, but decided to answer it, hoping it was the church.

"Hello?"

"Hello. Is this Alice?" A cheery, upbeat voice was on the other end.

"Yes," Alice said, her heart beating.

"My name is Mary Beth, and I'm one of the Stephen Leaders at First Presbyterian Church. You talked to Jim this morning, is that right?

"Yes."

"I'd like to get a little more information from you so we can match you with the best caregiver for your needs."

"Okay." Alice hesitated, and she wondered if this chipper Mary Beth could sense her anxiety.

"Alice, I understand your problem may be confidential. Confidentiality is one of the most important parts of our program. You can trust me."

There was a pause, as if she was waiting for Alice to give the go-ahead. "Okay," she said finally.

"Can you tell me a little more about your situation? I understand you lost both of your parents and then your sister. Is that right?"

"Yes," Alice said. "My parents were killed by a drunk driver."

"How tragic! And how did your sister die?"

Alice panicked. She wasn't going to tell this person. Maybe this wasn't such a good idea after all.

"Alice?"

She couldn't say anything.

"It's okay. You don't have to tell me. Maybe that's something you'll be able to share with your caregiver. We understand sometimes there are situations too painful to speak about. I will pass that on to her. And by the way, that helps me understand your situation a little better."

Alice wondered if she knew what had happened.

Mary Beth continued, "Sometimes circumstances like suicide are complicated and hard to explain."

Alice let out a breath. "Yes."

"I'm going to check my list of Stephen Ministers, and one of them will give you a call, hopefully in the next day or so. Would you like for me to call you back and give you the name of the person?"

"Yes, that would be helpful," Alice said.

"Wonderful. I will give you a ring. It was so nice visiting with you, and again, I'm sorry for your losses."

Alice hung up the phone, again feeling both anxious and relieved, but more relieved this time.

A few days later Alice received a call from Mary Beth. A caregiver had been assigned to her, and her name was Laura. She would be contacting Alice soon to schedule a meeting time and place.

On Friday morning, the following week, Alice arrived at First Presbyterian Church at nine o'clock. It was a traditional-styled church, red brick, white trim, tall columns at the entrance, and a steeple. Alice was to go to the side entrance, and Laura would be waiting for her. From the sound of her voice, Alice envisioned an older woman, sophisticated, but calm, dressed in stylish clothes with maybe a string of pearls around her neck.

There was a heavy-set woman with blazing red hair waiting outside the church. She wore a brightly colored tent-like top over leggings. She appeared to be in her fifties. Oh dear, is this Laura?

"Are you Alice?" the woman asked. It was the calm

voice she had heard on the phone. "I'm Laura. Let's go inside."

Alice followed Laura into the church.

There was a large open area with some tables. Light filtered in from the skylight above. A teacher pushed a large stroller holding six or eight toddlers past them.

"We have a day care here," Laura explained. She led Alice up a set of stairs. "I thought we could meet in the library. It's quiet and private up there." Alice heard organ music playing a familiar hymn. "That's our organist. He likes to practice in the mornings."

The library was a cozy room, lined with Bibles, commentaries, and famous Christian authors on every wall. There was a large wooden table in the center of the room with heavy wooden chairs.

The two women got situated and Laura explained the guidelines of the Stephen Ministry program. "We will meet for about an hour once a week," Laura said. "And everything you say to me is strictly confidential. Confidentiality is a big part of Stephen Ministry. My main job is to listen. Listen and care. And support and encourage. I'm here for you," she said.

Alice didn't say anything. She felt tears beginning to form.

After a while, Laura broke the silence. "I understand you lost both your parents and your sister." She glanced at Alice's left hand. "You have a family? Any other relatives?"

"I'm married and have two teenage daughters. I have some aunts and uncles, but they live out of town. We don't see them very often."

During the hour Alice managed to avoid saying Lou's name or explain how she died. She wasn't ready for that. But she liked Laura and felt at ease with her. They left the church together and planned to meet at the same time next week. Alice found herself laughing as she shared some silly story about Phoebe at the end. It was nice. Nice to be laughing.

It was chilly outside, but the sun had finally come out. Since she was already out Alice decided to go to the store. She added ingredients for soup to her list—chicken, white beans, chilies, onion, and tomatillos. When she got home, she started the soup. Then she went outside and gathered some firewood. By the time Flory and Phoebe came home, there was soup on the stove and a fire in the fireplace.

Over the next several weeks Alice continued her visits with Laura. She looked forward to the time spent with her. She was safe. She cared, and she listened.

Toward the end of February during their visit Laura made a comment. "You know, Alice, you seem to be adjusting well to your parents' deaths. But you haven't mentioned anything about your sister. I don't think you've even told me her name or how she died. Can you share that with me?"

Alice froze. The charade was over. She knew she had to tell her, but she didn't know what the outcome would be. Would Laura tell her that she could no longer help her? That was Alice's fear, but she knew she had to be honest.

Alice took a deep breath. "I have to admit I've been avoiding this. But at the same time, this is why I need help." She paused to see what kind of reaction, if any, Laura gave. She merely nodded, as if to say, go on. "My sister's name is Lou Ella Sutton. She was killed during the mass shooting in Mineral Wells. Lou was responsible for killing eleven victims, and she was the twelfth." Alice said it. For the first time she spoke the words she had dreaded. She admitted the truth. Her sister had murdered eleven innocent victims.

There was silence between the two women. Alice watched Laura, expecting rejection. But it didn't happen.

Finally, Laura broke the silence. "What a terrible burden you've been carrying. I'm so sorry." Tears filled her eyes.

"You mean you aren't going to ask me to leave because of who my sister is?"

"Why would I do that?" Laura asked. "You came here for help, and you need it. Why would I abandon you when you finally open up? I can hardly imagine the suffering you and your family have gone through. How are they doing?"

And the dam burst. Alice talked nonstop for the remainder of their time together. She told about the police's visit, the media, how Flory and Phoebe had been treated at school, their failing business, her inability to cope, and the pending sale of the farm.

"I can see how the two are tied together—your parents' deaths and Lou's. I don't know how anyone could function under those circumstances. We must stop now, but we didn't even get to why Lou murdered these people. I know it said in the paper there was mental illness. Maybe we can talk about that next time."

Alice left the church feeling like a burden had been lifted. She had admitted to what Lou had done. At the same time, however, it was like opening a Pandora's box. All the feelings of guilt and shame and grief returned. She wanted to go home and crawl into bed. This ascending and descending, this roller coaster of emotions was exhausting. Why did she think she deserved to have a normal life again?

Chapter 43

"Tell me about your sister," Laura said.

Alice sat across from Laura at the table in the church library. "Where to start," she said.

"How about your first memories of her," Laura suggested.

Alice leaned back in her chair. "There was a picture on my dad's desk of Lou and me," she said. "I was just a baby, so Lou must have been six. She's holding me in her arms and looking at me as if I was the most important person in her life." Alice turned to Laura. "Of course, I don't remember it, but I always loved that picture."

"So, you and Lou were close?" Laura asked.

"When we were young, we were very close." Alice said. "Lou taught me everything she thought was important, like tying my shoes, how to swing, and ride a bike. There was a special tree on the road near our farm. It had a long branch shaped like the letter L. We liked to sit up there. One day we saw Dad driving home. When we yelled and waved, he stopped and backed up. We thought we were so clever!"

"She sounds like she was a wonderful big sister," Laura said.

"She was. Every Friday we helped Mom make Sutton cookies," Alice said.

"What are Sutton cookies?"

"They were my mom's special recipe. She used to

make them for bake sales, potluck suppers, or anytime she needed a dessert. We made a batch every Friday after school. Now my girls make them."

"How did Lou get along with your parents?"

Alice took a sip of coffee. She stared at the books lining the walls. "Lou was closest to my dad. She was more of a tomboy and loved to help him around the farm spending hours doing who knows what. Whenever Dad let her drive his old pickup in the pasture, Mom would get mad. Occasionally, Lou found an injured animal, and she'd bring it back to the house. Once she brought back a skunk. Mom about lost it." Alice chuckled. She hesitated before speaking again. "They enjoyed hunting together. Dad said Lou was a natural." Alice became quiet.

After a few minutes, Laura asked, "Is there something else you wanted to say?"

"No." Alice didn't want to think about it. If Dad hadn't taught Lou how to use a gun, would that have stopped her from killing those individuals?

Laura moved on. "What about your mother? Did she and Lou get along as well?"

Alice shook her head. "Mom and Lou seemed to butt heads. Mom would call Lou out on something or try to orchestrate her life, and Lou would retreat to her room. I was six years younger, so I didn't pay attention to their spats when she was a teenager." Alice paused and stared at the bookshelves again. "You know, Mom and Lou were so different. Lou was much more like Dad. But Mom, well, she was more…how do I say it? She cared about appearances. She was an artist and very talented. But she liked to have things a certain way. Her way." Alice shrugged her shoulders. How much of her mother did she have in herself, and how much of her dad?

Laura didn't say anything.

"When my parents finally told me what was wrong with Lou, they never spoke about it again, as if it was taboo. Especially Mom. Lou was diagnosed with schizophrenia when she was twenty, but they didn't tell me what was wrong with her until she was twenty-four. Looking back, it was so strange."

"But how could they not tell you? Didn't you realize something was wrong with your sister?"

"I guess I was preoccupied with my own life. If Lou was twenty when she had her first psychotic episode, then I was fourteen. I remember she'd act strange, do weird things like blockade her room, not eat certain things, and sometimes wear an old helmet when she left her room. And she'd say weird stuff like the government was spying on her, but I just thought she was odd. Then she'd disappear. When she came home, she acted like a zombie sometimes. I never knew what was wrong with her, and I don't think I really cared. How could I have been so selfish!" Alice took a tissue from her purse and wiped her nose and eyes.

Laura remained silent.

"Did you know the word, schizophrenia, was never spoken in our house? I never heard either of my parents speak of it. At the end of my senior year, my parents and I visited their attorney, Barney Anderson, who helps us now. That was when they told me, but Barney did most of the explaining. If something were to ever happen to my parents, I would become co-executor of their estate with Barney. They had set up a trust for Lou." Alice paused. "And then they died."

Alice stared at the books again. "Thanks, Mom," she

said. "*Schizophrenia.*" She crossed her arms, suddenly feeling uncomfortable. "When I told you what Lou did, that was the first time I had said Lou *killed* those innocent people. I couldn't say it. And I got upset if my family said it. Just like Mom."

Alice closed her eyes to prevent tears from forming. She was tired of crying. She took a deep breath. Opening her eyes, she said, "I feel guilty because I got to live a normal life, and Lou didn't."

Chapter 44

Lou had an appointment with a new social worker. She didn't want to go. She hated meeting these people who called themselves professionals. All they wanted to do was ask her questions. It was exhausting. She carried with her a fidget cube. It came from her self-soothe box, and Lou liked to have it when she went someplace new or met someone she didn't know.

She sat in the empty waiting room. The interior door opened, and Lou saw a woman come out. The woman seemed squishy and soft and reminded Lou of her grandmother. She had a nametag that said Loretta. She smiled and extended her hand.

"You must be Lou Ella. I'm Loretta."

"I know," Lou said. "That's what your nametag says." She continued to fiddle with her fidget cube.

Does she think you're stupid and can't read?

She glanced down and laughed. "So, it does." When Lou didn't shake her hand, she dropped it. "Are you ready to come into my office?"

"I guess so." Lou stood up. She wore a leather jacket over Carl's plaid flannel shirt. Her blue jeans were dirty, and her work boots, caked in mud, left tracks as she walked.

Loretta led the way into her office, directed Lou to a chair and offered her some water. She asked some preliminary questions, and Lou merely grunted in answer. Finally, she set down the folder containing Lou's history.

"Tell me, Lou Ella, are you happy?"

"No."

What a dumb question.

"Do you think you'll ever be happy?"

"No."

Again, stupid. And she thinks you're the dumb one!

"Never?"

"It's too exhausting." Lou kept her eyes down. Her hands stayed busy manipulating the fidget cube.

Loretta said nothing.

Don't say it! I know what you're thinking.

Finally looking up, Lou said, "I used to be happy…"

I told you not to say it!

"Tell me about it," Loretta said.

Don't tell her about when you thought you were happy. It's all a lie.

"When my little sister was born. When I had a best friend, Nora. When Alice and I used to make Sutton cookies with Mom." Lou paused, trying to remember more times when she was happy. "When I would go hunting with Dad. Anytime with my dog. When Dad let me drive his truck. When I found an injured animal and nursed it back to health. When I worked at Anne's Doggie Day Care…" Lou stared beyond Loretta and spoke as if she was stating a list.

"Those sound like really good times," Loretta said. "Can you think of any more?"

"No," Lou said.

Loretta didn't say anything. Lou's hands stayed busy with the fidget cube. Finally, she spoke. "If you don't feel happy, then how do you feel?"

The cube fell on the floor. Lou bent down to pick it up. "Tired," she said.

"Can you explain?"

Lou had an exasperated expression on her face. "Answering questions like this is tiresome." She indicated with a nod of her head in the direction of Loretta.

Why don't you tell her how you really feel? That she's a pain in the ass!

"Well, how can I help you, if I don't know what's going on with you?"

"You can't help me," Lou said.

There you go! You tell her! Bitch!

"Okay. Let me rephrase myself. How can I support you? Will you tell me that?"

"Stop asking questions. That's what you can do." Lou spoke with no emotion.

Loretta said nothing.

Good job! That's how to shut her up!

"Can I be your friend?" Loretta asked.

Stop it! I'm going to vomit!

"I guess." Lou said.

"What's important for friends to know about you, Lou Ella?"

"First of all, don't call me Lou Ella. My name is Lou."

"Okay, Lou."

Lou picked up the fidget cube. "It's important to have someone I can call on if I need help," she said.

No, it's not!

"Okay. I would like to do that for you."

Lou glanced at the social worker and nodded her

head.

"What kinds of things would you need help with? Maybe picking up a prescription or…"

"No." Lou seemed to struggle.

Shut up! Don't say anything more. I'm warning you!

She didn't know whether to tell Loretta how she could help or not. "Sometimes…the voices, well, I can't tell if what they're saying is real or not…and sometimes it's too much, and I'm scared."

You're an idiot!

"You could call me if you felt afraid."

"Spies are trying to steal my thoughts and do experiments on them. The government hired the spies. Sometimes I can be a danger to myself. And sometimes the voices tell me to hurt other people." Lou spoke as if she was reading from a list.

Untrue! Untrue! Liar! Liar!

"Do you? Hurt other people?"

"No."

A thought occurred to Lou. "How do I know you're not one of them?"

"I'm not a spy," Loretta said. "I wouldn't know how to be one, and I don't know how to steal someone's thoughts. Trust me."

She is a spy! Don't trust her!

Lou shrugged her shoulders, as if to say, whatever.

Loretta hesitated. "Since you know I'm not a spy, and I want to be your friend and help you, can I ask you something?"

"Maybe…"

"If you don't want to answer, you don't have to."

Don't answer her stupid questions!

"Some questions stress me out. They make me

anxious. Then I can't sit still, and I start to pace. I can walk for hours."

"The only reason I want to ask you this question is because I want to be a helping friend. And friends must be honest with each other. Right?"

"I guess so," Lou said.

Loretta leaned toward her. "Lou, are you taking your medicine right now?"

Don't tell her!

"Yes," she said. "I don't want to, but my dad said it helps me. I told him I don't need it, but he explained to me when I stop taking it, I end up in the hospital."

"Is that true?"

"I guess so."

"And you don't want to go back to the hospital."

"No. They hook me up to a machine and put drugs in my veins. I get so drugged out I can't talk."

"Does the medication help you?"

"I guess so."

No, it doesn't!

"How?"

"The voices are not as loud, so I can ignore them easier."

"Do you hear the voices now?" Loretta asked.

"Yes."

"But you can ignore them?"

"Yes."

You are worthless, totally worthless!

Lou stared at the fidget cube. She knew Loretta was watching her.

"Lou, what do you wish you could do?"

"I wish I didn't have to put on a face, you know, pretend to be normal. It's exhausting. If I don't feel like speaking, I wish I could just be silent. Or not go to my doctor's appointments if I don't feel like it. Or anyplace." Lou paused, and she showed the first sign of emotion. "I hate it when I see someone who knew me before, because I know I'm not who I used to be."

There was silence. Then speaking softly, Loretta asked, "What do you see in your future?"

"Nothing. A long empty road of nothing. Nothingness every day. The same thing. Hopeless."

"What would give you hope?"

Lou turned and looked at Loretta. She shrugged her shoulders.

"Lou, I know your parents care. And I care."

Lou glanced at Loretta. Her face had changed. She had a pig's snout instead of a nose, and she smelled like pancakes with syrup.

Chapter 45

2012

Donned in her oversized sun hat, Florence was on her hands and knees weeding her vegetable garden. The tomato plants had a few tiny green tomatoes. Peppers, okra, beans, and squash were all thriving. But so were the weeds.

Florence leaned back on her heels and stretched. She wiped her brow with her shirtsleeve. She preferred gardening in the morning before it became too hot, but it was already sweltering. She glanced toward the house. Lou was inside, probably in her room. Carl was in the barn working on his John Deere. Alice and her family were coming over that evening for hamburgers to celebrate their anniversary. Florence shook her head. The wedding ceremony was supposed to have taken place at the farm. Alice was crushed, but it couldn't be helped. She sighed.

Florence tried to block out those days when they first realized something was wrong with Lou. It had come on gradually at first. Then Lou began to withdraw and say strange things about the government trying to read her thoughts. Florence remembered the first time Lou came downstairs wearing her bicycle helmet. She refused to take it off because it was protecting her thoughts from being stolen by the government. It was so bizarre to Florence she couldn't even grasp what was going on. Why would Lou say something so ridiculous? The change in Lou was frightening. Then, after her sophomore year, Lou never went back to school.

Schizophrenia. The word conjured up images from bad movies of zombie-like bodies all dressed in white, slumped in chairs, strapped in beds, leaning against walls. Some stared into space. Some were moaning or yelling. It was horrifying.

The psychiatrist had told them, "Your daughter is schizophrenic. There is no cure. She will never be the same again."

Florence had felt like someone had knocked the air out of her. She couldn't catch her breath. Carl, sitting in the metal chair next to her, had squeezed her hand so hard she thought he had broken it. The doctor might as well have told them Lou had had her head cut off, and it would never grow back. Then he handed them a printed sheet about the disease.

"Read this," he said. "If you have any questions, call the office. We will see your daughter in two weeks, and she has enough medication to last until her appointment." Then he was gone.

After the doctor left, Carl leaned over and whispered to Florence. "We'll get through this." Dear Carl. He always saw light at the end of every tunnel. He never gave up. Carl used to call Lou the animal whisperer. She was always bringing home a stray pet, or an injured animal, or abandoned babies. Lou had planned to become a veterinarian, and she would have been a good one. Florence rubbed her forehead. Those were dark days.

After the first psychotic episode at Buffalo Springs, it became a revolving door of hospital stays, released

293

with medication and appointments, temporary compliance and back to the downward spiral toward another psychotic episode. Florence didn't know how to get them off this horrific merry-go-round. Carl, once again, was better at getting Lou to understand. But even he couldn't pierce the bubble of non-reality surrounding Lou when she became psychotic.

And there was always the question, what if *she* had done something to cause Lou's schizophrenia? But Carl had told her that was an old wives' tale. Florence stared at her hands, her fingertips stained from the weeds and the dirt. She hoped he was right.

Florence resumed pulling weeds, and soon there was a pile of them next to the pepper plants. She stood up and brushed the red Oklahoma dirt from her shorts. She dumped the weeds into the wheelbarrow. Then proceeded to do some pruning on her rosebushes.

Florence had planted a rose bush on either side of the front door, for each baby she lost—pink roses for the girl and yellow roses for the boy. She had had complications when she was pregnant with Lou. But when Lou was born, she was a healthy baby. Then came the two babies in between—a late-term miscarriage, followed by a stillbirth. When Florence was pregnant with Alice, she felt like she was waiting for disaster to happen again. But six years after Lou, came little Alice.

Florence planned the family evening in her head as she continued doing yard work. Carl was going to grill hamburgers. She had fresh corn on the cob she planned to husk in the afternoon. For dessert, homemade ice cream and Sutton cookies.

It would be nice if Lou offered to help this afternoon. But she knew that wouldn't happen. She didn't have much success initiating a positive response from Lou. Florence hoped Carl could talk to her. She felt her neck tighten.

Chapter 46

"I have blood on my hands," Alice stared at her hands. Of course, there was no blood.

"Why do you say that?" Laura asked.

Alice was silent. She didn't want to admit what she thought. Slowly she spoke. "I feel I'm responsible for the deaths of those people."

"The ones from the shooting in Mineral Wells?"

Alice nodded.

A minute passed, then another. Laura didn't ask any more questions.

Finally, Alice spoke. "If I had been more aware of Lou's needs, if I had *tried* to help her, or even cared…" She put her face in her hands and sobbed.

Laura pushed the tissue box across the table, but she didn't speak.

Eventually Alice took a tissue and wiped the tears from her face. Her mascara left dark circles under her eyes. "I used to have this recurring nightmare—before I started seeing you. Someone was falling, and I tried to reach out and grab an arm to keep that person from falling. I always woke up before they fell. But I was never able to help. And I never saw the face. Except one morning." Alice paused and took a deep breath. "It was Lou's face." She began to cry again.

Alice's eyes pleaded with Laura to answer the impossible question. "How do I undo all the mistakes

I've made in the past? If I had been there for Lou, if I had been on top of her medical issues, then she might not have slipped through the cracks." Alice slumped in the chair. It was her fault those innocent people had died.

"I disagree," Laura said.

"About what?"

"You aren't responsible for the deaths of the people who died in Mineral Wells that night. You didn't pull the trigger," Laura said.

"No, but I could have done something to prevent Lou from doing so." Alice wadded the damp tissue in her hands.

"Alice," Laura said after a moment. "You're the one who told me your parents never spoke of Lou's schizophrenia after the meeting when you were eighteen. How were you supposed to know what to do when they wouldn't talk about it?"

"Yes, but..." Alice felt the need to defend her parents.

"I'm not faulting your parents. I want you to understand that. I think the system of how we deal with mental illness is probably more at fault than anything." Laura sighed. "Think about it. There is a stigma attached to mental illness. No one talks about it. Families are ashamed. Our society doesn't know how to handle them." Laura reached into her purse and pulled out a brochure. She pushed it across the table. "Alice, I read about schizophrenia after we started meeting. It's the worst of all mental illnesses, and there's no cure. They used to house the seriously mentally ill in asylums. Then they shut down all the hospitals, but there was no place for them to go. Today, many of them are either homeless or in prison, and those are the worst places for a person if they are mentally ill."

"So, what am I to do?" Alice was at a loss.

Laura picked up the brochure. "Call this organization. Or go by there." She handed Alice the brochure.

Alice read it and immediately felt overwhelmed.

What to do in a crisis? Who do I contact if I'm worried a loved one might hurt himself or others? How do I get help? What are the signs of an imminent psychiatric crisis? Support Groups. Resources. Educational programs.

"I could go with you," Laura said softly.

"Thanks," Alice said. "This is something I could have used ten or twenty years ago. but no one will want to deal with me now. I'm the example of what *not* to do. No one wants to be around the sister of a mass murderer." She set the brochure on the table and stared at her hands, as if seeing the blood no one else could.

"I do," Laura said.

Alice looked up. Laura smiled and nodded.

"Do you think you're the only person whose family member has done something terrible? That's what that organization is here for. Do you remember what I said to you when you finally told me about Lou? That's what I'm here for. For people who are hurting, and you're hurting."

"Yes, but what about the families of the victims? How do I go there? How do I navigate the guilt that never seems to go away?"

"Have you thought of writing them a letter?"

"I've thought about it, but I don't know where to start. What would I say? How would they take it?"

Laura shrugged her shoulders. "I don't know. But a

genuine apology," and she patted her heart, "from the heart, can often break barriers. Think about it."

Laura glanced at her watch, and Alice stuffed the used tissue inside her purse. She pushed back the chair and stood, ready to leave.

"I just thought of something," Laura said.

Alice paused.

"Were you able to forgive the man who killed your parents?"

Alice froze. Jordan Hall. How could she ever forgive him? He killed both her parents. He was drunk and crossed the median, hitting them head-on, walking away with a broken collar bone and a couple of cracked ribs. This was different, she wanted to tell herself.

Alice shook her head.

"It's complicated, isn't it? But at the same time, they're connected. Don't you think?" Laura walked around the table and put her hand on Alice's shoulder. "Think about it."

The two of them walked out of the library together. They shifted to small talk as they descended the stairs. Toddlers walked past in a line, each one holding on to a rope. One teacher was in front, and one was behind. They sang, "Jesus Loves Me."

Alice watched them go by. How young and innocent they were. Who would they become? What would their lives be like? Did Jordan know his life would change on that night? Had he sung "Jesus Loves Me" as a child?

She didn't know the answers.

Chapter 47

Alice sat up in bed. The setting moon seen through the window illuminated the room, casting faint shadows. Her face was wet, and so was her pillow. Had she been crying? Both her parents were dead, yet she had heard them speak. She must have been dreaming. It was as if they wanted to convey something to her, and she *felt* her dad pat her on the leg. It brought back memories of him coming into her room. He'd sit next to her, and he'd pat her leg. Reassurance, support, comfort. That's what he gave her, and she sensed that now.

Alice flopped the damp pillow over and closed her eyes. Next to her Rodney was on his back, snoring. It was a long time before she fell asleep. When Rodney's alarm went off, she woke up with the usual feeling of dread that greeted her each morning. On cue, a sick feeling in the pit of her stomach appeared out of nowhere. Yet, her dream lingered. Hope mixed with anxiety. *What was the point?* collided with a belief that something better was out there. It was unsettling and confusing and hopeful at the same time.

Alice then remembered it was the anniversary of her parents' deaths. Maybe that was why she had the dream. It had been three years. "I miss you, Mom and Dad," she whispered.

Alice thought about the day her parents were killed. How she hated the man who killed her parents! How could she forgive him?

Jordan Hall.

Alice climbed out of bed and went into the bathroom to wash her face and brush her teeth. She spit in the sink, and said, "He snuffed out their lives."

"Who snuffed out whose lives?" Rodney walked past her with a towel and turned on the shower.

"Jordan Hall," Alice said.

Rodney dropped his shorts and stepped into the shower. "Name sounds familiar. Who is he?" he called over the sound of the water.

"He's the one who killed my parents. Today is the third anniversary of their deaths." Alice shouted back.

She remembered the emotional testimony Rodney gave at his hearing. Alice was too upset, and Lou had disappeared. She thought of the satisfaction she had felt when the judge found him guilty of vehicular manslaughter, and he shuffled out of the courtroom in cuffs. He had gotten what he deserved. Jordan Hall had been sentenced to eight years in prison.

The words tossed around came back to Alice—gross negligence and reckless behavior versus no prior convictions, and something about medical school. The verdict would ruin any dreams he had for his future. He had that coming. But he had been accepted to medical school. It only took one time getting behind the wheel when drunk to kill her parents. No, she could never forgive him.

Rodney stepped out of the shower, wrapped in his towel. "Those were sad times," he said.

"Do you remember what we were doing when we found out?"

"Of course, I do."

****

March 22, 2013

"Flory should be home from the movies soon," Alice said to Rodney. It was Friday night, and they were watching an old Steve McQueen movie. Alice was already in her pajamas, and Rodney had on a pair of sweats. Neither of the girls was home. Flory had gone out with some friends, and Phoebe was spending the night with Sadie.

The doorbell rang.

"That's funny," Alice said. "Flory must have forgotten her key. Put the movie on pause while I answer the door," she said.

It wasn't Flory. There were two police officers at the door. From the expressions on their faces, Alice knew something bad had happened.

"Are you Alice Bennett?"

Immediately she thought of Flory and couldn't speak.

"Mrs. Bennett, may we come inside?" The taller of the two officers spoke. His tone was gentle.

Instead of letting them in, Alice called out to Rodney. "Something's happened! There are two police at the door."

Rodney came up behind her, and Alice felt herself shaking. *Dear God,* she pleaded, *please don't let Flory be hurt.*

"Are you Mr. Bennett?" The taller officer seemed to be in charge. The other officer was a woman.

"Yes. Come in and have a seat in the living room," Rodney said, and he led the way. Alice and Rodney sat next to each other on the sofa facing the large picture window. The woman sat in the armchair, while the taller officer stood behind her.

"Mr. and Mrs. Bennett, I'm Officer Chris Spencer, and this is my partner, Officer Sally Johnston." The two of them looked at Alice. "Mrs. Bennett…"

"No!" Alice didn't know what had happened, but she knew it was bad. She covered her mouth. And waited.

Officer Johnston spoke. "Mrs. Bennett, I'm very sorry to report to you there was an accident on I-35."

Why would Flory be out there? It didn't make sense.

"Carl and Florence?" Rodney asked.

"Yes." She nodded her head.

"Are they okay?"

"No," she said, shaking her head.

"Dead?" Rodney put his arm around Alice and held her tight.

They both nodded.

Alice covered her face and sobbed. Her parents. Dead. She had talked to them that afternoon. They had made reservations at a small dinner club to celebrate their seventieth birthdays.

"What happened?" Rodney asked.

Officer Spencer explained a young man, drunk, had crossed the median and hit them head on. They died instantly.

****

"I'll never forgive him," Alice said. She realized her hands were shaking.

Memories of her parents' deaths surfaced throughout the day. Alice found it hard to concentrate. There had been an abundance of support from the community. Yet none of it had eased the pain. When they had the hearing, Lou had already disappeared. Alice didn't know where she was, but that was the least of her worries.

Eventually, Alice found a way to return to normal. Now she was in another tailspin, yet she struggled to see the correlation. The dream from the night before disappeared from her mind and was replaced with a resurgence of anger at Jordan Hall.

On Friday, when she met with Laura, Alice announced, "Wednesday was the anniversary of my parents' death."

"How was that day for you?" Laura asked.

Alice told her about the dream and about Jordan Hall. She mentioned the anger she felt.

"You're struggling with your anger toward this man who killed your parents. I wonder if any of the victims' families are having the same problem? I wonder if finding out about Jordan might give you some insight into their situation?"

Alice regarded Laura. "I know what you're saying is probably right, but I can't wrap my mind around it. I mean, he killed my parents. What am I supposed to do with that?"

Laura didn't reply.

"Both of their lives snuffed out in an instant. There was nothing they could do." She began sobbing.

Laura spoke. "Then you know exactly how these eleven families feel." She paused. "And that's really hard."

Alice laid her head on the table. She shook her head. How was she supposed to reconcile the pain of the loss of her parents with the guilt she felt for what her sister did to the eleven families? Her greatest fear reared its ugly head once again. What could she have done? Could she have prevented Lou from pulling the trigger?

Eventually Laura spoke. "The first thing you told me, after you said it had been three years since your parents' death, was the dream you had. Tell me again how it made you feel."

Alice wiped her face. "Comfort. And assurance. And hope."

Laura nodded with each statement Alice said. She leaned across the table toward Alice and said, as if it was a secret between the two of them. "So, how best do you think you could navigate all this? The anger at Jordan, confusion, guilt, and the fear?"

Chapter 48

March 22, 2013

Carl locked his office door and walked across campus to the faculty parking lot. He caught himself searching for Lou, but, of course, she wasn't there. She no longer attended school. She hadn't for twenty-five years, but the habit of looking for her never left him. He missed Lou. He missed the person who used to be his daughter. Now he had to learn how to love the person who had replaced her.

"Your daughter is schizophrenic. She will never get better." That was what the doctor had told them. Did the doctor realize the death sentence he gave them? Why didn't he just come out and say, "The daughter that you knew and loved no longer exists." If they had been told Lou had cancer, the whole community would have rallied around them. But schizophrenia? He might as well have told us Lou's brain had been taken over by aliens.

Carl sighed. Leprosy would be better than this. Last Sunday Pastor Dunham had preached his sermon on the ten lepers. He had gone to great lengths to explain how much those individuals were avoided.

"Lepers, back in Jesus' time, were considered unclean. According to Hebrew law, they had to live outside the city walls and were required to call out, 'Unclean! Unclean!' to any passerby. The Jewish people believed that leprosy was punishment from God."

Punishment from God. Carl could not get that out of his head. Yet, he didn't believe that for the lepers, and he didn't believe it for Lou. Nor for anyone else with this horrible disease.

"...they were outcasts, untouchables, unloved, unaccepted..."

Carl didn't want that fate for Lou. He was determined to do everything he could to protect her and prevent that from happening. But how? It was hard when her behavior had become so bizarre. Every time there was a story in the newspaper about some homeless person attacking someone, or being attacked, or some humiliating act like urinating in public, or, worse, being found frozen to death or beaten to death, Carl became anxious. What if that happened to Lou?

After Lou's diagnosis, Carl became her primary caregiver, and Florence took care of the house and Alice. They both rearranged their teaching schedules, so someone was always available in case of an emergency. This arrangement became their way of life for twenty-five years.

Carl spotted a woman with her dog on a leash. Lou and Lucky. Lou and Charlie. Lou and Schroeder. His chest tightened. Schroeder had died last fall. Yet Lou hadn't seemed to notice. But recently, she seemed to be in a good space. She was taking her medication and going to her appointments. Maybe Lou was going to be okay. She seemed to understand she had to take her medication, and it was evident the new psychiatrist and social worker were positive factors.

Carl drove toward the farm. He rolled down his window and inhaled. Exhaling, he sighed again. This time it was with delight, instead of dread. He loved springtime. He loved getting on his hands and knees and helping Florence plant her vegetable garden. He loved the earthy smell of the soil, the freshness after rain, the expectation of new leaves waiting to open. It reminded him that life *was* good, and he was a lucky man. Sure, like everyone else, they had their share of challenges. But also, great blessings.

And tonight, he and Florence were going into the city for an early celebration of their seventieth birthdays. Carl turned into the drive and parked his truck near the barn. He entered the house through the kitchen, turning on the tea kettle as he walked past.

"Hi, Lou, I'm home," he called out as he climbed the stairs. He seemed to have a bounce in his step.

"Hi, Dad."

Carl peeked in at his forty-five-year-old daughter. She sat cross-legged on her bed viewing something on her laptop. He walked over and sat next to her on her bed. "What are you reading about?"

Lou turned the screen so he could see. There was a photograph of wild horses. "I'm reading about how to train wild horses."

"Well, if anyone can do it, you can." Carl stood up and kissed Lou on the top of her head. "You know Mom and I are going out tonight."

"Yes."

"I'm going out on the back porch and enjoy the fresh air. Do you want to come out?"

"No thanks."

"Okay. I'm making some iced tea if you'd like some."

"Okay."

Carl stood at the door and blew Lou a kiss. When was the last time he had done that? She reached up, grabbed it, and patted her cheek. He smiled.

Chapter 49

March 22, 2013

Florence finished sweeping the paper scraps into the trashcan. Damp paint brushes lay on the counter to dry. She walked carefully to avoid the long strips of butcher paper still wet with paint covering most of the floor. They were signs for the school-wide fundraiser. Florence's art classroom had been taken over that afternoon by the student council making signs.

She glanced around the room. Florence loved her space. She had been teaching art at the high school for over thirty years, and she cherished the years Alice took classes from her the most. She was so talented.

Florence walked over to her desk and picked up the photo of their family—all seven of them. It had been their wedding anniversary, and they had hired a photographer to take the family photo at the farm. The flowers were spectacular, and the Oklahoma sky was a brilliant blue. There were Alice and her crew—the girls sitting on the ground, Alice and Rodney behind them— then herself, Carl, and Lou. Everyone was dressed for a day at the farm, shorts and T-shirts. That is, everyone except Lou. She had on what she always wore—blue jeans, a leather jacket, and her heavy work boots. Florence remembered trying to get Lou at least to take off the jacket for the picture. That almost became a disaster, as Lou started to walk away. Only Carl could convince her to come back and be in the photo. How had something so simple as taking a picture become a production? Florence felt her shoulders tighten.

Schizophrenia. She hated the word. It was a label, and nothing about the connotations was good. She sighed heavily just thinking about it. But Carl reminded her the treatment had changed dramatically since Lou's first psychotic episode in 1988.

"Lou has anosognosia," Carl told her after Lou's last release from the hospital. "She doesn't believe she's ill, and she believes the drugs are poison." The new social worker and psychiatrist working with Lou were making a difference.

That was when Florence began to better understand Lou.

Florence drove out of the high school parking lot. Thirty years of memories were in that building. She took her time driving home, going past old hangouts and places that had left an indelible mark on their lives. She drove past Rose Rock Park, a favorite of Lou and Alice when they were young.

****

"Come on, Al-Pal, you can do it," Lou said, encouraging Alice. "Just pump your legs and move your body back and forth." Lou watched Alice attempt to swing by herself, but her movements were more rigid than fluid. Lou gave her one more big push, and then ran over to the swing next to her. "Like this," she said, as she swayed in rhythm with the swing. Soon Lou was soaring. And then she jumped, almost flying before she landed.

Lou ran around behind Alice and pushed her again. "Try one more time," she said.

"Give me five big pushes and see if I can do it by

myself."

****

And she did.

Florence noticed the two rose bushes on either side of the front door as she returned home. New spring growth appeared on each of them. She had planted them over forty years ago for the two babies she lost.

Florence entered the old, stone farmhouse, greeted by the smell of spring. She made her way to the back porch where she knew the door must be open.

"There you are," she said. Carl sat on one of the old wicker rocking chairs. His gray hair curled over his collar, and the years spent outside gave his face a weathered appearance.

"Why it's my lovely bride," he said. "Come sit with me." Carl patted the rocking chair next to him. "I made some iced tea. Want some?"

"Good idea. I'll get it myself," Florence said. A strand of silver hair slipped down and tickled her nose. She blew it up from her face and patted it back in place. At almost seventy, Florence had aged well and gracefully.

A few minutes later the screen door creaked then slammed shut. Such familiar, comforting sounds. Florence joined Carl on the porch. It faced her vegetable garden, the grove of apple trees, and the barn. Beyond the trees was the pond. Florence glanced at Carl, thinking of how he had taught Lou and Alice the fine art of tadpole catching and then passed the tradition to his granddaughters.

The two of them sat together, each in their own thoughts. A cardinal chirped then flew past. Carl seemed so relaxed and peaceful. Finally, Florence broke the silence. "What are you thinking?" she asked.

"I'm thinking about how lucky I am." Carl leaned over and planted a kiss on Florence's cheek. "How about you?"

She shook her head. "Nothing. Just sitting." She took a sip of tea and gazed at the garden. The tender leaves of sugar snap peas were beginning to come up, and the green tips of onions poked out of the dirt.

"After fifty years, you can't fool me," Carl said. "What's on your mind?"

"You're thinking of how lucky you are, and I'm feeling sorry for myself. I was thinking of Lou and what we're going to do with her. Someday we'll be gone…"

"Don't say that. We're both healthy, and Lou's in a good space right now. She's taking her meds and goes to her appointments. Barney has all the information should anything happen to us. But it won't."

Florence wasn't convinced. She glanced at her watch, and then stood up quickly, almost spilling her tea. "We're going to be late if we don't leave soon." They had planned an evening out to celebrate their birthdays, which were mere weeks apart.

When Florence went upstairs to change her clothes, she noticed Lou's door was ajar. She started to enter her own room but changed her mind.

"Hi, Lou. What are you doing?" Florence asked as she knocked on the door. She found Lou sitting on her bed, just like she used to as a teenager.

"Reading," Lou said.

Florence ventured into the room. "What are you reading?"

Lou turned the laptop to show her mother. "It's an article about how to train wild horses."

"That sounds interesting," Florence said.

Lou didn't reply. She had resumed reading.

"Lou," Florence said, "you know we're going out tonight. If you need anything, call us. Or you can call Alice."

"I know, Mom," Lou answered but didn't look up.

Florence turned and walked to the door, but something prompted her to go back. She kissed the top of Lou's head. "I love you," she said.

"Love you, too."

Twenty minutes later Carl and Florence left the house. They never returned home.

Chapter 50

Alice had no idea what it entailed to visit someone in prison. First, she needed to find where Jordan Hall was serving his sentence. Then she had to submit a visitor's request form and get on his visitation list. There was a list of dos and don'ts, such as, what to wear and what not to, what could and could not be brought.

For reasons she couldn't explain, Alice had decided she wanted to meet Jordan Hall. How could she expect the eleven families to forgive her if she still harbored hatred toward him? Who *was* this person who had plowed into her parents? The facts the defense laid out at his hearing were that he had been accepted to medical school, and this was his first offense. At his sentencing the judge announced him guilty of two counts of vehicular manslaughter. That was all she knew about him. He was seven years older than Flory, and *his life was over*.

Six weeks later, before the end of school, Alice drove to the state penitentiary. Upon arrival, she stopped at the gate where a guard asked her name and to see some identification. There was a sign directing her to visitor's parking. She found a spot and turned off the ignition. Her heart raced. She felt like the walls were closing in on her as she stared at the concrete structure surrounded by a chain-link fence and barbed wire. Her anxiety had returned. Alice put her ID and keys into a zip-lock bag and left her purse underneath her seat in the car. Then she locked her car. Dressed in a pair of khaki pants and a striped top, she walked toward the imposing building.

At the entrance Alice showed her identification again. Her plastic bag went through the x-ray machine, and the guard scanned her with a metal detector. She was buzzed through two more sets of metal doors before she was led down a hallway toward the visitor's room. The metal doors slammed shut behind her, causing Alice to jump. Her breathing became rapid, and she leaned against the wall until the dizziness passed. She was locked in, and she couldn't leave unless someone let her out. This must be what the inmates experienced every day. Locked up with no way out.

The guard opened the door to the visiting area. Alice's heart was racing such that she didn't know if she could talk. She saw a thin, young man at a table by himself dressed in the standard orange prison uniform. His hair hung over his eyes, shabby and unkempt, and he had several days' growth of facial hair. He stared at Alice with dubious curiosity.

"Are you Jordan Hall?" Alice heard the tentativeness in her voice. It was as if she was afraid of being there. She was.

"Yes." He sat slumped at a low, round table with four plastic chairs around it. In fact, the entire room consisted of low, round tables with plastic chairs. Other inmates with visitors were seated around the room. The guard stood at the door.

"Hi, Jordan. Alice Bennett." She extended her hand. When he didn't respond, she dropped it. Alice waited for Jordan to offer her a seat, but he didn't. "May I sit down?"

He shrugged his shoulders.

Alice pulled out a chair opposite him and sat down. Neither of them spoke. She glanced around the room. At one table she saw a couple with their heads together, holding hands. Another table she presumed a father was visiting his son. She didn't know what to say. But seeing him in person, despondent, and knowing he was locked up like a caged animal for years gave her a hopeless feeling. There seemed to be no light at the end of the tunnel for him.

Before she could say anything, Jordan spoke. "Why did you come? I know who you are." He spit the words out of his mouth, as if he was trying to get rid of them.

Caught off guard, Alice found herself asking the same question. Why did I come? Maybe this wasn't such a good idea.

Jordan's expressionless face had changed to a scowl. "What do you want from me? I'm paying for it, aren't I? I'm doing my time."

"You know, I'm not sure why I came." Alice found herself saying something she didn't know she was going to say. "But it wasn't to accuse or torment you or bring up the past." She took a deep breath. "May I call you Jordan?"

He nodded.

"I need to make amends."

The scowl dissipated partially, like fog lifting as the sun burned it off. Alice could tell he still didn't trust her, and she didn't blame him.

Without warning something changed. Alice saw Jordan as another human being, not as a convict, nor the person who was responsible for the deaths of her parents, but a lost person, like herself. She couldn't explain it.

"Are you familiar with the mass shooting last year in Mineral Wells?" These were words Alice struggled with. Yet here she was, ready to tell him about Lou.

"Yeah. What about it?"

"Do you remember who killed those people?"

"No." He shook his head, as if with indifference.

"The killer's name was Lou Sutton, and she was my sister."

Jordan raised his head and stared at Alice. "Holy shit!" Jordan leaned back in the chair. Alice could tell he was trying to figure out the entire scenario.

Alice nodded. "You said it. Now I have an idea of what you're going through, except I'm not in prison."

Jordan seemed to have lost his suspicion of her. "So, why'd she do it? Was she crazy or something?"

"Lou was schizophrenic. She hadn't been taking her medication. I didn't even know where she lived. Then I found out it was my sister who killed them."

Jordan whistled. "Man, that's tough. You've got a shitload of angry people on your back, don't you?"

Alice nodded her head. "Yeah. We're kind of in the same boat."

The two of them sat in silence. An occasional laugh, a sob, the quiet conversations of the other visitors could be heard in the room.

Alice asked, "Why did you accept me on your visitors' list? I knew I was taking a chance when I realized you had to approve of anyone added to your list."

Jordan examined his right hand and found a fingernail that hadn't been bitten to the quick. He chewed on it until it began to bleed. He said, "You're the first visitor I've had since last summer. I figured anyone was better than no one."

Alice stared at his shaggy head in disbelief. She didn't know what to say. Finally, she asked, "What about your family? Surely, they come to visit."

Jordan shook his head. "My parents disowned me when everything happened. I have an older sister, but she just had a baby, and she lives a couple of hours away."

The guard at the door interrupted their conversation. "Visiting time is over."

Alice and Jordan pushed back their chairs. They stood facing each other. He was almost a foot taller, and she was almost twenty years older. An unspoken understanding seemed to pass between them.

Jordan held out his hand. "Thank you for coming."

Alice shook it. "I'm glad I did. Can I come back?"

"Yes. That would be nice."

Chapter 51

Springtime in Oklahoma was glorious. Splashes of the lime-green new leaves reminded Flory of the sponge paintings she made in kindergarten. Wild red buds popped with magenta blossoms. Maple trees dropped their seeds, the ones Flory and Phoebe used to toss in the air and watch whirl like mini helicopters. Phoebe practically bounced around the house and to and from school. Even Flory's spirits seemed to rise with the warm weather. That is, until reminders of her upcoming graduation and end-of-school events were plastered everywhere in the school. All promises from last spring about her upcoming senior year disappeared.

"Next spring, we'll go shopping for your prom dress and for a graduation outfit," Alice had promised. This was supposed to be the best year of her life. But it wasn't going to happen.

Flory had lost her honor society status, and no one had noticed, including her parents. Most of her classmates had already been accepted to universities. She overheard talk of spending weekends at state universities and colleges, visiting sorority and fraternity houses, including Oklahoma A&M in Mineral Wells, where the shooting had occurred.

Flory didn't know what she wanted to do, and no one had asked her. She had never felt so alone. Should she even go to college? She knew money was tight.

Maybe she should just find a job. But what could she do? What did she *want* to do? Flory had dropped out of basketball when it became obvious that she would be the only senior girl not to be on varsity. She had become a nothing. What do I want to do with my life? Besides getting away from Junction, she had no idea.

Flory sat alone in Alice's car in the driveway. Phoebe had stayed after school and didn't need to be picked up until five. Listening to music on her phone, she heard a tapping on the window. Peering into the passenger side was their neighbor, Mrs. Callahan. She was old. And nosey. Not who Flory wanted to see, but it was too late. She couldn't ignore her. That would be rude.

Slowly Flory gathered her backpack and opened the car door. "Hi, Mrs. Callahan. What can I do for you?"

"I looked out my window and saw your mother's car in the driveway. Then I saw someone was in it. And I waited to see who it was. And when you didn't come out, I got worried maybe something was wrong. I put on my sweater and walked over. And that's why I'm here." She paused. "Are you okay?"

"Yes, ma'am. Thank you. I was just sitting in the car. That's all."

Mrs. Callahan had shrunk to about five feet, and Flory was almost five ten. Her back curved and her shoulders hunched up, as if she was an old turtle standing on its hind legs. Her hair was completely white, and curls fluffed around her face. Underneath her cardigan sweater, she wore one of those day dresses Flory saw in the older women clothing section at the mall.

"You've gotten tall," Mrs. Callahan exclaimed. "I need someone tall. Can you spare a minute for your old neighbor?"

Flory wanted to say she was busy and had plans. But the truth was she had nothing to do. She was available, much as she didn't want to be.

"Well, I guess I have a few minutes. What do you need?"

Mrs. Callahan took Flory's hand and led her across the street, like a giant dog being pulled on a leash. "Come with me, and I'll show you."

In the pocket of her sweater, she pulled out a jumble of keys. Adeptly she unbolted and unlocked the front door to her house. It was a smaller version of their home. Heavy curtains framed the same picture window. Dark, antique furniture was in the living room. It didn't appear as if anyone had sat in the chairs or turned on a lamp in ages. A slight mustiness permeated the house.

"Which daughter are you?" Mrs. Callahan asked.

"I'm Flory, the older one."

"Named for your grandmother, right?" Mrs. Callahan smiled at her. "She was such a charming lady."

"Yes. She was," Flory agreed.

Mrs. Callahan beckoned her to follow, past the living room, the dining room, and down the hall. Flory noticed that instead of three doors in the hallway, there were only two. And they were both shut. She half expected Mrs. Callahan to knock on the door before entering.

The room facing the back of the house was Mrs. Callahan's bedroom. When she opened the door, light from the open window streamed into the hall.

"How pretty," Flory said. Light and colors dominated the room, and the view from the window revealed flowers already in bloom. It was as if she had entered a different house.

"Thank you." Mrs. Callahan continued into a small hallway between the bedroom and the bathroom. There were closets on either side.

"Here." She pointed to the shelf above the clothing rod. "Up there. Can you reach those boxes on that shelf?"

Flory stepped into the closet.

"Careful. They're heavy," Mrs. Callahan said.

Flory lifted two boxes and set them on the carpet in the hall.

"Follow me and put them on the dining room table." Flory obeyed. The boxes were old and taped with masking tape that no longer stuck. One was labeled Callahan, and the other had Hibbitt written on it.

Mrs. Callahan opened the Hibbitt box. Inside were stacks of old black and white photos. She dug through them until she found what she was searching for. It was a picture of a mother with three children. It must have been taken in a photo studio a long time ago. Mrs. Callahan pointed to the baby sitting on the mother's lap.

"That's me," she said.

Flory peered at the old photo. "You were a cute baby."

She continued pulling out old photos. At the bottom of the box were framed ones, and it was too difficult to reach them. The table was too high, and she was too short.

"Florence, can you get those framed pictures out of the bottom of the box? I can't quite reach them."

"Sure. It's Flory," she said, correcting her neighbor. She carefully lifted the framed photos. There was one of a man on horseback with a woman standing next to him.

"Those were my grandparents, and that was taken

right before the Land Run," Mrs. Callahan said. "My father was born in 1907, the same year Oklahoma became a state."

"That's cool." Just then Flory's phone dinged. It was Phoebe. "Oh, that's my sister. I'm supposed to pick her up. Do you need me to help you with anything else?"

The older woman sighed. "No. But maybe you could come back and lend me a hand with some other things around here." Mrs. Callahan waved her hand as if to indicate the space around. "I would like to pay you."

"Sure, I'd be happy to help," Flory said. Her phone dinged again. She glanced at it. "I guess I'd better go. I enjoyed looking at your pictures. Bye."

Mrs. Callahan walked Flory to the door. She sensed her neighbor watching as she crossed the street. She must be lonely, Flory thought. Then she pulled up Phoebe's text.

—*Let's stop and get a slurpy when you pick me up.*— It was followed by a smiley face.

—*Sure.*— Flory texted back.

Flory and Phoebe sat in the car at the drive-in restaurant. It used to have teenage carhops on roller skates take orders when their grandparents were in college. It was still a popular after school hangout. They sipped their drinks in silence, trying not to get a brain freeze.

Flory's phone dinged. It was Rodney.

—*Can you pick me up? Your mother borrowed my truck, and she is still using it.*—

—*Sure.*— Flory texted to Rodney.

"Come on, Phoebe, we have to get Dad. Mom has the truck."

"Where's Mom?" Phoebe asked.

"He didn't say."

"Well, at least she's out of the house. That's a good thing."

Flory made a face. "I hope she goes to the store while she's out. It would be nice to have some food."

Phoebe turned toward Flory. "Why do you have to be so grumpy all the time? I swear, you're always thinking the worst of everyone and everything. Sometimes you're hard to be around, you know?"

"Thank you very much, Miss Pollyanna. Maybe you'd feel this way, too, if your boyfriend broke up with you—*by text*—and started dating your best friend right after Aunt Lou did her thing. And you were the only senior who didn't make the varsity basketball team, even though you had a guaranteed spot. Or maybe you think it's normal for all my friends to drop me. I really didn't want to go to prom my senior year or be a part of the Senior Skit. Do you want me to continue?"

"No. But we're all having troubles, you know."

"So, make me feel guilty for not being all chipper and happy."

Phoebe sighed. Neither sister spoke the rest of the way to Sutton Cards.

Rodney climbed into the back seat and patted both daughters on their shoulders. "Hi girls. How was school?" he said.

"Fine, Dad," Phoebe said.

Rodney inspected the back seat of the Honda. "Well, this is a new perspective. I don't think I've ever been in the back of your mother's car." He chuckled.

There was no response from the front seat.

"I said, I've never been in the back seat here. Don't you girls think that's funny?"

"Sure, Dad," Flory said. "Real funny." She glanced in the rearview mirror and saw her father gazing at her. She stared at the road.

"Okay," Rodney said, "let's try this one more time. Hi, Flory. Hi, Phoebe. How was school?"

"Hi Dad. School was fine," Phoebe glanced at him in the back seat. "You know, you do look funny back there."

Flory knew it was her turn. It was like the old manners games they used to play when they were younger.

Rodney cleared his throat, and Flory kept driving in silence.

"Flory, when is graduation?"

"I don't know. I'm not going."

"What do you mean you're not going? Of course, you are. You're going to walk across the stage and get your diploma with your class."

Flory eyes flared. She glared in the rearview mirror. "Why?"

She watched Rodney's chest rise as he took a deep breath. "Why not?"

Flory turned into the garage. "I don't want to talk about it!" She slammed the car door and ran inside. She stood at the door to her bedroom and threw her backpack across the room, nearly knocking over the lamp on the table next to her bed. Books and papers spilled out. She plopped on her bed, fuming. They just don't get it.

Heavy footsteps on the carpeted hall alerted her Rodney was coming. She wished her bedroom door had a lock. She just wanted to disappear. She heard the soft tap on the door. Flory turned her back to the door and put her pillow over her head.

"Flory? Tell me what's going on. We can work this out."

She felt his weight on the mattress as he sat on the edge of her bed. She moved away from him.

"Please sit up. Let's talk."

"Leave me alone," she said, her voice muffled under the pillow.

Rodney spoke. "Come on, Flory." He removed the pillow and pulled her to sitting. She resisted his efforts, going limp like a rag doll. "Tell me why you don't want to go to graduation."

Flory moved away from him and crossed her arms. "There's nothing to discuss. I'm not going."

"But we want to celebrate your graduation with you. This is a major milestone. We want to be there for you," Rodney said.

She turned and glared at him. "You don't get it, do you? You and Mom just don't get it. The day Aunt Lou *murdered* all those people, my life changed. Forever!" Flory's arms were crossed tight, as if to keep herself from throwing a punch. Tears ran down her cheeks. She let go of one arm to wipe her face, then resumed her rigid position. "None of them want me to be there—no one in my senior class. And I don't want to be with people who hate me for something I had absolutely nothing to do with, other than the fact she was my wack-o aunt."

Flory felt Rodney put his arm around her. She repelled from his touch. "Leave me alone," she said.

Neither of them spoke. Finally, Flory got up and stomped out of the room.

"Flory! Where are you going?" Rodney yelled. "Come back here this instant."

Flory slammed the door to the garage and got in

Patsy King Hosman

Alice's car. She sat there, breathless from her anger. She didn't even try to wipe away the tears. When she realized she didn't have the keys, she returned inside and stood at the door of her bedroom. Rodney was still sitting on her bed. He appeared sad, but she didn't care. Flory saw what she was looking for. She grabbed the keys and slamming the door to the garage a second time, left.

Chapter 52

Alice found herself at the library. It seemed a better option than staying at home. She struggled with the letters she wanted to write to the victims' families. She was in a different place now, thanks to Laura and Jordan, yet what could she say to them? How could she tell them how sorry she was? Or how she wished she could have prevented Lou from her actions? Did they feel the way she had toward Jordan Hall? Of course they did.

What had caused her to change her feelings about Jordan? Maybe it was Laura. Maybe somehow, she let go of the hurt and anger she had been clinging to. All she knew was when she came face to face with him, she didn't see an uncaring, out of control, drunk driver. She saw a broken man.

Alice shuddered. She never gave Lou the grace Jordan received from her. Alice stared at the blank legal pad in front of her. "Forgive me, Lou." A single tear fell on the lined, yellow paper. How could she expect these families to forgive her if she still struggled with shame and guilt toward Lou? She had much work to do.

Alice examined the list. Hannah Cummins. Her twin brother had died. Alice's older sister had died, too. Maybe this could be a starting place. Alice closed her eyes and tried to picture this woman. Was she short or tall? What were her hobbies? How close had she been to her brother?

Of course, they had been close. "I'm so sorry," she whispered. The temptation to crawl into her hole pulled at her, but Alice resisted. She stared at the blank legal pad. It was no use. Her brain was empty. Discouraged, she gathered her things and left.

The next day she met with Laura.

"I keep hitting a wall," Alice said.

"What do you mean?" Laura had changed her hair color from fiery red to brown with pink tips in a spikey haircut.

"I can't seem to put in writing my thoughts. Try as much as I can, I haven't been able to write a single letter." Alice slumped in her chair.

"Why do you think you're hitting a wall?"

"I don't know how to tell them I'm sorry my sister murdered their loved ones." Alice shook her head. "How do you put that into words?"

"What is it you want to say to them?"

"I want them to know how sorry I am for what Lou did."

"Why do you want to tell them that?"

"Well," Alice stammered. "Because I should. Because I feel so terrible. Because I want them to know—oh, I don't know what I want." Alice felt even more confused.

"You want them to know you're a good person, and you wouldn't ever do anything like what Lou did. Is that what you're trying to say?"

Alice hesitated. What Laura said was probably true, but it sounded so trite and shallow. "I'm making it all about me, aren't I?"

"I don't know," Laura said. "Are you?"

Alice shrugged her shoulders and shook her head.

She couldn't speak.

The room fell silent. Finally, Laura spoke. "It seems to me, you're trying to find a way to relieve yourself of the all-encompassing guilt you feel for what Lou did. That's a reality." Laura paused. "But I don't think you want to ask these family members to be responsible for easing your pain."

Alice knew Laura was watching her, yet she sensed support, not condemnation. There was no shame, and her mind seemed to clear.

"I just don't want them to spend the rest of their lives in a living hell of hate and revenge. I don't want these people to torture themselves with bitterness that will hurt them more than anyone else." Alice paused. "Trust me. I know."

"Do you remember the shooting at the church in Charleston?" Laura asked.

"Yes. It was terrible."

"What did several of the family members do?"

"I—I don't know. I don't remember."

Laura sighed. "It didn't make the headlines. But you need to find articles about the families of the victims. They—not all of them—*forgave* the shooter. Like you, they didn't want their lives consumed by hate. No, they sought love and forgiveness. I think after you read about them, you'll know what to write."

Chapter 53

Graduation and the end of school came and went with hardly a blip on the radar at the Bennetts' home. There was the initial relief school had ended—no more studying and no more reminders of the lack of social life. Flory had gotten her way. She didn't walk across the stage for graduation. But now what?

Flory didn't know what she wanted to do. She didn't know if it was too late to enroll for classes in the fall. And where could she go? Should she try to enroll in school or find some boring job? Neither prospect seemed promising. Thankfully, Mrs. Callahan had continued to ask Flory to help her, and she paid generously. But it wasn't a real job. She needed a full-time job, but what? She was stuck.

Still in her nightshirt, Flory wandered into the kitchen, hoping to find something to eat. No one was around. Phoebe had probably gone on a run, and she assumed her mom was still in bed. She fixed a piece of toast and a glass of milk, standing at the counter as she ate.

The doorbell rang. Who could that be? Flory saw the silhouette of a man standing at the door. From the living room window, she noticed an ambulance across the street at Mrs. Callahan's home. This must be her son. Despite her appearance, Flory opened the door. Toast crumbs stuck to the sides of her mouth as she crammed the last bite in.

"Excuse me for bothering you," the man at the door said. He appeared to be several years older than her parents. "My name is William Callahan. My mother lives across the street."

"Oh, yes, I know her," Flory said. "Is something wrong?"

"Yes. She fell. I don't know how long she'd been there. But I found her on the floor in the bathroom. When she didn't answer the phone this morning, I got worried."

"I'm so sorry. I visited with her on Friday," Flory said. "I should have gone by."

"Are you Flory?" William asked.

"Yes. She and I have kind of become friends."

"She's told me about you. Thank you."

"Is there anything I can do?"

"Well, yes. I hope so. You see, I must go out of town for a meeting. I'm concerned she might have broken her hip. If she did, she'll have to stay in the hospital, and I hate to leave Mom there by herself. I was wondering if you could stay with her. I'd pay you, of course."

Flory hated that she'd fallen. She pictured the scenario being presented to her. Sitting in a hospital, maybe for days? Boring, but getting paid? Not so bad. And she liked Mrs. Callahan.

"I'll have to check with my parents," Flory said.

"Of course. I have to get back over there and follow the ambulance." He pulled out a business card, wrote his cell phone number on the back, and handed it to her. "Have your parents give me a call." Then he pulled out another card. "Here, write your number on this card, and I'll call you once I know what's going on with Mom." William grabbed Flory's hand and shook it briskly.

"Thanks so much," he added and ran back across the street.

Flory didn't see grown men run very often, and it appeared it had been quite some time since he had done any running. Then she realized she needed to get dressed.

"Mom," Flory called. No answer. She checked the garage, and it was empty. Flory frowned. Who knows where she is? Flory called Rodney and explained the situation, giving him William Callahan's phone number.

As Flory stepped out of the shower, she heard her phone ringing. "Hello?"

"Hi Flory. I just got off the phone with William. I told him you could stay with her. He's going to call you when she gets into her room."

"Thanks, Dad." Flory didn't know what to expect, but anything was better than being stuck in the house all day.

It was three o'clock when she heard back from William. Mrs. Callahan had to have surgery on her hip and was in recovery. Rodney picked up Flory and drove her to the hospital.

"How is she?" he asked.

"She's in recovery right now. They'll be moving her to room 308. That's where I'm to go."

Flory found the room with no trouble. The door was slightly ajar, and she heard voices in the room. She knocked softly, and the voices stopped.

William opened the door. "Hi Flory," he said. "Mom, Flory's here. I told you I asked her to stay with you while I'm out of town."

Mrs. Callahan nodded, then closed her eyes.

Flory cautiously entered the room. Her elderly neighbor appeared to have shrunk. She seemed like a small child in the hospital bed, as if she had taken a bite of the cake from *Alice in Wonderland* to make her shrink in size. One hand rested on top of the blanket and was hooked to an IV next to the bed.

Flory went over to the side of the bed and held her hand.

"Hey, Mrs. Callahan. I'm so sorry about your fall. I wish I had known you needed help." Tears formed.

Mrs. Callahan opened her eyes and smiled weakly. "Well, you're here now. And I'm glad you are."

"Have a seat," William said to Flory, indicating a chair near the bed. "This is Tanya. She was going over the doctor's orders for Mom."

Flory observed the woman in blue scrubs. She was probably in her mid-forties. Her platinum-colored hair was pulled back in a ponytail. She was heavy but moved briskly.

"Mrs. Callahan will stay here for about four or five days, so we can watch for any signs of infection or other complications. Then she will be transferred to skilled nursing for rehab."

"How long will she be in skilled nursing?" William asked.

"That can depend," Tanya said. "Recovery from hip surgery takes a long time. Unless she has help at home, she might stay in skilled nursing for a month or so."

"I don't get why it will take so long." Flory had been listening intently.

Tanya explained her recovery would involve getting her strength back, retraining her balance, plus making sure she was able to handle daily activities, such as getting dressed, getting up and down from a chair or in and out of her bed. She would need physical and occupational therapy to help in these areas.

"Are there any other questions?" Tanya glanced at the clipboard in her hand. "I think I've gone over everything then." She held up the call button and said, "Just press this if you need anything."

After Tanya left, William hovered by the door as he made several phone calls to reschedule his business trip. "Flory." William beckoned her to step outside.

"I was supposed to be in Boston today to give a presentation at a conference. They were kind enough to switch me with tomorrow's speaker. That means I'll be leaving tonight. I just booked my flight."

Flory nodded, not sure what that meant.

"I hate leaving Mom here," William said as he watched her sleeping. "I'm grateful your dad said you could stay with her. I know this is asking a lot, but I feel much better knowing someone is with her." He took out a wad of twenties and handed her five of them. "I should be back by Wednesday, Thursday at the very latest. I know this isn't enough money. Just use it for your meals, and I'll pay you when I return."

William grabbed her hand and shook it for the second time that day. "Thank you so much. Mom has spoken highly of you." His leather shoes squeaked as he tried to tip toe across the room. Kissing her on the forehead, he whispered, "Bye, Mom. I love you." She slept through it.

Flory realized he was leaving that moment. "Wait," she called. "What am I supposed to do?"

Glancing at his watch, William said, "Let's go to the nurse's station and talk to them."

William informed Tanya that Flory would be staying with his mother. She felt better when Tanya assured her that family and caregivers often stayed overnight with patients.

After William left, Flory called Rodney. "Dad, can you bring me some other things?"

Later that evening Alice and Rodney came to the hospital with Flory's backpack and dinner from Johnny's.

"Knock, knock." It was Alice. Flory quickly got up from the metal chair she had been sitting in most of the afternoon. Mrs. Callahan was asleep, and her dinner sat on the tray. Flory had coaxed her to have a few bites of Jell-O and some crackers before she dozed off again.

Out in the hall Flory could smell the hamburgers in the bag. "We brought dinner," Alice said. "How is she?"

"She's sleeping a lot. But Tanya, who's her nurse, said that's to be expected." Flory glanced at Mrs. Callahan. "Let me ask the nurses if I can go to the waiting room with you guys."

Flory returned with a thumbs-up sign. "Tanya said she'd check on her before her shift ended."

The three of them found a secluded corner in the waiting room. The television above was on an old movie channel. No one spoke for a few minutes as they consumed their dinner.

"Thanks for bringing me some food," Flory said after she had finished her hamburger. "Mrs. Callahan's son gave me some money for my food, and said he'd pay me when he returned."

"If you have any problems or need anything, just call us," Rodney said.

"I'll be fine. I'm two doors down from the nurse's station."

"Are you sure you won't get bored?" Alice wrinkled

her brow.

"No. I'll be fine," Flory repeated. "Besides, I like Mrs. Callahan. We've gotten to know each other."

"I put in a couple of books from Dad's library. I thought she might enjoy them. Maybe you could read to her," Alice said.

"Good idea. Thanks."

When Flory returned to Mrs. Callahan's room, she found a set of hospital sheets on the recliner in the corner of the room. I guess that's where I'll be sleeping.

Mrs. Callahan's tray was gone, and fresh water and ice filled the giant hospital cup. On the dry erase board Tanya's name had been erased. In its place was written Debora. Not Debra or Deborah, but Debora. Interesting, Flory thought. But then people probably thought her name was strange. She chuckled to herself.

Flory unfolded the sheet and tried to tuck it into the sides of the cushions. She found a rather hard pillow and blanket on a shelf in the cabinet. It was too early for her to go to sleep, so she opened her backpack. They had remembered her charger. Flory dug into the bag and found her earphones. It was still light outside, so she closed the shades and dimmed the lights in the room. Making herself as comfortable as possible, she leaned back in the recliner and closed her eyes.

Someone shook her shoulder. "Are you Flory?"

She opened her eyes and saw an unfamiliar face. Where am I? Then she remembered—at the hospital. Had she fallen asleep?

She sat up, taking out the earphones. "Yes. Sorry, I must have fallen asleep."

"I'm Debora. I have the night shift." A tall, angular middle-aged black woman stuck out her hand. Flory shook it. She had a strong grip.

"If you're going to stay with a patient, you can't use earphones." She spoke in a matter-of-fact tone.

"Oh, I'm sorry. I didn't think…"

"That's right. You didn't think. What if Mrs. Callahan needed something but couldn't find the call button? That's why you're here."

Flory sensed this wasn't going well. Tanya had been so helpful. Already, she felt like she was on the wrong side with Debora.

"I didn't think a young girl could handle this," Debora said. "I guess I'm going to have to come by here more often now. She crossed her arms and eyed Flory.

"I'm sorry. I won't use them again. I'll sit right here and stay awake." Flory got up from the recliner and returned to the metal chair.

Debora's face softened. "Hon, you don't need to stay awake all night. What good will you be in the morning? It's just those earplugs have a way of letting you tune out what's going on around you. Understand?"

Flory nodded and put them in her backpack. Debora had already moved on. She was examining Mrs. Callahan's chart. She checked her IV and the fluid in her bag. Then she gently woke her up.

"Mrs. Callahan? I'm Debora, your night nurse. I need to check your vitals." She smiled at her and brushed wisps of silver hair from her face. "How are you feeling, Hon? How's your pain?"

Flory watched Mrs. Callahan's face. She appeared a little groggy still. "I'm fine, thank you."

Spoken like a true Southern lady.

After Debora checked her vital signs, she said, "Mrs. Callahan, I need you to get up and try to use the bathroom. Do you think you can do that?"

"Of course, I can," she said.

Debora put one arm behind her and signaled to Flory with her eyes to get on the other side. "Miss Flory and I are going to help you." With Debora's guidance Flory assisted her in easing Mrs. Callahan to a sitting position and getting her legs swung around to the side of the bed.

"We're going to sit here for just a minute to make sure you don't feel dizzy or nothing."

Mrs. Callahan's thin legs hung down from the side of the bed. Her feet didn't touch the floor.

"We're going to lower the bed until you can get your feet on the floor," Debora said. With her head, she tilted it in the direction of the switches that operated the bed. "Miss Flory is going to push the button, and you're going to feel the bed go down. Don't be surprised."

The bed creaked as it lowered. Once Flory saw Mrs. Callahan's feet on the ground, she stopped.

"Mrs. C, I'm going to help you stand, and Miss Flory is going to get your IV and wheel it around to this side of the bed. Then the three of us are going to walk into the bathroom and let you go potty."

The three of them made their way the eight or nine steps to the bathroom. Flory held back as Debora helped Mrs. Callahan onto the toilet. When she had washed her hands, the threesome retraced their steps back to the bed.

Once she was comfortable in bed, Debora asked if either of them wanted a snack or juice. Then she looked at Flory and said, "Tanya was right." She smiled and left the room.

Over the next day and a half Flory learned how to help Mrs. Callahan get up and down from the bed. She helped her select her meals from the daily menu, and at three thirty they watched *Jeopardy!* together. Flory knew the current questions, and Mrs. Callahan knew the history ones. Neither of them knew the questions on sports.

"How did you know I love Wendell Berry?" Mrs. Callahan asked.

Flory set the book down that she had been reading to her. "I didn't. My mom brought it back from my grandparents' farm, and she put it in my backpack. It must have been an afterthought."

"Well, it was a great afterthought."

William returned Wednesday evening as Mrs. Callahan was eating her dinner.

Flory watched her eyes light up when William entered the room. She was glad to see him, too, because she was getting tired. The recliner wasn't much of a bed.

After greeting his mother and kissing her on the cheek, he questioned them both about how she was recovering.

"I'm doing just fine. And it's thanks in great part to this young lady." Mrs. Callahan tilted her head toward Flory. "She's taken great care of me, and we've become good pals. Haven't we?"

"Yes, Ma'am. We have," Flory said. She enjoyed her neighbor's company, but she was ready to take a shower and sleep in her own bed. Flory began to gather her things, putting them in her backpack. She folded the blanket and sheets and placed them on the recliner. "Here, Mrs. Callahan," she said, picking up the book they had been reading, "you can hang on to this until you finish reading it."

"No, you take it with you," she said. "Then you can bring it back when you return. And please, call me

Evelyn or Mrs. C."

"Okay, Mrs. C," Flory said.

William, who had been scrolling through his messages on his phone, said, "I'll be staying at Mom's house while she's here in the hospital. I'd like to talk to your parents about having you help her as she recovers. They'll be moving her to skilled nursing, and it might be good for someone to be with her a few days a week. Would you be interested?"

"Uh, sure." What else did she have to do? And besides, she enjoyed Mrs. C's company.

Flory stood next to the side of the bed and took both of Mrs. Callahan's hands in her own. They were ice cold. She held them in her warm hands.

"Oh, your hands feel so good," she said.

"Good-bye, Mrs. C. You take care of yourself. And I'll be back." Flory bent over and kissed her on the cheek.

"Good-bye, Flory. And thank you again." Mrs. C blew her a kiss.

Flory closed the door softly behind her. She leaned against the wall with her eyes closed and sighed. She didn't realize how tired she was.

"...can you believe there's been another shooting?" One of the nurses at the nurse's station spoke.

Someone read, "Nine dead in latest shooting." Flory opened her eyes. Suddenly her knees buckled.

"It's terrible," the conversation continued. "These killers need to be locked up. They need to catch them before it happens again."

"What was that woman's name who killed all those people last year?"

"Cruella? No, that's from the Dalmatian movie." There was a chuckle. "She should have been named

Cruella. It was Lou Ella. Did any of you know her?"

Flory froze. She texted Rodney. —*Pick me up. I'll meet you outside.*— She had to figure out how to get past the nurse's station without anyone noticing her.

Another voice spoke. "Her father taught my husband at COC. He said he was a nice man. He and his wife died in a car accident. It's a shame they died. Maybe they could have prevented this from happening."

"Doesn't she have a sister who still lives in town?" This was the voice who made the Cruella joke. "I can't remember her name."

Thank goodness, Flory thought. Then her phone dinged.

—*On my way.*—

Flory decided to go to the restroom which was in the opposite direction to settle her nerves. By the time she walked past the nurse's station, the conversation had moved on to what movies were currently showing. One of the nurses saw Flory. "Are you leaving?"

"Yes. Mrs. Callahan's son is back in town."

"Well, get some rest. You did a good job."

"Thank you," Flory said. She tried to walk casually toward the exit, even though she wanted to run. Rodney drove up not long after she got outside.

"How is Mrs. Callahan?"

"She's doing well. Her son is going to talk to you and Mom about hiring me to help Mrs. C when she goes to rehab."

"Is that something you want to do?"

Flory nodded her head. "Yes. I like her." She smiled, thinking that her closest friend was an eighty-year-old woman. "We get along." She thought of the conversation she overheard at the nurse's station. "Uh, Dad?" Flory hesitated.

"What is it?"

Flory saw Rodney's hands grip the steering wheel. How does he know when I'm about to tell him something bad? She took a deep breath. Maybe I shouldn't say anything.

"What did you want to tell me?"

Flory spoke. "Did you know there was another mass shooting this week?"

"Yes," he answered curtly.

"I overheard the nurses talking about it, and then they started talking about Aunt Lou and Granddad and how she had a sister still in town."

"What else did they say?" Rodney asked. Flory could see the veins in his neck stick out.

"That was about the time I decided to go into the bathroom. I didn't want them to see me and figure out who I was. I didn't hear the rest of the conversation."

Rodney turned into the parking lot of a strip mall. He put the truck in park and turned toward Flory. His eyes betrayed him.

"Is this the way it's going to be for the rest of our lives?" Flory's voice cracked.

Rodney shook his head. "I don't know." He leaned across the seat and hugged Flory. "I'm so sorry. I don't know what else to say."

Chapter 54

Phoebe opened the back door, and unexpected heat hit her in the face. It was mid-morning in early June, and already the temperature was stifling. Still not dressed, she brushed dead leaves from the chaise on the back patio. Sitting, with her knees pulled up, she stared at her phone and wondered if Sadie had gotten the babysitting job. Phoebe and Sadie had babysat together last summer. But when she contacted the family, they told her they already had found someone else.

She glanced at the pots on the patio that contained the dead remains from last summer's flowers. Leaves from the fall piled against the fence. The grass hadn't been cut in weeks, and weeds appeared to be taking over. Phoebe watched a chickadee land on the birdfeeder in search of food. But it was empty. That was exactly how she felt now, empty.

Phoebe thought of the farm, and it made her throat constrict, like she wanted to cry but couldn't. She wished Mimi and Granddad were still alive. Phoebe imagined her grandparents giving her a job for the summer. Wouldn't that have been great? She could help Mimi in her garden, and Granddad would take her all over the farm in his tractor.

A mosquito buzzed around her head and brought Phoebe back to her current reality—no summer job, nothing to do, no one to do it with, and no Mimi and

Granddad.

When she was little and said her prayers at night, Alice used to remind her, "Don't forget to pray for Aunt Lou." Now Phoebe understood. She felt bad. She felt awful for all the victims, but she also felt bad for Aunt Lou. None of it made sense. And she didn't know what she could do to help.

The mosquito returned, and Phoebe decided it was time to go inside. She opened the door and ran into Alice, causing her to spill coffee onto her Snoopy nightshirt. She wasn't dressed yet either.

"Sorry, Mom, I didn't see you," Phoebe said.

"That's okay. I was coming out to talk to you." Alice patted the damp spot on her nightshirt. "In or out?"

"I'm coming in. The mosquitoes started to bug me," Phoebe said. "Ha ha," she added, without laughing.

Alice led the way to the den.

Phoebe plopped down on the couch and tossed the pillows on the floor. "What did you want?" She studied her mother. When was the last time she had colored her hair, much less washed it? Her roots were distinctly grayer than before, and her hair appeared greasy. Phoebe used to think Alice had the mom-next-door kind of look, but that wasn't what she saw. Phoebe wondered if she would get dressed or stay in the coffee-stained nightshirt all day. She picked up one of the pillows from the floor and hugged it.

"I got off the phone with your dad, and he wants you to work for him this summer."

Phoebe's eyes widened. "Really? What would I do?"

"He's coming home for lunch, so he can talk to you about it."

A real job. Maybe her summer wouldn't be so bad after all. "I'll go take a shower so I'm ready."

By one o'clock, Rodney and Phoebe had arrived at Sutton Cards. Rodney led her to the back room where Liem and Ha were operating small presses. Ha was running off labels for a local bakery, and Liem was printing invoices.

"Hello, Miss Phoebe." Liem said. His eyes twinkled, and he reminded Phoebe of Yoda.

Ha bowed. "So good to see you, Miss Phoebe." She seemed to have shrunk since the last time Phoebe saw her. It felt good to be here.

"I want you to shadow Liem and Ha this afternoon. They will show you what they do and how you can help."

"Okay, Dad."

Phoebe spent the afternoon with Nguyens. They began printing an order for one thousand postage-paid return envelopes using the offset printer.

Liem explained, "The aluminum plate has the inked image of what will be printed. It's transferred to this cylinder here," he said, pointing to the cylinder. "It's called a rubber blanket, which rotates over the paper, putting the ink on it."

"Here is the finished envelope," Ha said. "Everything has to be precise. We work hard to make it perfect."

"Why is it called offset printing?" Phoebe asked.

"That's because the image isn't printed directly from the aluminum plate to the paper, but it is offset by the rubber blanket. See?"

"I get it now." Phoebe kept her eyes on the machine, watching the cylinder as it rotated onto the blank envelopes.

"What did you think?" Rodney asked as he locked up the shop, and the two of them walked to the truck. Hot Oklahoma wind blew dust around the empty parking lot, and a Styrofoam cup rolled by, getting lodged under the front tire of the truck.

"It was good," she said. She picked up the cup and threw it in the trash bin.

"I'm glad," Rodney said.

Phoebe looked out the window as they drove away. Her new job. She liked that thought. They drove past the 7-Eleven and crossed the railroad tracks. She had been around Sutton Cards all her life, but now she saw it from a new perspective.

"How long have the Nguyens worked for you?"

"Let's see. I took over the shop from my dad in 1996, the year your mom and I got married. I think they started working for us in 1998. Yep. The year Flory was born."

"I like them," Phoebe said.

"Yes, they're good people. They came over from Vietnam in the 1970's. Boat people. That's what they were called. I'd say they were more like survivors."

"I didn't know that."

"They had a young daughter, and Ha was pregnant when they arrived. The daughter died, but Ha delivered a healthy baby boy who is now a heart doctor."

The next day when they arrived at Sutton Cards, the Nguyens were already there and waiting. There was a girl with them, who appeared to be about Phoebe's age.

"Who's that?" Phoebe asked.

"I forgot to tell you. Their granddaughter, Kate, has been spending a couple of days at the shop each week when she's not in summer school."

Phoebe studied the girl standing beside the Nguyens. She was taller than either of them, and she stood erect, like she had a rod attached to her back. Her straight black hair was cut chin length, and she wore a pair of gym shorts and a Junction Memorial band T-shirt.

Junction Memorial band. That meant they had gone to the same high school.

Together they walked toward the Nguyens. "Good morning, Liem and Ha. Hi, Kate," Rodney said. "I forgot to tell Phoebe about you. Phoebe, this is the Nguyens' granddaughter, Kate."

"Hi," Phoebe said. She seemed familiar. "Did you go to Memorial last year?"

Kate nodded. "We were in band together, and I had Mrs. Granger for fifth hour English, right before you. Sometimes I saw you as I was leaving class."

"You were in band? What instrument did you play?"

Rodney interrupted them. "Kate is going to be here all day. You two can visit and get to know each other at lunch. We need to open up and get to work."

Kate followed her grandparents toward the building, and Phoebe said, "See you at lunch."

Phoebe spent the morning learning about some of the equipment in the bindery, the finishing department. Then Rodney had her run off some fliers on the duplicator.

At lunch Phoebe and Kate had a chance to continue their conversation.

"What instrument did you play in band?" Phoebe asked, picking up where they had left off.

"I played percussion—drums, triangles, you name it. But mainly I played the marimba."

"Wait, I remember you," Phoebe said. "You're

really good! You got to play a solo at the spring concert."

"It wasn't that big of a deal. The piece I played was easy. You know, so I wouldn't screw up." Kate laughed. Then she turned serious. "I thought it was shitty they didn't let you be in marching band last year."

"Thanks. I was bummed for a while. Then I decided to move on. You know, get over it."

Phoebe shrugged her shoulders.

"Are you going to try out for it this year? I think you should. Band camp is the end of July. You're going, aren't you?"

"I didn't sign up for it. Mr. Fixley and I didn't really hit it off last year. You know, after…" Phoebe didn't finish her sentence. She tore off a piece of crust from her sandwich. She wasn't used to talking about her aunt to anyone.

"Hey, forget I said anything. I just thought it would be cool to see you at band camp.

"It's okay."

Soon, Phoebe and Kate were exchanging information, learning more about each other. Kate and her parents had moved from Dallas. Her father was a surgeon, and her mother was an ER nurse.

"Wait," Phoebe said. "You moved here last year? Like you were new at school?"

"So were you. We both were, as freshmen."

Kate explained her parents didn't want her to go to a private high school in Dallas. Instead, they moved to Junction to be closer to her grandparents. "I like it here," she said.

"You like living in Junction better than Dallas?" Phoebe couldn't believe it. "Dallas is so cool. There's so much to do there."

"Well, I like it here. Everything's so close, and there's no traffic. Not compared to Dallas. And we can get away, out of Junction, in no time. There's this park we like to go to. It's about thirty minutes away. There are buffalo and trails and a creek that winds through. It's called…"

"Are you talking about Buffalo Springs? That's one of our favorite places." Phoebe couldn't believe it.

Phoebe and Kate continued to discover all they had in common. Ha came over and reminded Phoebe she had a job to do, and Kate had homework.

"Homework?"

Kate explained, "I'm taking pre-calculus this summer, so I can take calculus in the fall."

"What are you, some kind of brainiac?"

By the end of the day the two had made plans to get together over the weekend. Her life almost felt normal again.

Chapter 55

"Good-bye. Phoebe, call us when we need to pick you up." The metal back door to Sutton Cards slammed shut. Phoebe had left with the Nguyens and Kate.

Rodney sat in his office and stared at the bobble heads. His laptop lay perched precariously in a corner space on his desk. A large bottle of TUMS and a thermos of cold coffee added to the clutter.

Rodney pulled up the accounting records from last year and examined them. Should he sell Sutton Cards? He didn't want to, but he felt his options were limited. How could he generate more business? He wondered if Alice would design cards and invitations again. What would it take to get some of his former customers back? Why not call them?

Rodney took a deep breath. "Here goes," he said. He called A & E Electric Company first because he knew the owner. "Hello, is Bill around...Hello, Bill? Rodney Bennett here...I'm fine...No, I don't have any electrical problems. Not that I know of." He chuckled. "Listen, Bill, I was checking my records, and I haven't printed any invoices for you lately. I was hoping to get your business back...Really? That's great. I've got it here. You like triple copies, right? Thanks, Bill. Great talking to you."

That wasn't so bad. Rodney felt hopeful. It was a small account, but it was a start. Rodney spent the next half hour phoning former customers. He learned several who had gone with other local printers weren't pleased with the service and were being charged more.

Rodney glanced at his watch. It was time to leave. There was nothing left to do at work, but he wasn't ready to go home. He used to have meetings in the evenings. And he hadn't been to the men's group at church since last summer. It had been strongly suggested he not attend. At least not for a while.

Rodney's perception was, "We don't want you here. Your association with that horrible event will not be good PR for us." Rodney had felt like they considered him the guilty one. It would have been like harboring a fugitive, if they had allowed him to attend the men's group. He never went back.

He wished he had something to fill the void. He hadn't been fishing with his buddies since last summer either. It wasn't their fault, though. Rodney didn't want them caught up in all the mess. Also, he hadn't been called about softball this spring, which hadn't surprised him.

As a young boy, Rodney had spent his Saturdays with his dad at the printing shop when he wasn't playing baseball. As he got older, his father taught him the trade and, ultimately, Rodney took over the business.

Now, he contemplated selling it. He didn't know how he could stay in business with his client base declining. The only good news was he owned everything free and clear—the building included. But then what? What would he do? With a degree in accounting, he could keep books or be an office manager. But who wanted to have the brother-in-law of a murderer working for them? His reputation in the community had completely evaporated. How could these people be so fickle? They've known me all my life, yet suddenly, I'm a different person. But I'm not. I don't get it.

Rodney's phone vibrated. He checked to see who it was. Archie. His stomach began to burn, and he reached for the bottle of TUMS, letting his voicemail take the message. Rodney chewed the berry-flavored tablets as he stared at his phone. He took a swallow of cold coffee before listening to the message.

"Hey, Rod. Archie here." Rodney hated to be called Rod. "I think I have a buyer for your property. Phillip Jernigan of JP Construction wants to make an offer. He's been out several times and likes the lay of the land. He sees a lot of potential and is willing to pay close to the asking price. Call me when you get this. See ya."

That was Rodney's other pet peeve. When someone ended a conversation with see ya, instead of good-bye. Well, it sounded like good news-bad news. The good news was they might get close to their asking price. The bad news was the buyer probably wanted to develop the property, which meant tearing down the old farmhouse. Alice was not going to like this. Rodney sighed and popped another TUMS in his mouth. He wasn't ready to call Archie back. Maybe I'll give Barney a call.

"Hey, Barney."

"Hey, Rodney. What can I do for you?"

"Are you busy? I'd like to discuss some things with you," Rodney said.

"Sure, I'm free. Stella has a meeting, so I'm solo tonight. Do you want to grab a bite, or do you need to get home?"

"Dinner sounds great. I'll call Alice."

"I've got about thirty minutes of tying up loose ends

here. What do you say we meet at Casa Comida's in forty-five minutes?"

"That'll work." Rodney hung up his phone. Forty-five minutes. That should be enough time to run out to the farm before meeting Barney. He could always call if he got detained.

Rodney grabbed the spare key to the farm from his desk drawer, and five minutes later he was on his way. He felt a lump in his throat. Would this be one of the last times to go out here before they had to pack it up? As he got out of his truck, he saw cigarette butts scattered near the entrance to the farmhouse. Rodney bent down and picked them up, stuffing them in his pocket.

He decided to follow the creek bed that wound its way along the southern border of the property. On the other side of the creek was the Cooper farm. Rodney saw a bulldozer and an excavator standing idle. The farmhouse and barn were gone. A shiver ran down his spine. He suspected JP Construction had purchased the property, which meant Phillip Jernigan wanted to do the same thing to their farm.

This piece of information didn't sit well with Rodney. He merely wanted to immerse himself in this place and its memories. But that wasn't going to happen today. His brain had already switched gears.

Rodney turned back toward the house. As he passed by the pond, a flock of Canada geese landed on the water, squawking. What beautiful nuisances, he thought. How often had he helped Carl scrub the dock on the pond from the geese? And if they ever forgot to turn the old rowboat over, goose poop—as the girls had called it—would be everywhere. "Be sure to watch where you step," he remembered telling Flory and Phoebe.

"Hello, there," Rodney whispered to the geese. "Are you leaving, too? It won't be long, will it?" The geese ignored him as they paddled to the other side.

A wistfulness overcame Rodney as he thought of the impending change of seasons. In a couple of months, it would be fall again, which had always been his favorite season. Fall meant football. But last fall he had felt nothing, only numbness. It was just a matter of getting through each day, trying not to drown himself in the agony of the situation, like Alice had, and hoping he could keep the business. And he had kept it. For a year. But now it seemed inevitable. Winter would come. The geese were leaving. The farm would be sold, and the old farmhouse torn down. And possibly, Sutton Cards would be no more.

Where did that leave him? Rodney didn't have the answer.

Barney was already seated when he arrived at Casa Comida's. He loved this place. It was honest-to-goodness Mexican food. The waiter brought out the basket of crispy homemade tortilla chips, warm corn and flour tortillas, fresh salsa and queso. Both men ordered a large Dos Equis beer with limes squeezed around the lip of the frosted mug.

Barney lifted his mug, and they clinked. "Cheers," he said. The two men swallowed the frigid beer and sighed in unison.

In between bites of chips and salsa, Barney asked, "So, tell me what's going on?"

Rodney let Barney listen to the voicemail he received from Archie. Then explained his thoughts on the good and bad news about it.

Barney nodded. "You're right about both. Alice is

going to be distraught, and Phil Jernigan is going to want that property.

"I know," Rodney said. He was grateful for Barney's guidance and friendship.

The waiter came by with a fresh basket of chips and salsa, and they ordered.

"You and I have both known the property would probably be subdivided. How do you think Alice will take it?" Barney wiped the lime from his mouth after a drink.

"Not good," Rodney said. "I've been trying to tell her not to expect a buyer who wants to keep the house. Believe me, I've tried to discourage those thoughts." He shook his head and muttered to himself, "Not good."

"But on the plus side, we've got Phil, who's going to be hungry for that land. I think we can hold out for your asking price. I'd tell Archie the price is firm."

"Do you really think we can get what we have it listed for?" Rodney was hopeful, but skeptical at the same time.

"I do," Barney said, "and I think Archie probably does, too. He's a good negotiator."

"He'd better be," Rodney said. "He drives me crazy."

"Good salesmen usually do. That's why they're so good. They're annoying, yet they have what it takes to close a deal. And somehow, they manage to do it so both parties feel like they came out on top."

The food arrived, and the two men settled into their meals. Rodney knew he had to call Archie. But that meant telling Alice. He played with his empty mug. "Okay. I'll call Archie tonight and tell him we're firm on the asking price."

"That sounds good." Barney signaled to the waiter for another beer. "What else is on your mind?"

"Sutton Cards. I'm considering selling it."

The chili relleno on his fork fell back on the plate. "Are you sure that's what you want to do?"

"I think so," Rodney said. Then he added, "I don't know." He wasn't sure. "I don't want to sell it, but I don't see how I can keep the business going. I've contacted some of my old customers who might come back, but I don't know if Alice will ever design again. That was a big part of our business. Besides, I don't have the energy." He let out a sigh.

Barney took a sip of beer. "Didn't you once tell me you have some old equipment that's no longer manufactured?"

"I still have my dad's Heidelberg Windmill Letter Press. It's an antique, basically. There aren't many around, and it does more specialty printing features. We used it on the higher end wedding invitations Alice designed. But what does that have to do with the customers I have?"

"Maybe there's a demand for it out there. What's it called?"

"Heidelberg Windmill. It has two arms that look like a windmill as they feed the paper."

"You should spread the word. Who knows?" Barney said.

Rodney shook his head. "I don't know. Who's going to want to work with me? I feel like my reputation is all wrapped up in what Lou did."

Barney took another sip of his beer. "I wouldn't discount it completely. Give it some thought." He changed the subject. "So, what will you do if you sell the business?"

"I have no idea," Rodney said, shaking his head. "That's where I keep hitting a wall. I'm afraid no one will hire me."

The two men spent the rest of the meal discussing Rodney's future. Barney advised putting together a financial plan, paying off the car and the house with the money they would receive from the sale of the farm after taxes were paid. He also suggested putting together a strict budget.

"I'd say you have at least six months to figure out what your next step should be," Barney assured Rodney.

Rodney set his fork down on his empty plate and pushed it aside. "I have another problem," he said.

"What's that?"

"Your bill. I haven't received one this past year."

"That's because I haven't sent you one," Barney said.

"But you've spent hours every month helping us."

Barney just shrugged his shoulders. "I'm not sending you a bill, and that's final." He waved his hand to signal the waiter as he pulled out his wallet. "Besides, I'm basically retired. I keep my office to stay out of Stella's hair. I don't have any hobbies, really. Work is my hobby. I love what I do, and you're letting me continue my hobby. So there."

"At least let me buy you dinner." Rodney pulled out his wallet and took the tab from the waiter.

****

Rodney dreaded going home. Once again, he wished he had someplace to go other than home. He didn't know which he was dreading more—telling Alice about the potential buyer or calling Archie.

Rodney found Alice in the kitchen putting the last of the dinner dishes in the dishwasher. "How was your dinner with Barney?" she asked.

"Good," Rodney said. "It's always good to get Barney's take on business." He helped put the food in the refrigerator.

"So, what did you talk about?"

That was exactly what Rodney didn't want to tell Alice, yet he knew he had to.

"Do you have a minute? I need to tell you something."

Alice and Rodney sat across from each other at the old kitchen table from the farm. Another reminder for Rodney of what he was about to say.

"What did you need to tell me?"

Rodney took a deep breath and let it out slowly. "I got a call from Archie this afternoon." He noticed Alice perked up. "I didn't talk to him. He left a message."

"What did he say? Does he have a buyer? This could be answered prayer."

"I wanted to talk to you before I called him back. But, yes, I think he has a buyer." Rodney paused. "I think the buyer wants to develop the land."

He watched Alice's expression fall.

"Does that mean what I think it means?"

Rodney nodded.

"What are you going to tell him?" Alice spoke, as if it was hard getting the words out.

"That's what Barney and I discussed this evening at dinner. Phillip Jernigan wants to buy the farm." Once Rodney started, he didn't want to stop until he told her everything. "I went out there after I got the call, and I realized the Cooper place had been torn down. Jernigan bought that property. So, it makes sense he would want the farm to expand his development. What this means is he's going to want it bad, and we have a good chance of getting our full asking price for it."

It was a relief to get it out.

Alice's face contorted, as if she was trying not to cry. Finally, she spoke. "I'm trying to separate what I'm feeling—and that's lots of screaming and wanting to crawl into my hole—and what I know is practical and reasonable."

"That's what Barney and I discussed," Rodney said, interrupting Alice.

"Let me finish," she said. "Let me get this out. I've been carrying this hope inside me, if we could find a nice family to buy the farm, then I could live with it. I could let go of the farm and all it's meant to me. The history of how my grandfather bought the land and built the house for his bride. How Dad was born there, and how he and Mom raised Lou and me." Alice began to cry.

Rodney watched helplessly, but he didn't speak.

"Part of me feels like I'm failing my family who came before me. This part is very powerful. It's like I'm destroying everything they ever stood for. And it's tearing me apart." Alice didn't speak for several minutes. The only sound was the dishwasher going through its cycles.

"But there's another part of me," Alice continued, "that's known all along this was going to be the eventual outcome. I could only hope for a different result, but deep down I knew it wouldn't happen." She paused. "It's going to be hard, but I know it's what we must do. We have to sell the farm. For the victims, for our girls, and for our future. But especially for the victims' families, so they can have a semblance of a future without their loved ones."

Neither spoke. The rumbling of the dishwasher continued. Down the hall muffled conversations could be heard. Rodney didn't want to break the silence. He waited.

After several minutes Alice spoke. "Call Archie. Tell him our price is firm."

Chapter 56

Rodney was both relieved and sad. He and Alice were in agreement with the sale of the farm, but that didn't make it any easier. They signed the papers, and the farm was sold. They drove out to the property one last time. Saying a final good-bye was more painful than Rodney realized it would be. He could only imagine what Alice was feeling. The farm had always been part of her life.

After the sale was complete, they escaped to a quiet café for lunch in the midtown area of Oklahoma City. From their corner table by the window, they could see other shops and a park nearby. All the tables had white tablecloths with a single red rosebud in a small vase.

The server brought Rodney a beer in a chilled glass. He took a sip and let the cold fizz go down his throat. He studied Alice as she read her menu. The stress had taken its toll. When she glanced up, he noticed the crow's feet reflecting the constant smile she used to wear were accompanied by creases between her eyebrows and lines pulling her mouth down. But he loved her. They had survived the worst year of their lives. It wasn't always on steady ground. No, there had been plenty of times when Rodney was ready to quit and move out, and it wasn't over yet. There was more to come, but he knew they would make it.

What was it that had kept them together during the

bleakest periods? he wondered. Why had he stayed on those days when he couldn't handle seeing Alice in bed, or dreaded going to work because there was hardly enough work to pay the bills? He knew. He had made a vow. Rodney had made a spoken vow before his family and friends. But more important, he had made a vow to God. Rodney had promised to stay with Alice for better or worse. When Lou murdered those eleven individuals, that was the *worse.* And he had kept that vow.

Their paradigm had shifted. *Normal* had a new meaning. Things taken for granted were cherished because life was fragile. It could change in a moment, in the flash of a fired gun. Rodney never again thought in terms of us and them because his family had been both *us and them.* He had seen his daughters treated like rabid dogs to be avoided. Alice had created her own universe—a cave, a prison—in which she barely existed. And Rodney had been left to try to carry on, all because of a deranged act by his sister-in-law. He was grateful for the handful of friends, like Barney, who never abandoned them.

Rodney knew if it had been his child or spouse or sibling who had been gunned down in cold blood for no reason, he would carry the anger and bitterness and vengeance he knew these victims' families must carry. How would he have been able to move on? There could be no forgiveness of someone who took the life of one of his precious daughters.

How many families out there were suffering this torture? he wondered. There had been numerous mass shootings over the recent years. Yet, several individuals had reached out to them. These were the invisible sufferers whose own relatives had been the shooter. They had reached out as if they, too, were victims of the shooting. And it was true. Alice lost her sister in the shooting. Did that make Lou a victim? But she had been the shooter.

Rodney had seen what bitterness could do to a person. He didn't want his life to go there, and he didn't want that for the families who had suffered from Lou's hands. But what could he do?

"Rodney?" Alice interrupted his thoughts. "Have you decided what you want?"

Rodney held the unopened menu in his hand. He glanced at is quickly. "I'll have the Reuben. How about you?"

Alice chose the chicken Caesar salad. "You seem quiet," Alice said as she squeezed lemon into her iced tea. "What's on your mind?" Then she rolled her eyes. "What isn't on your mind?"

Rodney nodded, agreeing. "I was just thinking about how grateful I am we survived this past year." He caught Alice's look of surprise. "I know. It's been the worst year of our lives. But the fact is, we did survive it. We may have plenty of obstacles ahead of us, but it didn't split us apart. And that's what I'm thankful for."

Alice took a sip of tea. "Me, too. I know I made our family's life miserable on top of all that was thrown at us." She reached across the table and put her hand on his arm. "What do we do now? How do we help the families of the victims?" What was going to be their plan moving forward?

Rodney answered, "Now that the farm has sold, Lou's portion will go into her estate along with her trust and will be divided among the families. Or at least the ones who have sued her estate, according to the judge."

"But that really doesn't amount to much when it's divided by eleven, or seven," Alice said.

Rodney nodded, doing the math in his head. "I know." He shrugged his shoulders. "What else do you suggest?"

"I don't know," Alice said. "I wrote letters to the families. I even tried doing a pastel sketch of one of the victims."

Rodney cringed. The thought of receiving a drawing of a deceased family member by the sister of the murderer was not his idea of how to help a grieving family. And he didn't see the point in writing a letter to strangers. He knew if he had gotten a letter from someone who was related to the person who had harmed one of his family members, he wouldn't want to read it. But maybe Alice would. What these people probably wanted was some form of action taken and money for retribution. That's what I'd want, he thought.

The server brought their lunch, and Rodney saw Alice glance around the restaurant as it was beginning to fill up. There was a soft crescendo of voices rising and falling, never getting too loud. The ordinariness of the lives around them was astounding. Yet here they were in a restaurant, acting normal, without fear of being recognized. How long had that been? Was it because they were too far from home? Or had others moved on?

As Rodney was about to take a bite into the second half of his Reuben, he sensed someone staring at them. Putting his sandwich down, he noticed a couple seated a few tables away. They seemed vaguely familiar, but he couldn't place them. The man, lean and tan, wore a golf shirt with the insignia of the local country club. The woman, fashionably dressed in a casual way, appeared agitated and unsettled.

Rodney whispered, "Do you recognize the couple behind you? The man has been staring at us, and the woman appears to be upset."

Alice turned around, trying to be discreet. Rodney noticed the panic on her face when she turned back.

"What's the matter?"

"It's one of them," Alice whispered. "What do we do?"

"One of who?" Rodney could hear the fear in her voice.

"It's one of the parents of the victims. I feel terrible." He watched as Alice tried to take a drink of her tea. It splashed out of the glass onto the white tablecloth. "I never thought I would see one of them face-to-face."

But Rodney wasn't convinced. "How do you know it's them? And who are they?"

"Trust me. I know. I have a file on all the victims and their families. I wanted information for when I wrote them each a note."

"So, who are they?"

"Elizabeth and Robert Randolph. Their daughter, Kathryn, was one of the victims. She was a senior at Oklahoma A&M, majoring in marketing, had interned in New York, and was promised a job in Dallas. Robert is an attorney with one of the bigger firms here in the city, the one that bought the old Herschel Building. Elizabeth is a stay-at-home mom, and she has one child still at home." Alice paused. "But that's all I know."

Rodney stared at her. Did she know this much about the rest of the victims' families? He didn't know whether to be impressed or creeped out. He wouldn't want strangers knowing all kinds of facts about him and his family.

Finally, he asked her. "How do you know this?"

"It was in the paper," Alice said. "I went online and read articles about the families—the obituaries, stories from local papers, stuff like that." She wiped a tear that had fallen on her cheek. "But now, I don't know what we should do." She leaned across the table. "Are they still staring at us?"

Rodney nodded, trying to appear nonchalant, but feeling far from it. He was beginning to feel the same panic and anxiety he saw Alice express. Was this the way it was going to be from now on? Would they always have to watch their backs?

"What should we do?" Alice whispered.

Rodney took another sip of his beer. He wiped his mouth with the cloth napkin. He knew he had to be rational and not caught up in Alice's emotions. "We do nothing," he said.

"What do you mean? We can't sit here and pretend we don't know who they are. We can't act like they don't recognize us. We need to go over to their table and speak to them."

Was she crazy? Did she think that was a good thing to do? Taking a deep breath, he said, "We didn't do anything to their family. Yes, Lou was responsible for their daughter's death, but we must find a better way to reach out to these families. I don't think going over to their table and creating a scene is the right thing to do."

Alice didn't say anything. She kept her head down and jabbed at her salad.

Rodney had lost his appetite. He turned his head and stared out the window, not seeing anything. Out of the corner of his eye, he saw the Randolphs pay their check.

He kept his eyes focused on the window but tried to watch the couple peripherally.

Presently, he saw them stand up. Then they were gone. He turned and watched them walk out the door and past the window. Rodney's chest tightened. Maybe they should have gone over and said something. He didn't know. There was no book of rules for how to interact with victims' families.

"They left." He tilted his head toward the window.

"I feel so terrible," Alice said. "It's like it happened all over again." She slumped in her chair. "When will this feeling go away?"

Rodney shook his head. He didn't know.

****

After dropping Alice off at home, Rodney returned to work, yet he didn't feel like working. He remembered how he used to love the smell of ink and freshly printed paper and the rhythmic clacking of the presses running. He was also grateful he never sold his father's older machines, like the Heidelberg Windmill Letter Press.

But instead, he felt like a deflated balloon. Empty. Seeing the couple in the restaurant reminded him Lou's actions would continue to haunt them. As he got out of his truck, he felt his phone vibrate. Not recognizing the number, he didn't answer it. A couple of minutes later, his phone dinged. He had a voice message.

"Hi Rodney, this is Mark Proctor at Southwest Printing. Can you give me a call? I have a client who needs a job done that requires a letter press. We don't have one, but I thought you might. Thanks, pal."

Rodney stared at his phone. *Wasn't that what Barney asked me about when we had dinner?* Quickly, Rodney called Mark back.

"Hi Mark. Rodney Bennett here. I got your message about needing a letter press. Yes, I have an old Heidelberg Windmill Letter Press, and it's an amazing piece of machinery."

When Rodney got off the phone, he realized he had found a niche for his craft. He and Mark discussed the possibility of Rodney becoming a job shop for other printers. His skills as a printer and having the Heidelberg Windmill Letter Press could allow him to transition to offering services to other printers as well as doing specialty printing himself. He hoped Alice would start designing soon. Maybe he wouldn't have to sell the business after all.

Chapter 57

Flory glanced at Mrs. Callahan as she sat in the recliner with her eyes closed. Flory shut the book, *Gift from the Sea*. Then she saw one eye open.

"Keep reading, please. I love to listen without the distraction of my surroundings," Mrs. C said. She shifted in the chair and closed her eyes.

Flory continued reading. William entered the room, and she paused. He bent over and kissed his mother's cheek. "Hey, Mother. Hey, Flory," he said. "Have you been behaving this afternoon?" He had a twinkle in his eyes as he spoke.

Flory listened to the playful banter between them. She shut the book and stood to make room for William.

It had been six weeks since Mrs. C had moved to the rehab for treatment and recovery. When William hired Flory to spend three days a week as a companion for her, she realized she enjoyed spending time with Mrs. C. They had formed an unlikely bond, and she was the closest thing Flory had to a friend that summer. Mrs. C taught Flory how to crochet, and Flory showed her how to use the cell phone William had purchased for her.

Flory stepped out of the room to give them some privacy and found a separate nook where she sat down. The television was on, and several patients sat in chairs watching the five o'clock news.

"Good evening, I'm Jessica Alberts. In two weeks,

it will be one year ago that the tragic shooting occurred in Mineral Wells. We start tonight's news going back to August 6, 2015. A local resident of Junction, Lou Ella Sutton, was responsible for the shootings. What do we know now that we didn't know a year ago? And how has this affected the community of Junction?"

Hot with embarrassment and anger, Flory felt her face flush, and her palms became sweaty. She stood up and raced to the women's restroom, hoping no one knew who she was.

Flory's phone vibrated. It was William. "Hello," she whispered.

"Flory, where are you?"

"I'm in the restroom," Flory said, still whispering.

"Are you okay? Why are you whispering?"

Flory realized it was too difficult to explain over the phone. "I'm fine. Do you need me?"

"I'm taking Mother to dinner and wondered if you needed a ride home."

"I can come back to the room now." Still flushed, Flory entered Mrs. C's room. "I'm sorry," she said, "the news was on, and I decided to leave the area."

"So, you hid," declared Mrs. C.

"Yes." Flory felt like she was being reprimanded.

"That's just terrible! A young person feels like she must hide because our community is following the media frenzy about an awful incident that has nothing to do with her," Mrs. C sermonized. "You have nothing to hide. You didn't do anything wrong. As for your aunt, she was a very sick woman. She would be horrified if she knew what she had done."

William said, "She's right, you know."

Flory's eyes watered. "My parents haven't turned on

the TV all week, and Dad throws the newspaper away before he reads it." She wiped her eyes with the back of her hand. "But what about those families who had someone die? I wish I could do something for them."

"Yes, that would be nice," Mrs. C said. "We'll have to think about that. Maybe we can come up with something."

"But I can't bring back their loved ones. I don't know what I'd do if that had happened to me," Flory said.

"It did." Mrs. C reached out and squeezed Flory's hand.

Chapter 58

Phoebe emerged from her bedroom. She had changed into a pair of running shorts and a tank top. Her hair was pulled back in a ponytail, and a single curl fell in her face. Brushing it aside, she filled her water bottle with cold water from the refrigerator and slid it into the pocket of her backpack.

Alice stood by the sink peeling carrots. "Where are you going?"

"I'm riding my bike to Arrowhead Park," Phoebe said. "I need some exercise."

Phoebe felt her mother's eyes on her, wondering what she was thinking. Maybe that this was something normal she hadn't done in almost a year.

"Are you sure it's not too hot?" Alice asked.

"No. I'll be fine. The back roads through the neighborhood are shaded," Phoebe said.

"Okay." Alice rinsed the carrots and wiped her hands on a dishtowel. "Make sure you have your phone. I'll text you when it's dinner time."

"Okay, Mom. Bye."

Phoebe grabbed her bike and helmet from the garage. She turned right and wound her way through the tree-lined streets backing up to the park. It was so convenient not to have to cross any major intersections to get to the park. The late July sun wouldn't set for at least three hours. Even so, the breeze felt cool as Phoebe biked. When was the last time she had ridden her bike to the park? This had been her refuge.

She and Sadie used to meet at the duck pond. They'd talk, listen to music, and sometimes do their homework. Phoebe's mind darkened momentarily as she thought of Sadie. It still hurt. School had been hard last year. Being an incoming freshman had been tough enough but having to navigate it alone had been almost impossible. Aunt Lou's actions had ruined her year, and not just hers, but her whole family's. Not to mention the eleven people who had died. They were never far from Phoebe's mind.

School started the middle of August, and Phoebe hoped her sophomore year would be better. At least she knew what to expect, and she had one friend, Kate, instead of none.

Still, she felt apprehensive. The one-year anniversary of the shooting was coming up. There were posters around town of the impending event, including photographs of the victims with the words in bold print: *WE REMEMBER*. Public Service Announcements aired on TV, stating, *"Guns don't mix with the mentally ill," "Pray for the families."* Roy Malone, the man responsible for killing Lou, was the hero of the week. Lou's face showed up on posters, in the newspaper, on the television, and even on social media. There was no way to avoid reminders of what Aunt Lou had done and what her family had endured the past year.

Phoebe locked her bike and walked toward the duck pond. She heard the ducks and geese quacking and honking as a handful of children threw bits of bread to them.

There was a large elm tree beyond the pond where Phoebe liked to go. She found her spot and settled in. She took a drink from her water bottle and pulled out a sketchpad from her backpack. She noticed a woman sitting on a bench nearby. Her clothes were dirty, and her hair was matted. She had a ragged canvas bag at her feet. She could have been forty, fifty, or sixty. It was hard to tell. Was she the same woman Phoebe sometimes saw at the library, the one who pushed a grocery cart? Phoebe began to sketch her.

Aunt Lou could have been that woman. She could have been homeless. Phoebe knew Aunt Lou had disappeared when her grandparents died. Where had she gone? What had she done during those two years, and what had happened to make her believe she had to kill innocent people?

Phoebe had googled schizophrenia several times, and what she read frightened her. Where had Lou fit into the descriptions? Had she been delusional? Paranoid? What went through her mind? How could she have believed her behavior was normal? What was the distorted logic that caused her to murder eleven innocent victims? Did she have voices tormenting her and convincing her of something unknown, something horrendous? Was Aunt Lou a victim herself?

Phoebe was only twelve when her grandparents were killed in the car accident. It was fleeting remembrances, such as seeing them at a soccer game, or family dinners at the farm that created a tightness in her chest. The memories were all she had now, especially since the farm had sold.

Yet they were momentary, not a constant emptiness, like it would have been if her parents had been the ones who had been killed. What if Flory or her parents had been killed last year in Mineral Wells? What if she was like one of those who lost a mother or father or sister or brother? The hole in her life would be too large to fill. The emptiness would be unbearable, as if someone had ripped her arm off.

Phoebe realized in the beginning she could only focus on how Aunt Lou's actions had affected her own life. It had been too painful a year ago, to imagine what those families were going through. Maybe that's why her mother couldn't get out of bed so many days. Phoebe wondered if her family would ever have a day when they didn't think about it in some way. She didn't know the answer.

She continued sketching the woman on the bench and saw the woman staring at her. She smiled, and the woman smiled back. She had beautiful eyes and dark holes in her mouth where there used to be teeth. What a contrast. What a shame.

"I like your drawing. Is that me?"

Phoebe jumped. She hadn't heard the woman approach. The woman leaned over, and Phoebe could smell her foul breath. Startled and uncertain, Phoebe answered, "Yes. It's you. Would you like it?"

The woman broke into a wide grin. "I sure would," she said. "Can you put my name on it? I'm Rosemary, but my family used to call me Rosie."

Phoebe wrote the woman's name, and then at the bottom she signed it, *by Phoebe.* "Here you go."

The woman took the picture and held it as if it was something of great value. "Thank you."

Phoebe's phone dinged. *—Time to come home.—*
—K.—

Phoebe stood up and brushed the dirt off her shorts. "I have to go," she told the woman, putting her sketchpad into her backpack.

The woman grabbed her hand and shook it. "Thank you so much for my picture. I love it. I really do."

"You're welcome." She walked toward her bike, turning to glance back at the woman. Phoebe watched as she carefully folded the drawing and put it in her tattered bag. A mixture of emotions, like the discomfort she used to feel when around Aunt Lou, and at the same time feeling good for doing something for someone, filled Phoebe's heart. She lingered on the thought of doing something for others.

****

After dinner Phoebe found Flory in her room. "I need your help," she said.

"Now what?" Flory rolled her eyes.

"I want to put flowers by the graves of the people Aunt Lou killed." Phoebe waited for Flory's reaction. "If I could drive, I wouldn't have to ask you. I have money from working, so I can pay for the flowers myself. I just need help delivering them."

"You've had a lot of crazy ideas, but this one has to be one of the craziest."

Phoebe pleaded, "Please Flory. I can't do it by myself, and Mom and Dad would probably have a fit and not let me. I really want to do something for these families, and I can't think of anything else I could do myself."

Flory sighed. "I guess so."

After contacting each of the cemeteries to find out the hours and any protocol, Phoebe realized her idea of delivering flowers was complicated. She ordered flowers for Kayla's family in Dallas, Olen's mother and sister in Joplin, and Amber's mother in El Dorado at a cost greater than she anticipated. Recruiting Flory's help, they found an abundance of fresh flowers at Corsin's grocery store. At the craft store they purchased mason jars and ribbon. Phoebe found a box of cards Alice had designed to use for an enclosed note, and they came up with an excuse for needing the car all day.

On Friday morning, August 5, they loaded the mason jars filled with sunflowers, dahlias, and alstroemerias into Alice's Honda. Calculating the time, they had eight deliveries to be completed by seven in the evening.

Their first stop was at Rose Hill Cemetery in Junction where Jamie Coverdale was buried. They entered the stone building at the entrance to the cemetery. Phoebe carried the flowers. Suddenly she realized what she was doing. There was a grave out there where the body was of a young female not much older than herself. She felt her knees buckle.

An older woman sat behind a desk. "May I help you?" she asked.

Phoebe turned to Flory. Her throat felt constricted, and she didn't know if she could talk.

"We wanted to place flowers at a grave, but we don't know where it's located," Flory said.

"Name?"

"Jamie Coverdale." Phoebe lifted the flowers to show the woman what they had brought.

The woman clicked on the computer. The she pulled out a map of the cemetery and circled number sixty-four with a yellow highlighter. Handing them the map, she said, "Take the first left, then follow it past the Angel Statue. Go to the right…" The woman continued explaining where Jamie Coverdale's grave was, as she drew a line on the map for them to follow. Phoebe hoped Flory was following the directions because her mind had turned to mush.

They thanked the woman and left. In the distance they saw several cars parked along the side of the narrow road that wound its way through the grounds. There was a green open tent set up, and Phoebe saw the mound of dirt waiting to be piled over the coffin after it was lowered. She swallowed to prevent herself from gagging. Why did she think this was a good idea?

Jamie Coverdale's grave was about one hundred yards from the burial. As soon as they opened the doors the air was filled with recorded organ music. Phoebe hated the sound. Instead of the intended feeling of reverence, the music sounded morbid, and it made her want to put her hands over her ears.

They walked toward a small hill, and Flory found the grave marker. It was a flat granite stone that said, *Jamie Lee Coverdale, 10-8-94 to 8-6-15, In our hearts forever.* There was a metal vase with silk daisies in it. Phoebe placed their flowers next to the daisies. Flory handed her the card. They had written her family a note and signed it. Phoebe pulled a stray weed. Then they stood back to admire at their handiwork.

In Guthrie, they placed the bouquet at Mickey Martinez's grave. Kathryn Randolph and Blake Youngblood were buried in Oklahoma City. Then they drove to Norman and put flowers at Ken Goodson's grave. They found Michelle Fisher's marker at Garden View Cemetery in Mineral Wells. Taylor Almon was buried in Tulsa, and Danielle Eckles' grave was in a small church cemetery in Wewoka.

Phoebe was exhausted by the time they finished.

"I don't know, Flory. What if they get angry? What if this was a bad idea?"

Flory stared ahead as she drove down the highway. "Don't think about it. We did it. What's done is done."

Chapter 59

There was no way to avoid it. Junction was back in national news. The media had begun promoting the one-year anniversary like it was a national holiday. Reporters again reminded the people of Junction a murderer had lived in their midst. For days the *Junction Times'* front page ran photos from the previous year with an ongoing headline stating, "First Anniversary of Mineral Wells' Massacre."

The satellite trucks had returned to town. Alice saw them not only parked outside their home, but reporters and cameramen were stationed in front of Arrowhead Park, on the campus of the college, interviewing the mayor, and even in restaurants. What was this small town like, they wanted to know? How could a female mass murderer have come from here? Was there something about the town that bred this kind of behavior? The citizens of Junction furiously defended their community. They considered Lou a freak of nature.

An entire marketing campaign on the wholesomeness of Junction had begun weeks prior. To Alice, it felt like she was watching a bad movie. To make matters worse, her family's name was once again brought before the public. If Lou was guilty, then Alice and her entire family were guilty by association. Junction's small-town values were touted, and Lou was condemned for the abhorrent crimes she committed.

Alice found herself again barricaded in her bedroom. She couldn't go out of the house. The heavy, dark blanket returned to cover the front window in the living room. The four walls of their home again shrunk.

The day before the one-year anniversary Alice met with Laura. She dropped Rodney off at work and used the pickup, because Flory had said she and Phoebe needed her car all day. The anticipation of the impending remembrance brought back memories of when she learned about the mass shooting and what Lou had done. It was all she could do to get out of bed, drive Rodney to work, and meet with Laura. She would rather crawl into her hole.

Alice arrived at the church looking like she had just crawled out of bed. She had. But at least she was there. If Laura was surprised, she didn't show it.

Laura gave Alice a quick hug and ushered her upstairs to the library. Alice dragged herself up each step. She had no energy. She plopped into the chair and slumped. She was drained. Her mind was in a fog, and she could barely function. It was a miracle she was there.

"This is so hard," Alice said. "I wish tomorrow was over. Or better yet, I wish we could skip tomorrow." Alice pondered this then added, "But the media won't let us. That's for sure."

Laura nodded but said nothing.

"The satellite trucks have returned to our street, and once again our family is part of the news."

There was silence. Not the uncomfortable, awkward kind, but mere silence.

Finally, Laura spoke. "What are your plans for tomorrow? Have you given any thought to how you're going to spend the day?"

Alice shook her head. "I have no idea. All I know is I want tomorrow to be over."

Again silence.

Laura asked, "What are Flory and Phoebe doing tomorrow? What about Rodney?"

"I don't know. We haven't talked about it, and I didn't think to ask them. I guess I'm wrapped up in my own misery…"

Laura continued to prod. "Are each of you doing your own thing tomorrow? It's going to be a hard day for all of you. What might be best for your girls?"

Alice stared at Laura, amazed. "There you go again. You get to the heart of things, don't you?" A slight smile crept on Alice's face. "It's not just about me, is it? I have a family who is suffering, too." Alice sensed a shift in her thinking. It was slight and seismic at the same time. She removed herself from the center of the picture and considered what would be best for the family.

"You know," she continued, "our get-away place has always been Buffalo Springs. We used to pack a picnic and spend the day there, always coming back refreshed."

"That sounds like a wonderful idea," Laura said. "Is there any way you could make it more meaningful? Or do you just need to escape?"

"I'm not sure what you mean."

"Do you merely want to escape or use the time together to honor Lou's life? Do you want discuss the realities of what happened? It might be a good time to get things out in the open." Laura paused. "Do you remember what you told me about your parents after you learned about Lou's condition?"

"Yes. Schizophrenia was never mentioned. We acted like there was no mental illness in our home, even though it was on display almost every day after that." Alice considered what Laura said. "I like that. Honor Lou's life and allow them to ask questions. Don't cover up schizophrenia. They need to know the truth." Alice felt like she had stepped out of a warm shower, cleansed and refreshed.

Chapter 60

August 6, 2016, came on a Saturday because of leap year. It was overcast in the morning with a cool breeze, but meteorologists were predicting record-breaking heat for the day. Jose Martinez had set his alarm, but he was already awake. How had this day started a year ago? He had talked to his son, Mickey, the night before who had told him about his date. On Thursday, they hadn't spoken, and he missed Mickey's text. The next day he was dead.

Jose was grateful for work because it was about the only thing that kept him going. That and his church. He put on a clean shirt and a pair of pants and fixed himself some coffee. Like every Saturday, Jose was going to Mass. After Mass, he would drive to the cemetery and visit Mickey's grave. Then he'd go to work. He had become used to the silence in the house, but today it was unsettling. With his coffee in hand, he went outside and picked up the paper on the porch and added it to the pile of unread newspapers. What was the point in reading and rehashing what had happened? It was too painful. He pulled out one of the three chairs at the kitchen table, pushing the pile of papers aside.

"Camilla. Mickey. I miss you both so much." Jose trembled as he spoke. He didn't say anything else, but sat in the silence, knowing they were together. Jose glanced at his watch. It was time to go to Mass.

After Mass, Jose drove to the cemetery and parked his car outside the gate. It was a small cemetery with gravel paths, but no road. I forgot to bring flowers, he thought, dismally.

Mickey's grave was next to his mother's. There was a large oak tree nearby shading the area. Jose noticed a mason jar with fresh flowers in front of Mickey's grave. There must be some mistake. These flowers belong to someone else.

Jose bent down and picked up the mason jar, admiring the simple arrangement of flowers he knew he would be giving up. There was a card underneath the jar. His name, Mr. Martinez, was written on the envelope. Jose couldn't think of anyone who would have done this, but he felt pleased and less alone. He opened the envelope and pulled out a card. There was an image of a cardinal perched on a dogwood branch on the outside of the card. Inside on the left-hand side in the corner was printed, *"When a cardinal appears in your yard it's a visitor from heaven."* A hand-written note was on the right side.

Dear Mr. Martinez,

We are so sorry for the loss of your son, Mickey. We cannot imagine the hurt and sadness you feel. We wish more than anything we could take away your pain or do something for you. We hope you will not be angry with us for wanting to send you the flowers. And we hope you will forgive our family. We had no part in what our Aunt Lou did, and it haunts us every day.

With deepest sympathy, Flory and Phoebe Bennett

Jose was conflicted. On the one hand he felt violated, like they had infringed on his privacy. How dare they think they have a right to invade my grief! On the other hand, someone else had remembered this awful day and reached out to him. He picked up the flowers and the card and took them with him when he left.

****

Diana Coverdale sat in Jamie's room. She hadn't changed it in the year since Jamie was killed. She liked being there. Since Rick had moved out, she spent more and more time in Jamie's room. Her friends told her it wasn't healthy, but they didn't know what it was like to lose their only child. She was accused of pushing Rick out because of her obsession with Jamie. Get some help, they said. But they didn't understand.

She just wanted to die. Then she could be with her precious Jamie.

Diana's phone vibrated. She intentionally placed her phone face down. If she didn't see who it was, then she didn't have to answer it. Unless they left a message.

Her phone dinged. She had a voicemail. Sighing, she turned her phone over to see who had called. It was Rick.

"Hi, Diana. I know you're probably going to the cemetery today, and I thought maybe we could go together. Call me."

That was going to take too much energy to call him back and plan a time they could go together. Instead, Diana lay down on Jamie's bed.

A couple of hours later Diana felt someone nudging her.

"Diana, wake up." Rick jostled her shoulder. "Did you get my message?"

She struggled to wake up. "Yes. Sorry I didn't call you back. I fell asleep."

"When I didn't hear from you, I got worried." Rick stroked her hair. "Come on. Let's go to the cemetery."

"Now?"

"Yes, now."

Rick and Diana drove to Rose Hill Cemetery. Jamie's gravestone was on a small hill where Diana kept silk flowers in a vase. She noticed immediately the mason jar with flowers.

"Did you bring these flowers?" she asked Rick.

"No, I don't come here that often." He bent down and picked up the card that was underneath the jar. "Here's a card," he said and handed it to Diana.

When she pulled the card out of the envelope, she admired the drawing of the cardinal. "That's nice, but I wonder who it's from?" When Diana read the message inside the card, she felt like she had been socked in the gut. She gasped.

"What's wrong? Who's it from?" Rick took the card from her and read it. His face turned red.

"Why would they do this?" Diana started crying. "Don't they realize it's like salt has been poured into my wound?"

****

Seth Fisher sat on his bed in his mother's old room playing video games on his phone. He heard his grandmother's steps in the hallway. She tapped on the doorframe.

"Seth," she said. "Grandpa and I are going to take flowers to your mom's grave. Do you want to come?"

No. He didn't want to go. That was the last thing he wanted to do. All day there would be reminders of what had happened a year ago. Seth just wanted to go off by himself. He wished he were sixteen instead of thirteen, so he could get in a car and drive away.

"Seth?" His grandmother opened the door and stood

at the entry.

He glanced up. He still had on the clothes from the day before which he had slept in. His hair was greasy, and acne covered his face. He hated what was happening to his body.

"Did you hear me?" Her tone was quiet. It wasn't the demanding one she used when he intentionally ignored her.

"Yeah, I heard you," he said.

"Grandpa said he'd take you fishing after we go to the cemetery. I'll pack a lunch for you men."

Seth hated it when she called him and Grandpa men. But, on the other hand, going fishing sounded nice. "Okay," he said.

"It's supposed to be a scorcher today, so dress light and wear a hat."

Why did all women feel like they had to tell you what to wear and what to do? Seth nodded his head but didn't say anything.

Twenty minutes later, the three of them were in Grandpa's pickup on their way to his mother's grave. He had only been there one time, when they buried her. He knew Gran and Grandpa went often, but he always declined. Garden View Cemetery was located outside of Mineral Wells on the rolling plains. There were neat rows of headstones and markers and not a tree in sight. The three of them walked to the spot where Michelle was buried. Gran had picked daisies and zinnias from her garden and tied a piece of twine around them.

"What's this?" Gran bent down and picked up the mason jar with fresh flowers. They were beginning to wilt in the hot sun. She saw the card addressed to Mr. and Mrs. Fisher and Seth. "And there's a card, too."

Grandpa took the card and mason jar from her so she could put her own flowers by the grave. "Do you want me to read the card? Maybe it will say who the flowers are from."

Seth stood by his grandpa so he could see what the card said. The handwriting seemed like it belonged to a teenage girl. It was too cutesy.

After reading it, Grandpa crumbled the letter in his large fist, and his face turned red. He threw the jar on the ground, and Seth watched it shatter. "Where were you when your crazy aunt did this to our precious Michelle?" His voice growled in a way Seth had never heard before.

He watched his grandfather stomp away. His grandmother bent down and tried to pick up the broken pieces of glass and the scattered flowers. So much for going fishing.

****

Cheryl Youngblood ignored her phone. Reporters had been calling them all week. What was life like, a year later? they wanted to know. It was none of their damn business. They were living in a tomb—that's what it was like. Their sons had retreated from life, quitting soccer and baseball, and avoiding their friends. Cheryl didn't know if they were grieving or ashamed of what had happened to their brother, Blake, because no one talked. Kevin was the same. Their marriage was barely surviving, and he wouldn't agree to see a counselor. When he was home, he spent time in his office with the door shut.

She picked up her cell phone, like she did on so many days, and went to her voicemail. "Hi Mom. It's Blake. I made it to Mineral Wells just fine. The guys I've met are cool. We're getting ready to go get pizza and hang out. I'll call you tomorrow. Love you."

She'd never hear his voice again.

Even though it was Saturday, Kevin was at the office. He didn't even tell her good-bye. Cheryl considered asking him if he wanted to go to the cemetery. No, she didn't want to ask him. She wanted to spend time with Blake by herself.

The boys' bedroom doors were shut. No need to disturb them. She knew they wouldn't want to go.

The cemetery, which used to be on the edge of town before Oklahoma City grew, was now in midtown surrounded by an older neighborhood with a large Episcopal church nearby. Kevin's family had several plots, and Blake was buried next to his grandfather. Cheryl came to the cemetery often. It comforted her to sit on the stone bench nearby. She was going to plant some bulbs once it got cold enough, so there would be tulips in the spring.

Cheryl noticed the mason jar with flowers right away. She was pleased. Someone else had remembered Blake. She picked up the card underneath the flowers. When she read the note, she began to sob. Did they think putting flowers on Blake's grave would help anything? Cheryl felt like the sacred ground had been contaminated.

Now her day was ruined. Her time with Blake was tarnished. Who were these girls anyway? That woman was their aunt! A shiver passed through her body. What would she have done if someone in her family had done this?

****

On Saturday morning Leslie Cottingham was emptying the dishwasher and heard the doorbell ring. No one rang her doorbell. Not since she and her son, Sammy, had moved to the duplex.

There was a man at the door with a bouquet of flowers. How odd. Who would be sending them flowers? Surely not her ex. He had already moved on to a new girlfriend and her kid.

Leslie absentmindedly wiped her hands on her apron and unlocked the front door.

"Are you Mrs. Cottingham?" asked the man holding the flowers.

"Yes," she said.

"These flowers are for you." He handed them to her and said, "Have a nice day." Then he left.

Leslie stood at the door holding the flowers. It was a small bouquet of daisies and yellow button mums. There was a sympathy card attached. She set the flowers on the kitchen table and read the card.

"Sammy! Come here," Leslie yelled, alarmed. The flowers were from relatives of that woman who killed Amber. But why would they do that?

"What's wrong?" Sammy stumbled into the kitchen, barely awake.

"That woman who killed Amber, her nieces sent us flowers." A chill went down her spine.

"I don't get it," he said. "Why did they send us flowers?"

"I don't know," Leslie said. "I don't know whether to scream or cry."

Sammy picked up the card and read the note. He said, "I think it's kind of awkward and weird. Like, we're going to feel better because they sent us flowers? Do they think that's going to bring my sister back? Maybe they should call Dad. They seem to think along the same lines."

****

"They have it all wrong," Ann Goodson said. She set the newspaper down. "Why do they always have to over-dramatize and sensationalize everything?" Ann sat outside on the patio. A soft breeze rustled the newspaper. It was supposed to be a scorcher later that day, so Ann wanted to take full advantage of the pleasant weather before it turned hot. She planned to go to the cemetery soon.

"I wish you were here, Ken," she said. "I know you'd agree with me. I know you would have dived into this story, if it hadn't been about you and the others who died."

The whole thing hadn't made sense. The only reason that woman would have murdered Ken and the other ten was because something was terribly wrong with her. Ann viewed Lou Sutton as a victim of schizophrenia. However, some of the articles she'd read tried to equate violence with mental illness, inferring they went together. Ann disagreed. Instead, she believed violence happened only if serious mental illness went untreated, and that's what must have taken place. But why? she wondered. She had read books and articles about schizophrenia, the worst of all mental diseases, and it made her want to reach out to those afflicted.

The former high school English teacher had started volunteering at one of the homeless shelters and at the support organization for the mentally ill. Trying to find ways to volunteer and help had eased some of the pain and loneliness she felt with Ken gone.

An hour later Ann arrived at the cemetery. A row of crepe myrtles acted as a barrier for privacy from the traffic. A native pecan tree shaded Ken's grave. Ann noticed the mason jar with flowers and wondered who had put them there.

When she read the note, Ann began to cry. They weren't tears of anger, but of gratitude.

"Ken," Ann said to the grave marker, "Lou Sutton's family brought flowers." In her purse she had a bottle of water, which she poured onto the flowers to give them a drink. "How did they know I love sunflowers?" She examined the picture of the cardinal on the notecard and read the saying that was on the inside.

It was going to be an okay day.

****

Elizabeth Randolph's phone rang. It was Robert.

"I'm on my way," he said. "Are you sure you want to go out there now? It's ninety-three degrees in the shade."

Elizabeth sighed. Robert had left her no choice. He had decided not to cancel his golf game that morning. "Yes. I want to go now."

"What about later this afternoon?"

Elizabeth shook her head, even though she knew he couldn't see her. "The mosquitoes, dear."

"Oh, yeah. You're right."

"I'll be ready when you get home. Bye." Elizabeth put her phone in her purse. She had on a light-weight sundress. Her over-sized sun hat, which she wore to protect her skin, was on the counter next to her purse.

She couldn't believe it had been a year. Elizabeth thought of the last conversation she had had with Kathryn. It had been about her future. About moving to Dallas and talk of a possible wedding once Paul finished law school. Her face clouded. All that was gone forever.

Her beautiful, only daughter.

Her beautiful, only daughter.

The last year had been a fog. She didn't see how her life would ever get better again. Elizabeth saw no hope for normal. But she knew Robbie needed his parents. She tried, but it was so hard. Her therapist had prescribed anti-depressants, but she didn't like the way they made her feel. She seemed agitated and tired all the time. But the worst was the weight gain. Elizabeth was proud of her size four figure. So, her choices were to get fat or be sad. She chose being sad.

Robert entered through the back door. "I'll be ready as soon as I take a quick shower," he said. "Is Robbie coming with us?"

Elizabeth ran her hand across the quartz countertop. It was a habit—to feel for any missed messes. "No. He said he didn't want to go. It would make him sad."

"It *is* sad." Robert kissed her on the cheek. "I'll be out in a sec."

A stone wall surrounded Memorial Cemetery, and there was a tall bell tower in the center. Robert drove his Mercedes through the expansive grounds. Elizabeth kept a silk flower arrangement at Kathryn's grave. She noted to herself it was almost time to change it to fall mums. That was when she noticed the mason jar with fresh flowers. What is that doing here?

The mason jar seemed small and insignificant next to the spray of silk flowers. Robert bent down and picked up the card underneath the jar. There was a round dirt stain on the outside of the envelope from the jar. He brushed it off.

"Mr. and Mrs. Randolph," he read.

Elizabeth watched him open the envelope and pull out the card with the cardinal drawing on the outside. He read the note, and he scowled. "Is this some kind of cruel joke?" Robert wadded the card and stuffed it in his pocket.

"What did it say? Who's it from?" Elizabeth couldn't understand his reaction.

"You don't want to know," Robert said.

****

The timer went off, and Frances Eckles pulled the last pan of oatmeal cookies from the oven. They had been Danielle's favorite. She put them on the rack to cool. Frances was going to send some of the cookies to Kayla's parents. They had stayed in touch since the two girls had been killed.

Bianca and David Merrell had paid for Danielle's funeral expenses. There was no way Frances and her husband, Roger, could have afforded it. The Merrells had been her lifeline. She couldn't go to Kayla's service, but the Merrells had driven up from Dallas to attend the small service for Danielle. They were the only black couple in the church, but it didn't seem to bother them. It bothered Roger, though.

Frances glanced at the clock. It was getting late. She wanted to get to the cemetery before Roger and her sons came home. Frances had cleaned the house from top to bottom, to honor Danielle. Then she made cookies.

It had been a hard year, but she was grateful for all the people who had been supportive. There were her boss and the people at work, the ladies at church, and, of course, the Merrells.

Roger—well, he could go to hell. He was drinking even more. And when he was drunk, he was mean. He went around yelling about the murdering bitch who had killed his precious daughter. Frances had given up. She only stayed married because she couldn't afford to move out. Thankfully, Roger and the boys had gone fishing that day. She doubted he had remembered what day it was.

Danielle was buried in the small cemetery behind the Methodist church where Frances attended. She often came out to the cemetery after church. It was a good time because her heart was calm. When she arrived, she saw a cardinal fly past her and perch itself in a redbud tree. It seemed to tilt its head.

"Hi, little guy." Frances acknowledged the bird. Then she saw the mason jar with the flowers. Someone had brought flowers for Danielle. She wondered who had done it. Probably one of her friends from church, she thought. There was a card underneath the jar. It said Mr. and Mrs. Eckles on the envelope. Whoever brought the flowers didn't know them very well, because they wouldn't have included Roger on the card. It seemed strange at that point.

Frances noticed the bright red cardinal on the outside of the card. "Here's a picture of you," she said to the bird. On the inside she read the printed saying, *"When a cardinal appears in your yard it's a visitor from heaven."* She felt goose bumps on her arms. Then she read the hand-written note.

All the memories of that horrible day a year ago came rushing back—the waiting, then finding out the worst had happened. God, why did you have to let Danielle die? Frances had asked that question more times than she could count. And the only answer she had ever received was silence. She wanted to shake her fist at God, and she had. Then later she went on her knees and thanked God for bringing the caring people into her life.

What would she have done without them? She knew they were God's helpers.

Frances searched for positive signs in the worst of times. That was how she had gotten through the past year. So, when she saw the cardinal in the cemetery, she knew it was a sign. She knew Danielle was telling her to forgive the family of the woman who had murdered her.

****

Misting rain fell as David and Bianca Merrell drove to the cemetery in Dallas to visit Kayla's grave. Clouds had descended on Dallas making it a melancholy day. It fit their mood.

David turned off the ignition and faced Bianca. "What are you thinking?"

She sighed. "I'm thinking how grateful I am we had twenty years with Kayla." She wiped a tear as it fell on her cheek. "And you?"

David shook his head. "My thoughts aren't as wholesome as yours." David struggled. It had been a hard year. He had watched Bianca suffer, yes, but with grace. She seemed to find silver linings everywhere.

"Come on, let's get out." David opened the back seat door and removed a large bouquet of fresh flowers. The two of them walked side by side to Kayla's grave. Her headstone read, *Kayla Louise Merrell, A Beautiful Soul.* Her birth and death dates were below, and a simple cross was at the base.

David handed Bianca the flowers, and she knelt to place them on the ground. David stood erect as he watched his wife crumble. Soon she was sobbing, and he bent down and put his arms around her.

"Oh, God, it hurts so much," Bianca whispered. David held her. He shut his eyes tight to keep his own tears from forming. He had to be strong. The two remained locked together for some time. In the distance a siren could be heard. The back of David's knit shirt was getting soaked.

He stood and slowly pulled Bianca to her feet. The knees of her white slacks were brown from the mud. He brushed a wiry curl from her face. David took her hand and began to walk back to the car. It was too wet to stay much longer.

But Bianca resisted. "I don't want to leave yet," she said. "You can wait in the car. But I want to spend a little more time here today."

David looked at her, not sure if she meant it or not.

"No, really. David, wait in the car. I want you to. I want to be alone."

"Okay," he said and kissed her damp, dark cheek.

From the car he watched Bianca, as it appeared she was having a conversation. What was she telling Kayla? He felt his heart pound in his chest. It hurt as if it was breaking. Now he understood what was meant by a broken heart. Grieving the loss of his only daughter and youngest child and watching his wife in her pain and grief were almost more than he could handle.

By living in Texas, the Merrells had been saved from daily reminders by the media of the one-year anniversary that the families in Oklahoma had to endure. On the other hand, no one in Texas understood what August sixth meant to them.

When they returned home, there was a note on the door. Flowers had been delivered, and their neighbor had them.

"I wonder who sent them?" Bianca said. "Maybe it was Frances. I've been meaning to call her."

When David returned from the neighbor's house, he handed Bianca a small bouquet of alstroemeria in shades of white and pink.

"Who sent it?" she asked. Setting down the bouquet, she pulled out the card.

David watched her read a rather long note silently. Her expression changed from sorrow to anger, then back to sorrow. "Who sent them?" He couldn't stand it any longer.

Bianca gave him the note. He felt rage build up inside of him. Did they think a cheap vase of flowers was going to alleviate the pain they felt? He wadded up the card, and he was ready to dump the flowers in the trash.

"Stop! Don't throw them away. I—I don't know why. I want to keep them." Bianca picked up the crumbled note and read it again. She looked at David. "They must be hurting, too."

****

Hannah Cummins offered to pick up her mother, Sylvia. She didn't want to ride in her mother's smoke-filled car. By driving, Hannah determined how long they would be at the cemetery.

How she missed Olen! Without her twin, Hannah felt like one of her legs had been cut off. A part of her was gone. But Sylvia's grief bordered on morbidity, grief for grief's sake. And it was too much.

It was just the two of them now. When Hannah's father had died of a heart attack six months before the shooting, she had hoped they would become closer. They only had each other now. But Hannah began to dread Sylvia's phone calls. She felt like her mother had a death wish. Hannah didn't.

More than anything she wanted to go to the

cemetery by herself. That would have to wait until tomorrow. Hannah drove past the cemetery on her way to work at the hospital. "Hi Dad. Hi Olen," she'd say. It was a nice way to start and end her shifts.

Hannah picked up the framed photo of the two of them taken on their twenty-first birthdays. She kept it on a small shelf in the kitchen. They each held a bottle of Corona and wore over-sized sombreros. They had their lives before them. It was her favorite picture of them.

Hannah heard her phone buzz inside her purse. She knew it was her mother.

"Hi, Mom. I'm leaving. I'll be at your house in ten minutes. No, I didn't forget we were going. We had already agreed I was going to pick you up at ten. I was about to call you." Hannah rolled her eyes. "Okay. I'll see you. I'll honk my horn when I get there. I'll wait in the car. Okay. Bye."

Sometimes Mom could be exhausting. "Sorry, Dad," Hannah said and glanced up. As she opened her apartment door to leave, she saw a man standing with flowers.

"Are you Hannah Cummins?"

Startled, Hannah nodded her head.

The man handed her the flowers. "Here," he said. "Have a nice day."

Hannah stood stunned. She backed into her apartment and set the bouquet of sunflowers on the kitchen table. Who would have sent her flowers? She pulled out the card and read the message.

Flory and Phoebe Bennett? Hannah felt a mixture of rage and confusion. Relatives of the woman who had murdered Olen had the nerve to send her flowers. How dare they think by sending flowers everything would be fine. She picked up the typed-written note and read it again.

Hannah sat down in the chair by the kitchen table and cried. She cried for Olen, thinking of how he had died alone, with no family around him. She cried for her dad. If he had still been alive, maybe things would have turned out different. She cried for her mother, who had not been able to move past that horrible day. She cried for herself, how lonely she had felt since her brother had been killed.

Hannah's phone rang. She knew it was her mother, but she didn't answer it.

****

"Old MacDonald had a farm, ee-i-ee-i-o…"

Angie Almon glanced in her rearview mirror at fourteen-month-old Lizzie. She was such a happy child.

"And on this farm, he had a cow, ee-i-ee-i-o…"

Soon they were moo-moo-mooing and quack-quack-quacking and oink-oink-oinking. What a joy Lizzie was. How she wished Taylor could see her.

Angie choked. How many times did she think those thoughts to herself? She felt that familiar ache in her chest and the burning in her eyes, as she fought back the tears. Just like that. Angie felt like her life went from joy to sorrow with hardly any in-between.

Her parents had offered to come with her to the cemetery or to stay with Lizzie while she went, but she wanted to take Lizzie. They didn't know how often she and Lizzie went to see Taylor. She knew someday she would have to tell Lizzie what had happened to her daddy. But for now… Angie quickly brushed a tear away.

It had been a hard year. No, an awful year. Angie

went back to work not long after Taylor died. She hated putting Lizzie in day care. She and Taylor had agreed she would stay at home until Lizzie was old enough to go to school. But now she was a single parent, and she had no choice.

Angie liked going to the cemetery. It was peaceful there. They drove through the wrought-iron gates. At Taylor's gravesite, she parked her car. She had a view of the skyline of downtown Tulsa.

"Come on, Lizzie. We're going to visit with Daddy."

Angie lifted her out of the car seat. She squeezed her gently and kissed her cheek before setting her down. Lizzie stood up and toddled over to the jar of flowers while Angie was busy retrieving her blanket and toys. She discovered them before Angie.

"Look, Lizzie, flowers," Angie said when she saw them. Who put flowers at Taylor's grave? Angie saw the card underneath the jar and picked it up. Her name was written on the envelope. She pulled out the card with a drawing of a cardinal on the outside. When she read the message inside, Angie began to sob. Memories of the news reports, the police officers coming to her door, the agony she felt all came rushing back.

"Taylor!" Angie sobbed. Lizzie stopped and watched her mother. Then she began to cry, too.

****

Rodney stood at the kitchen door and observed his daughters. On the counter were eight slices of whole wheat bread. Flory spread mustard on half the slices, adding cheese and ham. Phoebe took Sutton cookies out of the oven and placed them on the rack to cool. This time Alice would be coming with them to Buffalo

Springs. Phoebe's idea finally worked.

Phoebe saw Rodney. "Dad, what are you doing?"

"Just watching my two favorite daughters," he said. "Are you girls about ready?"

"We are," Flory said. "The question is, is Mom ready?"

"I'll get her." Rodney walked back to the bedroom and found Alice sitting on the edge of their bed. She was crying as she held two framed photos. He picked up one. It was of Alice when she was a baby. Six-year-old Lou sat in a rocking chair holding her. The other photo was the one taken on Carl and Florence's wedding anniversary with the seven of them. The contrast between the two was enormous.

"Hey, I know it's going to be a tough day, but we have to be available to Flory and Phoebe today. They need us." Rodney put his arm around Alice.

"I know. It's just so hard. I realized I was fourteen when Lou had her first psychotic episode, and Phoebe was the same age when she had her last one."

Tears streamed down her face, and he followed her gaze to the painting hanging on the wall. It was the one Florence had painted of Alice and Lou when they were girls.

"I wish I could stay home," she said.

"But you can't," Rodney insisted. There was no anger or annoyance in his tone. He continued, "Remember what you said Laura told you—that today would be a day to honor Lou and the good memories."

Alice nodded. "You're right. It's just hard," she repeated. "Today is for Lou—and for the girls.

Rodney nodded. "Yes."

Phoebe stuck her head in the door. Rodney watched

her sum up the situation. "Mom, are you okay?"

Alice wiped her face with her hand and put the framed photographs back in their place. "Yes and no," she said. "I'm really sad, but I want to be with you all."

"Come on. Let's go. It'll be good to get out of town today," Rodney said.

Yes, it was going to be a difficult day, but they would get through it.

Chapter 61

Working for Mrs. C had been a godsend. Flory discovered she enjoyed being around the elderly and realized what she wanted to study. COC had a two-year associate degree for physical therapy assistants. Two years was much more economical than four—or seven for a physical therapist—and her parents had been relieved.

Flory's first day of college felt like she was back in grade school. Here she was, living at home and having her mother drop her off at the campus. She had envisioned going away to school. At least away from Junction. Instead, she was stuck at home. Another dream shot down.

Okay, she told herself. I can focus on how miserable I am, or I can go to school. Which is more important? Do I want to make something of my life, or do I want to stay stuck? She knew the answer, but it wasn't easy. A big part of her was still stuck. It was hard not having friends. Maybe I'll meet people in my classes who have never heard of Lou Sutton. Junction was too small for that to happen. Everyone knew everyone else. That was why Flory had wanted to leave. Yet, here she was, going to college in her hometown. This was *not* part of her plan. Aunt Lou had done a real number on them.

Flory wanted to go where no one knew her. She wanted to start over with no expectations from anyone—

her parents, her classmates, no one. How long would she have to run away from life? How long before Aunt Lou was a faded memory, just another old story? How long before she could be her own person without worrying about what was being said behind her back? Her face burned as she recalled the nurses who had talked about her family as if *they* were criminals, too.

Just get me out of here, she screamed inside her head. She wanted to go where no one had ever heard of Junction, Oklahoma.

"Junction? You're from Junction," they would say. *"Isn't that where that woman who murdered the people at the Mineral Wells bar was from? Did you know her?"*

What would she say? *"No, I never knew her."*

They would respond with, *"Can you imagine someone doing that? How horrible! What kind of person murders strangers? She must have been a sick-o!"*

Flory had this imaginary conversation often. What would she say to this? *"Yes, she must have been a sick-o."* Or, *"I feel sorry for her."* She could never say what she really felt. *"She was my aunt, and I hate her for what she did."*

But then, Flory would regret her thoughts. She knew Aunt Lou couldn't help her behavior. Deep down Flory felt sorry for her. It was a cruel disease. What if she became schizophrenic? That was her other unspoken fear.

Flory had two classes in the morning and one in the afternoon, with a three-hour break in between. This will be good, she thought, I can get most of my reading done while I'm here.

After her morning classes Flory found a spot in the library and pulled out a textbook. It didn't take long for her stomach to start growling. Flory wanted to skip lunch, but her body told her differently. She didn't want to be the only person eating alone. Closing her book and loading her backpack, Flory trudged toward the Student Union. Glancing around, Flory saw several students eating alone with their laptops open or scrolling through their phone. That was a relief. She spotted an empty table near a window and settled in.

By the end of the day Flory felt more at ease. No one had recognized her. No one had asked her if she was related to a murderer. She was just another student.

Flory saw Alice's car in the visitor parking lot. As she walked toward it, she heard her name called.

"Flory." It was Abby Sullivan, a student she knew from high school.

"Hi, Abby," Flory said. Anyplace would be better than here talking to Abby.

"I didn't know you were going COC," Abby said. "I've seen several other classmates from high school. Isn't that great?"

Flory nodded.

Abby continued talking, but Flory didn't pay attention.

Finally, she said, "I've got to go. Nice talking to you." Flory turned and walked away from the parking lot. Please, Mom, don't get out of the car and call my name. Please stay in the car. Immediately her phone rang.

"Flory, I'm in the parking lot. Where are you going?"

"Sorry, Mom. I forgot something. I'll be right back." Flory hung up the phone before her mother could ask anything else. She hoped Abby wasn't following her.

Maybe it was better to be alone than around people who knew you.

Flory went inside the closest building and found the restroom. She washed her hands. Staring into the mirror, she wondered, who would want to be friends with that person? What had happened to her confidence? It had evaporated.

"Okay, Flory," she told herself. "You can do this. It's called going to school. Don't get stuck." Flory slung her backpack over her shoulders and walked toward her mother's car.

Chapter 62

The rain from the day before had cooled the temperature. Newly planted mums and pansies perked up from the drink of water. The brown grass didn't seem so brittle under Flory's sandals as she walked across campus. Perhaps it would start feeling like fall, instead of the oppressive heat of Indian summer.

Her classes were going well, and she had made a few acquaintances. However, she remained anxious, not wanting to get to know anyone too well for fear they would find out to whom she was related. After running into Abby the first week of classes, she avoided anyone from her high school. Flory decided to eat in study areas that permitted food instead of the cafeteria. But being a loner was not her style. She longed for friends and craved conversation. Flory found herself watching classmates walk together across campus and feeling a twinge of envy. She wished she had someone waiting for her after class like others she saw.

Flory went to her favorite spot, a large leather chair in the shape of a baseball glove. But someone else was sitting there. Disappointed, she found herself glaring at the top of the head of the person sitting in *her* chair. It was some guy with dark hair, lots of it, like a mop on his head. His T-shirt caught her attention. There were various fruits with faces and arms and legs, each one speaking a different word—fairy, care, chapel, Montana, escape What did it mean?

"Confused?"

Flory heard a deep voice, and it startled her.

The guy sitting in her chair repeated himself. "I said, are you confused? With my shirt?"

He appeared older than her eighteen years, but he had a nice smile. She smiled back, embarrassed he had caught her staring at him. Finally, she admitted, "Yes, I don't get it. There's a cherry, a pear, an apple, a grape, and a banana—and they're all speaking. Then the orange at the end of the line is crying. Is there some secret meaning?"

The twenty-something stood up. "What it is, is my favorite T-shirt. See if you can figure it out." As he spoke, he pulled his shirt tight so that Flory could see the entire design. "Now say everything you see," he told her.

"I just did," Flory said, and she repeated the names of the fruit on the shirt.

He laughed. "No, there's more on the shirt. What about the words?" Then he pointed to each talking fruit as she said it.

"Cherry-fairy, pear-care, apple-chapel, banana-Montana, grape-escape, and a crying orange." Flory shrugged her shoulders. "I still don't get it."

"By the way, I'm Jesse," he said.

"I'm Flory. Nice to meet you." And it was.

"What do all the talking fruits have in common with each other?" Jesse asked.

Flory ran through the line of fruits once again, mumbling to herself. Then she got it. "They all rhyme."

"That's right. Now, what about the orange?" Jesse said.

"Well, he's crying because he doesn't have a word

like the others."

"Because? Come on, you can figure it out."

Flory was enjoying herself, and it seemed this good-looking guy named Jesse was, too. "Because...I don't know. Tell me."

"Because nothing rhymes with orange!"

Flory laughed. "That's funny. I like your shirt."

"Thanks," Jesse said. "So, what are you studying here at the world-famous campus of COC?"

"I'm studying to be a physical therapy assistant. How about yourself?"

"I'm gen-ed right now. Just trying to get my feet back on the ground. I've been uneducated for a while." Jesse used his fingers to make the quotation marks when he said uneducated.

"I see," Flory said. But she didn't see. What did that mean?

"You're wondering what I was doing, aren't you? I was in the rodeo circuit. Right out of high school. But the injuries started adding up. I decided I needed to find a way to earn a living that didn't abuse my body." Jesse shrugged his shoulders. "So, here I am." He added, "I could have benefitted from knowing a PT personally." He raised his eyebrows.

This guy is flirting with me. She hoped she wasn't blushing. "PT-*A*," she corrected.

"What's the difference?"

"About five years of school. I can't afford that, so I'm taking the shortcut." Flory was enjoying herself and decided she wanted to continue this banter. "By the way," she said, "you're sitting in *my* chair."

"Your chair?" Jesse turned and examined the chair. He had one of those physiques she used to call an upside-down triangle—broad shoulders and small hips. His pecs and biceps were squeezed into his T-shirt. He had a dimple when he smiled, and his eyes were dark brown and narrow, like he spent all his time in the sun, squinting. "I don't see your name on it," he said.

Flory laughed. "Someone must have taken my name tag off."

Jesse glanced at the paper bag she held. "Have you eaten? I was trying to study, but my stomach began overruling my brain. I'm starving." He laughed.

"I usually eat while I study in here. I was trying to find a place to sit, since *my* place was taken." She pretended to be annoyed.

"Would you like to join me while I grab a burger in the cafeteria? I promise, I don't bite."

"Sure. That'd be fine." Flory decided walking into the cafeteria with him might not be a bad thing.

Flory learned Jesse had grown up on a ranch, and his family had been in the ranching business for generations. For him, riding horses was like breathing. His dad had put him on a horse when he was two, and, as he said, the rest was history. When he asked Flory about herself, she became vague and evasive. She told him her parents owned a small business but didn't say what it was.

On Friday, they had agreed to meet by the baseball glove chair. Flory arrived at the appointed time, but he wasn't there. What if he doesn't show up? What if he has a girl friend? She saw Jesse walking toward her and breathed a sigh of relief.

"Hey, Flory. I was afraid you weren't going to show up."

"Hey yourself. I was worried you weren't going to come."

They both laughed as they walked toward the cafeteria. As they began to eat, Jesse pulled out a copy of the school paper. On the cover was an article titled, "School Shootings: Are College Campuses Safe?" Flory froze. She felt like running away, but her feet seemed nailed to the floor.

"What's the matter, Flory? You look like you saw a dead person."

Flory didn't know what to say. She didn't know how to explain, or if she should explain why she appeared so upset. What if Jesse assumed what everyone else did? What if he thought she must be awful because of Aunt Lou? She decided she didn't want him to know.

Trying to regain her composure, Flory said, "I guess I'm tired of the articles about shootings. If you ask me, it's old news." She knew she didn't sound convincing. Her words didn't match the expression she had on her face. She knew that.

"If you say so. But I think it's important. There have been so many random shootings. I just don't get it."

Flory remained silent.

"I've been around guns all my life. I learned to shoot when I was a kid. But I also learned about gun safety. My question is, what kind of person would go into a bar and start randomly shooting at people, like what happened last year in Mineral Wells? It doesn't make any sense to me." Jesse shook his head, but he didn't take his eyes off Flory.

She felt her heart beating, and sweat dripped down her back. "Well," Flory stammered, "I heard the woman who shot those people last year had some mental issues. I don't know, maybe she wasn't right in her head when she did it." Flory had never defended Aunt Lou. It was a strange experience.

"If you ask me, they should lock people up like that. I'm glad somebody shot her."

Flory couldn't take it any longer. "I've got to go. I have a test next period, and I need to study. Thanks for the lunch." She picked up her backpack, along with the uneaten sandwich, and rushed out of the cafeteria. She knew Jesse was watching her. She could feel his eyes on her back. I can't do this. She choked down a sob.

As she left the cafeteria, she wondered, now where do I go? If I go back to the baseball glove chair, he might find me. She liked Jesse and thought he liked her. Aunt Lou once again had to come between Flory and any hope of having a relationship. It wasn't fair. I just want to be normal again, maybe have a boyfriend.

Flory was unable to concentrate in her afternoon class. She was grateful there wasn't a test, like she had told Jesse. When Alice picked her up, she was unusually surly, more so than normal.

"How was your day?" Alice asked.

"Fine." Flory spoke abruptly. Alice raised her eyebrows and pursed her lips, but neither spoke.

****

Flory ran across campus. She knew she was late, but she didn't care. Instead of studying, after lunch she and Jesse had thrown a frisbee. Flory pulled her hoody around her as a gust of cool air blew. She thought back to earlier in the day. She had gone to her regular spot, the giant baseball glove chair and began reading an assignment. Before she finished a page, she sensed someone watching her. Glancing up, Flory saw Jesse standing in front of her.

"That's my chair," he said, smiling at her.

"No, it's mine," Flory said. She laughed. "When I saw you in it last week, I was initially pissed someone was in *my* chair."

"You're like Goldilocks, aren't you?" Jesse settled into the oversized chair next to her. Flory closed her book and scooted over.

"So, can you tell me what happened last week? Did I do or say something to make you mad?" Jesse turned toward Flory, and he brushed a stray hair from her face.

"No, not really. It's hard to explain."

"Well, try me. I can understand most things explained to me," Jesse said.

Flory shifted her weight and caused Jesse's arm to touch hers. "Maybe I will…later," she said, "but not now." Flory wanted to make sure she could trust him. But how? Would he reject her once he found out? She hardly knew him, but she wanted to get to know him better. He did say he was glad someone had shot Aunt Lou, and it was hard to get past that.

Jesse shrugged his shoulders, as if to say, whatever. He picked up her lunch sack and opened it. "What have we here?" He pulled out an apple. "Mmmm." Jesse pretended to take a bite.

"Stop it," Flory said. She grabbed the apple and her sack lunch, laughing.

Jesse's stomach growled. He held his hand over his stomach to stop the noise. They both laughed again. Others in the room appeared annoyed and shushed them.

Jesse stood and slung his backpack over one shoulder. "Come on," he whispered, "let's go someplace where we don't have to be quiet."

Jesse bought a ham sandwich and a bag of chips from the cafeteria, and they found a spot outside. The sun was shining, and it felt good.

Once settled, Jesse said, "By the way, I think I should tell you I don't drink."

"Well, I'm not supposed to," Flory said, "because I'm not twenty-one."

"Yes, but I *really* don't drink. Not anymore."

Flory didn't know why he was telling her this. It seemed kind of strange.

Jesse turned toward her. Flory wanted him to touch her again, like when he had brushed the hair from her face. "I'm a recovering alcoholic. My dad's in recovery, too. And my older brother, well, he's in rehab. I just wanted to be up front with you. Just in case."

In case we decide we like each other? Flory wondered if that was what he wanted to say but didn't. She wanted to say she liked him, and she had secrets, too. But she wasn't ready to share hers.

"So, you don't drink, and I can't drink. That's fine with me."

"Okay. No drinking then." Jesse seemed relieved.

"What happens if you take a drink?" Flory had never been around anyone who admitted to being an alcoholic.

"I can't. I'll relapse. And it gets more difficult to hit rock bottom, and you get hooked on harder stuff. It's bad. I'm watching my big brother lose his life." Jesse paused. "He's gone to rehab I don't know how many times. It never seems to take. Dad and me, I guess we got lucky. Maybe we like what we do too much. Alcohol and horses don't mix. And certainly not guns."

Flory thought about what he said.

"Hey, can I give you a ride home?" Jesse asked.

"That might be better than having my mom pick me up." She laughed.

Flory met Jesse after her last class. He was leaning against a tree in his cowboy boots and jeans and another crazy T-shirt. All he needed was a cowboy hat. His hair was thick and wavy and kind of long. She wanted to run her fingers through it.

"Hey," Jesse said as Flory walked up.

"Hey yourself," Flory said. It had been a long time since someone had paid attention to her the way he did. It was nice. He was nice.

Jesse walked around to the passenger side of his pickup and opened the door for Flory. This keeps getting better.

Jesse turned on the ignition. The radio blared country music, a song by Jerry Jeff Walker. He turned it down. "So, tell me where we're going."

"What if we take a detour before you take me home?"

"A detour sounds fine with me."

Flory directed Jesse to Arrowhead Park. There were a handful of walkers and joggers on the trail that circled the park. At the pond several children fed the ducks, and a boy and his dad were fishing. A mother swung her toddler on the swing at the playground. Scrub oaks and sumacs along the creek beside the trail were starting to turn. The sun had returned, and it was nice to be outside.

"My best friend, rather my former best friend, and I used to come here a lot. It was better than talking on the phone or texting."

"What do you mean by former?" Jesse asked.

"It's complicated. But she dumped me, along with my old boyfriend and most everyone else at school," Flory said.

"So, what did you do to get everyone to turn against

you? Kill someone?"

Flory couldn't believe what she heard, and her face showed it.

"What did I say?" Jesse stammered. "It was a joke. I didn't mean it. Did I screw up again?"

"It's nothing. Never mind." Maybe this wasn't such a good idea. She crossed her arms. Suddenly the breeze felt cool.

They walked in silence for several minutes. Flory sensed Jesse trying to make gestures to repair the unknown damage he had done. He started to put his arm around her, then stopped. He turned to say something, then didn't. His long strides prevented Flory from walking ahead of him.

Finally, Flory turned to him. "I guess I'd better go home now."

Jesse grabbed her arm. "Whoa! That's it? You're not going to tell me what's wrong? Just give me the silent treatment? At least tell me what I did wrong."

Flory stopped, but she kept her eyes down. "It's really, really personal. No, I didn't kill anyone. I didn't get pregnant. I didn't rob a bank either."

"You're not going to tell me, or you don't want to tell me. Is that it?"

Flory nodded.

"So, I have to guess. Or maybe walk on eggshells, because I don't know what I'm going to say that might upset you." Jesse let his words hang in the air. There was a bench ahead near the trail. Jesse took her arm and led her toward it. He sat her down, and he sat next to her.

"Flory," he said. "Look at me." He gently turned her head toward him. "I'm sorry I upset you. That wasn't my intention. I don't know what I did or said. I bared my soul to you at lunch. Do you know how many people I've told that to?"

Flory shook her head. She felt mute.

"Let's just say I don't say anything unless I have to. And I didn't have to say anything to you, but I did." Jesse waited. "I told you because I wanted to. I wanted to be honest with you. I thought maybe we had something going. Something clicked for me, you know?"

Jesse's eyes pleaded with her. She felt so bad. She wanted to believe him. Finally, she admitted, "Something clicked for me, too." She saw relief spread over his face when she said that.

Jesse took a deep breath. "How about I give you some space? We don't know each other that well, but I want to get to know you. I won't text or call you the rest of the week. If you think you're ready to open up, maybe we can get together Friday night. I know a place where we can build a campfire and have a picnic."

"I like that idea." Flory wanted to say more. "Jesse, I'm sorry." She touched his arm. "And thanks."

"Don't mention it," he said.

A breeze came up as the sun went behind the clouds. Flory shivered. "I guess I'd better go home now."

They walked back to his truck, and Jesse opened the passenger door for her. *I wonder if he does this every time?*

Blake Shelton's voice came on when Jesse started the ignition. "Do you like country music?" he asked.

"I never listened to it much."

"You gotta listen to the words. That's what makes it country. Words are primary. Melody is secondary."

Chapter 63

It seemed Friday would never come, but finally it did. Flory spent her lunch hour at the giant baseball glove chair, hoping to see him. But Jesse remained true to his word. There were no calls or texts, not even a visual sighting of him. How was she to know if they were still on for that night?

I guess I'll have to text him, she decided.

—*Hey, J. It's me. Are we still on for tonight? Hope so.*—

Flory reread her text before sending it. I guess it sounds okay, she thought, and clicked SEND.

Flory waited. No answer. Maybe he was in class, or maybe he had changed his mind. Try as she would, her mind convinced her he had changed his mind. When Flory's afternoon class let out, she felt her phone vibrate. She gathered her books and walked into the hall before she checked her phone. It was Jesse.

—*I'm counting on it. Bring your appetite and a warm jacket. Can I pick u up at 7?*—

—*Sure*—, she texted and added a smiley face. She hoped that wasn't too cheesy, but that was how she felt, all smiley.

When Alice picked Flory up that afternoon, she tried to act nonchalant, as if it was the start of another boring weekend. But she wasn't successful because her mother noticed.

"Flory, you look so happy, like you aced a big test or got asked out on a date."

"Mom!" Flory tried to act embarrassed, but she smiled, adding, "I did."

"You did what? Ace a test or get asked out on a date?"

"I'm going on a date," Flory said. "Well, it's not a real date, more of a friend date. More of 'can we be friends or not' kind of date." She kept smiling. She couldn't stop.

"Well, it appears to me like you're hoping you and what's-his-name can be friends," Alice said. "Who is this guy?"

"Remember last week when I told you I was getting a ride home?"

Alice nodded.

"Well, that's the guy. His name is Jesse, and he's taking classes at COC, too."

"Is he in one of your classes?" Alice asked.

"No, I met him while studying." Flory said, remembering the encounter. She had never had a cute guy flirt with her like that. "He's nice. Mom, you and Dad will like him," she added.

****

Flory stood in front of her closet. She couldn't decide what to wear. Jesse had said to dress warm. Maybe Phoebe could help her. "Phoebe," Flory said as she stood in her sister's doorway, "can you help me?"

Phoebe glanced up from her phone. She still had at least one friend.

"What do you need?"

Flory ambled in sheepishly. "Well, I kind of have a date, and I'm not sure what to wear."

Phoebe dropped her phone. "A date! Who's the guy? Where is he taking you?"

"His name is Jesse, and he's taking me someplace where we're going to build a campfire and have a picnic. So, I must dress warmly, but I want to look, you know..."

"Sexy?"

Flory rolled her eyes. "Kind of. I want to look appealing, casual and comfortable, but cute, and attractive."

"All those things you aren't," Phoebe said, laughing. Flory grabbed a pillow and threw it at her. "You know I was joking. Imagine me, little sister, helping you get dressed for a date. I like it."

The two of them pulled out half of Flory's closet as they tried to put together the perfect outfit for her date. Flory checked the weather on her phone. It was supposed to be cold. "Maybe I should bring a thermos of hot chocolate. What do you think?"

"Better yet how about taking some Sutton cookies with you?" Phoebe said.

"Good idea."

Between the two of them they figured out Flory's outfit. Skinny jeans tucked into her boots, her favorite fitted turtleneck with a fleece vest, knit hat, scarf, gloves, and her grungy jacket, in case it got really cold. She found a tin of Sutton cookies in the freezer, and she took a half dozen.

Flory was checking her makeup one last time when she heard the doorbell ring. Her heart fluttered, and she dropped her lipstick on the bathroom floor. She hadn't felt this nervous in a long time.

Her entire family was curious to meet Jesse. Before

she could make it down the hall to the front door, she heard Rodney's voice. "You must be Jesse. Come on in. Flory's almost ready, I'm sure."

Flory ran back and grabbed her phone and stuffed it into the pocket of her vest, taking one last glance in the mirror. She forced herself to walk, as if it was last week instead of over a year since she had been on a date. She stopped before entering the room. From her vantage point she could see her entire family and the back of Jesse's head. Poor guy. Then she remembered the cookies.

She ran past them to grab the cookies. "Flory," Alice called.

"Just a minute. I forgot something." Flory returned to the living room, and Jesse smiled when he saw her. "I guess you met my family," she said.

"I did."

An awkward silence followed. There was no point in introducing Jesse because it had already happened. "I guess we'll be going then," Flory said.

"Nice meeting you," Jesse said. He shook Rodney's hand and nodded to Alice and Phoebe.

"Nice family," Jesse said as they backed out of the driveway. The country music station played at a low volume.

"Thanks." Suddenly Flory felt shy. She didn't know what to say. Talking and joking on the campus were different from being picked up at her house. A nervous silence filled the truck. She didn't know where they were going. Should she ask him, or would that seem rude?

Jesse broke the silence. "I hope you like chicken."

"Is that what I smell? It smells delicious," Flory said.

"Thanks. I kind of cheated, though." Jesse turned toward Flory. "You look nice."

Flory felt herself blush. "So, where are we going?"

"Back to our place," Jesse said.

"Our place?"

"My parents' ranch. It's on Bison Creek past Blue Stem Road. We have a spot on our property where we build campfires. As long as it's not too windy. Fire threat, you know."

Did that mean she was going to meet his parents? She thought of her own family and who they were, more specifically, to whom they were related. She suddenly felt nauseous. Flory rolled down the window.

"Too hot in here for you? I can turn down the heat." Jesse adjusted the temperature.

"No, I just felt a little car sick. I don't know why," Flory said.

"I guess you're not used to fast driving," Jesse joked. "Seriously, are you okay?"

"I am. Sorry about that." Flory wasn't sure how the evening was going to go. Why couldn't she just go on a date without having to worry about her dead aunt ruining everything?

Jesse turned into a gated entrance. He pushed a remote, and a large wrought iron gate swung open. "Here we are," he said as he drove through.

There was a gravel road that wound through the land. It reminded Flory of the farm, except more expansive.

In a panic, Flory blurted, "Did you know of anyone who was at the bar that night of the shooting?"

"Whoa! What brought that up?" The tires crunched over gravel as Jesse followed the road.

"I have to tell you," Flory said.

"Tell me what?"

"I have to tell you before I meet any of your family, because you might not want them to meet me. So, I have to tell you now."

Jesse put the truck in park. "Who said anything about meeting my family? Whatever you have to tell me, it's okay. Can we start the fire and get comfortable first?" He scooted over and put his arm around her. "Please?" he said, squeezing her shoulders.

"Okay," Flory agreed. She was relieved.

Jesse continued driving. It was getting dark outside. Outlines of buildings were in the distance. Flory saw what must have been his house to the right with the windows lit up. They drove past fenced areas until he reached an open field.

Jesse unloaded firewood from the back of his truck. Then he handed Flory a bin containing their food. She could smell something wonderful wrapped inside pieces of foil. "I was going to have my mom help me make Dutch oven apple crisp, but I ran out of time."

"I almost forgot," Flory said. She put the bin down next to the firewood and ran back to the truck. "I brought cookies."

Jesse showed Flory how to build a fire, and soon they could feel its heat. He got two camping chairs and set them up. He placed an old rack on top of the firewood and added a kettle to the rack. "Coffee, tea, or hot chocolate?" he asked.

"Hot chocolate," Flory said.

"Me, too. Here." He motioned for her to sit in one of the camp chairs. "Have a seat." Then he handed her a blanket. "In case you get cold."

"Thanks," she said and unfolded the blanket, wrapping herself inside of it. Flory felt herself begin to relax. She was amazed at how he had thought of everything. This was nice. "So, tell me how you cheated."

"I picked up a roasted chicken at the store, and I cooked the vegetables before I put them in the foil. We're just warming our food."

Flory laughed. "I like your idea of cheating," she said. "I guess I cheated, too. I got the cookies out of the freezer. We made them earlier. They're our favorite, a family recipe of my grandmother's. They're called..." Flory stopped.

The kettle began to hiss. The water was boiling, ready for the hot chocolate mix. Jesse pulled out two mugs from the bin and emptied cocoa packets into the mugs, then added the bubbling water.

He hadn't noticed, Flory thought, relieved. She took one of the mugs and blew on the hot liquid.

"What were you saying," Jesse asked, "about the cookies?" He had noticed.

Flory took a deep breath. Here goes. "We call our cookies Sutton cookies because the recipe is from my grandmother, Florence Sutton." There. She said it.

Jesse peered at her in the dimming light. He appeared confused. "Is this supposed to be some kind of quiz?"

Flory repeated, "*Sutton* cookies."

Jesse shrugged his shoulders and shook his head. "Great. They're named after your grandmother, and so are you. I don't get it." Jesse set his mug in the canvas cup holder attached to the chair. "What are you trying to tell me?"

Flory sighed. Why couldn't he connect the dots, so she didn't have to come out and say Aunt Lou was the murderer? But she realized she was going to have to state the truth. This wasn't going to be easy, she knew.

In the year since the shooting, it seemed *everyone* knew what had happened, and so there was no need to speak of it. *They* were either supportive of her family or against them. In fact, Jesse was the first person she had encountered who had no idea of her family's past. She knew to be fair to him she had to be honest about Aunt Lou. The same way he had been honest about his drinking. Jesse had taken a risk in telling her his private, untold story. Now it was her turn to do the same.

Flory began to feel unusually warm. She pushed her chair back from the fire and removed the blanket from her shoulders. She pulled at the collar of her turtleneck to allow some cool air on her skin. Flory was aware of Jesse watching her.

She turned toward him. It was now or never. She wished it could be never.

"You shared with me your struggle with alcohol, and you didn't have to. But you did. Now it's my turn. I'm about to tell you something I've never told anyone. I've never told anyone because I didn't have to. Everyone already knew."

Flory paused. This was hard. Please, say something. But Jesse remained silent, waiting for Flory to drop this unknown bomb. The shadows from the fire danced across his face, and she couldn't tell what his expression was.

"My aunt, Lou Sutton, is the one who murdered those people in Mineral Wells." Flory sensed Jesse stiffen. He backed his chair away. She knew it. He was one of them. It was over. The fire crackled. The blanket had dropped to the ground, and suddenly she felt cold. Why was he like everyone else? Why had she hung on to the hope he might be different? She wanted to say she was sorry. She wanted to tell him the rest of her family wasn't like that. She wanted to tell him she was normal and lonely.

Flory's eyes stung. Please don't start crying. With the palm of her hand, she tried to wipe the already forming tears. She didn't care that her makeup was going to run. What was the point?

If she could, she would get up and leave, but she couldn't. She had to depend on Jesse to take her home. This was a mistake, a terrible mistake. Why did she even think starting a new relationship was possible? She felt like she was condemned for life.

Flory stood up. "I guess you need to take me home." She walked toward Jesse's truck. She opened the passenger door and felt him grab her arm.

"Where are you going?"

She turned and faced him but couldn't see his expression.

Then he wrapped his arms around her and held her. Neither spoke, but Flory began to cry. This time it was tears of relief.

Finally, Jesse released her. Stepping back, he wiped her face. Then he took a bandana from his back pocket and tried to remove the smeared mascara below her eyes.

"I must look like a mess." What a normal thing to think about, she realized, and laughed. "I'm so sorry. My aunt really wasn't a horrible person, if you can believe that." She began to cry once more.

Jesse took her hand, and they walked back to the

campfire. "No, I'm the one who needs to apologize. Now I understand."

He pulled her close and kissed her. Flory felt herself go limp, as if her cares had evaporated. They pulled apart, and Jesse stirred the coals. "Here," he said. "Sit down while I put our dinner on the fire. I'm starved."

Flory watched him get out the foil wrapped chicken and vegetables and place them on the rack over the flames. When he was finished, he pulled his chair back toward the fire and sat next to her.

"Flory, I'm so sorry. What a terrible year you must have had. I cannot even imagine. How did you and your family manage?"

"We didn't. It was awful." Flory told Jesse about Aunt Lou's schizophrenia. She described what had happened at school, and how she and Phoebe were treated by their former friends. Flory explained Alice's inability to function and how angry she was at her, and how Rodney tried to hold everything together, all the while losing business.

"Tell me, was there anything good that happened?"

"Mrs. C," she said. "She's our eighty-year-old neighbor, and she was my only friend. As a matter of fact, if it weren't for her, I wouldn't have met you." Flory leaned over and kissed him. It felt so normal.

Their conversation continued as they ate.

"What a jerk I was! I'm sorry I reacted the way I did. It shocked me. That wasn't what I expected to hear."

Flory found herself sharing thoughts about the past year she hadn't told anyone else.

"I don't know what it would be like to be in your place. But you're not your aunt."

In turn, Jesse opened about his own concerns.

The fire began to die, and only embers remained. Yet they stayed seated by the fire, now closer to each other.

Jesse turned to Flory. "I have an important question to ask you."

"Okay?" The old fear returned, and Flory tensed.

"Where are those Sutton cookies?"

Epilogue

Alice stood in front of the bathroom mirror, applying mascara. Her hair, cut in a bob, had streaks of gray. Rodney told her he liked it that way. She wasn't the same person she was four years ago. Older, yes. Wiser, hopefully. Thankful, most definitely. For the briefest moment, she had a glimpse of Lou and her parents in her mind. It was a memory of happier times. She smiled and whispered, "I love you all," and blew a kiss.

"Who are you kissing?" Rodney came up behind her, putting his arms around her. He, too, had begun to gray in what little hair he had. "Are you ready?"

"Almost," she said. "And a little nervous."

"You'll be fine," he assured her.

Neither spoke for a moment. Alice was thinking of all their family had gone through in the past four years and how Rodney had never given up. She stood on her toes and kissed him. "Thank you."

"What was that for?" Rodney put his fingers to his lips where she had kissed him.

"For being you. For keeping our family from falling apart. For not giving up on me. For reinventing your business. For everything."

Alice watched his face turn bright red, and she laughed. "That's what I love about you, Mr. Member of

433

the prestigious Craftsman Club."

Alice, who had gone back to school at Laura's encouragement, was giving a personal talk about her sister and the repercussions of allowing mental illness to go untreated. She had become an art therapist for patients suffering from schizophrenia.

"I ran into Leo when I stopped at the store, and he told me he and Edith will be there. So will Liem and Ha."

Alice turned around and said, "I got a message from Ann Goodson, and she is coming. So are Jeremy and Gina. And she's pregnant." Alice began to tear up. "I didn't expect this kind of support," she said. Jeremy's new wife, Gina, had a brother who was bipolar and suffered from depression.

From the bathroom they heard the door to the kitchen slam and Phoebe calling out. "Mom, Dad, where are you?"

"Back here," Alice said.

Phoebe came into their room, and by her expression, Alice could tell that something was wrong.

"What's the matter?"

"Mom, there was another mass shooting. They haven't identified the shooter yet, though."

Alice's chest tightened. That old feeling was trying to make its way back. "What happened? Tell me about it." As Phoebe explained what she had heard on the radio, Alice thought back to the notes she had received— the ones she couldn't open for almost a year—from others who had suffered similar experiences. It had become one of her personal missions to continue writing to the families of the victims and of the perpetrator, especially when the shooter suffered from some form of mental illness. The importance of getting treatment for those who suffered from schizophrenia was paramount. Untreated, they could resort to violence, and she only knew that too well. But what a source of comfort it had been to receive notes from other family members who understood what they were going through.

"Mom, Dad. Where are you?" This time it was Flory.

"We're all back here in the bedroom," Phoebe said.

Flory and Jesse appeared at the doorway. "Shouldn't we be leaving soon?" She had that glow about her that comes from being in love. On her left hand was a ring, and the wedding was scheduled for the spring.

Alice gazed at the couple. She couldn't be happier for Flory. They all loved Jesse.

"Okay. Everyone out. Let me gather my thoughts for three minutes, then I'll be ready to go."

Alice shooed her family out of the bedroom. She went into her office and shut the door. The walls were covered with artwork and notes from those she worked with at the clinic. On her desk was a note from Angie Almon. They had set up a scholarship fund for Lizzie, her daughter. And for Seth Fisher, too. He was now a junior in high school. His note was tacked on the wall. Alice closed her eyes and focused on each family—the Randolphs, Jose Martinez, the Coverdales, Ann Goodson, Seth Fisher and his grandparents, Angie and Lizzie Taylor, the Merrells, the Eckles, Leslie and Sammy Cottingham, the Youngbloods, and Hannah Cummins and Sylvia, her mother. She and Hannah had been writing each other.

Fifteen minutes later they parked at the high school. Alice was giving her talk in the auditorium. Rodney gave her a quick kiss. "Break a leg. " he said. "You'll do great."

Alice stood backstage. There was a single podium on stage. Behind it was a banner that said, *"How to Care for your Loved Ones who Suffer from Schizophrenia."* Her hands shook as she held her notes.

God, give me the words.

Laura came up behind her. "It's just about time," she said. Her hair was back to fiery red. She pointed out to the audience. "Look at the size of the crowd."

Alice peered out. She saw a sea of faces. There was Ann Goodson on the front row. It appeared she was saving some seats. Then she noticed three individuals coming down the aisle—a Hispanic man, a black woman, and a white woman. It was Jose Martinez, Bianca Merrell, and Frances Eckles. She saw their neighbor, Evelyn Callahan, and her son, William. Barney and his wife were there, along with Mrs. Mullins, the Nguyens, Kate and her parents, and Jeremy with his wife, Gina. Leo and Edith Porter came down the side aisle and sat next to Barney. Then she saw Rodney stand up and make room for Jordan Hall. Alice smiled. He had been released on parole, and they were helping him get back on his feet. Alice recognized many who were in the audience, including some from the clinic where she now worked. But there were many there who she didn't recognize. It was a large crowd, and she was surprised.

The lights in the auditorium dimmed, and the chatter quieted. The stage manager signaled to Laura.

"I guess it's my turn." She gave Alice a quick hug and walked on the stage.

Alice watched Laura walk to the podium. She didn't hear what Laura was saying. All she heard was Lou's voice encouraging her. *"Come on, Al-Pal, you can do it!"* Yes, she could do it, and she would.

A word about the author...

Patsy King Hosman has lived in Oklahoma most of her life and currently shares her time between Oklahoma and Florida with her husband. She is the mother of four adult children and the grandmother of triplets. Patsy loves to spend time out-of-doors—being in nature, gardening, taking long walks on the beach, and celebrating sunrises and sunsets. An avid cook and baker, she has been making sourdough bread for over forty years. Patsy is a Stephen Minister. She believes having the privilege to live and learn can be a blessing. So can writing about it.

Thank you for purchasing
this publication of The Wild Rose Press, Inc.

For questions or more information
contact us at
info@thewildrosepress.com.

The Wild Rose Press, Inc.
www.thewildrosepress.com